THE
DETRIMENT

ABOUT THE AUTHOR

A former Scotland Yard investigator with twenty years' policing experience, including counter-terror operations and organised crime, David Videcette has worked as a Metropolitan Police detective on a wealth of infamous cases. He currently consults on security operations for high-net-worth individuals and is an expert media commentator on crime, terrorism, extremism and the London 7/7 bombings.

To find out more about David and to subscribe to his newsletter, visit: www.DavidVidecette.com/about-david

THE
DETRIMENT

We all have secrets we say we'll never tell…

DAVID VIDECETTE

The second title in the
DETECTIVE INSPECTOR
JAKE FLANNAGAN SERIES

The Detriment

Published by Videcette Limited

Copyright © Videcette Limited 2017

Ebook ISBN: 978 0 99342 632 2

Paperback ISBN: 978 0 99342 633 9

The moral right of the author has been asserted.

Typesetting and copy-editing by www.tenthousand.co.uk

Find out more about the author and his upcoming titles at:
www.DavidVidecette.com/about-david

FOREWORD

His clothes had partially burned from his body. His hair was on fire. His whole torso was alight.

I watched in horror as people tried to douse the flames on the burning man using fire extinguishers; a man who had poured petrol over himself and set himself ablaze, after ramming a flaming Jeep into the bollards outside the main terminal building at Glasgow Airport.

A police officer tried to grab him, but the man's skin came off in his hands.

It had a surreal feel the moment I saw it – I'd never witnessed anything like it before.

It was obvious to us, almost immediately, that it was connected to the two car bombs we'd found outside a London nightclub, thirty-six hours before. The ones we were busy investigating that Saturday morning during the summer of 2007.

How could it have happened? How had they slipped through the net again, almost two years to the day since fifty-two members of the public and four terrorists had died on London's streets? My heart sank.

We were the Counter Terrorism Command and we couldn't stop them – not with all the resources at our disposal, and not with the help of the security services. We'd still failed.

Despite all the changes, the upheaval, the amalgamations – and despite stopping a group intent on bombing transatlantic airliners in 2006 – we'd still failed.

Or had we?

I can't tell you the truth, but I *can* tell you a story…

1

Sirens blaring, Jake sped down Whitehall and past the black gates of Downing Street. He wondered whether Prime Minister Gordon Brown, in his first week in charge of the country, had any inkling that a car bomb was about to explode outside a packed nightclub.

The traffic was heavy, even at this early hour of the morning, with black cabs, buses and rickshaws all jockeying for their slice of the road, all seemingly unaware of the urgency of Jake's journey, despite the lights and noise bellowing from his unmarked car.

Tourists took blurry holiday snaps with flashes that barely registered in the dark night sky, while revellers made their way home from bars and clubs. Jake swerved narrowly to avoid several pedestrians as they sprinted across the road, despite the green lights indicating his right of way.

There were people everywhere. If the caller's report about the smoke they'd seen in the suspect vehicle was true, then they were all in big trouble. Jake could already envisage the carnage. The instant 'kill circle' of a car bomb might only be several feet around the site, but the blast could wreak devastation in a huge radius, causing mayhem and injury up to 500 metres away.

Despite the car's closed windows, the wail of the two tones was loud enough to hurt Jake's ears as he drove. Lord Nelson watched from his column as Jake screeched around the corner and through Trafalgar Square.

Westminster Borough Police had already closed Haymarket to traffic. Jake drove the wrong way up the one-way street then slammed on the brakes, pulling up sharply next to an old Mercedes saloon parked outside the doors of the busy-looking nightclub. The dampened sounds of a chest-rattling beat emanated from within. The black and orange sign above the entrance proclaimed its name to the street as Tiger Tiger.

A young female officer with rosy cheeks, wearing a badged bowler hat, rushed over to greet him. Jake flashed his card.

'DI Flannagan, Counter Terrorism Command. Is this the car that was reported?' he asked, pointing at the willow-green Mercedes.

With its lights on in the dark street, the vehicle looked to Jake like a waiting taxi, hovering – ready to pick up punters leaving the nightclub.

'Yes, sir. It stinks of petrol; someone reported seeing smoke inside,' she replied.

Jake glanced up and down the wide carriageway. Several officers were trying to clear pedestrians from the pavement area, while the Tiger Tiger door staff struggled to keep the clubgoers from wandering over to get a look at all the commotion.

On closer inspection, the vehicle looked a little too old to be a minicab. He felt the bonnet of the old, W-reg Mercedes. It was still warm.

The car couldn't have been there long.

He dropped to his knees and peered underneath. No sign of any leaking fluid, but his nose confirmed the female officer's fears and worse. A damp, sweet hydrocarbon smell indicated she'd been right about the petrol, yet what was more worrying was the stench of rotting vegetables. It was mercaptan, the pungent-smelling substance deliberately added to gas canisters to warn of leaks.

'Shit!' said Jake, realising there was gas coming from something inside the car. He felt his pulse quicken, knowing full well the risks that fuel bombs carried. Petrol and gas burned quickly and easily, mixing with the surrounding air and igniting together. They were much more energetic than conventional explosives and could create a devastating shock wave.

The nightclub next to him had enormous, floor-to-ceiling frosted windows, which ran the width of the building and faced on to the street. Through the glazing, Jake could make out the figures of people gyrating on the dance floor.

Thursday. Ladies' night. Club classics and party anthems. The place was packed. There would be hundreds of people crammed inside.

Jake closed his eyes for a split second. Potential outcomes rushed through his head.

Numerous deaths from horrific burns.

Damage caused by the shrapnel from the glass.

The inevitable stampede among the inebriated injured.

Trampled bodies.

A nightclub in flames.

'Go into the club and tell the doorman to evacuate *everyone* through the fire exits at the back. *No one* comes out of the front!' Jake shouted to the female PC, who retreated quickly.

A growing crowd had amassed on the street. A handful of local officers were trying to herd them away from the Mercedes.

He couldn't wait.

There was no time.

He had to know. Was it a bomb? Or was it a false alarm?

If it *were* a bomb, he had to try and defuse it – *now*.

2

Jake had been in the Reserve Room when the call had come in, drinking tea and chatting with one of the girls on duty. He was on nights, consigned to office duties only. He wasn't supposed to be out in the field – he knew that. The local borough police were the first port of call. They would clear the streets and try to keep people away. But this was the West End – evacuations were neither quick nor easy at the best of times, let alone when there were thousands of drunken revellers milling about on one of central London's main arterial roads.

The bomb-disposal team was on the other side of London dealing with another call. Seconds and minutes counted in situations like this. Jake had felt a sudden and overwhelming compulsion to attend. He wasn't going to sit in an office, barely a mile away from the scene, and wait for a bomb to go off while the EXPO guys hotfooted it across town.

And now he was here. Now what?

Jake tried the driver's door. It was locked.

From years of grunt work investigating car thefts, Jake knew how unreliable central locking could be on older makes and models of car so he tried each of the other doors in turn. To his relief, when he pulled on the handle to the rear passenger's-side door, it popped open.

The stench of fuel and gas was stronger now. It seeped into his mouth and nose.

He felt sick.

Where the hell was Geoff, the explosives officer?

Inside the car, the back seat was strewn with cardboard boxes and a duvet. Jake pushed the bedding to one side. It was cold and soaked through. Smelling his hands, he realised it had been liberally doused with petrol. Underneath, he found two propane gas cylinders – one tucked into each of the footwells behind the front seats.

This was deliberate – an improvised explosive device.

Someone had created a bomb.

He moved to the front to scrabble around for an initiator, something that could create a spark to ignite the fuel and gas. He had to find it. Maybe the cigarette lighter?

Nothing.

Jake's heart was pounding so hard he thought he could hear it in his own ears as it fought to get out of his chest. The base of the Rihanna track 'Umbrella' thundered from inside the club, just a few feet behind him. He wondered why word hadn't reached the DJ that there was a car bomb outside.

Why was the music still playing?

Panic started to set in. His hands began to shake as he searched through the glove compartment.

Still nothing that could ignite and initiate the explosion.

Sitting between the two front seats, in the centre console, was a pile of leaflets. He rummaged beneath them and found two Nokia mobiles.

Two wires protruded from the bottom of each handset, leading to the back of the car. Without thinking, Jake yanked the phones toward him, frantically trying to break the circuit.

One of the phones came free in his hands, the wires dangling from the bottom of it. No longer connected to anything, it began to ring, vibrating in his grasp as the screen flashed on and off.

He dropped it and then grabbed at the wires still securely attached to the second phone. As he did so, the second phone started to ring.

Jake closed his eyes and waited for the bang.

3

He didn't know how long he'd been kneeling in the car, doubled over the centre console with his eyes shut. It felt like a long time.

He thought about a lot of things. His two daughters. His ex-wife Stephanie. His on-off girlfriend Claire. Ted, his cat.

The first thing he felt was a gentle pressure on his shoulder. And then a voice, getting louder and louder.

'Jake!' Geoff, the explosives officer, grabbed him by the shoulder. 'Get out of the car. Step away. Come on!'

Geoff pulled him toward an alley, out of sight of the car.

'Leave it – leave it alone. Move away!' said Geoff, as he dragged him further and further down the alleyway. 'We've got the cordon in; people are being evacuated from the back of the club. Stop now. You don't need to do any more – we'll handle it from here.'

'It's OK. It's OK… It's dead. I think I've stopped it…' said Jake, shaking.

'Mate. You shouldn't have been in there. I don't know whether you're crazy or a genius,' replied Geoff, grabbing Jake by the shoulders to steady him as he slumped in exhaustion.

'*You* remember what it was like last time, Geoff. I couldn't just sit there and do nothing… I couldn't face it all again,' said Jake, tears streaming down his cheeks.

4

'Take a seat.' Helen motioned to the sofa as Jake entered.

The spoils of her promotion were immediately evident to Jake's eyes. Most of the offices on the fifteenth floor were long and narrow, with a single window overlooking St James's Park Tube, but becoming a superintendent meant Helen now got one of the larger rooms, a highly prized sofa and two windows.

The mood was oddly sombre. There were no smiles, no congratulatory handshakes, no pats on the back saying 'well done'.

'Morning, Jake. Thanks for coming in,' said Helen as she sat down opposite him.

'Morning, ma'am,' said Jake, keeping his tone formal.

'How're things with you then? Everything all right?'

Jake knew that Helen wasn't usually one for asking about well-being. She expected her team to leave their private lives at home, to get on with their jobs. This already felt distinctly like a 'welfare chat'. He was even less fond of them than Helen was.

'I'm not too shabby. Had a lucky result last night... I'm guessing that's why I'm in here?'

Helen shifted in her seat and half smiled. 'I love your direct-ness, Jake. Yes, I've been asked to have a chat with you about your decision-making last night.'

'My decision-making? In what way?'

'You went to the Haymarket. Got into a suspicious vehicle. Tried to defuse one of the bombs?'

Jake frowned. 'I did.'

'Talk me through it. Why you did that.'

'I was in the Reserve Room. I saw the incident come up on the CAD. It looked like something we should be involved in. It was clear, once the borough officers arrived on scene, that it was something big. The on-call team was at least an hour away. Explosive specialists were half an hour away. It was the middle of the night. The call seemed genuine. I didn't think we could wait that long. I decided my experience was best used at the scene, not here in the office.'

Helen nodded. 'OK. Go on...'

Jake recounted to Helen exactly what he'd found at the scene.

'And I hear the phones started ringing while you were there trying to defuse the device?' she asked.

'Trying to defuse it? I *did* defuse it. The phones started ringing while I was trying to pull the wires out of them – while they were in my hand.'

'Does that not scare you a little, Jake?'

'Well of course it does. But there was no time to be scared. I was just trying to save the people on the pavement, Helen. I couldn't face another bombing while I was at work – not again, almost two years to the day – sitting in the office doing nothing. And I stopped it. I defused the bloody thing.'

Helen stared at him but said nothing. Jake couldn't decipher her expression. He was confused. He'd done the right thing. He'd neutralised the threat. Why was Helen talking to him like this?

'Jake, the explosives specialists believe the reason your car bomb didn't go off – indeed that neither of the car bombs went off—'

'Neither of them? What do you mean?'

'Yes, sorry, I thought you were aware. You must have been asleep. We found a second VBIED early this morning.'

A car – or truck – bomb was known as a vehicle-borne improvised explosive device or VBIED. It meant the device would be delivered to the target and detonated inside the vehicle.

'No, I wasn't aware,' replied Jake, shaking his head.

'A second car bomb was found not far from Trafalgar Square, just outside the Department for Culture, Media and Sport in Cockspur Street. The car had been left at a bus stop. Council wardens ticketed it and towed it away to an underground pound on Park Lane. Identical car, identical device to the one you found in Haymarket. They'd originally been just a few hundred yards apart. Luckily that one didn't go off either.'

'Why didn't it go off?'

'The detonators were no good. They're not sure why. Maybe too damp – possibly had too much fuel poured on them. They think it should have detonated when the phones rang. Had it not blown then, they think it should have detonated when you pulled all the wires out of the phones.'

'You're suggesting that me pulling out the wires actually put people at risk, rather than helping them?'

'I'm telling you what I've been told, Jake. Either way, had the detonators been good, you probably would have been dead. Worse still, there's the suggestion, at the moment, that you could have caused them to explode by pulling on the wires, yes.'

'That's total rubbish – it really is…' said Jake angrily. 'I don't know if the detonators were good or not; I doubt whoever is saying this stuff to you, just a few hours after they've been recovered, knows at this stage either. What I saw was a car that smelt strongly of petrol and gas – and hundreds of people inside a nightclub. I did what I thought was best for them.'

Jake shut his eyes. He couldn't believe what he was hearing. He'd tried to do his best in an incredibly difficult situation. He remembered the car crash on his way to stop the 7/7 bombers, the scenes of devastation in Tavistock Square, the mangled flesh and debris from the exploded double-decker bus, the bodies laid out with tablecloths for shrouds. It all came flooding back.

'Jake…' Helen sighed. 'You've been back at work for six months – you know your cards are marked. People are going to find fault with you where they wouldn't normally with others. You know how this stuff works.'

'So replace "hero" with "crazy" or "liability" – that's what this is then, is it?'

'You were given a written warning for not following procedure, Jake. There are questions being asked about you. "Loose cannon" was the phrase used about you at the commander's briefing this morning. That's not good. Not for you, nor me.'

'But...'

Helen raised her hand to cut him off. 'Jake, I'm on your side. You know I am. The commander is worried about you; I'm worried about you – that's all. He's asked me to have a chat. Rein you in a bit – make sure that you're all right...'

'Rein me in? I've been stuck in that Reserve Room as duty officer for the last six months. You couldn't rein me in any more, ma'am. I want to be let loose. I thought that's what we were going to discuss this morning. I thought I'd get a pat on the back. Maybe a well done. Or perhaps even a commendation. But no – I've had a bollocking instead. You couldn't make it up.'

'Policy, procedure, rules, Jake. That's what this is about. During your girlfriend's missing-persons enquiry, you ignored all of those. That's why you got the warning. Last night, you were duty officer – office bound. Yet somehow you ended up in Haymarket defusing a car bomb...'

'There was no one about. I had skills that were best used on the ground...'

'Jake. Don't overstep the mark. Don't break the rules and put yourself on offer...'

'For God's sake! Are you really blaming me for trying to do my best? Blaming me for trying to save lives?'

Jake stopped himself. He was getting worked up. He knew that sort of attitude would just strengthen the case against him. He tried a different tack.

'Look, I want out of the office, Helen. I've done my time. I've done what's been asked of me. Last night there were lives at stake. I had to make instant decisions. You know I was just trying to do my best – stop that car from exploding. I did what was expected in an emergency. What anyone would have done.'

Helen's face softened.

'No, Jake. That's not what anyone would have done. That's the problem with you. You're headstrong and totally unaware of your own mortality. But I know you have the best intentions when you do these things.'

Jake sensed his chance. He'd been sitting tight in the Reserve Room for long enough.

'Then let me pick up on this one. I'm perfectly placed to handle the nightclub job from last night. You know I'll deliver results.'

Helen was one of his strongest supporters. She couldn't turn him down on this surely?

'The commander has given it to DI Castle. I'm happy that you help out on it from an intel point of view, but Mark is the lead. You need to toe the line.'

Jake nodded.

'There is a "but" to it though, Jake.'

Jake's heart sank 'What's the "but"?'

'The commander wants you referred to Occupational Health. He wants to hear from the professionals that you're all right, instead of me vouching for you all the time. I've booked you an appointment for Monday. You will attend,' she said, looking him straight in the eye and holding his gaze.

'Of course.'

'Good. There's another little matter I need you to look into for me too.'

5

Helen retrieved a newspaper from her desk and passed it to Jake. It was a copy of *The Guardian*:

'Egyptian "spy for Israel" found dead outside London flat,' read the headline.

'Was he poisoned? Another case like the Litvinenko one?' Jake asked.

'I don't think so. I need you to pop over to Belgravia police station, touch base with the officers dealing with it. Make sure it's being dealt with properly, that nothing's been missed, and help them out with anything they might need. Commander wants us to have oversight of it. Nothing heavy.'

'Happy to, ma'am.'

'I'm sure it won't take you too long. I think the locals have it wrapped up to be honest. Looks like he's jumped or fallen from his balcony. When you get back, go and see DI Castle. Operation Seagram's the name we've been assigned for the car-bombs case.'

'I'll need Lenny…'

'I hear Mark's given him the office manager's role on Seagram.'

'Lenny. My Lenny? DS Lenny Sandringham?' Jake asked incredulously, his mouth agape.

Helen stifled a smile. 'Yes, your Lenny.'

'Oh for heaven's sake! That's just ludicrous. He's made Lenny office manager? That's like giving a goldfish a bicycle to ride.'

Helen gave him a stern look. 'Jake, what have I just said about toeing the line?' she cautioned.

'Oh come on, Helen. You know Lenny. How the hell is he going to be any use as office manager? Can't he come on the Belgravia job you just gave me? I *do* need him if we're going to have a proper look at the spy thing. Two heads are better than one,' said Jake, giving her his best puppy-dog eyes.

Helen sighed, resigned. 'OK, take him with you... You two can be liaison for the dead spy. And we need someone to start work on the intelligence development cell for last night's car bombs. I know that's your forte. You and Lenny can take that on. Just don't cause any trouble. You're working *with* DI Castle – it's *his* job. You know he's close friends with the commander?'

'I do know, yes. That's why he got the job here...'

Helen rolled her eyes. 'Well for heaven's sakes, don't upset him...'

'Thanks, guv...'

Now that they'd concluded the work discussions, Helen changed the subject.

'How's Claire?'

Jake hated discussing his private life with anyone, most of all the boss. As if the job didn't already encroach enough on his home life.

'She's OK. I've not murdered her, not yet anyway... Nothing to worry about, guv.' Jake tried to sound as casual as possible. He fixed a smile to his face.

'I know you don't like being asked, Jake. Fact is I have to. They're still unsure of what went on and, well, you know how it is...'

'Everything is fine. I hardly see her. She works a lot; I work a lot. We live separately, we aren't an *item* any more, just good friends,' Jake replied reluctantly. He still had feelings for Claire, but it seemed the universe had other plans for them – plans that conspired to keep them apart.

'No plans to change that, move in together?'

'None.'

'Any reason why?'

13

'It's a long story – I won't bore you with it now. I'm single – just look at it like that. Better for work anyway.'

Helen eyed him suspiciously. 'Single?'

Jake knew about the gossipmongers who said he'd been seeing office staff, civilians, other officers… pretty much anything in a skirt that moved. If the rumours were to be believed, Jake was an alcoholic, womanising swine. He'd even heard that he'd engaged in a drunken threesome with two of the MIR office girls.

It was crazy, thought Jake. He'd never have done that drunk.

He nodded. 'Yes, single. Are we done, guv?' he asked, trying to move the conversation away from his private life.

Helen raised her eyebrows and then frowned. 'Yes. Just be careful, Jake… touch base with DI Castle first, and let him know what's going on; what you and Lenny are doing.'

'Thanks,' said Jake as he got up and left.

Jake and Mark Castle had history.

This wasn't going to be easy.

6

Jake made his way down the hall of the fourteenth floor to hunt for Mark in the Major Incident Room.

Mark had joined Counter Terrorism Command only recently, but Jake knew him from their time spent at Hendon Police College. They'd been in different classes but the same intake. Despite their contrasting characters, they had one thing in common, and that was Gaynor Lewis.

When Jake had joined the Met, he'd been sent on a residential course at policing college, which had given him the basic skills required to become a police officer. The college, a short walk from Colindale Tube station in north-west London, had originally been an RAF base. The RAF had left in the sixties and the huge site had become the Metropolitan Police's training school.

It was hard work – a really pressured environment with tests that had to be passed every Friday morning. University studies indicated that the Met was teaching the equivalent of a three-year law degree to their students in just eighteen weeks. Some just couldn't keep up and left.

Jake had lived on site in a pokey campus room with a single bed, a chest of drawers, a wardrobe and a sink. Yet he'd had no complaints. He'd made lifelong friends and enjoyed every minute.

They'd been young and free, with no obligations and no cares in the world besides learning and growing as people. Or so he'd thought.

Gaynor Lewis had been a fresh-faced nineteen-year-old with a figure that, even when clothed in dowdy police training kit, had unfailingly attracted male attention. One drunken night, Jake had ended up in a passionate embrace with her in the corner of the Peel bar – the bar used by new recruits. There had been jokey shouts from onlookers to 'get a room'. He was not the first of Gaynor's conquests – nor would he be the last.

Unbeknownst to Jake, Mark Castle had considered himself in a relationship with the lovely Gaynor – though the bubbly, fun-loving girl had seen things a little differently at the time.

Mark had been the oldest guy in Jake's intake by some years, and even back then his grey hair and laborious anecdotes had set him apart from the others.

Mid-kiss with Gaynor in the bar, Jake had heard shouting from an angry male voice. Breaking it off, he'd found Mark standing there, furious, trying to grab Gaynor by the arm and frogmarch her away.

As the rest of the bar looked on, Jake had remonstrated with him, attempting to calm the situation, saying that it was nothing more than a peck on the cheek.

However, when Jake had returned to his room that night, he'd spotted his reflection in the small mirror above his sink. Covered in Gaynor's deep burgundy lipstick, he looked as if he'd been attacked by a clown in full make-up. It would have been clear to Mark that it was more than a simple peck on the cheek.

After training school, Gaynor and Mark had both been posted to Brixton police station. Mark had pursued Gaynor at the same time as he'd pursued a career in uniform, swiftly rising up the ranks to become an inspector, and Gaynor Lewis was now Gaynor Castle. Jake wondered if she'd settled by choosing a dependable father figure so much older than herself.

Now a detective sergeant at Brixton, Gaynor was apparently pretty good at what she did, or so Jake had heard. Yet if the rumours were true, the training-school dalliance she'd had with Jake before she wed was really the least of Mark's worries.

Oh what fun this chat was going to be, thought Jake. An attempt to get Lenny back from Mark without a scene, as if he were trying to prise Gaynor from Mark's grasp in the Peel bar all those years ago.

As he wandered up the corridor, Jake took out his phone and rattled off a text to Lenny:

'Are you in the MIR now?'

'Yes, why?' came Lenny's response.

'I'm trying to bust you out of there. When you see me talking to Mark Castle just play dumb.'

'I don't have to act dumb. I've not got a bloody clue why they've put me in here!' Lenny replied.

Jake chuckled to himself as he slid the phone back in his pocket.

1

Friday
29 June 2007
1220 hours
New Scotland Yard, Westminster, London

Jake found Mark Castle in the Major Incident Room. Operation Seagram had taken over a small corner of the investigation floor, and the place was alive with people, all in a frantic rush to do something admin-related. Jake was never completely sure how everyone's tasks related to the operation.

He spotted Lenny sitting at a computer terminal in the corner. Older than Jake and neatly turned out as always, his old stablemate was a good copper with many years' service under his belt. Lenny smiled at Jake and rolled his eyes. Jake acknowledged him with a nod and made his way over to where Mark was talking on the phone.

'No, we don't know where they are now; Security Service are working on it as we speak. What's the score with the second device?' Mark barked into the phone as Jake waited patiently by his desk. 'Keep me posted on it.'

Mark replaced the receiver and looked up at Jake. 'Morning,' he sighed. 'Or is it afternoon now?' There was no flicker of emotion on his face. Jake couldn't be sure if Mark was having a sly dig or not.

'Hi, Mark, it's been a while…' Jake extended his hand.

'Been a long time.' Mark stood and shook his hand rather too hard.

'Not sure if Helen has spoken to you yet about this, but I'm going to be running the intel.' Jake paused, waiting for

Mark's reaction before he went any further. There was no point getting off on the wrong foot here.

Mark looked at him. 'No – no, she's not mentioned anything,' he said, sounding ruffled and shaking his head vigorously.

Mark had transferred to Counter Terrorism Command directly from his role at Brixton – a standard police station where he'd dealt with mainstream crime like assaults, shoplifting and bag thefts. He'd never been involved in large-scale investigations with hundreds of people running around after him, and Jake wondered how he was feeling about being thrown in at the deep end. This was a world away from anything Mark would have ever experienced, and Jake actually felt a bit sorry for him.

He tried to phrase it more tactfully. 'So I believe we're going to be working on Operation Seagram together. The boss has indicated that she'd like Lenny and me working on some form of intelligence development cell, so let me know if we're OK to run with it.'

'What? I was told Lenny worked on the 7/7 bombings, so I've made him office manager. I need someone who knows what they're doing. This is a major incident...'

Jake looked over at Lenny. Mark followed his gaze.

Lenny saw them looking and began shouting loudly across the room at a systems administrator, 'Erm, I'm a bit stuck. How do I go from "read only" to "input"? Do I have to logout again?'

'Why is your access level "read only"? I thought you were the office manager here?' replied the administrator.

Jake turned back to Mark and tried to suppress a smirk at the thought of Lenny kicking around the office all day, pushing pens and crashing the IT systems.

Mark continued staring across the office without saying anything. He appeared slightly bewildered at the scene that was playing out before his eyes.

Jake took a deep breath. He had to break the bad news to Mark and bust Lenny out of this.

'OK, Mark… Well Helen has said that as both Lenny and I worked together on developing intelligence in Operation Theseus, she thinks that we'd be best utilising our 7/7 experience on the ground. And Lenny isn't the man you want as office manager as you can see…' said Jake, motioning toward the ongoing discussions between Lenny and the administrator about system-access rights.

Mark's face tightened as he turned his attention back to Jake.

'I'm just thinking that you don't want to be changing office managers any later than this, do you? It's a good time to change, right at the start. Maybe speak to the boss. She can recommend someone with the right skill set for the role.'

Mark didn't look convinced.

There was banging from the other side of the office. Lenny was kicking his computer tower and swearing.

He was playing his part in this little ruse well – perhaps too well. Maybe he really was having trouble?

Jake lowered his voice a notch and gestured toward Lenny. 'To be honest, Mark… I really don't think you'd have much of an office left after he's been here for a day.'

They both looked over in Lenny's direction again. The blue felt of the office partition was shaking. Still having problems, Lenny popped his head over the dividing screen. 'Hey, did you just change my login details? It's saying now that I'm logged out. I didn't log out.'

Some of the other team members in the room groaned.

'I see,' said Mark, tight-lipped.

'Have a word with Helen. Just see what she says.'

Jake knew he was playing a cheeky game of workplace bridge. Usually whoever had the highest rank won the round, but they were both detective inspectors, and Jake held all the trump cards here. Helen had said it was OK to take Lenny, and Jake wasn't about to back down.

Mark's face was dark. 'I'm not sure what Helen's plans are with this *intel cell* yet, to be honest. Jake.'

Jake cut across him. 'Well I guess I'll be speaking mostly with the Security Service and trying to see how we can convert any intelligence into usable evidence. They're very separate things here due to phone tapping, and all the other murky stuff that goes on in the world of espionage. Have you worked much with the security services since you've been up here at Counter Terror, Mark?'

Jake knew the answer. That was why he and Lenny had been asked to take it on.

'Not really, no…' Mark looked back at the huge pile of papers on his desk and frowned.

How on earth could the bosses put Mark in this position? Here was a man with no experience of how these things worked suddenly running a major investigation. They were hunting terrorists and the commander had put their most inexperienced man on the job as a case officer. Some people did well out of baptisms of fire. Maybe that was the idea. But what if he messed up?

'Don't worry – I'll help you out. They can be a bit slippery sometimes with what they tell us over at MI5 and MI6. Lenny and I have had plenty of dealings with them, we know the ropes,' said Jake, trying to reassure him.

Mark nodded but said nothing.

'Helen's sending me on an errand,' Jake continued, 'over at Belgravia. It won't take long. I guess it's best we just muck in with the main investigation after that, until we get some intel through? Whatever you need doing.'

'There's an office meeting at 6 p.m. Fifteenth-floor conference room. I'll see you back here then,' Mark said firmly.

Having pretty much lost the battle over the intelligence cell, Jake knew Mark was now attempting to lay down the law in other ways – such as timekeeping.

'Thanks, Mark.'

Jake walked over to Lenny. 'Grab your coat, mate. We're off out.'

'Thank Christ for that,' said Lenny under his breath as he followed Jake out of the office. 'I didn't think I could play the fool for much longer.'

8

In the canteen at Belgravia police station, Jake sipped hot tea from a polystyrene cup. Sitting opposite him and Lenny was Jim – a uniformed sergeant that Jake hadn't met before.

'So the DCI says you lot at Counter Terror are taking this on? Not that there's anything to do, mind,' said Jim.

Jim was in his late forties and a little ragged around the edges; his dark hair, lank and thinning, needed a wash, and his forehead and cheeks were pale and shiny. Jake wondered if the man had had a chance to shower that morning. Maybe it was just the shift work. Earlies, lates and night shifts took an awful toll on the body over time. Never having a proper sleep pattern was one of the most gruelling aspects of the job – as Jake well knew. Plenty of statistics showed that retired police officers died around seven to ten years before those from other professions. Was it the shifts? Stress? Did they all drink too much? No one seemed to know – and what was more worrying, no one seemed to care. Police officers died young, and that was the way it was.

'There are some concerns around this guy's background,' said Jake. 'We had that rather nasty political assassination in London recently, if you remember – Litvinenko, the one with the radiation poisoning. They just want me to make sure we've dotted all the *i*s and crossed all the *t*s.'

This was straightforward stuff, but Jake had to be sure Jim had carried out his enquiries correctly.

'Assassination? Crikey.' Jim rolled his eyes. 'This isn't anything like that Russian geezer…'

'What have we got?' Jake pointed to the blue folder Jim was holding.

'Yeah, well…' Jim opened the folder and flicked through some loose sheets of A4 paper. 'The deceased was a bloke called… er… here it is – Dr Adham Marmora, born 1944, sixty-three years old. We found him dead in the rose garden—'

'In the rose garden?'

'Yeah, the rose garden. He had a nice place in a fancy apartment block, tucked away round the back by Trafalgar Square. Worth a fortune – a few million I'd say. Lived on the fifth floor. The rose garden is located at the front, five floors down obviously. He fell. It's that what killed him, I reckon.'

'He fell?' That sort of terminology already indicated how Jim felt about this. 'Anyone see or hear anything?' asked Jake.

'No. No one saw or heard anything at all. Just him and the maid in his apartment when it happened. I suppose it could have been suicide, but he didn't leave a note or anything.'

'The maid? Did she see anything? See him *fall*?'

'No. It's a big apartment. She was vacuuming when he fell.'

'You don't think she might have helped him in his *fall*?'

'Nah.' Jim laughed. 'She was a tiny little thing. Filipino. Really upset about it all. Worked for him for years. She wouldn't kill her employer, would she?'

'Depends on lots of things – depends what her motive might have been, I guess.'

'Motive?' Jim exclaimed.

Alarm bells were ringing in Jake's head. Jim clearly hadn't considered any other possibilities. He kept using the word 'fell' – he'd obviously already made his mind up.

As a detective, Jake knew that those who came to a crime scene with a prior belief about how or why something had happened were often blind to the obvious. They overlooked crucial pieces of evidence; ignored what they were hearing or seeing and banished things from their thought processes. It was a dangerous thing for an investigator to do.

'What do you know about this bloke? Marmora?'

'Not a lot. An Egyptian. Very wealthy. Runs a few companies. Has an ex-wife who lives abroad; son lives in London.'

'Do you know anything about his background?'

Only what I've seen in the newspapers since. They're saying he was some sort of...' Jim paused, 'spy. A spy for Mossad. I guess that's why you're here, because he was some sort of James Bond? But I'm telling you, he either fell or jumped off the balcony – there's no foul play in this.'

Jake wondered who Jim was trying to convince with that statement.

'No damage to the entrance door of the flat or anything?'

'No, nothing.'

'So who've you actually spoken to?'

'I've spoken with the ex-wife and the son on the phone. I took a statement off the maid, took a statement off the neighbour who found him in the rose garden, and I've spoken to the chauffeur too.' Jim smiled as if he was pleased with himself.

'Chauffeur?'

'Yeah, Egyptian like his boss. Big geezer. Nice chap. Was downstairs in the underground car park when it happened.'

'Does he have keys to the apartment?'

Jim said nothing.

'You didn't ask?'

'No, I didn't think it was relevant.'

'What if the chauffeur came upstairs, let himself in with the keys, lobbed Marmora off the balcony then went back downstairs?'

'No! The maid would have seen him!'

'You just said she didn't see Marmora fall.'

'Erm... yeah. She said she didn't see anything...'

'She doesn't see everything then, does she? Otherwise she would have seen him fall.'

Jim was silent again. Jake was beginning to lose patience.

'How did we find out he'd *fallen*?'

'Neighbour called 999 after seeing his body in the garden. Went up and told the maid. They'd asked for an ambulance, but we got a request through from London Ambulance Service to attend too.' The smile was gone as Jim concentrated on recalling the details. 'So, umm, we got there first, before the paramedics. And erm, he was well dead when we got there. No signs of life.'

'What time was that?'

'The 999 call was 13.35. We arrived at 13.47. He was pronounced dead at 14.00.'

'Did anyone take his temperature?'

'What?'

'Marmora. Did anyone take the temperature of his body?'

'No, we waited for the photographer. He took some photos. Then the body was taken off to the morgue. That's it. Why would we take body temperature? There was nothing suspicious.'

Jake sighed. 'You said he was *well dead*.'

'Yeah…'

'How long had his body been lying, five floors down in the rose garden, before anyone saw him, Jim? Body temperature would have told us that. It would have given us the time of his *fall* – not what time someone called the police or what time the ambulance was called or what time you turned up. We wouldn't be relying on the maid, who didn't actually see anything.'

'I don't get how that's relevant,' Jim said, flicking through his paperwork to hunt for the computer-aided dispatch message. 'We were assigned the call at 13.36 and we arrived at 13.47.' He held up the sheet to prove it.

'You checked the body for signs of life when you got there?'

'Of course!'

'Was the body warm or cold to touch?'

Jim paused, staring into space. 'It was cold,' he said eventually and sighed, realising his mistake.

'He was *well dead*, like you said a moment ago. He hadn't been lying in the rose garden for just a few minutes after his fall, had he? Or his body would have been warm to touch, wouldn't it?'

Jim stayed silent but nodded.

There was a formula for working out time of death based on normal body temperature. Algor mortis, or death chill as it was better known, started the moment a person died – the moment the heart stopped beating. A body cooled by only one-and-a-half degrees Fahrenheit every hour from normal body temperature. It kept cooling until it reached the same temperature as its surroundings. It wasn't exactly rocket science. Jake figured even Jim could work it out.

'He'd been dead a while before you got there, Jim, hadn't he?'

'Probably, yeah… Um, look, I don't know what time he fell. He was cold to touch…' Jim stumbled over his words and his pallid skin reddened slightly. He looked down at his notes.

'It means we have to treat what the maid says with some caution, Jim.'

'Yeah,' Jim conceded as he sighed again.

'Any other witnesses?'

'None.'

'Did you do any local enquiries? House-to-house enquiries, I mean?'

'We banged on a few doors. There was no one around – no one saw anything.'

'Where's the body?'

'I dunno. At the morgue, I suppose… Coroners' officer is dealing with it. Nothing else for us to do.'

Jake was shocked at how poorly the investigation had been handled so far. He thought back to his own career progression from officer to detective and the first week he'd spent out of uniform in the Criminal Investigation Department.

CID had felt like an initiation into a very secretive, working men's club. One CID officer had been chugging away on a huge cigar in the corner of the small office, a blanket of smoke hanging across the centre of the room like the canopy on a four-poster bed. A long-serving detective constable called Tony had sat Jake down to give him his Criminal Investigation Department induction.

'Right, first and foremost, never forget what I'm about to tell you…' Tony had begun.

Jake had held his breath and waited for that golden nugget. The holy grail of detective work. The hallowed initiation he'd been anticipating. There was something the CID knew that Jake, as a uniformed officer, didn't, and Tony was about to spill the beans. Jake had been on the edge of his seat awaiting that eureka moment – the piece of information that set a detective apart from those in uniform.

'You see him over in the corner?' Tony had pointed to the CID officer who was smoking and cursing over the case file. 'Well, the reason he is thoroughly pissed off is because the lids are lying fuckers. Never trust what those in uniform tell you. Ever. They'll tell you they've done something when they haven't. They're lazy bastards. All they want to do is drive around in their stupid cars with their blue lights on. They haven't a clue about investigating anything. Always check that things have been done properly by doing them again yourself! Welcome to the CID.'

That had been it. Tony had told him nothing else – just that he shouldn't trust his colleagues if they wore a uniform.

Jake had been in that very uniform only weeks before. Was this really what CID had thought of him back then, he'd wondered. Was this really all you needed to know to solve crimes as a detective? At the time, Jake hadn't been so sure. He'd thought there were plenty of good coppers in uniform out there who knew their stuff, had an inquisitive nature and worked hard to fight crime.

Yet, sitting in Belgravia police station now, the words of CID Tony came echoing back to him, and he wondered if Jim was actually telling him the truth. Had he even looked for any witnesses who might have seen a man fall five floors into a rose garden? How much had been missed? It would need doing again. All of it.

'Thanks, Jim.' Jake stood up and held out his hand for the file. 'I'll let your DCI know that we're going to take this job on. It's probably for the best.'

'Yeah, good idea,' Jim said willingly, as he pushed the paperwork across the desk to Jake.

Lenny said nothing until the pair of them reached the safety of the car park at the rear of the station.

'I take it you weren't happy with him keeping it? I thought we were just getting an overview of what they were doing?'

'You'd have been happy with him keeping it?'

'Other than messing up with how long the body had been there—'

'Lenny,' Jake interrupted him. 'It's a fundamental flaw in the entire initial investigation. The time of death is possibly one of *the* most important points. It's not like he said he died sometime between this time and that time – he assumed the time of death based on when the 999 call was made. It's a monumental mistake. That assumption has changed his entire pattern of thinking. If they've got the time of death wrong – by an hour, or half an hour – everything they've done since then is flawed too. So in answer to your question – no, I'm not happy them carrying on with it.'

'But we've got terrorists running around planting car bombs, Jake? Shouldn't we let them keep it?'

'No,' said Jake, looking through the paperwork for the coroner's details. 'I want you to spend the next few days on this for me. Go to the scene of his death, have a look for all the usual things, make sure they've not missed anything. Check and collect all the CCTV you can, speak to the neighbours and find some witnesses. Have a look where he fell – make sure they've not left anything around. Get inside the address he fell from, have a nose about.'

'You not coming with me, guv?'

'No, you take the car. I want this done properly. I don't want us with egg on our faces. I'm going to the morgue to see what's happened to the body. Talk on the phone later.'

'OK,' sighed Lenny. He didn't sound too pleased.

'Lenny, this is important. If we get any urgent work on Operation Seagram, we'll shoot off and do that. In the meantime, crack on with this, all right?'

Lenny shrugged and sloped off toward the car.

9

Every time Jake visited a morgue, he thought of Edwin Chadwick.

Back in 1843, Chadwick had produced a distressing report about Londoners whose living quarters consisted solely of one room. Should a family member pass away in Victorian London, the remaining relatives would have to live alongside that dead body in cramped conditions until it was buried – which could take a week or more. During this time, there was a risk that the decomposing corpse would release the contaminated contents of its bowels, and deadly viruses such as cholera could wipe out whole families.

Chadwick's shocking report showed that twenty thousand deaths took place per year among families who lived in a single room, and that many of these deaths could have been prevented by removing dead bodies promptly and safely. He proposed that 'houses for the dead' be built and the concept for the London mortuary was born.

Jake shuddered to think about how creepy and unsanitary life would have been living alongside a corpse for any length of time. He thanked Chadwick silently for his vision as he entered the rather handsome red-brick Victorian building on Horseferry Road.

John, the coroners' officer, rose from his chair as Jake stepped through the door. He was in his late fifties. An ex-police officer, they'd worked at the same station when Jake had been in uniform. His chubby appearance and mottled red face indicated that John still liked his drink.

'Jake! How have you been? I heard you were suspended.'

'Yeah, I was off for a while. Had all sorts of accusations thrown at me. Most of them were nonsense – you know what they're like. Been back for six months. It's old news.'

They shook hands.

'What are you doing here?'

'I've taken over the investigation of a death, Adham Marmora…'

'The spy who fell from his balcony?'

'Yeah, though I'm still looking into whether he actually fell or whether he was pushed.'

'But the local police said there were no suspicious circumstances?'

'I'm not sure they've covered all the bases on it. I want to give it the once-over, just to make sure. Has the post-mortem been done?'

'The PM? Yeah, of course it's been done – I released the body to his family this morning. It's on its way to Cairo for burial,' he said, looking at his watch. 'Flight left an hour ago.'

'Bollocks!'

'The local sergeant said it was just a fall – nothing suspicious. No witnesses, no nothing. The PM showed that he died from a ruptured aorta, consistent with a fall from height. Lab technician did the job – didn't need a pathologist.'

'Did you take any body samples?'

'It was a straightforward PM. We took ordinary samples for toxicology – that's it. What's the problem?'

'The problem is his background. He's not just Joe Bloggs. That coupled with a poor initial investigation that concluded the wrong time of death… I'm worried we've missed something.'

'I can get you copies of everything we've done, get you some photos. The inquest date has been set for 15 August. What do you want me to tell the old man?' he asked, referring to the coroner.

'Don't tell him anything yet. Let me see what I can turn up.'

10

Jake taped the laminated sheet of paper around the lamp post outside the old Troxy cinema.

How far did cats usually travel from their homes? Would she really go this far?

The road was busy. He'd travelled the length of it several times over the past few days, calling both of her names. Jake had been half expecting to find a small, furry black body squashed and dead in the gutter somewhere. He was relieved that he hadn't – though he did wonder if the road sweepers might have picked her up.

He'd been waiting for the phone to ring all morning. Mark Castle had allocated all the jobs he needed doing prior to the office meeting the previous night, which left nothing for him and Lenny to do. It riled Jake slightly, because he was sure they could have helped out, but Mark obviously wanted to play his cards close to his chest.

Counter Terrorism Command was now so big it could handle a major terror attack without everyone being involved. At three thousand police officers, it was twice the size of some entire provincial police forces.

Lenny was still doing the house-to-house enquiries on the dead spy investigation. He'd found no decent CCTV footage, which, for a central London location, was pretty disconcerting.

Jake taped another appeal to a lamp post. He wondered how many sheets he needed. He had seven left.

Had he made enough? Did anyone really read these things anyway?

Cat Missing
All black, female, no collar, answers to the names
of Edwina *and* Ted. Reward if found.

Jake hadn't seen Ted in the last five days. It was unusual, especially as she'd been home so much over the past few months. Jake had been working regular shifts, with set times for leaving work, and they'd both been getting along fine. She'd been eating really well – perhaps a little too well now he thought about it, and he just couldn't understand why she wouldn't come home. He hoped someone had just locked her inside, thinking she was a stray or something, but as the days rolled on, he'd become more and more worried.

Jake walked back to the Brewery Tap pub on the corner of Caroline Street, directly opposite the entrance to his flat above the sari shop. Despite its close proximity, he'd never actually been inside. Drinking was something he did elsewhere, not this close to home. The place had always looked down at heel, as if it were about to go out of business.

Inside, he tried to catch the attention of the barmaid, a thin woman in her late fifties with a pink skinhead. The place was deserted but her gaze was fixed on the TV that hung on the wall.

'What can I get you?' she asked in a thick Irish accent, eventually tearing herself away from the news bulletin. Jake glanced up and saw a car on fire. A policeman was struggling to put it out with a fire extinguisher.

'I'm not here for a drink. I'm being good.'

'We're a long time dead you know? God won't thank you for being sober. Have a beer, man!'

'No, honestly, it's fine. I wanted to ask a favour.'

'Shoot – what do you need?'

'I live opposite, above the sari shop, and I've lost a cat – a black one. I was wondering if you'd put this poster on your wall.'

Jake held up one of his laminated posters. 'So your customers could see it. I'm hoping someone knows where she is…'

'An old woman used to live there, didn't she? She was Irish?'

'My grandmother, Eva. She died a few years back. I've lived there ever since.'

'Eva, yes, I remember her. Thought I'd not seen her around for a while…'

'She'd come in here?'

'Once or twice. Liked her Irish whiskey, though not often. Sorry to hear that she's passed on, my love. Give us a poster – I'll put it on the wall for you.'

'Thank you. I would have asked in the sari shop, but there seem to be new people in. I don't recognise them. Any idea what's happened to the family that were running it?'

'No, but it's funny you should mention that. They had a blue Citroen, a people carrier that they parked out the back. I was just thinking this morning that I'd not seen it for a few weeks. They must have sold up and left.'

'Maybe. Strange they didn't say goodbye. I was quite fond of the girl that worked there,' said Jake, looking out of the pub at an older Indian woman he didn't recognise. She was standing in the shop window draping a blue sari over a mannequin.

The barmaid turned her attention back to the TV as the news presenter's voice became more and more animated. The screen showed a burning vehicle crashing into some bollards. The barmaid turned the volume up.

'What's that car crash about?' asked Jake as he passed her a cat poster. She took it and stuck it up near the pockmarked dartboard.

'Glasgow Airport. Some bloke crashed into the terminal building. Very strange. The driver caught fire – a policeman put him out!'

'Has he done it deliberately – driven into the building deliberately, I mean?'

'I don't know, my love, it's just happened. That's life.'

Jake had never heard of a burning vehicle driving into an airport building before. Cars rarely caught fire when they had accidents these days. It looked like a deliberate act. What was going on?

'Thanks for putting the poster up. I'm sorry I can't stop for a drink right now. Maybe next time,' said Jake, eager to find out exactly what the incident at the airport was. He waved to the kind barmaid as he walked out. On the street outside, he pulled out his phone and dialled the Reserve Room.

'It's DI Flannagan.'

'We're a bit busy, sir. Is it urgent?' came the flustered voice on the other end of the line.

'Not especially. What are you busy with?'

'DI Castle is up in Liverpool on Operation Seagram. We've got a ton of vehicle checks to do, and then we've got this Glasgow Airport thing with the burning vehicle, which is looking a bit suspect…'

Mark had mentioned nothing to Jake about Liverpool, let alone going there with the team. Yesterday afternoon he'd said there was nothing for Jake to do. And here Jake was searching for his cat, while Mark searched for terrorists.

'Who do you have there, supervisor-wise, in the office now?' asked Jake.

'It's Saturday afternoon, guv…' the officer said with a note of sarcasm in his voice that told Jake everything he needed to know.

'Don't worry. I'm on my way in,' Jake replied, hanging up the phone.

11

In the event of a terrorist attack, the Reserve Room was the nerve centre for absolutely everything. When Jake arrived, it was incredibly busy – people talking loudly on phones, trying to move officers from place to place, teams being coordinated to conduct all sorts of enquiries.

'What have we got?' asked Jake, throwing his coat on to an empty chair next to a DC he vaguely recognised.

'Just after 1500 hours a Jeep Cherokee tried to ram its way into the main terminal building at Glasgow Airport. It was stopped by the crash barriers. There were two occupants of the Jeep, and they set it on fire deliberately. One of the occupants then set himself ablaze. The other occupant of the car, a big guy by all accounts, got out and fought with various people as they tried to put the fire out or intervene. The Jeep was loaded with propane gas cylinders, much like the two cars that we had here in London yesterday, guv. We're pretty certain it's connected. We think it's a failed terror attack.'

'OK, good work. The two occupants of Jeep – both arrested?'

'Yes, guv. One is very badly burned. Strathclyde Police don't expect him to live. He's been taken to hospital.'

'Any idea who they are and where they live?'

'No information yet.'

'I want four counter-terror officers from the on-call team to leave in a car for Glasgow immediately. They're to act as the initial liaison with local police.'

'Yes, guv, I'm on it now.'

'Has anyone got any video, CCTV, the registration number of the Jeep?' Jake shouted over at two officers at computer terminals on the other side of the room.

'No, nothing, not yet,' the older of the two officers, in a T-shirt and jeans, replied.

'OK. Call the local police up. Get a liaison point going, and get the name of someone who we can use as a conduit for information until our officers arrive.'

'Yes, sir,' the other officer replied as she picked up the police almanac and began scanning through it for the right phone number.

'And what the fuck is Mark Castle doing in Liverpool?' asked Jake.

'No one seems to know, guv. He's got two people from his team with him,' replied the older officer.

Jake shook his head and let out a sigh. 'Who's the on-call senior today? Has anyone informed them of the events yet?'

There was a rota that showed which teams had which responsibility in which weeks. It meant the Reserve Room knew which teams had their bags packed and ready to leave at a moment's notice, should there be a terror attack.

'It's Helen Brookes, guv. We've not called her yet. We were waiting to get further information before we did.'

'Leave that to me. The most crucial question at this stage is – have we got any milk to make tea? I say we all need a cup to get us going!'

12

A summer downpour. This part of Docklands always looked at its worst in the rain, thought Jake. Not a single piece of greenery would benefit from the deluge; just concrete and tarmac as far as the eye could see.

Occupational Health was located on one of the upper floors to the rear of Limehouse police station, a post-war building sorely in need of demolition. The huge, gleaming towers of Canary Wharf a few hundred yards up the road just rubbed salt into its wounds.

Jake had always associated Occupational Health with skivers, those on long-term sickness or – as in his own case – management trying to cover its own arse. He wasn't looking forward to this appointment at all. It had elbowed its way in sharply between important tasks, slap bang in the middle of his morning.

In the small waiting area, Jake studied his surroundings. The furniture appeared old and decrepit. A dog-eared, road safety poster screamed 'Arrive Alive'. It felt very much like he was in a doctor's waiting room, anticipating some nasty test results.

'DI Flannagan?' A dowdy woman in her sixties, with a tight curly perm, a long creased skirt and a purple cardigan, appeared from a corridor.

'That's me!' Jake raised his hand and rose from his seat.

'Follow me,' the woman said. She didn't offer her hand to shake or say who she was but turned on the flat heels of her

37

comfortable-looking shoes and headed back on up the corridor in the direction she'd come from.

Jake followed her into a small room that looked like it had once been the station commander's office – acres of space, an en-suite toilet and shower, and a sofa with cushions and coffee table. It smelled faintly of paint, as though it had recently received a makeover.

'Sit down,' she barked at him. 'You've been referred to me because your command unit is worried about you. "Taking unnecessary risks" it says here.'

She pointed at a rather long report on top of the very fat file on the desk in front of her.

'That's all about me?'

'Yes, written by your supervisor.'

'And that folder, what's all that about?' Jake nodded in the direction of the file.

'This is your personnel file.'

The Met computerised very little. They were gradually migrating across to digital records but personnel files were still paper. They contained everything. Original application forms, vetting forms, letters of thanks from victims of crimes, even Christmas cards that had been sent by victims – all somehow found their way in there.

'I've read it. Interesting,' the woman said, pulling open the file and thumbing through it as she spoke. 'Lots of commendations for detective ability, professionalism, determination and several for bravery… Impressive on one level, but there is a pattern here – a pattern of rather foolhardy behaviour. Bus chases, defusing explosive devices… There are also details of your disciplinary history in here, your recent suspension and issues about your current vetting status.'

'I'm really sorry. This is my first time here. Who are you? What rank are you?'

'I'm Shirley Laughlin. I'm your advisor. I don't have a rank – I'm a civilian. You get an hour with me. We talk about whatever you want. I write a report containing my conclusions as to your mental well-being.'

Shirley the shrink? Surely this was a joke?

Jake struggled not to laugh.

'Is this like a pass or fail test?' he asked. 'I don't understand.'

'No, it's not pass or fail. I listen to what you have to say; I write a report. That report may make some recommendations, depending on what you tell me.'

'What sort of recommendations?'

'Well we identify where there are problems, performance issues, problems at home. We make recommendations that will help take people out of very stressful roles, so that they can recuperate – and get back to being their best – all in agreement with the individual.'

'I have no idea why I'm here, Shirley, if I'm honest. This all seems a bit pointless…'

'It says in the report that you struggled with the loss of your mother and grandmother, a very nasty car accident and then you were dealing with the 7/7 bombings… How do those things make you feel?' Shirley pressed on, not listening to him.

'There's nothing wrong with me. Honestly. You're talking to the wrong bloke – I am absolutely fine…'

'Can I call you Jake?' Shirley's approach changed suddenly. She now looked all mumsy and less authoritarian.

'Fine, but—'

'Jake, I understand that you feel a bit odd. You've been referred here. That doesn't happen every day. That means your manager thinks there's something wrong. She's trying to help, not catch you out.'

'This is ridiculous. My manager only referred me here because she was forced to as a box-ticking exercise. What do you want me to say? I'm mad? I drink too much? I like having a lot of sex? I drive too fast when the music is loud? My diet is heavily reliant on microwave meals and I should eat more vegetables? I support Charlton Athletic. That last one must *surely* be a sign of madness, *Shirley*?' said Jake, raising his voice.

'Well… that last one is beyond help to be honest with you.' Shirley chuckled. 'I want to know what you think triggers your drinking?'

'I don't know, I've stopped it…'

'And sex? How many partners are we talking about?'

'I'm a man. I'm no worse than most, I don't think. Do we really need to talk about that?

'You brought it up.'

'I can talk about anything? Anything I want?' Jake asked.

'Well, within reason. I must warn you that I'm not a doctor. So nothing you tell me is confidential. And if I see fit, I will inform your supervisors of any disciplinary matters. Let's try and get off on the right foot here. Your current role, are you enjoying it? Is it fulfilling you?'

'It's OK. I'm a very hands-on person in terms of investigations. I like to be out in the field doing things, not stuck behind a desk doing spreadsheets on overtime and counting how many paper clips my team used last month. As you'll know from my file, I've been stuck in the office a lot recently after coming back from suspension.'

'And has that changed recently?'

'Yes. I made the decision to leave the office and deal with a car bomb the other night. I don't think upper management were very happy about it.'

'What makes you say that?'

'Well instead of getting another commendation for bravery like the ones in that personnel file there,' said Jake, pointing to it, 'I've been referred to Occupational Health to have a chat with you about it, haven't I?' Jake shrugged and smiled at her.

Shirley sighed and smiled back at him. He wondered how many people answered her questions like this and if he was an unusually difficult customer.

'It's nearly the second anniversary of the 7/7 bombings. Do you have any feelings about that?' she asked, changing her line of questioning.

'Like what? What do you want me to say about it?'

'I don't *want* you to say anything about it. I was asking how you *feel* about the anniversary.'

'Well I wish the bereaved families were spending it with their loved ones instead of visiting their graves, and I wish I could have stopped it – if that's what you mean?'

'Could you have stopped it?' Shirley asked, looking puzzled.

'Hindsight is a wonderful thing. Maybe – who knows? But I wasn't about to let it happen again the other night, that's for sure!'

'Do you feel responsible for that, Jake?'

'I'm not responsible for it, no. But it wouldn't have happened if I could turn back the clock.'

'But we can't turn back the clock, Jake. We just have to move forward.'

'Yes, we do. Look, I don't know what I'm doing here, I really don't. I don't feel like there's anything wrong. I was drinking a lot back in 2005, when I was stressed out. My marriage had just broken down, the bombings happened, my mother and grandmother passed away, the car accident... They were all triggers – I recognise that. I know my own mind. That's all stopped, and my life is a lot calmer – I hardly drink at all now.'

'You sound like you've been through an awful lot, Jake. That would take its toll on anyone. I'm sure many people couldn't deal with those things in isolation, let alone all at the same time.' She paused and stared hard at him for a moment before continuing. 'Look, I can't force you to do anything, but I want to say that sometimes talking about things – it helps. And that's all I want to do with you. Help you identify if there are areas in your life that you could be doing better in.'

'I just want to get back to work, Shirley. I've got lots to do. I've got a meeting later, and I've got a ton of stuff to do to be ready for that meeting. All this rigmarole is just someone covering their backside if I do something stupid. I'm not going to do something stupid. I don't want to die – I just want to stop other people from dying, and I won't do that sitting here talking to you, will I?'

Shirley shook her head at him. He couldn't work out if she was agreeing with his last statement or disagreeing with his whole attitude.

'Do you know what post-traumatic stress disorder is, Jake?'

'I've heard of it. Can I leave now? Can you stop me from leaving?'

41

'I can't stop you leaving, no. But look – I'm going to book you in again for another appointment, Jake. Perhaps we can talk more again then? OK?'

'OK. Great,' he said, though he actually meant neither.

'Sometimes, especially in the case of police officers, we can bottle all our emotions up. Things can be playing away in the back of our minds, causing damage that we don't realise is happening, and this manifests itself in odd ways – too many sexual partners, risky behaviour, drinking, drug taking – all symptoms of PTSD,' Shirley said as a passing shot.

'I've not got PTSD.'

Jake stood up, shook Shirley's hand and left.

13

Waiting in reception for his chaperone to come and get him, Jake thought how much of a chore it was to get in and out of the Security Service building. Visiting the home of MI5 was like going through a hard-line version of airport security. Everything was X-rayed, you were searched, and then – when you entered a holding area and thought you'd made it – you discovered that you'd actually only reached reception, where Jake now was.

Here he had to leave any electronic device he had behind, unless it had been pre-approved for use in the building and had a certain level of encryption on it – so when it left the building with any information on it, it was properly protected. That ruled out pretty much any device the police had access to, so he was limited to notepads and pens only.

Jonathan Grant, a twenty-something university graduate, appeared on the other side of the security booth separating Jake from the inner sanctum. Jonathan spoke quietly with the security staff and Jake was ushered through.

Jake had met Jonathan a couple of times before. Though well spoken and clean-cut, Jake thought he always looked a little pale – as if he could do with a bit more Vitamin D. Thames House was rather like much of the Yard once you got inside: people in offices, sitting at desks, hunting through electronic data or writing reports – being out in the sunshine wasn't something these people did very often.

Jonathan took Jake up on to the second floor via an ornate staircase at one end of the main corridor. There were lifts, but the staff shunned them because they took so long. They settled into a small meeting room that overlooked Horseferry Road.

'How have you been, Jon? Long time no see,' said Jake, taking off his suit jacket and sitting down. The meeting room was very warm.

'Yes, it's been a while. I've been working on a project that's trying to streamline our internal processes a bit more, make sure that we share things more quickly with the right people in critical cases and incidents. Been out of the loop as far as operations are concerned.'

'Well it's good to see you back.'

'You're here about your Operation… What's your name for it? Seagrass?'

'Operation Seagram,' replied Jake.

The Security Service had their own naming system for operations, which was quite separate from the police. It was often confusing if neither party knew the other's operation name.

'Seagram. OK. What is it you need from us?' asked Jonathan.

'I want to get an idea of what you guys know, to see if it helps us.'

'Well you know how our systems work. I can't just print things off and give them to you now. You have to ask questions and I'll try and give you the answers, if I can. I gave DI Mark Castle some intelligence on Friday evening. Have you not seen that?'

Jake paused. Mark had been told specifically that Jake would handle the area of intelligence development.

'No – I've not seen that. But, to be honest, he's been away from the office. Things were a little hectic over the weekend.'

'Yes, he went to Liverpool – to do some research on the intelligence we gave him.'

Jake grimaced. Mark had run off with the bloody material that he and Lenny were supposed to be working on? 'So what specifically did you give him?' asked Jake, almost through gritted teeth.

'Well we did some work on the call patterns of the mobile phones that were found in the two cars. Very basic. We hopped from those on to two other phones that we believed were linked to them. We provided DI Castle with some names on Friday evening. It's now clear that these were associates of the two main suspects. I think he made some arrests as a result of it, didn't he?'

Jake was fuming. Mark had cut him out of the loop deliberately. He wondered how much Helen knew about all of this.

'There's obviously been a breakdown of communication at our end. I'll discuss that with DI Castle when I see him.' Jake moved on swiftly. 'I take it you know the names and details of the two Glasgow Airport suspects?'

'Yes, we have those.'

'Have either of them featured in Security Service operations before?' Jake opened up his notepad with one hand and held his pen in the other. This was how the police did business with the Security Service. Initially the case officer would give you generic information. Then it was up to you to home in on what you thought might be useful. It was like a game of twenty questions.

'One of the suspects is sort of known to us – Fadhil Ghalib. The other guy – Sudeep Murthy – isn't on our radar.'

'What do you know about Fadhil Ghalib?'

'Ghalib arrived in the UK from Iraq in 2004. He lived in Cambridge at first. We don't know a great deal about him; he pops up as a contact of other extremists that are on our radar but there's nothing specific. Name and phone traces only – we've never actually done any work on him. We have traces of him that show he's regularly visited extremist websites – just as a passive visitor that is. He views extremist material rather than talking to other jihadis through those websites. He's never been a target of ours.'

Jake noted down what Jonathan had said.

'And what about Sudeep Murthy?'

'Only what we've got from the Saudis.'

'The Saudis?'

45

'Yeah. The Saudis have provided a fair amount of intelligence on both subjects to us in the last twenty-four hours via Vauxhall Cross.'

Vauxhall Cross was how MI5 referred to their counterparts over at MI6 – the Secret Intelligence Service, which supplied the British government with foreign intelligence. Their building was situated across the river, on the south-bank crossroads by Vauxhall Bridge.

'What sort of intelligence?'

'It's all historical. Just what they'd been involved in on their home turf. Both have been involved in Islamic extremism. Fadhil Ghalib is an associate of Harith al-Dari, the Sunni spiritual leader of the 1920s Brigade in Iraq. They're a fairly hard-line group involved in the Iraqi insurgency. Sudeep Murthy is suspected of a bomb attack in his native Bangalore; his parents were leaders of a Muslim extremist party in India. I'm not sure any of it is any use to you as it's a few years old. It's not recent intel.'

'How the hell did both of them get into the country? Why weren't they refused entry?' asked Jake, confused.

'We don't know. We were given the details after the events, not before. As I understand it, the Saudis have only recently searched their systems. They handed over what they found after seeing the London and Glasgow attacks on the news.'

'Why have the Saudis got it, if it's intelligence that appears to be from Iraq and India?'

'I don't know. You'd have to speak with Vauxhall Cross about that.'

'Who's the case officer over there?'

'I'm not sure. I'll find out. See if I can get you a name.'

'Great. Can you also provide me with all the phone numbers, addresses and email addresses that you have for Fadhil Ghalib on your system please, just so I can check we know about them. Then I'll come back to you with some more questions.'

'Sure. It'll take me a few days. And you know how it is – I'll have to send it to you via secure email.'

The Security Service transmitted information to the police via a special system. It was received and printed off on the eighteenth floor of the Yard, where Jake would have to collect it.

They shook hands and Jake left with a nagging feeling that something about it all didn't sit right. He just had no idea what it was.

14

'Thank you all for coming,' Helen said, raising her voice to address the room and quieten the twelve middle-aged men in suits and ties all talking amongst themselves. She had gathered the team of detectives leading various parts of the investigation, together with analysts and representatives from exhibits and the high-tech unit in the conference room.

The chatting abated as people opened notepads and picked up pens, waiting for an update and further instructions.

'First of all,' Helen continued, 'I want to say thank you for your hard work so far. I know some of you have worked very long hours over the course of this past weekend. It's all been very fast moving and we've not had much of an opportunity to catch our breath yet. I just wanted us all to have a quick update with where we are and who's doing what. As I'm sure you're all aware, we have now linked the Glasgow Airport attack to the two car bombs in London. This will now be one investigation.

'Not many of you know DI Mark Castle. He's been assigned as case officer.' Helen indicated Mark, who was sitting on her left-hand side. 'Mark's new here, and to some extent he's been given a bit of a rude introduction to Counter Terror with this one.' Helen caught Jake's eye for a split second. 'This is a fast-moving investigation, and it's becoming increasingly more complex. We need to work effectively together and talk to each other so I'll be making this a regular slot – Tuesday afternoons,

1 p.m., here – until further notice. Without exception, I will expect you, or a team member deputising for you, to attend...

'Right, Mark. Where are we with the suspect interviews?'

Mark took the floor. 'My interview team are still questioning the suspect from the airport bombing – the one that didn't set fire to himself that is – Fadhil Ghalib. He's not saying too much. They're also continuing with the questioning of his Liverpool associates. We know the bombers purchased a car there, decided they didn't want it and left it at Liverpool Airport – empty. Again, nothing much coming out of the interviews at present.'

'And the suspect who set fire to himself?'

'Sudeep Murthy is still alive, or so I'm told. Doctors have said he's in a coma. We've got the local police guarding him. He's in critical condition and being moved to a specialist burns unit. It's not looking good for him at all. Ninety per cent burns, not expected to survive.'

'Is it a medically induced coma?' asked Helen. 'Can we do anything about it, talk to him before it's too late?'

Mark shook his head. 'I don't know.'

Helen looked at him. She didn't give much away, but she didn't look pleased. 'Have you spoken to the doctors yourself, Mark? This is important.'

'Well no, he's in Scotland.'

Helen frowned, looked down at her notes and changed the subject.

'Jake – could you update everyone on your activities please?'

'Well on Friday there was apparently nothing for me to do on Operation Seagram so I was sent home.' Jake paused slightly for emphasis and to demonstrate that it wasn't of his own choosing. 'Then I found out about the Glasgow attack from Sky News as I searched for my cat, which is currently missing...'

There was some stifled laughter around the room.

Helen looked up and frowned at him – she wasn't amused. Jake moved on. 'And so I ended up back here in the Reserve Room. I dealt with the information flow from Scotland as the situation at Glasgow Airport developed over the course of Saturday and Sunday... while Mark was in Liverpool.' Jake did his best to disguise his displeasure about not being kept up to date on the Liverpool visit.

'After I found out the names of the bombers,' he continued, 'I did some digging around and found that one of them, Fadhil Ghalib, worked at the Royal Alexandra Hospital in Paisley as a doctor. I managed to speak to Ghalib's supervisor. Very nice guy. Ghalib was supposed to be at work on Saturday, the day of the airport bombing. His supervisor received an email at around 0530 hours on the day of the Glasgow attack. The email claimed to be from Ghalib's sister. It said that he had been seriously hurt abroad and wouldn't be coming to work. Obviously that was a lie – he wasn't abroad, and he hadn't been hurt at that point. I got an IP address from that email and passed it to the Security Service in the hope that we might identify who had sent the email. They traced it to a village in Houston, just outside Glasgow – a six-mile drive from the hospital. In Mark's absence, I dispatched a team up to Scotland on Saturday.' Jake paused again, briefly. 'We obtained a search warrant for the house in Houston and discovered that it was the bomb factory.'

Helen smiled at him. 'Great.'

'I've handed the enquiries over to Mark on that now.'

'Excellent work, Jake.'

'Mark, the bomb factory – how're things going there?'

'I'm waiting for exhibits to update me on that.'

'What local enquiries have been done on the address?'

'Exhibits are searching it and—'

'Mark,' Helen cut him off. 'Did you organise any local enquiries to be done among the neighbours of the bomb factory yet? Exhibits won't organise that for you. You'll need a team up there to do it.'

'Well, err, yes, I know, but my team are all tied up with the suspects. I've not exactly got round to it yet.'

'That's the sort of thing you need to tell me about, Mark. Then I can allocate you more people – but you need to tell me. You've got your whole team involved in the suspect interviews?'

'Yes.'

Helen moved swiftly on. 'Who's here from exhibits?' she asked.

'Exhibits, yes, that's me – DS Snow.' A small chubby-faced man raised his arm. 'DI Knight sends his apologies. He's busy with the burned-out Jeep from Glasgow. It was moved down from Glasgow Airport on Sunday morning to the forensic explosives laboratory in Kent. We're slowly going through the motions with it. Early indications are that the Jeep was set up to explode in a very similar way to the cars in London. Petrol, gas canisters, that sort of thing. Interestingly we've recovered a laptop from the Jeep. It's pretty burnt and beaten up, but we've managed to get the hard drive out of it. I took the liberty of passing it straight to the high-tech unit for them to mirror the drive and see what there is on it. Hope that's OK?'

'Of course. Glad to see that some people are using their initiative,' said Helen.

'Jake.' Helen looked over at him 'Intelligence – where are we with that?'

'Well I met with the Security Service case officer about Seagram yesterday, opened the channel as it were...'

'Good,' Helen said encouragingly.

'There are a few minor traces of Fadhil Ghalib in the UK,' continued Jake. 'He's visited some extremist websites, that sort of thing. We also have some intelligence that has come from the Saudis. Not sure how useful that is to us yet, as I haven't had sight of it in its entirety, but it's on its way.'

'Are the traces any use to us?' asked Helen.

'I'm waiting for the full details to be sent to me. What I will say, before I go any further, is that the Liverpool enquiries were done straight off the back of Security Service intelligence around some of the associates of the bombers. And I know Mark is new here, but jumping in with two feet, to action *intelligence* – well it's something we need to be very careful of.'

'That's a good point,' agreed Helen. 'We must remember that *intel* isn't *evidence*. I've appointed Jake as the lead on the intelligence cell. He knows the ropes here, knows the pitfalls and the problems that can be created when we action intelligence that we take from the Security Service. I don't want us doing that again. OK?'

Mark nodded but didn't look up from his pad on the table.

'I've asked the case officer at Thames House to put me in contact with someone over at Vauxhall Cross to discuss what the Saudis know. For some reason, they've got a lot of intelligence on these two guys,' said Jake. 'It doesn't appear that they've appointed a case officer over there yet,' he said, referring to MI6, 'so I'm just waiting at present. It's likely to be a few days or a week before we have anything too much to do.'

'OK,' Helen replied.

There was a pause.

Jake wanted Helen to know he was keen to be involved in this job so he decided to push his hand a little. 'If you need anything doing in Scotland, I'm happy to be involved, get some people together, go up there, sort out those house-to-house enquiries – if we're struggling for staff?'

'Good idea, yes. Liaise with Mark and get those enquiries at the bomb factory underway. That's helpful, thanks.' Helen looked around the room. Mark was still staring at his notepad as she spoke. 'Anyone else got anything?'

There was silence.

'Good. See you all again here next week. Same place, same time.'

15

Jake lay down on the bed in his hotel room, the contents of the minibar gone.

He struggled to focus on the intricate tartan pattern plastered across the feature wall of his room. The alcohol had weakened his pupils' reaction time.

The TV had been his only company after the long journey up from London. The rolling news channel had played footage of the Glasgow Airport attack ad nauseam.

Jake felt like he'd gone back in time two years. A hotel room miles from home. Terror attacks. Alcohol and loneliness.

Why the hell had he volunteered for this? Was it just to try and get one over on Mark Castle?

His thoughts turned to the argument he'd had with him earlier that day about the bomber's work computer. Jake had wanted to remove Fadhil Ghalib's terminal from the hospital he'd been working at before the attacks. When Jake suggested it might be important, Mark had insinuated that Jake was just finding new ways to carve out work for himself. 'Don't be a wanker,' had been Mark's exact words.

Did Mark not realise that he was just trying to help? Not picking holes? Why did everything have to be so difficult with him?

Things had escalated from there.

'Do what you want,' Mark had said, like a petulant child, before hanging up the phone. Jake had heard laughter in the background, as if Mark had been playing to an audience. He'd caught snatches of another voice, a detective sergeant on Mark's team that Jake had little time for – Gavin Bonson. A smarmy little troublemaker in Jake's opinion.

On the television, the burning Jeep had driven repeatedly into the metal bollards at Glasgow Airport; the bomber had doused himself in petrol and set himself on fire, ablaze from head to toe. Raiding the minibar had seemed to Jake like a good diversion at the time.

It was his own fault – of course it was, despite trying to find someone or something to blame for his drunkenness.

The buck had to stop with him, didn't it?

He'd been so good over the past few months, but as the room began to spin a little, Jake thought about his discussion with Shirley, and about what triggered his drinking.

He knew it wasn't simple boredom that made him drink; knew that it was something deeper that he didn't really understand.

Maybe she was right. Maybe he did need to talk.

The blazing Jeep appeared in his head again – the flames engulfing one of the terrorists as he was grappled to the ground; his skin disintegrating in the police officer's hands. His body burned down to the nerves.

Then it hit him. That's what this was about tonight. The thoughts came flooding back, as if the door to a vault had been loosened by his drinking, his inebriation giving him the courage to look inside after a very long time.

He picked up his mobile and dialled Claire.

Ring. Ring. Too long. He hung up.

He tried again. This time she picked up the phone.

'Hey! It's me.' He tried to quell the excitement in his voice.

'You sound drunk. Why are you drunk, Jake? I thought you were off the booze?'

'I've had a few. Not many. I'm all right.'

'What do you want? It's way past midnight.'

'I just wanted a chat, to hear your voice. Wondered when I'm seeing you again?'

'What's the matter?'

'Nothing.'

'I'm trying to sleep, Jake.'

'I just want to have a chat, discuss—'

'Jake – it's late, you're drunk and that's bad news, on both counts,' Claire said, annoyed.

She sounded like she was getting ready to put the phone down on him. She was right, it was late, but he didn't want her to go. Maybe he should just be honest?

'I called you as a distraction,' he said, plucking up his courage.

'From what?'

'I can't watch the flames any more.'

'What?' she asked, confused.

'On the TV.'

'Oh, Glasgow Airport?'

'Yeah.'

'Then switch it off,' she tutted.

'I did, ages ago. But every time I close my eyes, it's there again.'

'Why?'

'Work have referred me to Occupational Health, said I might need to talk some things over about what triggers my drinking. I've been lying here on the bed thinking about it.'

'And seeing the fire has brought something back?' she asked.

'Yeah. It's opened a Pandora's box of stuff that I probably should have left well alone.' Jake sighed.

'What sort of stuff is it?'

'It's from 1996.'

'I thought you were going to talk about the bombings, 7/7...'

'No.'

'Then tell me. It's clearly upsetting you. I'm a good listener,' she said, her voice mellowing.

'Christmas Day. I was working. Got called to a house fire.'

Claire laughed. 'Someone leave the turkey in the oven too long?'

Jake took a deep breath. 'You could say that.'

There was a pause.

'Tell me.' Claire's tone changed as she realised her joke had been misplaced.

Jake thought back to that day; a memory he'd kept locked away until now.

He was standing at the door of the second-floor maisonette, smoke and flames billowing from the windows like it was only yesterday.

'It wasn't the turkey that was the problem,' said Jake slowly. 'The fire was already raging when I arrived. Young couple outside, arguing with each other, both drunk, both very upset...'

'What were they arguing about?'

'The baby,' said Jake, feeling a lump appear in his throat.

'The baby was dead?' Claire asked tentatively.

'Not at that point, no. She was upstairs in her cot – I could hear her crying. Mum and dad were arguing with each other about who should have grabbed the baby.' Jake grimaced. 'They'd both jumped out of the first-floor bedroom window on to the balcony because of the smoke, but none of us could get back inside because the front door was double-locked. I tried kicking it in, but the door was so hot that the rubber soles of my shoes were sticking to it. I couldn't get in the windows, as the flames were too strong, so we had to stand there and wait for the fire brigade. The baby carried on crying, then screaming, for what seemed like an eternity – right up until the fire engine pulled up. Then it went silent. Eventually they put the fire out. The firefighters found the baby...'

As he told the story, Jake began to slip into the present tense, so vivid were the memories. It was like he was actually standing there once again, watching the fire brigade spraying water over everything in sight.

'Looks like the baby is all right, it's a little girl... Her pink skin is a stark contrast to everyone else. We're all covered in soot and smoke, filthy. I'm relieved that she doesn't look burnt. She's naked. Totally unmarked. My heart misses a beat, hoping that she's still alive. I go to help her, but one of the firefighters shouts, "Don't touch her," as they lay her on the ground.'

'They didn't want you to help?' asked Claire.

'They'd been hosing her down for five solid minutes before they could pick her up and remove her from the flat, even though they'd been wearing gloves. She was still too hot to handle with bare hands. And then I realise why she's pink and clean. She's been hosed down so much. She was cooked in her cot… like a sausage in its skin. Dead.'

'Why have you never told me about it?'

'You file it away. Not to be looked at or thought about.'

'Don't they give everyone in the emergency services counselling to deal with this stuff?'

'Nope.'

'Then how do you go back to work once you've dealt with something like that?' she asked, horrified.

'You condition yourself not to think about it – easy to do unless something forces you to look into the place the memory is stored. When you see something on the TV, like today.'

There was silence.

'I'm sorry, Jake. I'm sorry you're still carrying all this around.'

'You just have to lock it away and learn how to cope with it. And if you can't learn, you leave and find a job where you never have to deal with this stuff.'

'I don't know how emergency services personnel don't go insane seeing that sort of thing day in and day out.'

'Someone has to do it. It's shit. Nobody likes it. But it has to be done. And you focus on the positives. File the negatives away.'

'Is everyone like you, Jake Flannagan?'

'The problem is everyone *else*. Because we've all got used to dealing with it. Police, fire, ambulance, rescue, whatever your role is – it makes you feel like there's something wrong with *you* for feeling bad about it. Everyone is either desensitised to it or just puts up a good front. So you learn to put on a front too. It's like unspoken peer pressure.'

There was a pause.

Claire yawned.

'What time are you on tomorrow?' Jake could sense her attention was waning so he changed the subject.

'I've got a breakfast meeting. Got to be in at 7.30 a.m. Early start,' she said. 'Ring me tomorrow. We'll discuss it more then.'

She was trying to get rid of him, wasn't she?

'It's fine. Honestly,' mumbled Jake, knowing he wouldn't and couldn't discuss this sober.

Claire yawned again.

'I'd honestly talk longer, Jake, but you know I really need to be able to function at these early briefings.'

'Get some sleep,' he said.

They wished each other goodnight and she hung up the phone.

He stayed on the line a while longer, not quite ready to accept she was gone, before, disappointed, he finally put the phone down. Being alone wasn't going to help. Alone with just his thoughts was never good.

The anger, the alcohol, the sadness... it wasn't a good mix. The need to have someone else there grew stronger. It made his loneliness worse. It made him focus on it. Drunkenness was like standing there with a magnifying glass – standing over himself and looking down.

Alone.

He lay there a few more minutes, hoping he'd fall asleep, but the thought of his recurring dreams held him on the edge of slumber.

The room slowed down and the spinning lessened. Sleep failed to come.

He got up. Picked up his coat.

He needed a new distraction.

16

Jake followed the directions provided by the guy on reception. He recited the man's words in his head as he walked: 'A nightclub? You want the Cathouse, that's quite close – pretty good too. Under the station bridge and turn left on to Union Street.'

The music in the club was blaring. It was a live band. He could hardly hear himself think, which was good – he didn't want to think. The place was young. Rockers. Mostly in black with tattoos and beards. Dirty looking.

Why was he here, amongst these twenty-something revellers? A hostage to his emotions... scared of being alone – scared of his memories.

Everyone seemed to be dancing, which meant the bar wasn't busy.

'I'll have a whisky please,' Jake shouted to the barman, who had to lean across the bar just to hear him.

'That'll be the Scotch then?' the young guy with huge hoop holes in his ears replied in a broad Glaswegian accent.

Jake nodded. 'Yeah, that.'

'Single or double?'

'Pint...' Jake smiled.

'I'll get you a double, pal.'

Drink in hand, Jake watched the packed dance floor from the bar. Everyone seemed to be jumping up and down on the spot. It made him feel old.

A girl extricated herself from the middle of the jumping mob and came over to the bar. She was in her twenties. Slim. Bright red hair with a blunt-cut fringe. Glasses. A tattoo on her right arm. Attractive, in a rock-gothic sort of way. She wore a T-shirt bearing the name of a band he'd never heard of and a short denim skirt.

'Hi,' she shouted at him.

He nodded back. 'Hi,'

The music was very loud. She came closer and stood on her tiptoes to speak into his ear. 'What are you doing here?'

Jake smiled. 'Getting a drink. You?'

The girl laughed. 'I meant here, in this place? Doesn't seem your sort of venue, with your work suit and nice shoes. It's all piercings and denim in here normally, and, well…'

'I'm old. I know,' Jake finished her sentence for her. 'I just needed a drink, and some company. Didn't want to be on my own, and this was the closest place.'

'You're from down south? You working up here?' she asked. She sounded like she might be from Yorkshire, but he couldn't be sure.

'Yeah, I'm working. I'm a long way from home.'

'What do you do?'

Rule number one: never tell strangers what you did for a living. Ever.

Most people reacted very oddly to Jake telling them he was a counter-terror detective. Some were incredibly hostile. All had stories to tell about their experiences with the police. Usually very long-winded ones about how something had gone wrong. Telling people his actual job title was to be avoided at all costs.

Rule number two: say something intriguing instead.

In Jake's experience, people loved a puzzle. If he could arouse their curiosity, it provided instant entertainment.

Rule number three: make them laugh.

Play the ninja clown. Or was it the clown ninja? Whichever – making them smile was the most important rule of all.

'I'm a caretaker,' he said enigmatically.

'A caretaker? Like at a school or something?'

'No. I take care of things. Someone has a problem, I sort it out. I take care of it...'

The girl burst out laughing. 'Like a hit man, you mean? You're a hit man?'

'Sort of. I could tell you, but you seem nice, and I don't want to have to kill you because I've told you too much,' he replied, smiling back at her.

She laughed again.

All three rules complied with – she was hooked.

He was just happy to be talking to someone who wasn't a victim, or a witness, or a suspect.

He hadn't told any lies. He was here, in Glasgow, taking care of a problem someone had created. He didn't know who'd created it yet, but he would.

He was glad of the company. It would keep his mind active, and on something else.

'What's your name?' he asked her.

He'd stay a while.

17

She'd insisted that he come back to her place because she had to be up for an early shift. Jake was tired and drunk and in no mood to argue with her.

They'd stumbled through the door of her grey-brick halls of residence opposite the hospital but made so much racket that her flatmates had chucked them out. Jake hadn't even known what time it was.

She wasn't about to be put off though.

'I know the place, I know the place,' she'd said, dragging him by the hand and smuggling him into the main hospital building.

He had to hand it to her – she was determined.

Successfully inside the building, she yanked him into a side room. Pulling up her denim skirt, she unbuckled his trousers and pushed him down on to a plastic chair before she climbed astride him.

He felt the soft skin of her breasts in his face as she pulled off her T-shirt and bra and threw them on to a chair alongside them. She groaned above him, the smell of her perfume filling his nose.

He looked around the dimly lit room, trying to focus.

White or cream walls.

Low-wattage candle bulbs.

Several chairs, all neatly lined up and facing the same direction.

She bounced up and down in his lap, the rose on her right arm hypnotising him. She moaned gently and then a little louder.

What was her name? He couldn't remember. She was only nineteen though – he remembered that. He was old enough to be her father.

'Fuck me harder, you old bastard,' she shouted.

Jake glanced to his left.

There was a cross on the wall.

He could hear her talking dirty, but all he could focus on was the cross.

There was a man on the cross – a crucifix.

Through the sweaty, alcoholic haze, it dawned on him.

They were in the chapel of rest. He was having sex with a nineteen-year-old in the chapel of rest.

In a hospital.

The place where people prayed for their loved ones and remembered their dead friends and relatives.

'You love it, don't you?' she kept saying, over and over.

He couldn't think of any appropriate words to use. Not here. Not now.

He closed his eyes, tried to focus on the sensations in his groin – tried to think about the nubile, young girl he was with.

But this place… A place of death. A place of grief. A place of loneliness.

Had he no respect for the dead?

'Harder,' she said as she sank her nails into his shoulders and threw her head back. 'I love fucking dirty old men.'

He grabbed her hips to lift her off, trying to hold her still as she gyrated up and down on him.

He was ashamed at even being here, but his shame just made him more aroused.

Without any warning, he ejaculated.

'Fuck!' he shouted with a strangled yelp.

He felt a pain at the top of his chest, as if the overwhelming shame and disappointment at his own actions were bearing down on him, squashing him.

She grabbed his hand and pulled it to her, grinding against his fingers. 'I'm coming,' she said in a hot whisper into his ear before her body shuddered.

Had anyone seen them?

He held her, waiting for her to be still. She slumped over him, panting, sweating.

He felt utterly conflicted. Why did he continue to take all these stupid risks?

'I've got to go,' he said into her ear, gently pushing her upright. 'You need to get me out of this place.

18

The bombers' rented property was a brick semi in a small village, a seventeen-mile drive from Glasgow. Clearly built in the seventies, the house had decorative grey pebbledash on its upper half, with a neat lawn and some decorative bushes to the front.

Standing alongside Lenny, outside this average-looking house in this average-looking village, Jake had a creeping sensation of déjà vu. This, coupled with the hangover, was making him feel slightly sick.

Kevin Knight, an experienced exhibits officer with a world-weary look, briefed them on what had been found inside. They could have done it in the office, but Jake wanted to attend the scene; needed to get a feel for the place himself. It was important that the words he heard during the briefing matched up with the gut feel he got about a place.

Kevin reeled off the details: 'Quiet road, neighbours have been very helpful so far. The house is a two bed. One large living room downstairs, with a kitchen off that. Upstairs there are two bedrooms and a bathroom.'

'Found much?'

'Very messy in the living area. Loads of component parts scattered everywhere. We found wires, a circuit board, bulbs and a soldering iron on the table and chairs.'

'When you say component parts – are they similar to the London devices we found in the two cars?'

'Identical – it's the right place. There are pliers, batteries and tape on the floor. Large amounts of matches – dozens with the heads broken off. Loads of diagrams of electrical circuits. Two modified mobile phones with wiring attached to an initiation device. Definitely enough materials to construct at least another two car bombs.'

'Anything else?'

'We also recovered plastic gloves, superglue and plastic syringes. There's tons of stuff – we're looking at over a thousand exhibits before this is out.'

'You sure this is where they did everything?'

'I can't say for certain, but it looks like it to me. And there are clothes in the cupboard upstairs. They were living here.'

'What about at the hospital where the guy worked? Desks, drawers, lockers, that sort of thing. Have they all been searched?'

'That's all been done. We found a car related to those items in the hospital car park. Nothing in it.'

'Did we take his work computer too?'

'I don't think so.'

'OK. I'll get over there and collect it,' replied Jake. 'We'll need it. Colleagues say he spent a huge amount of time on the computer at work – it's likely to be full of stuff.'

'The new bloke didn't mention the work computer to me or I'd have taken it when we were there on Monday. Where's he from, that bloke… DI Mark Castle, is it?'

'Local borough.'

'He's really odd. Ask him a question and he doesn't seem to know the answer. He'll just snap back about something else,' said Kevin, less than impressed.

Jake said nothing as they walked round to the rear of the property.

Kevin pointed to the garage. The windows were covered with black bin bags and bubble wrap. 'Tenants blocked the view,' he said.

Jake nodded. 'OK, Kevin, thanks. I'll get my lot doing the house-to-house later and see what else we can find out about the guys and the property.'

'Sure. If you need anything, just let me know, guv.' Kevin turned and went back to the house.

Lenny puffed up his cheeks, trying to scope the neighbourhood out. 'What do you reckon, Jake? Three or four days to do statements from everyone in the street?'

'Maybe. I'd much prefer to have it wrapped up sooner if we can though. We've got some loose ends to tie up at the hospital, but that can wait until tomorrow. Let's make a start here.'

They wandered round to the front and down the drive. 'This place, Len, is what I would term "naturally bland". Like vanilla blancmange. Faceless, nameless, characterless... There's no way the neighbours would have missed these guys moving in. And people are nosey. Something always turns up. Let's brief everyone, get them going.'

Identifying everyone who lived in the local radius by knocking on doors and asking the occupants was often tedious but always necessary.

'Guys, can I have your attention over here please,' Lenny called to a group of six detective constables standing by their cars – all waiting for instructions on what to do next.

The officers gathered round. Lenny got down to business: 'I want a list with everyone's names on it. Make sure you speak to everyone on that list, take a statement from them, find out what they know about our two bombers and this house, if anything.'

Plans in place, Jake finished with a pep talk. 'This is one of the single most important things you will be doing in this investigation. There is no substitute for putting in the hard yards. We're in a small village. Two men of Asian appearance renting a house together *must* have got curtains twitching, people talking. If there were other visitors to their house, it's likely the neighbours knew about it. They may well have seen them and what cars they drove. Invaluable information. Things we can work with, move forward with.'

Not that Mark Castle would understand, thought Jake.

19

Friday
6 July 2007
1030 hours
Royal Alexandra Hospital, Paisley, Renfrewshire

As Lenny drove, Jake slumped back into his seat, letting his head loll back against the headrest. It was still early, but he felt as if he'd done a day's work already. They'd had a team meeting over breakfast at the hotel, during which the house-to-house enquiry team had fed back their findings.

In the village of Houston, one of the elderly neighbours had remembered seeing a mini parked outside the bombers' house. The car had stuck in her memory because of the unusual green and purple lettering on the side, and because it never left enough space for the supermarket delivery van to pull in – much to the neighbour's annoyance.

The perpetrator had been a local rental agent conducting viewings. Jake and Lenny had tracked him down and he'd confirmed that he'd shown the two bombers around the property.

'Interesting what that letting agent said, don't you think?' said Jake, turning to Lenny.

'What do you mean?'

'That he thought they were odd when he was showing them round.'

'Yeah, but that's just him marrying it up with what we know now.'

'Possibly. But he did say he couldn't understand why one of them needed another place when they already had lodgings in the hospital halls of residence?'

'So?'

'And right from the outset, when they first enquired about a rental property back in May, they went on and on about insisting on a house *with* a garage.'

'What are you thinking, guv?'

'It just makes me far more confident that the Houston house was rented *specifically* to manufacture the explosive devices.'

Jake's phone buzzed with a text-message notification. It was Claire: 'Are you around tomorrow? Fancy doing something?'

Jake messaged her back: 'I can be.'

'See you at 7.30 a.m. I'll pick you up. Bring some shorts,' was the response.

Jake frowned at the early start.

'Everything OK?' asked Lenny.

'Yeah, fine. Just thinking,' replied Jake, without looking over at him.

'Listen, Len, I'm going to get the train back home tonight. Leave you here with the team. Everything's going well. You'll be done by tomorrow night. You don't need me here.'

'Are you all right, boss? Late night for you last night? You look awful.'

'Something I ate – kept me up most of the night.'

'You didn't go out for a sneaky beer after we'd all gone to bed then?'

'You know I'm trying to stay away from the booze,' said Jake, waving Lenny's question away.

'Well I've seen you hungover, probably several hundred times, Jake. And you look hungover.'

'Leave it, Lenny.'

'I might be your DS, but I'm also your mate…'

'I know.'

'Don't go back down that road again, Jake. You've put it all behind you. It's madness to start it all again.'

'I know. I know,' replied Jake. He was disgusted enough at himself as it was. He didn't need Lenny to point the finger.

They pulled into the car park of the hospital, got out of the Mondeo and walked toward the building.

Jake recognised it instantly. The square and boxy eighties architecture; the black bricks and white window frames; the ridiculous circular tower part, right at the front, that served as the reception area – and looked like an odd architectural afterthought.

This was a familiar venue.

This was where he'd been dragged two nights ago, by the redhead from the nightclub.

As they entered the hospital, Jake hoped against hope that he wouldn't bump into her. His heart was hammering away in his chest. He felt dirty. It had been wrong on so many levels.

Most of all, he didn't want Lenny to see her.

Why was that? Was it because she put his drunken debauchery back on the table as a work-related issue? Was it because she represented his major weakness – that he too often surrendered to his feelings? His stupid, reckless impulses.

They navigated their way around the hospital, thanks to guidance from staff and patients along the way, and found the diabetes department, where one of the bombers, Fadhil Ghalib, had worked as a locum. Jake asked to see the consultant who oversaw the unit.

'So how can I help you gentleman?' asked Dr Bedi, a fifty-something, rotund man of Indian descent. Jake looked at the grey carpet tiles, the wood laminate desk with steel legs, the pot plant perched on one corner. It reminded Jake of his GP's office. He eyed the plant on the corner of the desk. Was it even real? Were they even allowed live plants in hospitals these days?

'Fadhil Ghalib – I wonder if you could give us some background on him?'

'Yes, Fadhil applied for the job here after getting temporary registration from the General Medical Council to practice.'

'Forgive me,' said Jake, 'I'm not completely in the picture in terms of your procedures.'

'OK. Well, Fadhil qualified as a doctor in Baghdad in 2004, and he first registered as a doctor in the UK in August 2006. In other words, the General Medical Council here recognised that he had done some training but they had to check that this

70

was up to standard. So he was given limited registration by them from 5 August 2006 to 11 August 2007.'

'So what does that allow him to do?'

'The limited registration is awarded to recent medical graduates. It allows them to work in Britain for a year, but in accordance with standard procedure, he could not move jobs during that time and had to be supervised.'

'And you supervised him?'

'I did. He was a very lacklustre doctor. He spent most of his time surfing the internet. He'd lost all interest in his work – so much so that one of our female staff reported him to me. She filed a complaint. I disciplined him for it. She was in tears when she heard the police had arrested him – she felt she should have done more.'

'What sort of websites was he looking at?'

'Mostly Arabic-language sites, things that I couldn't read, but judging by the photos and videos – at least some of them were extremist websites.'

'Did he give any explanation for looking at these? Did you report it to anyone?'

Dr Bedi sighed and shook his head. 'Do you know much about Fadhil, inspector?'

'Not too much, no.'

'Fadhil was born in Aylesbury, Buckinghamshire, but he moved to Iraq when he was young. He's the son of a rather brilliant Iraqi doctor who did his training here on a scholarship. The following year the family returned to Iraq. They lived in a very upmarket part of Baghdad, a six-bedroom villa. The entire family are very well-to-do. He's got five siblings. They became doctors, pharmacists and an engineer. That's his background.'

'They don't sound like Islamic extremists.'

'No. And that's why I wasn't overly concerned about him looking at the sorts of websites that he was. Fadhil loved Iraq. He said Baghdad was militarised during the Iran–Iraq war in the eighties – that one of the most dazzling cities in the Middle East had been ruined by Allied forces following the Gulf and Iraq Wars.

'You think anyone going through that torment would look at those websites? Is that what you're suggesting?'

'I'm saying that it's possible. His family eventually fled Iraq and sought haven in Jordan. Had to move into a one-bedroom apartment. Fadhil remained in Iraq, which was by that point tearing itself apart in a sectarian bloodbath brought about by the US and UK invasion. I'm not sure how involved in the fighting he was. But he did tell me that he lost fifteen close friends and family. I think he was very angry, and the websites were just a symptom of his anger about things. I didn't see them as a problem, it was just that he was doing it far too much.'

'And what do you think about him being arrested?'

'I'm extremely surprised. He doesn't strike me as a violent person. It seems to me that the other man was the lead in all of this – the one who set fire to himself.'

'If you speak to the police officer who tried to stop them blowing up Glasgow Airport, you'd probably think differently,' said Lenny quickly.

Jake gave Lenny a look and continued, 'But I guess it's all about perception, Dr Bedi? We see what we want to see. You saw a broken, angry man. Not one who wanted to kill people?'

'Agreed,' replied the doctor.

'You said that he was given registration by the GMC to practise for a year. Were there any plans for him after August, when it ran out?'

'We probably would have passed him – he probably would have been given his competency.'

'OK. The desktop computer that Fadhil used – we're going to need to take it, to examine it for evidence.'

'Several people use that computer, not just him.'

'We need to be sure there's nothing on it. Can you show me where it is please?'

Twenty minutes later, Jake and Lenny had bagged up the computer and were following the exit signs.

'What d'you think about all that, then, Jake?'

'When did his cohort, the one with the ninety per cent burns, arrive in the country?' asked Jake.

'May, I think. Just a month before the bombings.'

'So they've rented that house more or less as soon as his mate arrived. He's moved out of the hospital halls of residence into the rental place, and that's then become a bomb factory. It was rented for that purpose. He's up to his neck in it. He's not a frightened fool who's a bit angry about his hometown being in the middle of a war. He's a killer. I don't feel sorry for him.'

'What about his medical registration running out next month? Do you think that's got any relevance?' asked Lenny as they neared the exit.

As Jake turned to answer, he caught a flash of red hair over a blue nurse's uniform down a side corridor.

'Jake?' called a female voice.

He turned his eyes to the floor and kept walking, but Lenny had already paused to look.

'Jake?' came the voice again.

He stopped and turned. It was her – the rocker girl from the club.

'Hey, how are you?' he said, smiling as he walked back to where she was standing.

Lenny looked confused but said nothing.

'What are you doing here?' she asked, eyeing the computer unit he was holding.

'Working, I'm working…' He was embarrassed. He didn't want her knowing what he did for a living. 'Can I call you later? I'm a bit busy.'

'You don't have my number. You left in such a hurry you didn't take it. Fine, let's leave it there.' She looked hurt and upset. That's not what he wanted.

'Hang on, give me a minute.' Jake turned, gave the computer unit to Lenny and asked him to wait in the car. Lenny looked at him suspiciously, but still he said nothing.

Jake returned to face the girl standing in the corridor. 'Look, I'm really sorry…'

'What are you sorry for?'

'I was very drunk and you're—'

'I had a great time. You were the perfect gentleman… most of the night.' She smiled at him.

'I wasn't when we got here,' replied Jake, thinking of their choice of venue.

'I'm free later, if you fancy meeting up?'

'I can't. I've got to get back to London.'

'What is it you do?'

'Just taking care of some stuff…'

She shook her head. 'That old chestnut? You're a police officer, aren't you? One of the blokes in that Glasgow Airport thing, he worked here. That's what you're doing here, isn't it?'

It wasn't a lucky guess. His and Lenny's bags had 'police evidence' written all over them.

Jake winked at her but said nothing.

'My friend, she works in the burns unit where he's being treated, you know.'

'Really?' Now she had his attention.

'She said that he's going to die.'

'Does he talk or say anything?'

'I don't know. Maybe.'

'Your friend. Can I talk to her?'

'It'll cost you a drink or two – tonight.'

'I'm going home on the train later. But I'll buy you a drink before I go?'

20

'Morning', said Jake, as he climbed into Claire's BMW, which was parked outside his flat. He threw his small rucksack on to the back seat, inhaling the new-car smell.

'Morning!' She leaned across and kissed him. He wasn't expecting it.

He lowered the sun visor and slid open the mirror. Her lipstick had left a coral-coloured smudge at the corner of his mouth.

He tried to remember the last time they'd been in a passionate embrace and couldn't. They'd both invested so much into their relationship over the years – he didn't want to feel a failure by letting it go totally. Maybe they could sort out their differences? There were so many good things about their partnership, but trust was a real issue. Every time he felt like they had a stable foundation to build on, one of them did something completely unexpected, and those foundations crumbled.

'A kiss? Is it my birthday?' He smiled, wiping away her lipstick. He was slightly suspicious at her unexpected display of affection.

'Not today. Maybe soon though.' She winked as she pulled out into the traffic and headed toward the City.

Yes, she was a challenge, and yes, he enjoyed being kept on his toes. But he often wondered if she was too challenging.

The early-morning sun glinted off the windows of the buildings as they drove. Commercial Road was notorious for nose-to-tail traffic, but at this time on a Saturday it was plain sailing. The shoppers who would soon be trying to get into the West End to grab a bargain were still asleep, along with those City workers who only frequented the route on weekdays.

'Where are we off to then? What's this *big* surprise you've organised?' asked Jake keenly.

'We're going for a nice bike ride. That's why I asked you to bring shorts.'

'OK. That's a bit different. Are we hiring bikes somewhere?'

'Well, yes, that was the plan. Unless a fully loaded bike rack miraculously appears on the roof.' She rolled her eyes playfully at him. 'Yes, *obviously* we'll hire some. Didn't you know I was a keen cyclist? With all the rain and floods this summer it's been difficult, but I do try and go regularly.'

'Do you?' Jake had no idea that she went cycling. She'd never mentioned it before.

'Yeah...' She turned and smiled at him. 'I like a good ride.'

Claire navigated her way past the pale grey, ragstone walls of the Tower of London, down Tower Hill and on to the Embankment.

Jake thumbed backwards in the direction of City Hall, the bulbous, motorcycle-helmet building they'd just passed. 'Did you hear that the Mayor is looking at having a London cycle hire scheme, a bit like the one they have in Paris? Bikes you can pick up at one place and leave at another?'

'I saw that too. "Ken's Cycles." Won't they all just get nicked? Great idea if they can make it work though.'

'We're going the wrong way for Paris though. I take it we aren't going there? Ken hasn't got MI5 doing secret testing of cycle-hire schemes, has he?'

Claire giggled. 'Ha! No! Nowhere quite that glamorous.'

'Where are we off to then?'

'The Forest of Dean.'

'Where's that?'

'Gloucestershire.'

'Gloucestershire? Why do you go cycling in Gloucestershire?'

'It's a fascinating place. Lots of interesting things there.'

'It's a two-and-a-half-hour drive?'

'You'll love it. Look, I'm driving. You get to sit next to me and talk to me the whole way too. What's not to like?'

'There is that. *And* I've had a peck on the cheek this morning. But still...'

'It's my neck of the woods. Used to spend a lot of time there as a kid. Talking of kids – how are your two girls?'

She'd changed the subject. It was subtle but obvious to Jake's overly suspicious mind.

'They're good. I saw them a couple of weekends ago. Growing up fast. I've still got a lot of bridges to rebuild with them – Tayte in particular, now she's that bit older – but they're both well.'

'And Stephanie, is she OK?'

'Sort of.'

'Sort of? What's up?'

'I don't know. I can't put my finger on it. I've known her for ten years, and we were married for seven of those. We have two children together. And I still don't know what makes her tick sometimes. We still struggle to communicate...'

'What do you mean?'

'Sometimes she's angry at me, and I have no idea why – other times she seems over the moon to see me, and I have no idea why.'

'Maybe that's why you split up. You've never really been able to explain that to me, Jake. Maybe that's what the issue was originally?'

Jake thought about that for a moment.

The radio was on in the background. He was trying to concentrate on Claire's question, but the announcement completely ruined his train of thought.

'Breaking news. Counter-terrorism police in London have charged a man in connection with the failed bomb attack on Glasgow Airport. More on that when we get it,' said the female presenter.

Jake slumped back in his seat. He felt totally detached from the investigation. It wasn't right that he was finding out these things from the media. Mark was keeping him out of the loop on purpose.

'Maybe,' was all he could think to say in response to Claire's question.

They weaved their way through Parliament Square. 'And what about you, Jake? Are you all right?' she asked after a long pause.

'I think so…'

'Tough day today, being the anniversary of 7/7 and all that?'

'It is what it is. I'm trying not to think about it. One day everyone will know the real story of what went on, and we'll look back on it very differently.'

'You never talk about it. You never talk about anything. That baby incident you mentioned the other night – that's the first time you've ever said anything.'

'There are lots of things that I've never told you. What's the point?'

'So I know how you feel about these things.'

'That's difficult when *I* don't know how *I feel* about any of them.'

'Well when you're ready, I'll listen. Like the other night on the phone.'

But she'd only been able to listen to him for a few minutes the other night, before she'd ended the conversation, saying she had to be up early. Sharing this stuff would just burden her too. That's why talking about it didn't actually do any good, he thought. No one cared how it destroyed you from the inside out – not really. And nobody could help.

Jake closed his eyes and kept them shut. He tried to concentrate on the movement of the car to drown out his thoughts and gradually drifted into sleep.

He found himself standing back in Tavistock Square after the 7/7 bombings. The attacks that should never have happened. Attacks so useless in timing that they could never have achieved their aims.

The smell, the feelings, the anger, the helplessness.

A London underground tunnel invaded with screams, blood and fire. Acrid, ultra-fine black soot covering everything. The smell of metal filings and burnt flesh in his nose, his mouth, his lungs...

People trapped inside; hundreds of them, their terrified expressions pressed against the windows. He had to get them out.

Faces on the walls of the tunnel; the ones that had been blown off the occupants of the Tube trains and the bus above ground.

Skin jagged at the edges where it had been torn from a head by the huge blast, then plastered on to the tunnel wall in a red sticky mess.

He woke briefly, blinking foggily against the morning sunlight as he pulled himself out of it.

Some nights – the worst nights of all – the faces were no longer strangers. He could see Claire, Stephanie, the girls… his mother and grandmother.

He'd not told Shirley about the nightmares. He'd not told anyone. The constant waking, being ripped from his sleep by dreams so vivid and clear that he could taste them when he woke, sweating in his bed…

He didn't know if it was post-traumatic stress. Did it even need to have a name? Admission would be pointless, and God forbid, it might even lead to a formal diagnosis. It would certainly mean a move from Counter Terrorism Command.

He certainly wasn't going to admit anything. The nightmares would go away eventually. Time was a great healer, as his mother had often reminded him when he'd hurt himself as a child. And as he found himself drifting back to sleep once more, he knew, deep down, that he *was* hurt.

21

'How long have I been asleep?' asked Jake blearily as the car's tyres crunched on the gravel of the bike-hire centre.

Claire pouted. 'Nearly all the way. I must have been riveting company.'

'I was getting my energy levels up for this bike ride. Is it booked under your name?' he asked, rousing himself into action.

'I'll sort it out. You wait here. Get your shorts on.' Claire traipsed off toward the cycle-hire centre, which consisted of a log cabin with some high fencing to one side to deter thieves.

Sitting in the back of the car, Jake wrestled uncomfortably with his jeans.

He saw Claire returning with two mountain bikes as he got out of the car. She laughed and shouted over to him before resting the bikes against the verge, grabbing his left buttock and squeezing.

'Do you *mind!*' said Jake with a note of exaggeration. 'What do you think you're *up to?*'

Claire winked. 'Oh you know what it's like... sometimes you just can't help yourself.'

Jake grabbed her waist, but she pushed him away, refocussing on their plans for the day.

He couldn't fathom her out.

'You ready? We're tackling some pretty rough stuff out there with all this rain we've had. Leave your phone in the car. Don't want you losing it in the mud or it getting broken. That's why I don't take mine,' she said matter-of-factly.

'No phones? Really?'

'Trust me, Jake. Leave your phone in the car. You'll thank me later,' she said, smiling.

Jake grabbed his mobile from the pocket of his fleece and switched it off to save battery. Leaning into the passenger side of the car to stow it safely out of sight, he noticed a map of the Forest of Dean stuck down one side of the glove compartment.

'You know where we're going? You need a map or anything? I don't want to be lost without my GPS,' Jake called over, closing the glove box.

'Nah. I'm OK with the cycle routes and the forest. It's taken me a few months to get my bearings, but I'm pretty good now.'

'What about bears and stuff in the woods?' joked Jake.

Claire laughed. 'Oh, there's far worse than that around here!' she said as she locked the car before jumping on her bike and pedalling off into the woods.

22

'Hang on!' called Claire.

Jake had overtaken her and started up the next muddy incline of the forest.

He turned to look at her. 'What's the matter?'

'Come back here. I want to show you something,' said Claire, beckoning him to follow. She was already off her bike.

Jake rode back down the hill to where she was standing on one side of the black, boggy track.

Jake panted, slightly out of breath. 'What's up?'

'Well I'm going in here…' she said, disappearing into the undergrowth with her bike, as she hid it from sight.

'What? Why?' Jake gave her a bemused look.

'Because I've got a listening device in the house on the other side of that.' Claire pointed at a nine-foot-high, ivy-covered wall bordering the cycle track.

'What? You're here working?'

'Sort of…'

Jake looked at her, unsure what to say, his mind suddenly scrambling over all of their movements up to this point.

'That's why you told me to leave the phone in the car. That's why you didn't bring yours… so our handsets won't ping on the local mobile-phone mast? So we can't be cell sited near here?'

Claire smiled and shrugged.

'There was me thinking that we came here for a nice bike ride and to spend some time together,' said Jake grumpily.

'It *is* a nice bike ride and we *are* together!'

'Get on with it then. Download the bloody thing!'

'Ah – it's not that type of listening device. The owner regularly sweeps his house for transmitters. He knows about all that sort of thing. I couldn't risk him picking up the radio waves.'

Jake nodded. He understood her dilemma. Certain listening devices transmitted their contents directly from where they were, using radio waves – much like a mobile phone did. But the radio waves could easily be located by someone with the right knowhow by sweeping the area with a receiver to pick up their signal. The signal would quickly lead them to the source.

'Can't you just turn the transmitter on and off? I've done that before. Just download it when you're nearby?'

'No! Those can still be found too. You coppers really have no clue about this stuff.'

'At least we tell our colleagues the truth about why we're taking them on bike rides though,' said Jake, annoyed. 'Where's the device?'

'It's behind an electric socket in the wall of his office. I've had it in there for a month. Time to get it out.'

'I can't *believe* you brought me here to do this, Claire. I came back from Glasgow specially.'

'I didn't bring you here to do it! I'm more than capable of doing this myself, thank you! I put the thing in there – it's what I do for a living! I don't need the Old Bill for this – and I don't need you just because you're a *man* either,' she snapped back.

'If I'm not here as the muscle, then what am I here for?'

'It's my uncle's house. He's not in.'

'This is your Uncle Frank's house? Uncle Frank as in the Uncle Frank that you had all the problems with when you were little? For fuck's sake, Claire! Why on earth are we *here*?'

'Let's just get the device out. I'll explain later.'

'You sure he's not in?'

'No one's in. He's out seeing my cousin. You remember Kate?' Claire put her hands on her hips and gave Jake a stony-faced stare.

Jake *did* remember Kate – only too well. She was the cousin he'd ingratiated himself with in order to obtain highly confidential information from GCHQ, her place of work.

He felt himself starting to blush. So that Claire wouldn't see it, he ran at the wall as fast as he could. Half leaping and half scrambling, he grabbed at the climbing ivy vines and managed to pull himself atop the wall.

Jake lay down and offered Claire his outstretched arm. 'Give me your hand,' he called down.

Claire giggled. 'What *are* you doing?'

'Helping you! Like you asked!'

'Oh, Jake. Always throwing yourself into things and asking questions later,' said Claire, shaking her head. 'There's a gate down here…' she pulled a set of keys from her pocket '…and I came prepared.'

She marched off toward a recess in the wall, hidden by overgrown bushes.

Jake heard the clang of wrought-iron gates as Claire made her way into the garden. From where he was sitting, he could only just see the roof of Frank's house over the very tops of the trees. The gardens were vast and beautifully tended.

'You coming down from there?' Claire said, smiling as she looked up at him from the other side of the wall.

Jake manoeuvred himself so that he hung by his arms. As he let go, he felt his heel snag on a knot of ivy, which sent him tumbling backwards, away from the wall. He landed on his backside in the grass next to Claire.

'We *are* the expert in this, aren't we, Detective Inspector Flannagan?' she said, laughing, and walked off toward the house, leaving him sitting there, facing the wall.

Jake picked himself up, his rear end soaking wet and muddy from the ground, and hurried after Claire, who was now midway to the house.

'You've got keys to the house too?' Jake asked as he caught her up.

'Yes. It's a very simple task. Get in, unscrew the fascia of the wall socket, pull out the device from the wall, put it all back together then leave…' She looked down at the state of Jake's clothes. 'And don't you dare leave telltale marks all over the place while we're in there. You'd be better waiting outside as lookout.'

They neared the edge of the treeline, beyond which stood a large, two-storey, detached Victorian house with a huge orangery to the rear. Between them and the house lay a pristine lawn with freshly mown stripes. The smell of cut grass filled the small orchard they were now in.

'Looks and smells like they've had some gardening done this morning?' remarked Jake.

'No shit, Sherlock,' Claire mumbled as she ducked. Crouching down on her heels, she looked at the house, frowning.

Jake felt his stomach churn. This whole episode felt slightly surreal.

'Clearly you weren't expecting this?' he asked with raised eyebrows.

'Look, the gardener normally comes on a Friday. But Saturday there's no one here at all. I've been watching them for months to establish their pattern of movement before I even started putting devices in there.'

Lifestyle surveillance was Jake's bread and butter. Know your subject inside out was his mantra. Know which bed they slept in; what time they went to sleep; what time they woke up; what time they left the house for work; which way they turned when they came out of their front door; what car they drove and which route they preferred.

We all had habits. Obviously Claire had worked out what Frank's were.

But habits could always change.

'The gardener parks on the drive. I need to see if his van is round the front. If it's not, he's gone, and we're clear for another two hours until they get back. Wait here,' said Claire, and she got up and began to work her way through the orchard toward the side of the house.

For once, Jake did as he was told. He remained crouching and watched the back of the house and garden for any movement. Claire disappeared out of sight round the side of the house.

After a few minutes, she returned, stooping lower than when she'd left him. She waved her hand at him to stay down.

'Gardener's in the front garden doing the bushes. Can you bloody believe it? The one bloody day he had to change his routine! We'll have to abandon it for today.'

'Is there just one bloke?' Jake didn't like abandoning anything.

'Yeah.'

'And you said you've got a key to the house?'

'Yes, to the back door – that one there.' She pointed to the porch at the rear.

'How long will it take you to get the device out once you get in the house?'

'Less than two minutes.'

'Let me go round the front of the house and create a diversion then? Just engage him in conversation as I ride past the front...'

'You think he'll talk to you long enough?'

'Making people talk is what I do for a living. Leave it to me. When you see me cycle past the front through there...' Jake pointed to a gap between the building and the treeline '...wait a few seconds and then go for it. I'll talk to him for five minutes and give you time to get out and back through to where your bike is.'

23

Jake retraced his steps back to the huge, ivy-covered wall and made his way through the gate, which Claire had left unlocked. He pulled his bike from the undergrowth and doubled back in the direction that they'd originally ridden in, searching for the edge of wall that bordered Frank's very large garden.

When he found the edge, he navigated down its flank, through the trees until he came to the tarmacked road at the front of the house. A single carriageway, wide enough for just one car, cut through the fields and forest beyond.

Jake was panting now from the slight incline up toward the house. He had ridden as fast as he could, aware that Claire was counting on him and waiting to see him from the garden.

He stopped as he neared the front of Frank's property. He couldn't see Claire now that she was hidden in the darkness of the orchard, but he was sure that she could see him.

He removed the water bottle from the frame of his mountain bike and drank. He used the time and space this action gave him to survey the house, the layout of the garden and, more importantly, locate the gardener.

He spotted a man wearing a pair of heavy-duty, brown suede gloves, bending at the foot of a rose bush near the front entrance gate. There seemed to be no clear pedestrian entrance, just a large, main electronic gate – the type that slid to one side.

Jake replaced his water bottle and began cycling slowly toward the gate. He thought he might start by claiming to be lost and asking for directions, then take it from there.

As he got closer to the gate, he heard it rattle as it slowly began to slide to one side. Had the gardener opened it? Jake looked up and saw surprise lining the man's face. No.

Jake could hear a powerful car engine coming up the hill then, approaching at speed.

Getting closer and closer.

He didn't turn round.

This was very bad news. Was it Frank Richards? His wife? Their daughter Kate? Whoever it was, it meant more trouble for Claire, who was still busy somewhere in the bowels of the house.

Jake took his cue from the gardener, who was starting to get to his feet, raising his arm in a wave at the rapidly approaching car. Jake knew he had no choice – there was only one thing to do.

Mid-ride and without turning his head, Jake picked up his front wheel and swung it back around in the direction of the car, which was now so close he could feel the heat belching from it as it breathed down upon him. He knew the driver would have no time to react to his sudden change of pace and direction.

Jake braced himself for a collision. He heard a squeal of brakes and the screech of tyres as the rubber lost traction on the tarmac beneath them, and the driver tried to bring the car to a rapid and unexpected halt.

The large white Mercedes flashed in front of his eyes and an eerie silence fell as things started to move in slow motion. Then a huge bang echoed in his ears as the car hit him much harder than he had expected it to – travelling faster than he'd originally thought – then silence again.

He was on the bonnet – then the windscreen, two faces looking at him from inside. Then he went across the roof. The roof slid by him. Then he was in the air, nothing below him, the car gone. He hit the tarmac with a thud. Sound filled his ears again as he lay in the road behind the vehicle, looking skyward.

He lay still for a moment, trying to assess how badly he was hurt. Then there were three faces blocking out the glare of the sun.

'You complete lunatic! What did you do that for?' one of them cried. A man's voice. He couldn't focus at all. The brightness of the sun made it worse; the faces were just silhouettes.

Jake tried to pull himself together. Saying nothing and lying still were the best things for Claire right now. It gave her time. He was sure the gardener was one of the figures standing over him.

'Be quiet, Frank, for God's sake. He's clearly hurt,' a woman's voice said from among the silhouettes. 'You were going too bloody fast again. I've told you plenty of times before... Are you all right, my dear?' She put her hand on Jake's chest.

Jake lay still. Silent. Was he hurt? He didn't know.

'He's breathing. His eyes are open. Should I call an ambulance or the police? My phone's in my van ...' a second male voice said. *The gardener. It must be*, thought Jake.

This was good. Despite the fact that he didn't know if he could actually get up, all the people he was aiming to distract appeared to be right where he needed them.

'I think I'm OK. Just give me a couple of minutes,' said Jake, not moving from his position on the ground.

'Bloody cyclists with no road sense...' It was Frank's voice again. 'Have you seen the damage to my car?'

'Frank! You were partly at fault. You were too close and going too fast,' the woman chastised him. She had to be his wife.

'Can you sit up?' asked the other male voice, as they bent down next to him. Jake felt a gloved hand on his arm. *Definitely the gardener. Perfect.*

Things slowly swam back into focus. He was OK. A few grazes and a few bruises. He'd rolled across the whole car.

'It's dented *everywhere* because of that imbecile!' Frank was pointing at the white Mercedes. 'Three weeks old and look!'

Jake looked. A brand new Mercedes-Benz S-Class. *Sonderklasse* as they called it in German – the *special class*. It was their flagship model, top of the range. Easily £80,000 worth of car.

'You all right? Do you need an ambulance?' asked the gardener.

Jake winced and put his head in his hands. He groaned loudly several times over in an attempt to give Claire some vital additional seconds.

'Can I get you a glass of something, or some painkillers?' asked Frank's wife, crouched on the opposite side of him.

'No,' Jake replied quickly, knowing that would mean them going into the house. Claire was possibly already out by now, but he needed to be sure.

Frank had a furious look on his face and was clearly losing patience.

Jake took a look at the man who'd been shouting at him. He was a distinguished-looking figure, in his early sixties with a flamboyant old-school moustache. He was wearing a checked Oxford shirt, burgundy corduroys and a country-club-style jacket, all topped off with an expensive-looking cravat.

Jake decided to change tack.

'How's my bike? Is it rideable?' he asked.

'Never mind your bike! Look at my bloody car!' shouted Frank.

Jake stared closely at Frank Richards. Despite his smart clothes and angry demeanour, something looked out of place. His hair was a very dark shade, a uniform blue-black, which permeated into his forehead, whilst his moustache was a silvery grey. For a man of his advanced years and skin tone, the colouring looked all wrong. Then Jake realised that Frank dyed his hair. He wondered if this reflected some sort of vain and obsessive side to the man's character.

The gardener walked back around to the front of the car and returned wheeling Jake's rented bike. 'I think it's all right...' He straightened the handlebars that were sitting skew-whiff to the front wheel. 'Yeah, it'll be fine. What about you? You sure you're all right?'

'I'm OK.' Jake got to his feet gingerly and made sure to exaggerate his discomfort to full effect. Then, spotting his opportunity, and with the gate still open, he plucked the bike from the hands of the gardener, hopped into the saddle and pedalled off as speedily as his bruised body would allow.

The element of surprise left the bystanders on the drive open mouthed in his wake. Only Frank managed to compose himself fast enough to shout after him. 'Oi! You, you liability! I want your name and address…'

Jake ignored him. He rode downhill and back into the forest. He couldn't be followed by a car in there, and they'd have to be pretty handy sprinters to catch up on foot. He doubted that Frank had even spent long enough looking at his face to recognise him again. He'd been more interested in his bloody Mercedes.

His job was done.

He sincerely hoped Claire's was too, or they were both in big trouble.

24

Back at the cycle-hire centre at the edge of the forest, Jake found Claire sitting in her car.

'You took your time! I was starting to think you'd keeled over and died on your way back.' She laughed. 'I have to say, that sounded like some decoy stunt you pulled back there, Jake! You bloody saved the day!'

'Did you get the device out?' he asked, climbing off his bike somewhat carefully. Large areas of bruising to his right leg and back were already starting to make their presence known.

'Yeah, I got it. Are you all right?' Her tone changed as she watched him wincing.

'I'm fine. Just a bit sore...'

'I really appreciate it, Jake. It all went wrong today. The gardener there, and then Uncle Frank coming back early. It was crazy. I couldn't have done it without you.' She stepped out of the car and kissed him on the lips. He didn't respond.

'You'd better have a good explanation as to why we've done this *and* why I've become involved, Claire. This is pretty serious stuff – breaking in and bugging people's houses. I'm guessing you've got no official authorisation for that?'

'No, I don't have any *official authorisation*, but I *do* have a good explanation.' Claire looked off into the distance and went quiet for a moment. Jake could see her eyes filling with tears, though she held them back.

'Claire, I've already been in trouble at work for helping you with this stuff. When you decided to fake your own disappearance, that nearly cost me my job.'

'I was just trying to flush out whoever was looking at me. Someone was watching me. I didn't know who it was. I didn't know if it was Lawrence…' Her former boss. 'I wondered if he might have twigged that I knew about his drug habits and his dealing… Or maybe it was connected to the bad guys that we looked at in the 7/7 investigation. Or maybe it *was* Uncle Frank? You know there's all that family stuff that went on…' She tailed off.

'Go on,' he prompted.

'I did what I needed to do – to find out who it was. And then when it got too much, I had to get out for a while. That's all. I'm sorry you got caught up in it. I wasn't expecting you to launch the world's biggest missing-persons case on me, using all the Met's assets without actually telling them why – or doing any of the right paperwork – was I? I thought you'd know that I'd send you a sign.'

'It was Frank that was watching you?'

'I still don't know. It's possible. That's what I'm trying to find out.'

'You *still* don't know? It was more than eighteen months ago!'

'I don't know who it was. Whoever it was, they were able to get in my apartment and place a recording device in it.' She sounded angrier now. 'I'm still no nearer to understanding who that was. I'm constantly being looked at by my new boss – reduced access on intelligence, vetting under permanent review… It's pretty big shit for me too, you know! One more thing and I could lose my job. It's driving me mad not knowing who was behind it. I've got to find out!'

'I'm taking my bike back.' Jake walked off, leaving her standing there alone. He wanted her to understand he wasn't happy about this.

At the hire desk, the spotty teenager noticed that Jake's bike frame was scratched and the front brakes were not working properly.

'Mister, this bike is damaged. Did you fall off or something?'

'Yeah, I was going a bit too fast and lost my balance.'

'Have we got your credit-card details on the system? They'll have to charge you for this, you know?'

'They've got all my payment information in there, yes.' Jake knew that Claire would have batted her eyelids, paid in cash and provided fake contact details for insurance purposes.

'Great. Thank you, mister.'

Jake made his way quickly back to the car where Claire was sitting inside with the engine running.

He climbed in and slammed the door. 'Drive! Quick, before they find out that they don't have our details for the damage to that bike. Don't let them get the registration number of the car!'

Claire pulled off in a hurry. Jake looked back toward the hire shop and saw no one.

They reached the safety of the motorway fairly quickly, the fields and bridges slipping past the car as Claire headed back toward London.

'Right, I'm all ears,' Jake sighed. 'Give me this good explanation you mentioned. I'm not buying any of it so far.'

'OK...' Claire took a deep breath. 'You know I went to live with Uncle Frank when my dad was trying to help my mum with her alcoholism. I was coming up to fifteen at the time?'

'Yes.'

'You know that Uncle Frank was really weird with me...' Claire's voice trembled as she spoke. She stared dead ahead. 'Made me do stuff – stuff I wasn't happy about.'

'You have said something went on, yes.'

'I didn't tell anyone about it at the time. Dad was always working; I hardly saw him; my mum was a mess. There was nowhere I could go. I just had to put up with it. Get enough money together and get out as soon as I could. Find an exit plan. My exams weren't far off. There was nothing else I could do. You understand?'

'I understand.' He didn't, but she'd never really told him anything about it before and he just wanted to keep her talking, so he nodded. Inside, though, he was wondering why she hadn't told her father, or confided in a teacher, or even slid a knife into the man's throat. Who would have blamed her? Unless she thought they wouldn't believe her for some reason…

Claire continued, 'Well, Uncle Frank had some videos of me, videos that I didn't want people to see. He said that if I ever told anyone, he would show the videos to people. So I just bided my time. It was agreed I could go to boarding school. I moved out. Then I went straight to uni from there, miles away from him. I never saw him again. The only person I see occasionally is Kate.'

This added a new dimension to things – videos and recordings of abuse. In this day and age, with the internet, it could ruin lives.

He nodded. 'Carry on.'

'Then I got the job with the Security Service. Went to live in London. The past was the past. Gone. Done…' Claire's voice caught on the words. Jake could see her trying to hold it together.

'OK, and then what happened?' Jake had never felt it the right time to press her on this, but he was glad she was now confiding in him. It was something she did very little of.

'The videos are the problem. I've never told anyone what really happened. I mentioned some things about it to Anne, Mum's housekeeper. My dad knew *something* happened, but I've never gone into details about exactly what – and I never would, despite them blaming me for it. My work, they know nothing about it. The police were never involved, so there was no record of anything on official databases that work could find. And they certainly know *nothing* about the videos…' A tear ran down her face as she drove. 'I'm a blackmail risk, Jake. My vetting would be withdrawn at a moment's notice. I'd be out of a job. I love my job – I can't let that happen.'

'You've searched the house for the videos?'

'Yeah, I've looked everywhere. And who knows how many copies there are?'

'So why the bug?'

'Someone was watching me, like I said. I didn't know who it was. I befriended Lawrence, to try to work out if it was him. It wasn't, as it turned out. He was just utter scum. Of course, it could have been another intelligence service, but I didn't think so. That only left you and Uncle Frank.'

'Me?'

'You proved it wasn't you. I know you love me. That leaves Frank – and the videos have suddenly become a big issue for me again, all these years later.' Claire wiped her face with her sleeve. 'So I've spent months watching him. Using all the tricks I know to work out what he's up to.'

'Well he's obviously got plenty of money. That car he ran me over with was brand new; cost a fortune.'

'When he left the navy, he started working for an arms manufacturer, but Kate said he was seconded to some government department.'

'They have private-company staff working in government departments?'

'Yeah, it's like a trade delegation. Big business for the Government. I wondered if he was worried I might say something against him now he's rubbing shoulders at that level, and that's why he was watching me…'

'So you wanted to be ahead of the game?' Jake understood Claire's predicament. 'And what have you found out?'

'Not much. Only that he *is* involved in something – something that sounds illegal. I don't know if it's drugs, money laundering or what – but I need your help to establish what it is. That's why I took you along today. Showed you what I'm up to. Why I'm telling you about the videos. He *and they* could destroy me…'

'OK.' Jake didn't know what else to say.

'Will you help me – please?' asked Claire, a note of desperation in her voice.

He smiled. 'Of course I'll help you. Whatever you need.' She was shaken and very upset. He didn't actually know how he *could* help, but he couldn't bear to see her like this.

Her face lit up. A beaming smile. She clearly hadn't been sure that he would say yes. 'Thank you. You're my knight in shining armour, Jake.'

Yeah, and look what trouble I get myself into when I help damsels in distress, he thought.

25

Still covered in mud from the bike ride, Claire wasted no time. She fired up her computer and connected it via a USB lead to the small, black listening device she'd removed from Frank's house.

'That'll take a few minutes,' she said, clicking on the *download* option that popped up on her screen. Special software that Jake didn't recognise was slowly converting the digital recording on the device into something they could listen to.

'I'll play you the two dodgy-sounding ones I got last time,' said Claire, navigating her way through some windows on her Mac until they were looking at a screen that was organised into folders by date and time. Two were highlighted in red; the rest were blue. There were about forty in total.

'Listen to the files in red.' She clicked on the first one. 'I'm going to jump in the shower. No peeking!' She pecked him on the cheek and headed off toward the bathroom, leaving him sitting in front of the screen. He was too engrossed in what he was looking at to follow her.

The first folder was named: 03/06/2007 19.32–19.34.

He clicked on it. Frank Richards' voice boomed out of the computer's speakers.

'I know, I'll do it in the morning. Not now, love.'

Jake could hear the sound of a door being banged shut and then the clicking of the lock mechanism. He heard some more banging – perhaps a chair being moved or a drawer opening. Recordings were sometimes difficult to decipher.

'Hi, it's Frank. I got your message. What you've suggested sounds fine to me. When will you do it?'

Jake could only hear one voice on the recording; he assumed Frank was on the phone.

'Of course. The sooner the better. Just get them moved...

'Yes. Just send them by courier. Get a van...

'Someone will sign at the other end, yes, then I'll have them moved to somewhere else. You don't need to worry about that part...

'Great. Speak tomorrow. Bye.'

Jake moved to the next folder and clicked on it: *06/06/2007 13.01–13.04.*

The same sound of the door closing and being clicked shut again.

'It's me. Have you done it?

'What's the problem? The investigation has been halted...

'Just mix them up with another bunch of files that you're archiving and sending off into storage. Where are they now?

'You've just got to organise sending them somewhere else. You're the clerk. No one will suspect anything...

'So instead of sending them there, to the normal place, send them to my man's place... Yes, Thames Road. Unit 3...

'This really isn't the time to be getting cold feet, Jenny. It's a bit late for that. We didn't put you in there because we wanted to know what tea they drank, what type of biscuits they liked... What I'm asking of you is the sort of thing we had in mind...

'I need those documents sent to the warehouse, as I've told you...

'OK. Bye...

'What a wet bitch. I knew she was trouble...

'Hi, it's me...

Frank's tone had changed. It sounded to Jake as if he'd completed one call and dialled another.

'That Jenny, she's being a pain in the arse. Three times I've spoken to her about this. Three times she hasn't done it. Are you positive she's up to the job?'

'Well, maybe we should lean on her a bit, give her some encouragement. The money clearly isn't motivating her enough...

'No...

'She's worried they'll be able to audit who asked for the boxes to be sent off for storage...

'That's right, I doubt anyone will even bother to check. Yes, that's what I said...

'Talk to her. You know which buttons to press with her?

'Yes. Good.'

'Thoughts?' asked Claire, startling Jake as she walked back into the living room wearing just a towel, her hair dripping on the carpet.

'You seem a little overdressed?' he said, trying to grab the edge of her towel.

Claire giggled and shimmied away. 'Stop it. We're working! What do you think about what you've just heard?'

'No idea exactly what it's about. But you're right. There's something dodgy going on.'

'Most of what I've listened to in the other folders sounds similar. It's like he's up to his neck in something, but it's difficult to figure out with no context.'

'You've got no idea at all what he's up to?'

'Well it sounds like he might be blackmailing that Jenny woman.'

'Have you made a list of all the names you've heard, places that are mentioned?'

'He mentions very few names. The conversations are really bland. Much like you've just heard.'

'Phone records? Do you know *who* he's talking to? We've got the times and dates – that should be fairly easy...'

'This is unofficial, Jake. I've got no access to anything that requires proper authorisation. I've got to glean it from what I can see and hear. And anything that has public access records, obviously.

'Well I'll need to listen to everything you have. Then I can decide what to do, how we're going to play it. How much data do you have? Hours wise?

'Three or four hours maximum.'

'OK. Any headphones? I prefer headphones when I'm doing this sort of stuff. And painkillers. My leg and back are killing me from falling off that bike... And I'm hungry. A man has to eat!'

Claire threw him some headphones from her bag and laughed. 'You are a demanding detective, DI Flannagan. One takeaway tikka masala and some paracetamol coming up... Now get back to work.'

26

'Well, here I am again,' said Jake, slapping his palms on his legs as he sat down in Shirley's office.

She was wearing the same knitted cardigan and skirt ensemble that she'd had on the previous week.

Maybe that was a tactic she used to put people at ease? Familiarity – deliberately wearing the same outfits on the same days for the same clients.

'So how have you been, Jake?'

'Not bad, I suppose.'

'What does that mean?' she asked, her expression giving nothing away.

'It means I could be worse, but I'm not brilliant either.'

'How could things be worse?'

Jake thought about the question for moment.

'I suppose I could have died?' he joked.

Shirley looked concerned. 'How could you have died?'

Jake realised that, although he was saying this in jest, it was partly true. He just hadn't considered it before.

'I got hit by a car when I was out cycling the other day.'

'Wow, that sounds pretty serious?'

'You're right, it was. I was lucky…' Jake realised that he hadn't contemplated how he could have been seriously hurt – or even killed. 'I managed to roll across the top of the car.'

'How did that make you feel?'

'What do you mean?'

'How do you feel about being alive?'

'I suppose God has plans for me, though I have no idea what they are,' he quipped.

'You're not happy about being alive, Jake? You think you're only here for a purpose?'

'I don't know.'

'What did you do when you got home that day, after the accident?'

'I don't remember.'

'Why don't you remember?'

'I don't know.' Jake didn't really want to get into the whys and wherefores of what he and Claire had been up to on their bike ride.

'Did you have a drink?'

'Look, I don't have a drink problem,' he said sternly, trying to put his slip-ups from the week before out of his mind.

'I didn't say you did. I might have had a glass of wine had it been me though. But that's me. I might also have called my friends, my family?'

'I walked out on my wife and family. Don't see much of the kids. Mum and Dad are dead. My on/off girlfriend has a busy job, and I try not to make a habit out of talking much about death and dying.'

'Why did you walk out on your wife, Jake?'

'Look, Shirley, I appreciate you talking to me. But let's be honest with each other – I'm only here because they've said I have to come. I'm just jumping through the hoops for them, and this all seems very personal.'

Shirley laughed. It was the first time he'd seen any emotion from her. 'This isn't compulsory, Jake. They can't force you to come here.'

'What? So I can go?'

'Of course you can. But you were honest with me, so I'll be honest with you. I think you would really benefit from talking some things out. I see lots of people here. But I see very few people like you.'

'Like me?'

'Yes. Most people that come here come knowing that they have issues they need to address. They come to me to explore those issues. They understand that it's a two-way process. It's not for me to do the work for you, Jake. I can't put words in your mouth, but you need to understand that you have areas in your life that are particularly challenging, which means you would benefit from these sessions.'

'What do you mean?'

'Risky behaviour is one of the telltale signs. You've had two near-death experiences in the last two weeks, Jake. You've talked of sexual promiscuity too. You've said that you used to drink a lot, though that's now stopped…'

'And you think they are all signs of something?'

'Yes, very possibly – post-traumatic stress disorder being one of them.'

This again. 'I don't have PTSD. I'm fine.'

'All of those things I've just listed *could be* indications of something important. I don't think it's bad luck that you keep finding yourself in these difficult situations, Jake.'

'I'm a big boy – I can look after myself.'

'Putting yourself in those situations regularly makes it look like you don't care whether you live or die. Most people don't make a habit of it the way you seem to.'

'It's just part of being in the police.'

'Jake, it would be good for you to talk about it.'

'I don't want to talk. I just need to do my job, Shirley – that's all I want to do. I'm being sidelined here with this. I need to get back and do my job.'

'OK,' Shirley said reluctantly.

27

'Good afternoon. Thank you all for coming. Let's get straight into it, shall we?' said Helen from the head of the large table in the conference room. The rest of the room fell silent. 'Mark, can you give us all an update?'

'On Friday last week, I submitted preliminary papers to the Crown Prosecution Service for the events in Glasgow. They authorised charges against Fadhil Ghalib and Sudeep Murthy – although we have yet to speak with Murthy, as he remains in hospital at this time. Late Friday we charged Ghalib with terrorism and the attack on Glasgow Airport. We continue to question the suspects from Liverpool. I await evidence from the bomb factory in Houston and the two cars before I can go to the CPS about those charges.'

'Good. Jake, can you update us on enquiries in Glasgow please?' Helen asked, moving swiftly on.

'Yes, the house-to-house enquiries have been done. They confirm it was just two men that were using the house. Neighbours had seen the Jeep there on lots of occasions. One remembers two older Mercedes cars – a blue one and a pale, metallic green one.'

Helen nodded. 'Excellent.'

'He's given a statement and positively identified the models as W124 E-class saloon cars – which are the same types as the ones found in London. This gives us a link between the address and the cars.

'I met with Ghalib's manager at the Royal Alexandra Hospital too. He paints a very sad picture of Ghalib – almost turns him into a victim, in fact. Says that, although he was born in the UK, he grew up in Baghdad. Spent most of his life there, comes from a very wealthy, well-to-do family… He says that he thinks the motive for the attack could be Ghalib's anger about the destruction of Iraq during the 2003 invasion. I seized the suspect's workstation while I was there. That's likely to have evidence on it that shows he was visiting extremist websites.'

'Good. You also made contact with a nurse while you were up there too, Jake?'

Lenny smirked at the mention of the nurse. Jake shot him a stern look across the table.

'Yes I did… a nurse in the burns unit where Murthy is being treated.'

From out of the corner of his eye, Jake saw Mark look up from his notes. He had a frown on his face, evidently unaware of this new development. *Serves you right*, thought Jake. *Anything you can do, Mark Castle, I can do better. You keep me in the dark, and I'm sure as hell not going to bother updating you about my news either.*

Jake continued. 'I've only spoken to the nurse on the phone as yet, no statement. She works on the burns unit at Glasgow Royal Infirmary. I came across her through a contact in the NHS while on enquiries up there,' said Jake, staring hard at Lenny and willing him to keep his mouth shut. 'She says that Murthy spoke to her when he first arrived from Glasgow Airport – before he went into a coma. He was talking to her about money – money for building a mosque in Bangalore. She got the distinct impression that he was being paid for the attack by someone.'

Jake paused and waited for the information to register with the group. 'If that's true, it obviously changes the way this whole thing looks,' he added.

'It does make it look different, and that's an absolutely crucial piece of information. Why has the hospital not come forward with this of their own volition?' asked Helen. She looked at Jake and then at Mark.

Mark shrugged.

'Mark, I think we really need to press the hospital on this. Have you had any contact with the medical team at Glasgow Royal Infirmary?'

'Not really, the bloke's been in a coma…'

'Well clearly there's important information to be gained from the hospital. We need to have regular contact with them. I want to understand if this coma is induced or not, and whether they can bring him out of it. Can we get an account from him on tape?'

'I doubt they can. He's on his last legs. Why do we need to dig any further?' he said curtly.

Was Mark *really* trying to tell Helen, the Senior Investigating Officer, the direction the enquiry should take, or was he just stupid? Jake wasn't sure.

'*Because*, Mark,' said Helen bluntly, 'I'd like to understand if this nurse's interpretation of what Sudeep Murthy is saying is correct. If this is a simple put-up-and-paid-for job, *it is* very different. I want you to speak to the doctor in charge, Mark – understood?'

Mark nodded, said nothing and looked down at his pad.

'Jake, can you get a statement from the nurse? Will she provide one?'

'I'm not sure patient confidentiality rules allow her to do that, but I will ask.'

'Thank you. Exhibits?'

'Yes, that's me, ma'am,' replied Kevin Knight. 'Enquiries going well at both the bomb factory and with the vehicles. I'd say there were enough components to construct another two complete devices at the property. We've done a lot of work with the forensic explosives laboratory at Fort Halstead. We've got a meeting about the findings of that work tomorrow. We've also had some images back from the laptop we found in the back of the burned-out Jeep at Glasgow Airport.' Kevin paused as he opened the folder in front of him. 'There are at least three circuit diagrams in the memory, one of which was a timer circuit involving a Casio digital watch. The other two were remote-detonation circuits using mobile phones.'

'Who does the laptop actually belong to? Do we know?'

'It appears to belong to Fadhil Ghalib. Most of the documentation on it is his.'

'OK, anything else?'

'Yes, perhaps the most significant item is a deleted file that we recovered.' Kevin flicked through the notes in front of him again. 'The document looks a bit like a will, as if it was written by an author who was expecting to die in the airport attack. It's in Arabic and addressed to "Osama" and "the soldiers of Islam". It reads as follows.'

Kevin paused and looked down at his notes to recite the English translation.

' "The Kingdom of Evil has been fighting against our nation. Their armies are shedding our blood and violate our honour and dignity in Iraq and Afghanistan.

' "Their soldiers kill the young and old.

' "They do not discriminate between men and women. So why should we?

' "If the policy of their army is to kill women and children, then only a similar policy would deter them. These people can only be awakened by the sound of booby traps and the Mujahideen hailing 'God is great'." '

Kevin continued. 'It was found with eight letters — each addressed to different people or groups — that praised extremists in Iraq and talked of opening a new jihad front in the UK.

'One, written to "the soldiers of the Islamic states", reads:

' "I have learned from you the love for death. You have been surrounded by unbelievers, stabbed by your closest of friends but you have no fear. You have weakened the fears amongst them, inflicting them with wounds until the blood reached their knees.

' "I still wish I could return there to be with you and witness your heroism, if it were not for the opening of a new jihad front here to expand the jihad arena against our enemy." '

'All fairly predictable.' Mark pitched in.

'Why delete the files though?' Jake asked, almost talking to himself.

'What do you mean?' Mark shot back.

'The attackers didn't know why the London bombs hadn't exploded and presumably they expected the Jeep to blow up when they set light to it and drove it into Glasgow Airport. If they both really expected to die, why delete the file?'

'They'd know we would look for deleted files though. It's a ploy,' Mark stated, as if trying to tell him to shut up.

'Do you know how difficult it is to reconstruct a hard drive that's been blown to pieces?' asked Jake. He knew Mark had no idea how this sort of thing worked; that there were just a handful of people in the entire world who had the skills to do it – and even then, it would cost several hundred thousand pounds and still be hit and miss. 'We're looking at a deleted file in a hard drive from a computer that they then deliberately set on fire and tried to blow up. They were not expecting that laptop to survive. This isn't something that they wanted us to find. If it were, they would have left it at the house – but they didn't. We're lucky to be seeing that. We're missing the point with some of these things. It's not as simple and straightfor-ward as it looks. There's something deeper in the background here. The deleted files, the stuff the nurse told us about…'

Mark said nothing. He put down his pen, indicating that he was no longer going to note down anything Jake said, because he believed it held no merit.

28

The drive to the forensics explosive laboratory took place mostly in silence. Mark Castle and his crony Gavin Bonson were in the back, Lenny and Jake in the front.

As they drove, Jake replayed the charade that had just taken place in the corridor at the Yard.

'I don't need you to come with me, Jake!'

'But the boss wants me to come along.'

'I'm capable of doing this stuff on my own. I know you've been questioning my experience behind my back!'

'Mark, this is not about you or your experience – it's about working as a team. I'm supposed to be running the intelligence development cell. I cannot do that without understanding what the evidence is – what the intelligence is. You aren't sharing that stuff. I'm finding things out from the news on the TV and radio. It shouldn't be like that.'

'I'll brief you when we get back. Give me the car keys...'

Jake had seen Gavin Bonson, Mark's right-hand man, through the open office doorway. Leaning back in his office chair, Gavin had been craning his neck to watch the whole sorry spectacle, wearing a grin from ear to ear, like it was some big joke.

'Mark, you can either grab a ride with Lenny and me, or you can find another car – it's up to you.'

Jake felt he'd been firm but fair. After their tête-à-tête had finished, he'd made his way down the stairs to the underground car park, recounting the goings-on to Lenny. As they'd driven out, he'd been surprised to find Mark and Gavin standing by the exit ramp – waiting for them.

In the car, Lenny had tried to make small talk with Gavin, who in return had answered with single words and shut Lenny down at every attempt, clearly enjoying the climate of animosity.

Jake drove as fast as he could. It was ridiculous that grown men were behaving like this. He would have to have it out, once and for all, with Mark. They couldn't continue working like this. It was vital that everyone communicated with each other properly in a large investigation. Barriers just meant that things got lost or weren't followed up on. If political point scoring became the primary concern, then solving the case would just become secondary.

Gavin saw Jake looking in the rear-view mirror at him and gave a sarcastic smirk.

On arrival at the forensics explosive laboratory, Jake parked the car next to the single-storey building that held the conference room.

Jake was last out of the vehicle. As he closed his door, he noticed a brown leather wallet sitting on the back seat. He reached back in and picked it up. It was stuffed with little white slips of paper, which he presumed must be cash-machine withdrawal notifications – and a fat wad of cash. The wallet's press-stud fastening was straining to contain it all.

'Looks like one of you boys has left your holiday money on the back seat,' Jake called after the others, not bothering to rummage inside the wallet for the owner's identity. He held it aloft for them to see.

Gavin looked startled and began patting himself down frantically, checking all his pockets to see if his wallet was there. 'That's mine,' he shouted, running back toward Jake.

'Off on holiday somewhere?' Jake joked, handing it back to the red-faced man.

Gavin ignored him, grabbing the wallet without saying a word.

'That's all right, you're welcome…' said Jake sarcastically as Gavin marched off in silence.

Once at the door, they were greeted by Professor Bowman, a wiry man with a mass of grey hair and a master in his field.

'Hello, Jake, good to see you again,' Bowman said, shaking Jake's hand vigorously as they walked through the building. 'I didn't realise you were involved in this one. What's your role? I've been dealing with someone called Castle – not heard of him before…'

'This is Mark Castle.' Jake stepped to one side and gestured toward his peevish-looking colleague. 'Mark is the case officer on Seagram,' continued Jake. 'I'm assisting him – running the intelligence development cell.'

'Ah, very good. Pleased to meet you, DS Castle,' Bowman said, shaking his hand.

'I'm a DI actually – Detective Inspector Castle,' Mark said, looking even more disgruntled.

'My apologies, Mark – case officers are normally detective sergeants. Good to meet you.'

Mark frowned and cleared his throat. 'Well they've clearly decided to move it up a rank in this case. It's evidently an important one, and that's why they've brought me in.'

Lenny caught Jake's eye and did a silent but exaggerated wince.

'Yes, yes, they have,' said Bowman, more preoccupied with getting them all settled. 'Please have a seat. Can I get you a tea or a coffee?' he asked, waving them toward a conference table.

'Tea please, three sugars,' said Jake, smiling at Bowman.

Kevin Knight, the experienced exhibits officer from the house search near Glasgow, had already arrived. They exchanged pleasantries as Bowman made the tea.

Drinks dispensed, Bowman sat down and heaved a large lever-arch binder, several inches thick, up from the floor and put it in front of him on the desk.

'Probably the best way to do this is for me to talk you through each scene in the order in which they've been examined. As I see it, there are four separate scenes with explosive-related exhibits. They are: a) the green Mercedes found outside Tiger Tiger nightclub; b) the blue Mercedes found at the car pound that had been in Cockspur Street; c) the Jeep that crashed into Glasgow Airport; and then finally d) the house at which the bomb factory was found in Scotland.'

'Great!' said Mark, a little overenthusiastically.

'First of all, I want to say that all three cars contained viable explosive devices. It is mere good fortune that they didn't explode in the ways that they were designed to,' Bowman was reading from the binder in front of him.

Mark scribbled frantically into a notepad as Jake concentrated on taking it all in.

'We've not actually seen these sorts of devices here in the UK before,' Bowman continued, 'though they are not uncommon in Africa and the Middle East – particularly in Iraq. As I'm sure you're aware, the initiators of the devices in both London vehicles were made from mobile phones. Circuit boards inside the phones had been altered and had command wires soldered on to them. The command wire was attached to a homemade initiator, which consisted of a small light bulb with an exposed filament. The exposed filament was surrounded by hundreds of match heads. When the phone rang, the idea was that the filament would get hot and ignite the match heads.'

'And what would happen then? Can we prove that the devices were going to explode?' Mark blurted, stopping Bowman mid-flow.

'I'm getting to that,' replied Bowman calmly. 'The match heads were there to ignite a piece of cloth. The flame produced from that was expected to ignite a gas-air mix inside the car and produce a primary explosion and fire.'

'Why do you say primary?' Mark asked impatiently.

Bowman sighed. 'You must already know that both cars contained a large quantity of petrol and several gas cylinders?' he asked, looking up from his notes and raising his eyebrows at Mark.

Jake watched Mark scribbling on his pad. Here they were, with the country's foremost expert on explosive devices – a world-renowned specialist – and Mark was interrupting him with daft questions mid-sentence. It was embarrassing.

He thought back to when he'd first joined the Anti-Terrorist Branch, as it had been called. He'd made it his business to find out this stuff, investing time to seek out the people who could tell him this information; listening patiently to them without interrupting. He'd researched how a bomb actually worked and how the detonation process took place. Maybe no one had explained this stuff to Mark?

'Yes, of course I do,' Mark replied sharply to Bowman.

'Good. The gas-air mix would likely have ignited the petrol that was in the vehicle, causing a very large initial explosion. The propane that was contained inside the gas canisters would then boil, causing the gas to expand, and there would then have been a second explosion – a vapour explosion.'

'That couldn't have actually happened though, could it?' asked Mark animatedly, interrupting Bowman's presentation for a third time. 'I mean, gas canisters here are fitted with safety-release valves to prevent them exploding, aren't they? I dealt with a fatal fire, some years back, that killed two people in an industrial premises, but the propane-gas canisters remained intact. They're designed to release the pressure inside slowly, I think?'

Was Mark really trying to outsmart this international bomb expert on his knowledge of incendiary devices, or just trying to make everyone aware of his presence in the room, wondered Jake.

Kevin caught Jake's eye and rolled his eyes.

'That is indeed how the safety-release valves work, and it is very, very rare that they explode, you're right, but…' Bowman was looking annoyed now '…if you'd let me finish, in this case, they had modified the safety-release valves on the canisters. They blocked them with putty, so they didn't work.'

'Oh.'

'You aren't dealing with a couple of kids here. These weren't just two lads who fancied seeing the fire brigade turn up to put out some burning cars.' Bowman looked at Mark when he spoke, as if to make a point. 'These, in my *expert* opinion, were viable explosive devices. Properly designed. *And* designed to kill. By people who had a history and some speciality in improvised explosive devices.'

Mark seemed to have no idea that he was completely out of his depth. 'I wasn't trying to say—'

'Although each device failed,' Bowman spoke over Mark, uninterested in what he had to say now, 'it wasn't through want of trying or the design process. It is fair to say that we have all been very lucky that they failed. In all three occasions, something minor has gone wrong. These people knew what they were doing. Like I said, they clearly have some *history* in this field. This isn't information that you find on the internet. I know, because we search regularly. This has been taught to them. They were killers. We believe that the metal from the exploding canisters could have been projected up to half a mile. Even the petrol in the boot had been modified. It was mixed with oil, we think in an effort to make the burning mixture stick – on the gas cylinders perhaps, but it would just as easily have stuck to your skin, had you had the misfortune to have been nearby. There were nails in the cars too. These would have been hurled in every direction, at considerable force, in the event of an explosion.'

Jake, who had been listening intently to Bowman's findings, now felt himself drifting off course slightly. Almost like an out-of-body experience. He thought back to the night of the attacks, standing next to that green Mercedes, pulling at the wires attached to the phone, what Bowman was now calling a 'command wire'. He shivered slightly. It could have been *so* different by the sounds of things.

Why was he still alive? Why hadn't his skin been showered with specially modified, burning petrol? Why hadn't the nails cut through his body? Why hadn't he been torn in half by the metal from the exploding gas canisters?

Maybe Helen was right – maybe he had been slightly mad thinking he could defuse the device.

'Why didn't they go off properly then?' asked Mark, bringing Jake back down to earth.

'Well in the case of the blue Mercedes, they'd turned on the gas cylinders to allow gas into the car, but the window of opportunity to set off the devices was probably only a few minutes. The gas-air mixture became too rich, which may have been what ultimately foiled their plan in that instance.'

'The gas-air mixture?' repeated Mark. Jake wanted to gnaw his fist.

'Although the matches were ignited temporarily, and there was some initial burn, any ignition probably went out because all the oxygen in the compartment was consumed at once. You can't have fire without oxygen,' said Bowman.

Mark scribbled notes furiously into his pad, as Jake saw himself, in his head, burning to death outside Tiger Tiger.

'In the case of the green Mercedes,' Bowman's words dragged Jake back to the present again, 'the command wire was a few millimetres too short to have lit the filament on the bulb, so there was no initial burn of the matches. We don't know why the wire was too short. Perhaps it was a design flaw or someone inadvertently disrupted it? We don't know here.'

Kevin looked over at Jake and winked at him.

Jake felt sick. He'd pulled on the command wire and that's likely why it was short? He felt light-headed. Maybe he did need to engage with the counsellor a little – maybe Helen and the commander were right and he did need help. He was lucky to be here, in one piece. He felt the sudden urge for a stiff drink.

As for the Jeep at Glasgow Airport,' Bowman continued 'very similar design to the London devices, except the initiators weren't mobile phones. It was human initiation. The canisters just didn't get hot enough to explode – most likely because various people were spraying them with fire extinguishers almost straightaway.'

Kevin pitched in for the first time. 'There were various items at the house in Houston – the bomb factory – that matched up with the items we found in either the Jeep or the two Mercedes. There were modified phone circuit boards, cut match heads, modified gas canister release valves. All of which have been provided to the FEL so they can be tested and married up with the items we're speaking about here.'

Bowman nodded. 'Yes, thank you.'

'How long will it be before you can put all this in a written statement to me?' asked Mark.

'I'll be dealing directly with Kevin on exhibits. I'll get him to let you know,' Bowman shot back. He clearly wanted nothing more to do with Mark.

Lenny stifled a snort by turning it into a cough.

Jake would have laughed, but he was still feeling queasy and wondering where he might get a drink to calm his nerves.

29

The pub that Jake had plumped for was a Wetherspoon's, which, to Jake, meant that the beer would be good value, with no annoying piped music to ruin his chain of thought. The Sennockian had just had a refit. Gone were the dark woods and dingy walls that Jake remembered from his previous visit. This one had light oak panelling and comfy, modern sofas. It looked more like a large coffee shop than a bar.

The fact that it was a short walk from the station meant that he and Lenny could grab a drink then get the train back to the Yard. He couldn't bear to sit with Mark and his idiot sidekick in the car.

'You OK?' Lenny asked as they waited at the long bar, a ten-pound note clutched in Jake's sweaty palm.

'Lots going on in my head... Some things don't make sense,' said Jake as he replayed Gavin's reaction to Jake finding his wallet in the car.

'Like what?'

Jake didn't answer; a bustling barmaid had already arrived to take his order.

'What are you thinking?' Lenny asked again as they carried their drinks to the sofas by the large front windows.

'About what?' Jake replied absently. His mind was running in circles. Something was important, something he'd heard today. His subconscious was screaming at him, but he couldn't make sense of it.

'Anything… Sometimes it's like talking to myself,' said Lenny, half under his breath.

'Well I reckon the dinosaurs would still be around if it wasn't for an asteroid,' replied Jake, with a smile and catching Lenny off guard.

Lenny chuckled. 'I mean the job… The view that the fire didn't take hold in the cars due to a lack of oxygen, and that's the only thing that prevented them going up?'

'I think they were potentially deadly devices, just unreliable,' said Jake, examining the cornicing in the pub so he didn't have to look at Lenny.

'Not like the 7/7 lot. They knew what they were doing – tested and tested until they got it right, I suppose?' said Lenny.

'Yeah, you can't just cross your fingers and hope. You need the skills to do it, and then you need to practise it,' replied Jake wistfully.

'You all right, Jake?'

'Something's bugging me about all of this. It's all a bit too easy.'

'In what way?'

'How did we identify the 7/7 bombers, Lenny?'

'They left their ID at the scenes for us, then we followed them on CCTV back to a car they'd parked. They wanted to be found. Wanted to become martyrs.'

'If they'd not left that ID and we'd had no CCTV, how long would it have taken us to find out who they were?'

'Months.'

'Yet here we've got two blokes, who were identified within hours, despite us not having any identification and poor CCTV footage. And despite them carrying umbrellas to shield their faces from the cameras, after they'd parked up those two Mercedes in central London and abandoned them. We've had no easy clues left for us.'

'Agreed,' said Lenny.

'The intelligence that the Saudis provided paints these two as hardened jihadis, involved in the insurgency in Iraq. But their bombs didn't go off, and even though they weren't on our radar, we still managed to identify them within hours.'

'They did try to bomb Glasgow Airport too – they were dedicated...'

'But what sort of stupid plan was that? And they even messed that up.'

'What do you mean?'

'Bowman says those devices were viable. The Saudis tell us they were dedicated jihadis, yet it's gone wrong on three separate occasions and we identified who they were within hours. Something doesn't add up, I suppose?' Jake sipped his pint.

'Luckily for us and all the people in that club, it went wrong.'

'Yeah, lucky...' Jake was looking at the barmaid.

Lenny followed his stare. 'Do you fancy her?'

'Not really.'

'Why are you looking at her like that then?'

'How long do you think she's been a barmaid?'

'I don't know, a while? She's pretty fast at serving.'

'Exactly.'

Lenny looked puzzled. 'Is there a point to this conversation?'

'It's not lucky that she gets it right, is it? It's practice. Something doesn't sit right with me about these two "dedicated terrorists" getting it wrong.'

'You think too much, Jake. Just be thankful no one was killed or injured.'

'I am very thankful,' Jake mumbled as he browsed the menu. 'Do you fancy some lunch, Len? The food looks pretty good here.'

'Yeah,' he replied, picking up a menu.

'You can update me on the enquiries you've done on the dead spy while we eat.'

'That won't take long. There's nothing, zero,' he said, pulling a face before engrossing himself in the menu.

30

In the office, Jake was looking through some statements on Fadhil Ghalib that had been taken at the hospital where he'd worked. They painted a picture of a lazy man who cared little for his job, spent much of his time surfing the web and had been disciplined for spending too much time on the internet during working hours. Jake made a mental note to speak with the Security Service. Maybe they had traces of the websites visited.

His mobile rang. Stephanie's name and number flashed up, distracting him from the job at hand.

'Hey, how are you?' he said, pleased to hear from her.

It was unusual for her to be calling for a chat. She rarely contacted him unless it was an important family emergency. The last time it had involved rescuing one of the girls' guinea pigs from the cavity walls.

'I've – I've had an accident,' she shouted down the phone.

Jake stood up from his desk. 'Are you all right? Are you hurt?'

'I'm OK – just really shaken up and—' Stephanie began sobbing. 'I— well I didn't mean to, and my car... He just pulled out. The police, they— I don't know what to do. It's all such a mess...'

'Where are you?'

'I'm on a roundabout... I really didn't see him.'

'Where? What roundabout?'

'They're telling me I'm in the wrong. And I wasn't. Honest.'

'Where are you?'

'I – I was just on my way… Oh God, I can't believe it…'

She wasn't making much sense. All he could hear was crying, and then traffic noise between the sobbing and jumbled sentences. He had to help her, wherever she was. He picked the car keys up from his desk and made his way down to the car park while trying to coax the location out of her. The signal cut off as the lift neared the basement.

He got into the car and started the engine. She'd sounded in a complete state – possibly injured. He needed to reach her quickly.

He called her again.

'I don't know what to do. They've left me here,' Stephanie sobbed down the phone.

'Where are you?' said Jake, his voice firm and loud.

'I crashed my car.'

'I know. Where?'

'World of Leather roundabout.'

'Are you still there? Are you all right?' Jake released the handbrake and moved off.

'Yes, I'm still here. The police, they left me here…'

'What do you mean the police left you? Are you hurt?'

'No, no. I just don't know what to do. My car is all smashed up and I'm sitting on the side of the road. I don't know what to do… And what about getting the girls from school?'

Stephanie meant Clifton's Roundabout. It was one of the busiest junctions in south London – a major intersection bringing together the arterial routes of the A2 and A20 roads near Eltham. Locals knew it as the World of Leather roundabout because of the big sofa store on the south-east corner of the junction. On the north-east side was a service station.

The roar of vehicle engines, the stench of exhaust fumes and the danger of getting shunted meant it was certainly no place to be standing or sitting in a smashed-up vehicle, not knowing what to do.

She could be hurt and not realise she was in danger.

'Wait there. Stay out of the road and out of the car. I'll be there as soon as I can – I won't be long.'

'OK. OK. Thank you.'

'On my way.'

With the traffic, it would take him an hour to get there from the Yard, but he could get there in fifteen or twenty minutes with the lights on. He affixed the magnetic beacon to the roof and plugged its long cord into the cigarette-lighter socket.

Lights flashing and sirens blaring, he made his way down Victoria Street and toward Parliament Square on the wrong side of the road. The traffic was heavy.

31

Even though he was a long way back from the roundabout and weaving between vehicles, he couldn't miss Stephanie's silver VW Golf. It was embedded in a lamp post, which was bent double, its head resting gently on her roof. The car was a write-off.

Jake pulled up on to the pavement next to it. Stephanie was no longer crying, but she looked terribly upset.

He got out of the car.

She ran over and hugged him immediately. She'd not touched him in over two years – not since they'd split up.

'I'm so glad you're here. Thank you. I don't know what to do, how to sort this out,' she said, holding him tightly.

'It's fine. The car is easy to sort out. I'm just pleased you're safe – I was worried about you.'

'I'm OK, just a bit bruised,' she said, breaking the hug.

'What happened?'

'I was on my way to meet Vanessa for coffee. I was on the roundabout heading toward Blackheath, and this car just pulled in front of me, from nowhere. I had right of way – I was on the roundabout. I swerved to avoid him – it was totally his fault – and I went up the kerb and smashed into the lamp post. He didn't even stop. Just carried on. No one else stopped. I thought the car was going to catch fire – there was all this smoke coming from the engine…'

'You said something about the police on the phone?'

'Yeah, a policeman on a motorbike pulled up almost as soon as it happened. He seemed all right at first…'

'What do you mean?'

'Well I told him what had happened then he started getting nasty. I don't know why. He was really rude. Said it was my fault, I was obviously driving too fast… and I wasn't, it was just—'

'What do you mean he was rude?'

'He was really aggressive. It might just be me. I was so upset. You know I'm a careful driver. I've never had an accident before. He said he was going to report me, cautioned me and everything.'

'Look, we'll worry about that later. We'll get it sorted out. This is obviously not your fault. Go and sit in my car while I organise getting your Golf recovered.'

'I'm really sorry to drag you out from work. I really appreciate you coming to help me,' she said, touching his arm as she walked toward his car.

Jake was just thankful she was in one piece and he could help. The last thing he'd have wanted was for her abandoned vehicle to cause a huge pile-up when he could have sorted the whole situation quickly and easily.

Police training kicking in, Jake glanced across the road at the service station opposite. He quickly scanned the forecourt and the buildings in all the appropriate places, spotting several CCTV cameras facing back at them.

'Did that police officer go over there and have a look at the CCTV, do you know?' he called to Stephanie.

'No, he just took all my details down. Told me I was being reported and then left.'

'OK,' said Jake.

One thing at a time. Tracking down any CCTV footage of the incident would have to wait.

32

Jake hovered on the threshold of Helen's office. 'You wanted to see me?'

'Yes, come in. Sit down and close the door please, Jake,' replied Helen, not looking up from the pile of papers she had in front of her.

'This sounds bad,' said Jake, closing the door. He sat down on one of the blue fabric chairs by her desk.

'It could be worse,' she replied, looking up from her papers and putting down her pen. 'You were seen with your blue lights and two tones on Westminster Bridge in one of our Mondeos yesterday. What were you up to?'

Jake was puzzled. He had to think about it for a moment. Then he realised – he'd been trying to get to Stephanie after her accident.

He tried to stall for time. 'Is there a problem? What's happened?'

'Just answer the question, Jake. What were you up to?' Helen didn't look pleased. He needed a reason to use blue lights on his car, a good reason – and rushing to make sure your ex-wife was OK after a car accident wasn't one of them.

'What do you want me to say, Helen?'

'What do you mean?'

'I'm driving with two tones and lights on a lot these days. We seem to have a terror attack or false alarm at least once a week. I need more information before I can say what I was up to.'

'OK.' Helen sounded stiff and formal, not her usual self. 'So the *complaint*,' she cleared her throat, 'says that you—'

'*Complaint?*'

A senior officer using the term complaint in this way meant that it was already formal – already a problem, already on paper. Complaint wasn't what you wanted to hear when you weren't long back from suspension. A complaint was a real problem.

'Yes, Jake. Complaint. The *complaint* says...' Helen began reading from a piece of paper in front of her on the desk, ' "He was seen at Parliament Square and Westminster Bridge, yesterday, 12 July 2007, driving with the emergency equipment – that is blue lights and two tones on – travelling south. Checks of the system and internally within SO15, reveal no obvious reason as to why DI Flannagan would be using emergency equipment at that time" ' Helen looked up at him.

From her stern expression, Jake knew he had to have a damned good reason.

This wasn't going well.

Jake tried again. 'Maybe I was following what I thought was a stolen motorcycle? Who exactly was it that saw me?'

'Jake...' Helen sighed. 'One of Mark's DSes saw you with your blue lights and two tones on. He told Mark, Mark did some checks and couldn't find you assigned to anything or any dispatch. He's made a statement and, sadly, Mark has taken it further, above me, to the commander.'

Jake shook his head and said nothing. His immediate thought was Gavin Bonson, given how much the smirking idiot had appeared to relish the difficulties between Jake and Mark.

Saying nothing was the best thing to do. At least until he understood how this was going to play out. Parliament Square and the bridge were full of CCTV cameras. You couldn't fart without something being caught on camera. The stolen motorbike story was lame. A quick check of CCTV would show it was a lie. He pondered his next move.

'I can deal with it, Jake,' Helen interrupted his thinking, 'but you've got to be straight. Were the blue lights justified or not?'

He thought for a moment. He'd been rushing to make sure Stephanie was all right. Morally noble. But completely unjustifiable from the organisation's perspective. They wouldn't support him, not if he told the truth – he realised that much. He was on thin ice.

'*Jake?*'

He said the first thing that popped into his head. 'I was late for a meeting. I didn't breach any traffic regulations or exceed the speed limit...'

'A meeting? Really?' Helen raised her eyebrows. 'Where was the meeting and who was it with? That's hardly urgent business.'

Jake shook his head. He owed it to Helen to be straight, but telling her that it was personal would only make it worse.

She could sense he wasn't telling the truth, he was sure, but he'd given her enough ammunition.

Misconduct was a strange thing in the police. It could be dealt with very simply – words of advice or a simple sanction from a supervisor – or, as Jake knew to his cost, they could send it to the Department of Professional Standards, who, using a lower burden of proof than you required in a real-world police investigation, could dress something up to make it look entirely different. Suddenly your simple, 'let's just put the blue lights on because we're worried our ex-wife has been involved in a serious accident and nobody is looking after her' is turned into 'you stole the car, used it for personal reasons, without permission, and you use your lights and sirens every night on your way home for dinner'.

They'd know it wasn't true, that it was a one-off, but if they upped it to multiple abuses, they could change it from misconduct to gross misconduct, which could lead to the sack. It was the way they weeded out those who didn't fit. Those who were difficult to manage. And after having just scraped through one misconduct board, he knew he wouldn't be so lucky on a second occasion.

There was no way out of this. If he lied and they investigated it, and they found he was lying – that was far worse. By the same token, if he admitted it, it could still cost him his job if they dressed it up as something else.

'Helen… look, I know it was wrong, but…'

'It wasn't work related, was it?' Helen shook her head, clearly disappointed.

'No. It was Stephanie, my ex-wife. She'd had an accident.'

'Was she injured? How is she?'

'She's fine. It was a car accident. It wasn't life and death.'

'And you were going to assist?'

'I wasn't on an official call. She contacted me. She was stranded. She was in shock. A car pulled out in front of her at a roundabout. She hit a lamp post.'

Helen grimaced. 'Jake, this really doesn't look good.'

'I know, I know. But she was in tears. She'd been left there at the side of the road. The traffic officer attending said it was her fault and just abandoned her…'

'Traffic officer? The police were already there, with her?'

'She was in a right old state; could have been involved in another accident. It was in heavy traffic on a major junction. She was in hysterics on the phone. I didn't know if she'd had a head injury or what had gone on. I just had to get there… It was important. She needed me… she needed help.' Jake's face was pained as he tailed off.

Helen's voice softened slightly. 'I understand that you've had a rocky relationship, Jake. I know that you mean well. But as you also know, this behaviour isn't justified – the use of the car isn't justified…' Helen paused and shook her head.

'But,' she continued, 'I *do* recognise that you're trying to be a better ex-husband than you were a husband. And I know that you're trying to get your family life settled again after a rocky period. I also recognise that you've told the truth, and many people wouldn't in your situation. They'd have lied, made us collect CCTV and other evidence – I appreciate all of that. However it still doesn't excuse the fact that you broke the rules.'

Jake braced himself for the worst.

Helen continued, 'Look, I'll make a note of our conversation. Thank you for admitting your mistake to me. You're banned for three months from driving police cars, Jake. That's the end of it.'

Whether the commander liked it or not, Helen had just dealt with it. And Jake knew that in her own small way, she'd actually done him a huge favour.

In police discipline, there was only one bite at the cherry. Once someone had been sanctioned with a form of discipline, as Helen had just done, nobody else could have a second go at it.

'Thank you, ma'am. I appreciate it. I'm really sorry that you've had to deal with this,' said Jake as he got up and left the room.

To find Mark.

33

Mark was sitting in a quiet corner of the almost deserted cafeteria on the fourth floor. It reminded Jake of a cheap kitchenette straight out of an eighties sitcom, with its blue plastic chairs and steel-legged tables. Synthetic plants had been added in an attempt to brighten the place up, but they only increased the general feeling of dreariness.

He sat down heavily at Mark's table.

'Afternoon, Jake.'

Jake cut straight to the chase. 'Why did you feel the need to do that?'

'Do what?' asked Mark.

'Let's not fuck about, Mark…'

'No need to swear. Are you upset about something?'

'If you've got a problem with me, you could always talk to me about it first, *before* you go whining to your big-boss mates. I could have put you straight about why I was using blue lights.'

'Someone reported their concerns to me. I did some checks. Gave the commander the facts. The rest is down to him and what he decides to do. Nothing to do with me.'

'I thought we all played for the same side? Us versus the bad guys? I didn't think we tried to get each other into trouble. I thought we sorted our own trouble out?'

'Get you into trouble? I got you into trouble, did I? I think you've managed that all on your own. It was up to the commander what he did with it.'

'You want all the glory. You want to be the big fish, show everyone what you're made of, eliminate anyone that might take some of the limelight. That's why you didn't tell me about Liverpool, isn't it? It's why you've cut me out of everything you possibly can, isn't it?'

'You have a terrible reputation, Jake. No one likes you – not really. Helen's the only reason you're still here…'

'Really? Is that what you think?'

'It's not just what I think – most people think it. I can do without all your nonsense. I can do without you causing trouble.'

'It's not me that causes trouble!' Jake snarled at him.

'I don't need you around me or my team. I don't need you on some fancy crusade, trying to save the world. You're a maverick, and I never liked you.'

'This is all because I challenge your thinking by suggesting that you might be wrong about things.'

'I couldn't care less what you think. I just want to get on with my job without the distractions that you cause. Operation Seagram is my job, and I say what goes on, not you.'

'No, Mark, it's not yours – it doesn't belong to you. We were supposed to be a team and Helen is our senior officer…'

'Team?' Mark laughed. 'When have you ever worked as part of a team? You swan about doing what you think is best. You butt in when you're not wanted, and you poke your snout into too many things – things that don't concern you.'

Jake was struggling to understand what this was about. Was Mark talking about work, Gaynor or something else?

'Is this about your wife, all these years later?'

Mark shook his head and tutted at him. 'You disagree with everyone about everything. Cause trouble.'

'You mean I question things? The way a proper detective is supposed to do?'

'*Proper detective* – is that a dig at me, is it?' Mark shook his head and tutted again.

He obviously wanted an argument. It was childish. Jake had meant nothing personal by it other than that was how detectives did business – testing things, questioning things.

'So now you're suggesting I'm not a proper detective, eh?'

Jake had had enough. He was sick of babysitting. He couldn't hold it in any longer.

'Well, you're not, are you? You're a level transfer who did it the easy way, not the *proper* way. Who you know, not what you know,' retorted Jake, deciding that if Mark wanted this argument then he could have it.

'Fuck off.'

'I'm not going anywhere, mate.'

Mark smirked at him. 'We'll see about that.'

'And I'm still doing the intelligence work on Seagram,' Jake carried on baiting him. 'You've achieved nothing apart from making an enemy of me.'

'Just that you're taking the bus and Tube everywhere for now, waiting for the DPS to interview you, and have *another* misconduct board coming up?' Mark said, laughed at him.

'You're behind the curve, *mate*. Helen dealt with it informally, gave me a driving ban. That's all you achieved, nothing else.' Jake shrugged. 'Who gives a fuck about a driving ban?'

'Just a driving ban?'

'You look disappointed. Were you hoping for something more?'

Mark said nothing, but he looked down into his lap, deep in thought. Had Mark actually hoped that Jake would lose his job over this?

'Just another nail in your coffin,' Mark said looking him squarely in the eyes again. 'A few more and you'll be gone.'

'I don't understand you, Mark. Why don't you be a man and tell me what this is really about?

Mark shook his head and chuckled at him. It gave nothing away.

'I'm sitting here. Tell me. Be a man.'

'It's about you driving police cars with blue lights on when you shouldn't. Simple as.'

'Detectives know when someone is telling lies. We've been in the police the same amount of time – we're the same rank. This isn't about work, is it?'

'I know how to follow rules and procedures, Jake. It's not me that keeps getting myself in trouble, is it?'

'Really?'

'Really.' Mark was smirking at him again.

Jake resisted the urge to punch him.

The image of a happy, fun-loving Gaynor aged nineteen appeared in Jake's head. He saw her face fall as Mark appeared out of nowhere to drag her off. How the hell did she end up staying with him? Was that what all this was about?

'Is this really about Gaynor and something that happened over twenty years ago? I didn't force her, you know!'

There was still no glimmer of emotion from Mark. Jake had to get a hook on something, to try and tease out what was really going on here.

'It was totally consensual – all of it. She was a more-than-willing partner. I didn't tie her to the bed or anything.' Jake winked at him. He knew this would rile him, make him think there was more to it than just a kiss. But if he got a reaction, it might give him the clue he needed to understand what this stupid argument was really about.

Mark lowered his voice. 'Don't you dare talk about my wife. At least I still have one. Unlike you. You can't even run your own life, let alone a terrorist investigation – that's why Occupational Health are all over you.'

Jake was flabbergasted. The Gaynor jibe had failed to do the job and now it seemed that nothing in his personnel file was confidential. The commander must have told Mark about Jake's pledge to attend Occupational Health. Helen wouldn't have, and Lenny was the only other person that knew he was attending.

'This isn't over,' said Jake, jabbing a finger in Mark's face.

'Oh give it a rest.' Mark laughed, mocking him. 'You're a womanising alcoholic – everyone knows that. It won't be long before you fuck up again, and I get more complaints or catch you out somewhere… and that information will be going straight to the commander too.'

'Yeah, you've got the support of your big mate there – the mate who's going to smooth your path all the way through to superintendent.' Jake was still fishing.

'He looks after those that do the work...'

'No, he looks after people he thinks are no threat to him. People who don't challenge him. People who do as they're told. You're like a pet poodle. No guts. No teeth of your own. All fucking fluff and no substance.'

'I think you need a drink, Jake – you're getting upset.'

How had they gone from working on a case together to an official complaint going in about him? Was there any point to this? Was Mark just hell bent on holding something against him that had happened years ago?

Sod it, thought Jake. He'd given him enough chances to air whatever grievance he had.

'To be honest, I only drink when I'm fucking your wife, Mark – which means I drink a lot, you're right.' Jake pushed the table away from him as he stood up. The polystyrene cup in front of Mark wobbled and tipped over, tea gushing into his lap.

Mark jumped up, away from the table. His trousers were soaked and dripping on to the floor. Standing there, their gazes locked on each other, Jake felt his jaw clenching, adrenalin flowing into his bloodstream.

'*Discretion is the better part of valour, Jake...*' he heard his mother's soft voice in his head. '*Walk away. Don't give him what he wants.*'

She was right. He wasn't worth it.

Jake turned and left the room.

34

'This is the place that Uncle Frank mentioned on those audio tapes… Unit 3,' Claire said, stopping the car opposite the large blue shutters of a warehouse. 'Looks deserted though.'

'It's a Sunday. To be expected. Looks to me like a flop.' Jake glanced at the large *To Let* sign that was hanging from the wall above the door and the rubbish littered around the loading bay.

'A what?'

'It's a flop,' said Jake again.

'What the hell is a *flop*, Jake?'

'A flop address.' Jake frowned at her. She obviously had no idea what he meant. 'It's a place where fraudsters deliver goods they've purchased on the internet or over the phone using stolen credit cards. Usually a sublet place or a squat. Tracing the person who actually controls the flop is like trying to track down Lord Lucan. Then when we go and bang on the door looking for Mr So-and-so, whose name the stolen goods have been delivered in, the people in the flop don't have a Scooby Doo.'

Jake did an impression of the cartoon dog. 'I dunno a Mr So-and-so.'

Claire burst out laughing. 'Well I've learnt something today. I now know what a flop is – *and* that you do an amazing impression of Scooby Doo!'

'I'm full of talent. I'm pretty much wasted in the police, Claire. I always wanted to be a secret agent, you know? Working with you is almost a dream come true for me.'

'Stop being stupid.' Claire hit his arm playfully. 'Concentrate on the job. How do you talented cops deal with flops then, if banging on the door is no good?'

'It's all about getting inside,' said Jake, undoing his seat belt. 'There's always something illegal inside. And then you've got Scooby Doo by the bollocks. Wait here,' he said, getting out of the car.

The place was typical of industrial estates built in the eighties and nineties. Concrete-block buildings, blue corrugated-iron roofs and a loading bay next to a small warehouse. Each one was a separate unit with a pedestrian entrance alongside the vehicle entrance. If you'd been in one, you'd been in all of them – identical, wherever you were in the country.

He made his way round the side of the units. There was a brick wall at the back that formed the border between the estate and the fetid creek. Jake hoisted himself up on to the wall and, arms outstretched like a tightrope artist, made his way along its length to the rear. At the back of the warehouse, he shinned up a nearby drainpipe and on to the roof.

'Bingo,' he whispered as he walked carefully across it to a skylight. Through it, he could see a deserted office in the room below.

Jake tried tapping gently on the windowpane with his heel, to test the strength of the glass. As he did so, the skylight suddenly shattered beneath his foot, causing him to over-balance and plunge straight down into the office. He landed heavily on a large wooden desk, his ankle twisting underneath him.

As he struggled to his feet, he saw a small man of East Asian appearance wearing a black T-shirt and blue jeans. He was standing at the office door, staring straight at him with a perplexed look on his face.

Jake quickly produced his warrant card. 'Sorry about your skylight, sir. I'm a police officer. I was chasing a suspect across your roof and—'

Before Jake could finish, the man turned and fled down a galvanised steel staircase. As Jake attempted to give chase, his ankle collapsed underneath him. He heard the man's clanging footsteps recede into the distance and the unit's main door slam.

Jake hobbled slowly down the stairs and into the brightly lit industrial unit below. Before he'd even neared the bottom, he knew from the hum of the fans and the heat of the lights why the man had run off.

Lined up in trays on trestle tables as far as the eye could see were green, jagged-leaved plants under the glare of UV lights; their temperature regulated by rotating blades that created a cooling current of air. The plants were mature – almost fully grown. In one corner, a sleeping bag lay on the floor, surrounded by sweet wrappers.

'I can see why that Chinese fella just ran off,' said Claire when Jake let her in through the main door of the unit and showed her the warm, plant-filled interior. 'You were right about there being something illegal in most flops, PC Plod.'

'Vietnamese gang member would be my guess. They've a virtual monopoly on cannabis farms these days. They perfected their industrial-scale growing programmes in Vancouver, and now they've taken over the market in the UK. Bring the workers over, all illegal immigrants. Imprison them in one of these places, use them like slaves and threaten their families at home as a bargaining chip.'

'Well your Vietnamese gentleman is long gone.' Claire was walking through the plants, her arms outstretched, stroking their leaves. 'What are we going to do with this little lot?'

'I'll call it in after we've gone. Get it all confiscated. Tracing the actual gang leaders is mostly hopeless anyway. Nothing lost. Have a look round. See if we can find anything that might tie Frank to this little lot.'

'Well I never! I really didn't think he'd be involved with this sort of thing. Cannabis farms! Can you believe it? Is that how he's making his money?'

Jake wasn't listening. He'd limped off to explore a storage area he'd found next to the toilet. Stacked in the corner, chest high, were a pile of A4-sized boxes, about ten of them, one on top of another.

'How much money do you reckon Uncle Frank is making from this crop, then, Jake? Jake?'

Jake pulled open the top box. It was full of documents. Copies of bank statements, interview records, written statements.

He began flicking through them. The majority of the sheets were headed with a black and white emblem of a lion and a unicorn. It was a simplified version of the royal coat of arms – the logo used by the British government on official departmental documents.

Claire came up behind him, leaned over his shoulder and gently whispered in his ear, '*Honi soit qui mal y pense.*'

'I have no idea what you're on about, Claire.'

'It's Anglo-Norman. It's the saying written on that.' Claire pointed to the motto on the coat of arms that Jake was staring at. It means "shame on you for thinking evil". The French use it ironically nowadays, to insinuate the presence of hidden agendas or conflicts of interest.'

'Well, isn't that apt?' said Jake, laughing. 'I think we were completely wrong about Uncle Frank and the cannabis farm, Claire.'

'We were?' she replied, looking crestfallen.

'Yeah, I don't think he's into drugs at all,' said Jake. 'I can't believe we thought he was a cannabis dealer!'

'He isn't?'

'No. Not in the slightest.' Jake pulled out several letters from the sheaf of papers he was holding and held them directly in front of her face, pointing to the address. 'Remember the phone conversations where he was talking about documents?'

'Yeah.'

'For some reason, your lovely Uncle Frank has chosen a lock-up housing a cannabis farm in which to hide government documents that have been stolen from the Serious Fraud Office.'

35

They were in the living room, both of them sitting on the floor surrounded by boxes, folders and sheets of paper as they read document after official document headed 'Serious Fraud Office investigation'.

'Does any of this mean anything to you?' asked Jake, barely bringing his head up from the file he was reading. Claire had wrapped a bag of frozen peas around his swollen ankle using a tea towel. He'd been so engrossed in the documents that he hadn't stopped to argue with her.

'Yeah, sort of,' replied Claire. 'What are you going to do about the cannabis farm?' she asked, changing the subject.

'I'll call the local station and feed them some story as to how I found the place. Get them to deal with it. It's not important. What's important is all this,' he said, gesturing to the piles of information that lay around them. 'So this is a fraud investigation into bribes being paid to some Saudi princes for an arms deal back in the eighties?'

'It looks like it, yes.'

'And Frank works for an arms manufacturer?' Was that what she'd told him before?

'Not exactly, no. He works for a trade delegation, in a government department – something loosely attached to the Ministry of Defence. He's an MOD employee.'

'And this little lot is all about a deal between an arms company and the Saudis back in the eighties. It must be what he was talking about on the phone then?' Jake finally looked up at her.

'I guess so...' Claire mumbled.

'You sound pissed off. I thought you'd be happy. We've had a result today. I don't think it could've gone better!'

'Depends how you look at it.'

'You wanted to know what he was up to – we've found out. He's clearly wrapped up in this somehow.'

'Obviously.'

'Well that's good then, surely?'

'Which one of us works for the Serious Fraud Office, Jake?' Claire snapped.

'Neither of us. And your point is?'

'I wanted to keep this quiet, find out what he was up to ourselves. With me working in secret intelligence and you in law enforcement, I thought we'd have all those bases covered. I hadn't factored in the small matter of the Serious Fraud Office being involved – a place where neither of us has any influence!'

Jake looked at her, confused. 'I don't get you. This is a major result...'

'It's not a result, Jake! I'm sick of it.' She screwed up the piece of paper she'd been reading and threw it across the floor.

'OK. Calm down. I can deal with the Serious Fraud Office. It's no trouble.'

'I don't want a third party being involved. I wanted to sort this between me and you.'

'Sort it? You said you wanted to know what he was up to... You find out what that is and now you've got the arse. I don't understand. He's obviously not looking at you. His beef is with the Serious Fraud Office.'

'So who is looking at me, Jake? This fraud stuff just adds another dimension for me to worry about. It makes it more complicated – can't you see?'

'I don't see it like that, no. How?'

'I'll drop you home. You can take all this to your place. It'll be safer there... I'm tired.' Claire stood up and stretched.

'Well thanks anyway for a lovely weekend, Claire. I've had a great time. Breaking into places, almost getting killed and finding cannabis farms. Weekends don't get much better,' said Jake, half serious and half joking at the same time.

'I'm just tired, Jake. I appreciate your help, I really do. I just need a good night's sleep.' She hugged him and gave him a kiss on the lips.

'OK. No problem. Look, I'll tidy up. Can you just grab my phone for me? I think I left it in the bathroom.' Jake began picking up the papers from the floor. 'I'll contact the Serious Fraud Office tomorrow and say I've found some of these boxes of documents. See what I can find out. Keep it low-key.'

Claire wandered off to find his phone. He waited until she was out of sight then picked up the screwed-up document she'd thrown into the corner of the room, gently smoothed it out and placed it in the box with the rest.

'It's OK!' he shouted to Claire. 'Found it! I'm all ready.'

36

Jake stared at the dark wood of Helen's heavy office door – room 1524 – her nameplate in the holder. A personalised nameplate at the Met was a real symbol of having properly arrived. He knocked and waited for her invitation to enter. He took a deep breath, pushed the stainless-steel handle and went in.

'Morning, ma'am.'

Helen was sitting at her desk. 'Morning, Jake. I hear you had an eventful weekend?' she said, frowning.

'Yes, ma'am, a rather surprising weekend. I was just coming to talk to you about it, but someone seems to have beaten me to it,' he said, puzzled.

'You were chasing a suspect in Docklands, across a roof, happened to fall through a skylight and found a cannabis farm inside?'

'You know how these things happen.'

'I know how these things happen with *you*, Jake. They never seem to happen to anyone else!' she said, clearly not buying it. 'Who were you chasing and why?'

'I was just passing the industrial estate and I saw this guy acting oddly. Watched him for a bit. He climbed on the roof so I thought he might be a burglar. I confronted him. He ran, I ran. I fell through the skylight. He escaped, I landed on my ankle and couldn't keep up—'

'And of all the skylights you could fall through, these premises had a cannabis farm inside?'

143

'Odd, I know. Truth is stranger than fiction.' Jake chuckled. 'I called it in, waited for the local uniform to arrive, and then as I was leaving them to it, I found some important documents in the street. I think the suspect I was chasing may have dropped them.'

'What?' Helen's voice hit a new high note. She obviously hadn't been expecting that plot twist.

'It's a weird one, I know...' Jake smiled, trying to butter her up. She was looking at him sceptically. 'They were documents from the Serious Fraud Office. Rather embarrassing for the SFO but could be something much bigger. I thought it best to investigate it myself.'

'Investigate what?'

'The documents are part of a case file. I guess they've been stolen from somewhere or something. I've not told the local police about that side of it. Thought it best that I follow up on this part of it myself – go over to the SFO and have a chat with them this morning about it?'

'I don't know where you're going with this, Jake. I trust you, but thousands wouldn't...'

'I'm just doing my job. Investigating crime, messing with the bad guys. Hey, I found a cannabis farm – how many of your DIs do that on their weekend off?'

'Be careful, that's all I'll say.'

'Thank you, ma'am. I appreciate it. It's fine, nothing to worry about. I'll let you know what the guys at the SFO come back with.'

'Unless this has a terrorism connection, Jake, it's nothing to do with us. You know that. So you haven't got lots of time to play with it, whatever it is.' Helen had a serious look on her face.

'No, I understand. I know we have a lot to do on Operation Seagram.'

'Yes, well – I need to talk to you about that.'

'Oh?'

'What happened with Mark in the canteen after I banned you from driving the other day? Did you talk to him?'

'Yes. I expressed my displeasure at the way he'd handled it. Said I thought he could have handled it better.'

'And how did he end up with tea all over his trousers?'

'The table moved as I got up, the cup fell over into his lap. It was an accident.'

Helen shook her head. She looked upset with him.

'You do know how hard I had to fight for you to keep your position here after you were suspended, Jake?'

He didn't. It had never been mentioned to him. He knew that she'd submitted a very strong statement of support to his disciplinary panel, but he'd still ended up with the toughest punishment possible at that level – a written warning. And after all, he'd only been doing his job. The warning was because he'd not followed the right rules and procedures when trying to hunt down Claire. It wasn't like he'd done something for personal gain. OK, so he'd taken the car with him while on leave, but that was hardly the end of the world. Helen had said to keep hold of it.

He kept quiet. He felt that was his best course of action right now.

'You don't need all this controversy, Jake,' Helen continued. 'We've got a new commander. He's not like the old guard – he's making lots of changes here. He allowed me to deal with the blue-light incident. And then, straight after, Mark ends up with a cup of tea in his lap.'

She paused, obviously waiting for a response.

Jake said nothing. The silence hung between them awkwardly for a moment.

'I didn't know you'd fought for me to stay here at Counter Terror,' he said tentatively.

Now he thought about it, it was obvious to him. People were often moved for far less.

'You're a fantastic investigator, Jake. But I can't protect you from everything.'

'I'm sorry I've let you down; I shouldn't have let my emotions get the better of me.'

'I want you to take more of a back seat on Seagram – let Mark get on with it. I'll allocate you work from it, as and when

I need you – no more free rein in the investigation. I want you to stay away from him.'

'But—'

'Jake!' she interrupted. 'That's come down from the commander. Just do as I ask – please?'

'OK, fine.' There was no point in arguing. Mark had succeeded in creating trouble. Trouble that got in the way of the investigation, trouble that he could then use as evidence to get Jake taken off the job. It was clear that had been his intention.

'Look, just crack on with this SFO thing you've got your teeth into for now, whatever that is,' she said with a hint of scepticism.

Jake smiled and left the office.

He called Lenny on his mobile as he walked into the lift.

'Lenny, it's Jake. Meet me in the car park. We've got a little errand to run.'

On reaching the basement, he found Lenny had already beaten him to the Mondeo.

'Morning, Jake. How was the weekend?'

'Eventful,' said Jake, opening the car and throwing the key fob to Lenny. 'Drive. I'll fill you in on the way.'

'OK. Where are we off to?'

'The Serious Fraud Office, Elm Street.'

'Where's that?'

'It's up by Mount Pleasant.'

Lenny started the car and began backing out of their space in the crowded car park.

'The Serious Fraud Office. What's all that about then? Why are we going there?'

'You'll *never* believe what happened to me over the weekend.' Jake turned to Lenny and winked.

'Oh, bejesus, it's one of those jobs?' groaned Lenny.

'Ask me no questions and I'll tell you no lies.'

Lenny shook his head in disbelief as he drove up the ramp and on to the street outside the Yard.

'Don't worry – the boss knows where we're going. I've told her.'

'That's a start, I guess.'

Jake laughed. 'Let's just say that I came into possession of some secret documents over the weekend. They were kicking about on some industrial estate in Docklands. I'm just trying to find out how they got there.'

'Does the SFO know we're coming?'

'No. I thought it best we just turn up. I don't want to be fobbed off.'

'Why? What are the documents?'

'They look like they're part of an important case file. Not the sort of thing you'd expect to find outside of their offices.'

The traffic lights changed to red and the flow of vehicles came to a halt. As they waited to drive into Parliament Square, Lenny turned to Jake. 'Do I want to know more about this, Jake? Do I need to?'

'It really is as simple as I've said it is. Honestly.'

The lights changed to green, and Lenny pulled off. 'Nothing is simple with you, Jake. Just don't drop me in the shit. I'm happy to help, as long as it's legal...'

37

After much discussion in reception, they were eventually led up to the second floor and into a conference room, where they were asked to wait until an investigator was located who could help them.

The room looked fairly smart to Jake's eyes, with a beige carpet and modern wooden desks. The Government plainly treated the Serious Fraud Office better than they did the police. After a short time, a woman who looked to be in her mid-thirties entered. She was wearing a navy skirt suit, a white blouse and block heels.

'I'm Sara Dowbert,' she said, shaking hands. 'I'm a senior investigator here. I understand that you've found some documents?'

With mousy hair that looked like it refused to respond to anything, Sara was not quite fit or slender enough to be considered attractive by impossible, glossy magazine standards, yet Jake noticed how comfortable she was in her own skin, with a quiet confidence that he wished more women had.

'Yes, we have. They turned up on an industrial estate in Docklands yesterday.' Jake produced photocopies of four of the documents, a Swiss bank statement in a company name, an exhibit list and two written statements. He passed them to Sara.

Sara sat down at the large desk and thumbed through the documents.

'Was it just these pages?' she asked, looking up.

'That's what we've got with us at the moment,' Jake replied, skirting the issue slightly. 'They look to be from a case file. Have you lost any case files?'

'Not that I'm aware of. I do know which case this is. There's been a fair bit of controversy about it in the news.'

'Oh, what case is that?'

'The Al Yamamah case.' Sara sighed. 'You may have heard of it.'

'Al what?'

'Yamamah. It's Arabic. I've been told it translates to "The Dove" – although I'm not sure whether that's just PR spin or not.' She smirked. 'It was an investigation into Britain's largest ever export deal. We were looking at whether a British defence contractor bribed the Saudi royal family and others as part of an arms deal.'

'*Was* an investigation? You mean it's finished?'

'Pretty much, yes. We've been told to drop the case.'

'Who told you to drop it?'

'Oh, only the Prime Minister and the Attorney General. No one important,' she replied, glowering at the documents.

'Sounds like you weren't happy with that?'

'We worked on this case for years. There's plenty of evidence that several, very well-known individuals have made billions from bribes, backhanders and other kickbacks from the sale of weapons to the Saudis. We got told to drop it. I'm sure you can imagine how we felt about that, after three years of work?'

'I can imagine.'

'The Yanks are pursuing the Saudi side of it now. We've still got the arms contractor in our sights over here for various other deals, but these documents relate to the Saudi side of things – I'm pretty sure we've moved all that stuff to secure storage.'

'Where would that be? I'm thinking your storage facility may have been broken into or something?'

'Let me see what I can find out,' said Sara, getting up from the table. 'Give me a minute.'

She left the room, closing the door behind her, leaving Lenny and Jake alone.

'Where *did* you get those documents?' asked Lenny.

Jake winked. 'I found them.'

'This sounds pretty serious, Jake. Prime ministers and attorney generals…'

As Jake was about to answer, Sara returned with a stunning younger woman. Mid-twenties, he thought, slim, with long blonde hair. Perfectly made-up and immaculately dressed in a tight-fitting, above-the-knee skirt. She looked to Jake like she'd just walked off the set of a Hollywood movie.

'This is Jennifer. She's our office clerk. She handles all of our filing and sends documents off for storage.'

Jake stood up. 'Good to meet you, Jennifer,' he said, holding out his hand.

'Call me Jenny,' she said, shaking it.

Jenny. Jenny. Jenny. Was it the same Jenny?

He could hear Frank Richards' voice playing in his head, just as it sounded on the recordings Claire had made:

'This really isn't the time to be getting cold feet, Jenny. It's a bit late for that. We didn't put you in there because we wanted to know what tea they drank, what type of biscuits they liked…'

Jake didn't want to jump to any conclusions. He tried to keep it light, stapling a 'good cop' smile on his face. 'I've got a few questions for you, Jenny.'

'Yeah, no worries. What's up?' she asked, sitting down.

'Have you worked here long?'

'Nah, not really. Since November last year. So about eight months.' Jenny's looks were in stark contrast to how she spoke. Months were pronounced 'mumfs'. She sounded as if she'd originally hailed from a north London council estate.

'Oh, OK. You do the filing here though – of the case papers?'

'Sort of, yeah. I don't exactly file it myself, you know? Nah, I'm just a clerk. There are tons of papers. I fill out the forms – send them off for storage, you know? What's all this about anyway? Why are you asking me this stuff?'

'Sara didn't tell you why we were here?'

'Nah, she didn't.'

'We've found some of your SFO case papers somewhere they shouldn't be.'

'Well, that ain't my fault. Why are you interrogating me?' Jenny interrupted, sounding slightly hostile.

'I never said it was your fault. I'm just asking a few questions. How do you send the case papers away to the storage place, Jenny?'

'I fill out the form and organise a secure courier to pick them up. The courier takes them there.'

'That sounds nice and easy.'

'Are you saying I'm stupid?' Jenny interrupted again.

'No, not at all, just that it sounds—'

'Jenny, you can go back to your desk. I'm pretty sure I can sort this out,' interjected Sara.

Jenny got up from the table. 'I'd like to say it was nice to meet you, but...' She turned and left the room without finishing her sentence.

Jake looked at Lenny. He raised his eyebrows back and smiled.

'Sorry about that. Jennifer can be a bit abrupt. I'm sure she's just having a bad day.'

'I don't think I'm going to be on her Christmas-card list, somehow,' Jake joked back.

'No.' Sara suppressed a giggle. 'Maybe if you leave it with me, I can check the paperwork and give you a call in a few days?'

'Great. Thanks, Sara.' Jake shook her hand, recorded her office number in his phone and said goodbye.

An unusual reaction for an innocent party, he thought. Claire would be very interested in this. It sounded like they might just have had a lucky break.

38

On their way out of the building, Jake checked with the security guard on reception to see if there were any other exits. There was just the one. That was good news.

Lenny knew immediately what Jake was up to. 'If we're going to follow this Jenny girl, you'd better fill me in on why we're here, Jake.'

'Ha, there's no flies on you, Len,' said Jake, laughing as they crossed the road to the car. They'd parked facing the entrance to the building on a side street opposite. 'You saw it too?'

'A knockout in the looks department, but hardly Mensa material and *very* nervous about something. What is it you know about her? Spill the beans,' replied Lenny as they climbed back into the car.

'Look, all I know is that someone called Jenny might be involved in arranging for SFO documents to be moved and accidentally – how should I put it – *lost*.'

'Moved and lost? What for?'

'I don't know what for – not yet. But moved into the hands of people that shouldn't have them.'

'How d'you know?'

'Because I found some of them in Docklands yesterday!'

'How? How did you find them? Where has this come from? A snout?'

'Let's just say it's a reliable source. What I don't know is exactly *why* she's moving these documents. It might be a national security matter, and that's why we're looking into it,' he said, steering the conversation away from how he'd found them as quickly as he could. 'I obviously don't want to ask for Jenny's personal details from her place of work, at least not at this stage – so we'll follow her home and see if we can find out who she is that way, OK?'

'OK. How are we going to play it?'

'One of us on foot, the other in the car. Use our mobiles to communicate. If she's a bit wrapped up in herself and thinking about what she's going to have for dinner, it'll be dead easy.'

'So I assume I'm driving and you're walking?' asked Lenny.

'No. I've got a dodgy ankle. I'm the boss. I drive.'

'Have you forgotten that you're on a driving ban? You'll have to do the walking. And there's nothing wrong with your ankle. I've seen you on it this morning. Go and buy some painkillers if it's playing up.'

Jake shook his head. 'I was doing all the talking in our meeting just now. She might not have paid much attention to you, Len. But she'd spot me next to her on the street, wouldn't she?

'Two words, Jake – "driving ban".'

'Who's gonna know? We're just going to follow her home or to somewhere that can give us a full name to work with. She might have a car parked nearby. That would be checkable for a name and address. Then you can drive again. No one is going to see me.'

'I bet you thought that with the blue lights on. And someone did see you that time – that's how you ended up getting banned. Remember? Why risk it?'

'It's an operational need. We need to know who this girl is, so we've got to do it now.'

'You've got some sort of problem, Jake. Why can't you just play by the rules, do as you're told? Be a bit humble every now and again and take it on the chin, as they say?'

'Take it on the chin?' Jake thought for moment. Then he retorted, 'Muhammad Ali, the greatest boxer that ever lived, once said, "At home I'm a nice guy, but I don't want the world to know that." Humble people, I've found, don't get very far.'

'So I'm guessing that means it's me on foot?' Lenny sighed. 'OK, you're the boss. I can't stop you doing stuff, even if I do think it's stupid.'

'I'm not stupid. The world belongs to the brave – remember that. We've got a bit of a wait. It's only 12.30 p.m.,' said Jake, checking his watch. 'Go grab some rolls or something for lunch. I'll wait here. I'll have a ploughman's or something please.'

'Fantastic. Not only do I get to watch you break the rules, I get to do the footwork *and* buy your lunch too?'

'Here.' Jake dragged a twenty-pound note from his pocket and handed it to Lenny 'Get yours with that too, you moany old sod!' Jake winked at him.

'Less of the old!' said Lenny as he walked off.

Jake climbed across into the driver's seat and settled in for what was probably going to be a bit of a wait.

He watched the world go by for a bit. He could see what looked like a tramp, dragging some anti-war banners out of a shopping trolley and laying them along the pavement. The banners were certainly attracting attention from passers-by, but mainly in the form of a trip hazard, rather than from any sort of political sentiment.

Jake pulled out his phone and called Claire.

She answered after a couple of rings.

'Hi, Claire, it's me.'

'Hi. How's things?'

'Pretty good. The boss gave me some space to look into those documents.'

'OK, well done,' Claire said, not sounding like she meant it.

'Better than that, I've been to the SFO and I think I've located Jenny.'

'That was quick work! How did you manage that?'

'Right place, right time.'

'Lucky,' she mumbled.

'It wasn't bloody luck! She didn't just fall from the heavens and land in my lap, did she?'

'No, Jake. You were the one who fell from the heavens, through that bloody skylight.'

'Yeah, anyway, I'm not one hundred per cent it's her. Maybe about ninety-eight per cent, and I've got to locate her last name and where she lives without alerting the SFO.'

'What did they think about the documents we found?'

'The investigator didn't seem that bothered to be honest. She said that part of the job was over and done with. It's something to do with a defence contract and the Saudis taking bribes. They were annoyed that the job got shut down, but they're pursuing the arms company for something else now, I think.'

'Oh...' Claire was sounding less and less impressed with his work.

'Are you all right?' asked Jake, struggling to understand her attitude.

'Fine. What's the plan now?'

'We're going to tail this Jenny when she leaves work, see what we can find out about her.'

'How's the ankle?'

'It's fine, just a bit bruised. I'm playing it up with Lenny so I get to drive.'

'Keep me posted?'

'Will do,' said Jake as he eyed Lenny coming back with two white paper bags and two polystyrene cups. 'Gotta go. Talk later,' he said, hanging up.

'Couldn't get you a ploughman's. They didn't have any cheese. So I got you corned beef and pickle,' Lenny said, handing Jake one of the bags.

'Corned beef? You know I don't eat any animal with four legs!'

'What?' Lenny exclaimed.

'I eat any bird, but nothing with four legs.'

'I've seen you eat bacon and sausages.'

'Only when I'm hungover. It's not a conscious thing. What's in the other bag, the other sandwich?'

'That's mine!'

'We're a team, Lenny. We help each other out.'

'It's chicken salad and mayonnaise,' replied Lenny, throwing him the bag.

'Perfect!' said Jake, pulling it from its wrappings and biting off a large mouthful.

39

'OK, that's her – blonde hair, red handbag – go go...' said Jake as Jenny came down the steps of the SFO building and turned right toward Gray's Inn Road in the side mirror of his car. 'Stay in touch on the phone, Len. I'll take the car and move to where you think she's headed.'

'No. You do the walking, guv!' said Lenny.

'What?'

'I've changed my mind,' said Lenny. 'I'm putting my foot down. You can do the walking for a change. You might be the boss, but you're not always right. You nicked my sandwich and now you're nicking my driving job when you're already banned. I'm not letting you get in any more trouble than you're already in. You'll get the sack if you get caught. And then I'll have to partner up with some idiot like Mark Castle.'

'They won't sack me! Go – follow her.'

'They *will* sack you! No, I'm not following her on foot and I'm not letting you drive.' Lenny folded his arms and remained where he was.

Jake glanced in the mirror as Jenny disappeared round the corner and out of sight. He raised his voice. 'If I tail her, she might spot me!'

'It's better than you being spotted driving the car, Jake. We could have got a team together to do this...'

Jake got out of the car. 'I'll call you!' he shouted as he slammed the door and began walking swiftly up the street after Jenny.

They needed authority for this – he hadn't bothered to get that either. He could have got the go-ahead by phone, but he didn't want to risk giving anyone the opportunity of saying no to it.

Easier to get forgiveness than permission.

The introduction of the Human Rights Act had meant a whole raft of changes to the way police conducted surveillance and investigations, but in Jake's opinion it had made things much more complicated for the police, while offering little protection to anyone except the criminals.

The time of day was perfect – end of normal business hours. It was likely that she was heading home, hopefully to her *own* home, from which they'd be able to determine exactly who she was without having to go through the SFO.

The pavements were thronging with people as they scattered from offices and headed for the nearest bus, taxi or Tube. Jake knew how easy it was to lose sight of targets in large crowds. Dealing with City workers in rush hour was no exception.

A navy suit and pink newspaper seemed to be the unwritten dress code for everyone. They all looked identical. Jake had heard that something as simple as wearing brown shoes could lose you a job in the City – 'when in town, don't wear brown' went the motto. The prevalent blue uniform certainly didn't help him when conducting surveillance. It was like trying to pick out one individual ant from a seething, swarming nest of indistinguishable others. He was grateful for Jenny's red hand-bag, slung over her right shoulder, which made it simpler to fix her in his sights.

She had a good head start – he needed to quicken his pace.

Jake called Lenny on his mobile. 'Looks like she's going toward the Tube. Call you in a bit.'

The days of being forced to communicate via a cumber-some, covert radio system strapped around some part of the anatomy were petering out. It couldn't come soon enough for Jake. Surveillance communications were increasingly being conducted via mobile phones, which were much less conspic-uous and far less physically restrictive than talking into a concealed microphone wired up under your clothes.

Jake increased his speed to reduce the space between him and Jenny. He needed to be close enough to watch comfortably but far enough away to maintain his anonymity.

At the bottom of Gray's Inn Road, Jenny disappeared down a flight of stairs marked with the red and blue roundel sign – one of the most recognised and imitated logos in the world. There was no mistaking where she was headed.

Jake dialled Lenny again. 'She's heading into Chancery Lane Tube – Central Line. Let you know which direction she's going in when I can.'

Jake had spent countless hours behind suspects. He knew the Underground network like the back of his hand – which directions the lines went in, where they ended up, and which tunnels he could get a whiff of a phone or radio signal in.

His role below ground as 'the walker' was the straightforward bit. Up above, Lenny would be one step behind as he tried to work his way along a similar route that mirrored Jake's subterranean movements as closely as possible. A tricky job when there was scant information emanating from beneath the streets of the capital.

The Central Line connected east and west London via a forty-mile stretch of track. It was arguably the longest and deepest-lying route of any of the Tube lines. Phone communications were non-existent until a carriage emerged from the bowels of the earth into the daylight of the suburbs.

Inside the station, Jake queued up at a wide-luggage gate at one end of a row of entry barriers. This was costing him precious time he didn't have.

Jenny had plumped for a narrow barrier in the middle, where the hordes were deeper. Despite this, she was still ahead of him and nearing the head of the queue. Jake's heart began to pound – was he about to lose her to the Central Line?

As she reached the front and held out her right arm to swipe her travel card, a woman directly in front of her, who was pulling a purple wheelie case, stopped dead. Her luggage had jammed in the ticket gates and Jenny was momentarily stuck whilst the suitcase was disentangled.

This gave Jake just enough time to make it to the front of his line and pass through the barriers. He followed Jenny on to the escalators almost simultaneously. She moved with the commuting herd, as did Jake, without ever looking behind her.

At the bottom, she made her way on to the packed eastbound platform.

Jake's training had taught him that the platform could be an unforgiving space. This was the point at which targets would often stop and look around for the very first time; the point you were at your most vulnerable.

Jake held back slightly and withdrew into the cross-passage so that he wasn't in full view.

He ducked behind a couple deep in conversation about the new iPhone. It wasn't due to be released in the UK until November, but the American market was already going wild for it apparently. Jake shook his head. Who really needed a hand-held computer with a music player *and* a phone attached to it?

Jake pulled out his own mobile – a small silver Nokia with a tiny screen and a basic design that had changed little since its original release, aside from a reduction in size. Not a single bar of reception showed on his screen. He couldn't even send a text message down here. He doubted that would ever change.

There was a roar as the train approached. Jake put his head round the corner and felt a warm gust hit his face as displaced air was forced through the tunnel by the fast-moving carriages.

The train slowed. Jake moved purposefully through the mass of commuters, ensuring that he got on one carriage along from the now familiar red handbag. Standing by the door, he maintained a careful watch on the platform, just in case Jenny suddenly decided to get off at the last second. He was grateful when the doors finally beeped and closed, letting out a sigh of relief as the train pulled away from the station.

Jake could see her in the next carriage, one arm around a yellow pole, one hip resting against a padded perch of brightly coloured moquette. There were no seats available. Through the sea of people between them, Jake kept up constant visual observation via the windows that separated the two carriages.

Once on the train, Jake knew that very few targets looked past those positioned immediately around them. All the same, he'd made sure he was located just out of reach, in order to appear like any other inconsequential worker ant on their commute.

They moved through two stations, stopping at St Paul's then Bank. Jenny remained rooted to her spot, red handbag over her shoulder, as people filtered on and off the train around her. Jake noticed that she wasn't actively looking for a spare seat to come free – nor was she manoeuvring to sit down. This suggested her journey would be short.

Soon after leaving Bank, Jenny's body language changed. She began to fidget, telling Jake that this leg of her journey was drawing to a close. As they neared the next station, she adjusted her stance, placed her bag on her other shoulder and moved closer to the door.

Jake readied himself.

Liverpool Street.

She stepped off the train and headed toward the exit to the mainline railway station. Jake ducked in a few bodies behind her on the escalator. As they ascended, he pulled out his phone and waited, willing the reception bars to appear on the screen quickly. It wasn't until they'd passed through the underground exit barriers and he'd almost hit the main concourse that the hint of a signal appeared.

As he trailed Jenny to the departures board, he hastily called Lenny.

'Sorry mate, no bars earlier. I'm at Liverpool Street overground station. She's looking at the departures board. Looks like I'm getting on an overground train. Hang on! She's off and running. Call you back!'

Jenny had changed direction and was heading off toward one of the imminent mainline departures, but there seemed to be several trains about to depart and Jake had no idea which one she was aiming for.

She slowed to pass through the barrier on platform four. There were no staff nearby. Jake took his chances and leapt an unguarded barrier two along and then ran back toward Jenny, who was boarding the train.

'What train is this?' Jake asked a skinny white lad wearing a Burberry baseball cap.

'Shenfield via Stratford, mate.'

'Thanks,' replied Jake.

Essex, he thought. *Lenny will be thrilled.*

This time he made sure to get on the same carriage as Jenny. Overground trains were longer than their underground cousins, and spotting the target was more difficult.

Jenny had found a seat. Her back was turned to him.

He texted Lenny. He didn't want to talk while he was surrounded by people.

'I'm on an overground train. It's packed. Left about a minute ago for Shenfield. Goes via Stratford apparently.'

'Chav country,' was Lenny's response.

Jake looked up at the baseball-capped youth in front of him and smiled.

As the train went from station to station, Jake could see Jenny messaging someone on her phone, her frosted acrylic nails tap-tapping on the keypad of her phone. She didn't look up once.

She alighted at Romford and made her way up through the barriers to the exit. Jake flashed his warrant card at the staff and followed her.

Once out of the station, she turned left. He tailed her closely now, dreading the possibility that she might have a car parked in the immediate vicinity of the station. She crossed the road and turned left into a side street.

Jake was glad she was still wearing her high heels, which limited her to a slower pace on the potholed pavements. As each minute passed, his confidence grew. It became less and less likely that she had a vehicle stashed away somewhere.

Further along the street, Jenny's pace slowed, and Jake hung back slightly.

Then she stopped dead, delving into her red handbag. Jake backed up quickly, ducking into a driveway for cover.

He saw her fish out a key. She'd reached her destination.

He watched her unlock the black front door of a bungalow, numbered forty-two. Jake took down the registrations of the two new BMWs sitting on the driveway, and the number of the house.

As he was searching for the street name, he noticed movement out of the corner of his eye. It was Jenny's front door opening again. Jake flung himself back into a scratchy privet hedge, just one house along.

He flinched. What was she doing? Had she spotted him?

She came thundering out.

'I don't believe it!' she shouted out into the street.

Jake braced himself. He wondered how he'd get out of this one.

He heard her bustling about. 'You bleeding sod!'

Damn it. He'd done the hard yards and now she must have spotted him as he'd been taking notes in the street.

He heard the clink of milk bottles as she picked them up from the doormat outside. 'You've been home all day and not brought the milk in!' she screeched, slamming the door as she retreated back inside the bungalow.

Jake felt a wave of relief rush over him. He extracted himself from the sharp twigs of the hedge, slightly grazed, and retraced his steps back to the station.

On the way, he texted Lenny, who he imagined was probably fighting his way through rush-hour traffic in an attempt to reach him.

'Housed her. Two cars on the drive. Got the registration numbers and address. No rush. See you at Romford train station. And as I did the legwork, the pie and mash is on you!'

40

Jake took the Tube to Chancery Road. Sara had suggested that they meet for an early lunch close to her office, on Gray's Inn Road; she'd completed some enquires into the missing documents.

She was sitting inside a blue leather booth, dressed in a freshly pressed trouser suit and silk blouse. Her hair had been professionally blow-dried, and she was wearing lipstick. She looked much more polished than the last time Jake had seen her.

Surely all this effort wasn't for him? They'd only met once before.

She stood up and greeted him excitedly. 'Jake! Good to see you, thanks for meeting me here. I thought it best we spoke away from the office.'

Jake smiled. 'No worries.'

'I'm out with my girlfriends tonight, my birthday bash,' she said, unprompted. He wondered for a moment if she'd noticed him eyeing up her smart attire.

'Happy birthday! Did you get anything nice?' he asked.

'Not yet. Maybe tonight though,' she said, sounding slightly crestfallen.

'Well I hope you have a good night. How did you get on with finding out about those documents?' he asked, swiftly moving the conversation back to work.

'I've done a bit of digging. It seems that we *have* lost a few boxes of documents. I'm not sure how many yet. But a few — all of them from the Al Yamamah investigation.'

'What can you tell me about that investigation?'

'You hungry? Let's order,' she said, pushing a menu over to him. 'Have you had sushi before?'

'Yeah…' he lied, not wanting to appear unsophisticated. 'But I'm sure you'll know what's good here so why don't you order?'

She smiled. 'OK.' Then she rattled something off to the Japanese woman behind the bar, who dipped her head slightly and scurried off.

'So Al Yamamah… The deal dates back to the mid-eighties.' Her tone changed. 'It was 1985…'

Jake shook his head. 'I was just fourteen.'

'And I was twelve,' Sara added. 'Do you remember much about that year?'

'Yes, of course. The country was in a terrible state…' Jake began to reminisce. 'The Brixton riots, I remember those – 3.5 million people unemployed. The unions were causing no end of trouble. The miners' strike was still going on. Fire ripped through Bradford City stadium and killed loads of people. Bob Geldof held his Live Aid concert at Wembley. Scientists discovered the hole in the ozone layer and told us all that we had to stop using aerosols.'

'Yes, and Margaret Thatcher's popularity was at an all-time low – the Conservative Party were third place in the opinion polls—'

'And Paul Hardcastle's '19' was the biggest hit of the year! The song that went "na na na nineteen!"' Jake laughed at his own joke, surprised that he remembered so much.

'If you say so.' Sara smiled at him. 'Maggie needed some good news, otherwise she was never going to win a third term in office,' she continued, more serious now. 'Enter stage right Saudi Arabia, wanting to buy £80 billion worth of military equipment. It was the biggest weapons deal ever. Some say it was the biggest sales contract in history for anything ever.'

The waitress pushed a large selection of colourful plastic bowls and plates with translucent domed lids across the counter to them, each containing its own delicacy.

'Just what the doctor ordered,' said Jake. 'I'm no expert with chopsticks though,' he admitted, unsure of exactly how and where to start with all this food.

'Oh, you can't be worse than me. I cheat,' said Sara, pulling the wrapper off a set of disposable chopsticks. 'They come out of the packet attached to each other at the top, so I figured you don't actually even have to pull them apart; just hold them halfway down and shove your middle finger between the two sticks. It's a bit like eating with spring-loaded tweezers, but it does the job!'

Jake watched her pick up a piece of salmon on her first attempt and shove it into her mouth.

'Haha, that's so lazy!' said Jake.

'But yummy,' Sara said, nodding in agreement.

'So what was the problem with this humongous deal then?' Jake asked, tucking in.

'Well the Saudis didn't actually have any money to pay for this stuff, because they had a bit of a cash-flow problem. So instead they offered Maggie a supertanker of oil, for every single day of the contract. The deal meant that she could sell the oil and it would pay for the weapons the Saudis wanted.'

Jake nodded.

'Each tanker,' she continued, 'contained 600,000 barrels of oil. The oil was sold, and the money was placed into accounts controlled by the Ministry of Defence. The MOD then used this money to pay for the weapons. But the Saudi cash-flow problem also extended to their royal family – they didn't have any money either. So, alongside the weapons, the Saudis also had a thirst for cash – cash for themselves, kickbacks... bribes from the weapons purchases via the arms companies.' Sara plucked another piece of sushi off her plate and popped it in her mouth.

'Bribes?' asked Jake, his ears pricking up.

'Lots of them. Billions of pounds worth of kickbacks to ensure those close to the arms deal helped smooth its path. But that's not the half of it. From the sale of the oil, the MOD ran a slush fund for the Saudis. This slush fund was used as a virtual personal bank account by members of the Saudi royal family. It was completely off the books as far as the public and much of Saudi Arabia was concerned – and all but invisible to just a few contacts within the MOD and the main arms dealers.'

'Nice work if you can get it?'

'Lots and lots of money was involved. Thatcher and certain people at the MOD were up to their necks in it. Paying bribes and taking bungs. That's what we were looking at – all the historical corrupt payments – but we were made to drop our investigation in December of last year. Apparently the Saudis are too valuable an ally to risk upsetting.'

'Tony Blair stopped the investigation? How could he do that?'

'We aren't the police. We're a government department, and we don't have the same autonomy as you guys. We can be told to drop investigations. It's rare, but it happens. The PM and the Attorney General put pressure on the Serious Fraud Office director. They said that it was bad for inter-country relations, bad for intelligence—'

'Bad for intelligence? In what way?'

'I think the Saudis threatened to withhold intelligence about people operating in Iraq, and the PM was worried it would affect the war effort there.'

Jake's thoughts wandered to the intelligence that his MI5 contact, Jonathan Grant, had said the Saudis were providing about the Glasgow Airport bombers. That material had been about Iraq. Maybe the Saudis were helping in the war effort with the US and UK there?

'And the paperwork for your investigation?'

'That's the odd thing. The job is dead. There's a court challenge from an organisation called AGARMT about the shutting down of the investigation, but it's not going to go anywhere – we've sent the paperwork to storage.'

'AGARMT? Who are they?' asked Jake.

'It's an anti-war protest movement. They're against arms dealing.'

'Did you check to see where the files had been sent?'

'I did. Some batches went to the wrong storage centre. The paperwork had the wrong address on it. I'm waiting for a response from the courier about where they actually delivered them to, but I think Jenny just made a mistake. So, to be honest, I don't think there's any crime that's taken place that you need to be looking at,' she said. 'And besides, the Yanks are going after the defence contractor for some of the bribes anyway.'

'Oh, are they?'

'Yeah, the US Department of Justice announced their intention to investigate in the middle of June, but they've been in discussions with us for some time...' She paused to nibble on another piece of sushi before continuing, 'After our investigation was dropped they've been keen to have a crack at the whole thing themselves.'

'Will they need your paperwork? Maybe that's why it's gone astray?'

'I doubt the Yanks need it, to be honest.'

'Maybe some senior bod will intervene and stop it, like our prime minister did? Not wanting to upset important allies and all that?'

'The Yanks won't back off like we were told to, though they tend to go after the money and do a plea-bargain deal or something. They'll just give the company a huge fine rather than trying to prosecute the individuals like we do.'

'OK. Well I'm going to dig a little further on my side. I'm still not happy about how these documents ended up on the street. Can I contact you if I need anything?'

'Of course! You can contact me tonight if you want. Why don't you come along to my birthday bash? Let your hair down a bit?'

'That's a kind offer, but I'm not sure you want the likes of me crashing your do.'

'I wouldn't have asked if I didn't, would I?' she replied, with a wink. 'We're kicking off at Roadhouse in Covent Garden. Give me a call if you fancy it!'

'I know Roadhouse. They have good tribute bands on there…'

'That's the place. I'll even buy you a drink!'

'I thought it was your birthday?'

'It is!'

'Well if that's the case, it shouldn't be you who's buying the drinks.'

'I guess that's why you'll have to put in an appearance then!' said Sara, smiling at him expectantly.

'I don't think I'll be able to make it, but it's very kind of you to ask,' he said, getting up. 'You have a great night.'

They shook hands and he left, alone, to walk back to the Tube.

He knew that he shouldn't accept Sara's offer. Yes, she was pleasant and personable, but life was already complicated enough. Going out would involve drinking, and he really didn't need that. He had no idea where his relationship with Claire stood, or what she thought about it. And then there was Stephanie. Maybe it didn't mean anything that she'd called him after her accident – but maybe it did, and he wasn't really sure how he felt about that possibility – or any of it. Avoiding alcohol and attractive women for a while might make things clearer; help him make more sense of his emotions.

He'd give it a swerve.

He headed back to the office to find out how the investigation into Jenny was going.

41

Jake placed a cup of hot tea down beside Lenny on the table. The fourteenth floor was virtually dead at this time of day. All the indexers had gone home, which meant the small fridge and tea-making facilities in the Major Incident Room were left unguarded – just ripe for a raiding party.

Outside, it was raining hard. Swollen droplets beat against the windows, whipped up by the strong wind. Jake couldn't believe the summer they'd been having. Some areas had received a month's rain in just twenty-four hours, and the weather patterns didn't seem like changing any time soon. He gripped his mug tightly to warm himself up.

'So what have you found out?'

'Some very interesting stuff, guv.' Lenny smiled at him and opened the blue cardboard folder. He pulled out a small pile of A4 sheets, some of which were custody photographs – *mugshots*.

'Wow, you have been busy!' said Jake.

Lenny began flicking through the papers as he spoke. 'Land registry entry on Jenny's bungalow shows that it's owned outright, no mortgage, by a Mrs Sharon Reynolds.

'The new BMW X5 on the drive is registered to her too. I did HPI checks…' Hire purchase index checks – they showed if there was a loan or finance secured on vehicles. 'There's no finance on that either.'

'A £60,000 car and a £400,000 bungalow and both owned outright? Someone's got a lot of cash to spare!'

'Sounds like she's got some money around her, yes.' Lenny nodded in agreement.

'Do we have anything on the owner?'

'Yes, we do. There's a fair bit of intelligence held on Sharon by Clubs and Vice—'

'Clubs and Vice?' replied Jake, surprised. Clubs and Vice was a specialist unit. Traditionally it dealt with prostitution – primarily those that enabled it – the illegal brothels, the pimps and the human traffickers. More recently it had became involved in the intelligence and targeting of nightclubs and gaming casinos because of the various criminal crossovers – drug supply being one. Major criminals often controlled clubs, but many didn't own them. They just used them to launder their illicit cash. It was a very murky world.

'Yes. Sharon is a former glamour model from the eighties. Former Miss Essex. Quite a looker in her day…' Lenny pushed over a photocopy of page three of *The Sun*, taken from a 1986 issue. An attractive bleached blonde wearing just a skimpy pair of bikini bottoms smiled up at him.

'Pretty face.' Jake nodded, trying not to stare at her exposed breasts.

'This is a better one of her.' Lenny slid over a police mugshot in which Sharon, looking solemn, held a white board below her face, showing her name, the date, the station code, and the custody number that referred to an arrest.

The year on the board was 2006.

'She doesn't look as good in that one, Lenny,' quipped Jake.

'No – agreed. She runs a marketing and events company that basically organises pretty girls to man the stand at big shows. You know the type. If they're launching a new motorbike, they'll hire pretty, scantily clad girls who will drape themselves all over it. Promotional girls—'

'That pays *that* well?'

'Apparently not – that's why she's known to Clubs and Vice.'

'Oh, do tell.'

'They know her because she's a madam. She runs a high-class prostitution ring. She's been seen in a lot of West End casinos with her girls. Last year she had a big falling out with one girl, a Latvian, who claimed that she'd been trafficked here, for the purposes of prostitution. Made a nasty allegation against Sharon, who was arrested, but it never went anywhere. The Latvian refused to substantiate the allegation with a statement, so it got dropped. Looks like it was a dispute about money.'

'OK. Good. Anything on a Jenny or Jennifer?'

'The PNC shows Sharon has a daughter called Jennifer.'

The Police National Computer held extensive records on people, vehicles crime and property, and could often throw up useful links between persons of interest.

'Bingo!' Jake was pleased – it had been the right decision to tail Jenny after all.

'But,' Lenny cautioned, 'the electoral roll only shows a Sharon Reynolds living at the bungalow, and I've checked with the council. Sharon is claiming single person's discount on the council tax there. There was a Jennifer Reynolds living at the address two years ago, but according to the council, she moved out, no forwarding address.'

Jake sighed. 'Jenny doesn't live there?'

'I don't know. Sharon may just be having the council over and trying to save some money. I checked who the cars belong to.

'That other car, the white, 3 Series BMW on the driveway, is registered to some company up in Yorkshire. The company looks dodgy to me, like it's just registered as a front. However the only person insured to drive that BMW is a Jennifer Reynolds, born 21 July 1981 – I'm guessing that's our girl?'

Jake nodded. 'Sounds like it.'

'There's no finance on that BMW 3 Series either,' Lenny continued. 'In the last few months it's been stopped several times for speeding though. A Jennifer Reynolds, with the same date of birth as on the insurance, was driving each time, but she's never been prosecuted.'

'All male Old Bill that have stopped her, I bet. She flutters her eyelashes and sticks out her chest, and they let her off.'

Lenny looked bemused. 'Do you want me to find out the sex of the people that stopped her?'

'No, I was just saying—' Jake shrugged it off. 'Is there a PNC record for Jenny?'

'No, no trace. She's never been arrested or prosecuted for anything, according to that.'

'OK. Then the question is – what is this madam's daughter doing at the Serious Fraud Office, and why is she diverting the paperwork for the biggest arms deal in history to a flop in Docklands?'

Lenny frowned. 'I don't know.'

'OK. What I need you to do now is speak to the guys at the finance unit and see if they can find out anything about Jennifer and Sharon's finances. If they need to get production orders from court, tell them I've authorised it,' said Jake.

The National Terrorist Financial Investigation Unit confiscated millions of pounds from the hands of terrorists every year. It was as good a place to start as any.

'Will do, but...' Lenny remained seated, his brow still furrowed.

'But what?'

'What are you so interested in this for? We're the Counter Terrorism Command and this is just some lost paperwork. Whatever this thing is – and I'm sure you're right, there's something illegal going on here – it's not ours, is it? It's not terrorism?'

'If there's something going on that affects the economic well-being of the United Kingdom, that's a national-security matter – that might be a threat to the UK.'

'Oh come on, Jake, that's stretching it a bit.'

'Lenny – it's not just some local authority looking at Mr Jones who left his wheelie bin out on the wrong day of the week. It's The Serious fucking Fraud Office investigating the biggest deal in history. An £80 billion deal!'

There was a pause. Lenny looked back at the paperwork, then back at Jake. 'OK. You're the boss. I'll speak to the finance guys.'

'Good. I want to know what mobile phones are registered to that address and if there are any other addresses that Jenny and her mother are using. We might get that from the financial on the bank accounts…'

'Do you not want to ask the SFO? Won't they have phone numbers and addresses for their employee and her next of kin?'

'I'm not sure who we can trust there. I think it's best we keep it in-house at the moment.'

'That Sara seemed all right?'

'Maybe. Let's not involve them too much – not until we know what we've got. Let's call it a day today. See the finance guys in the morning. Fancy a quick pint? Just one? I'm staying away from the binge drinking.'

'Not tonight. Not for me, mate. I'll see you in the morning.'

'You won't, Len. I've got to go and see Occupational Health again tomorrow.' Jake sighed, annoyed that the day's progress would be hampered once again. Though he was looking forward to seeing if swapping his appointment to a Wednesday meant he'd catch Shirley out with her wardrobe choices. 'You crack on with it. I'll see you later on at some point.'

42

Just a short stroll from the Yard, the Feathers pub, with its gothic facade, reminded Jake of the TARDIS – small and dingy-looking on the outside, bright and airy on the inside.

Despite being the closest pub to the Yard, very few in the job drank there, and early in the week, the place was rarely busy. Jake hated to admit that he knew their opening hours off by heart – and exactly when peak trading fell.

He needed a drink. Something was bothering him, but he couldn't quite put his finger on what it was. He felt overloaded by all the material floating around in his head. The random jumble of information weighed down upon his shoulders, tormenting him. None of it seemed to fit together, though it felt as if it should.

'Pint of Stella please,' Jake called over to the barman, who was wiping the far end of the polished wood bar.

'No worries, mate,' he called back in an Australian accent.

There was a TV on the wall. On the news they were talking about next year's US presidential election. The Democrats had announced their candidates. There was a black guy among them that Jake had never heard of before – Barack Obama – talking into the camera. He seemed really polished and composed. Hillary Clinton was also among the candidates and the favourite to win. There was currently a dispute between them about who would and wouldn't be willing to meet with the leaders of Syria, Iran and Venezuela during their first year in office.

175

It always went with family dynasties, mused Jake – Bush followed by Clinton, followed by another Bush – presumably now followed by another Clinton. Different political parties, but always a continuum of the same main players in the background. How could these family dynasties continue to dominate the presidency otherwise? Jake concluded that the black guy, Obama, didn't stand a chance. He couldn't imagine America would ever elect a non-white president. They'd surely go for the white candidate, even if that candidate was female.

The barman plonked Jake's pint in front of him.

'That'll be £2.60 please, mate.'

Jake dug in his pocket for the cash without turning his gaze from the screen.

Families. It wasn't so unusual that there were dynasties in politics, he supposed. He saw it in criminal networks with organised crime families, and even in terrorism. He began wondering about Jenny and her mother. Did Jenny play a role in her mother's criminal network? It was highly likely.

Jake picked up his pint, but before he even took a sip, it hit him.

The uneasiness that he felt; the thing that was troubling him.

Claire.

If her uncle Frank were involved in criminality, there was a chance that Claire might be involved too. Things ran in families. Crime ran in families. Why had she really bugged her uncle? Was she telling the truth?

He thought about her attitude toward him on the phone as he'd told her about the SFO meeting, and about Jenny. He remembered watching Claire screw up a piece of paper and throw it into a corner after they'd found the SFO documents. Why had she screwed that up? What was she upset about? He'd picked the piece of paper up and placed it safely with the others in the box at home.

Jake put his drink back down on the bar, the liquid untouched – and headed for the door.

43

Claire opened the door to her luxury apartment. No words were exchanged. Standing aside, she motioned for him to come in with a slight turn of her head. Jake followed the path of the polished, dark wood floor that led to the living room at the end of the hallway.

He didn't sit down. He knew this was going to be difficult, and he felt out of place – almost as if he was at work and she was a stranger. Asking awkward questions and delivering bad news was what he did in the day job. It wasn't supposed to be this way in his personal life.

She sat down on the sofa and pulled her legs up underneath her, looking nervous. 'Go on then, what's up? You sounded annoyed with me on the phone,' she said with a wan grin.

'You were eager to involve me in this stuff with Frank. You took me to his house, wanted me to find out what he was up to—'

'I know, but—'

'Don't interrupt me,' he said, raising his hand. He was in full work mode now.

Claire went silent. The half-smile she'd plastered on had slipped.

'That day we found the SFO documents at Docklands,' Jake continued, 'you were very upset when I left. I couldn't work out why at first. It bugged me, but I put it to the back of my mind – tried to forget about it. I almost did. Then, when

I started to make headway on those documents, you became more and more cagey about it. Like I was some sort of pet dog fetching a ball, and then you'd got tired of the game—'

'Oh, Jake, listen. You really have no clue what you're talking about—'

'No, *you* listen, Claire,' he said, shutting her down again. 'I found Jenny, as you know. And just as we were starting to get somewhere, you withdrew – the complete opposite of what I expected. I couldn't understand it. Then I thought back to that night, when we were here, looking through the files we'd found. And I remembered that you'd got upset, screwed one of the documents up and thrown it in the corner...'

Claire crossed her arms and began looking at the floor. This was all the signal he needed. He was on the right track. She didn't even need to answer the next question he was about to ask – her body language was giving it all away.

'So I went back and looked at that document. The one with all the creases in it...'

Claire stood up from the sofa, wandered to the other end of the room and into the open-plan kitchen. He knew she was trying to remove herself from what he was about to say. She took a translucent blue glass from the cupboard above the sink, and filled it from the iced-water dispenser on the stainless steel fridge-freezer. She said nothing.

'So I look through it and see that it's a statement from a girl, whose phone number has been found on one of the phone bills that the MOD were paying for. The SFO have traced her through that number, interviewed her for their investigation into the Saudis and their huge deal. This girl says that she was a regular attendee at special parties, where she was paid to wait on Saudi princes who were over here on all-expenses-paid visits, buying arms. But even then I couldn't understand why that would upset you and why you'd want me to back off...'

'I can explain,' she replied, putting down her glass for a moment.

'I haven't finished yet, Claire.' He wanted to tell her what he knew first. It would be easier when she understood the extent of his knowledge. 'When I got to the end of the statement, then things started to make sense.'

Jake pulled the folded document from his back pocket. Claire's jaw clenched and her face burned red as he started to read from it ' "They took secret videos of me, having sex with the Saudi princes, said they knew my family, said they would show the videos to them, reveal to them that I was a prostitute – and I'd never seen myself as a prostitute. I have no idea how I ended up there really, but I'd sort of got used to the money." The statement goes on to say that a family friend had introduced that young girl into it. She was fifteen when it first started.'

Claire said nothing but took another sip of her water. Jake could see her hands trembling. He folded the piece of paper and put it back in his pocket.

'And then I put two and two together, Claire. And I realised. I realised why you were so eager to involve me, right up until you realised what it was all about.' Jake paused, and his tone softened, knowing that this would hurt her more than him. 'You didn't want me to go digging further, because you knew I'd uncover it – find out your secret – and it would be to your detriment. Because that's how you're connected to this, isn't it?'

'It's not like that!' Claire blurted. 'I did nothing wrong. Uncle Frank said he was taking me to a party. He was kind to me. Made a fuss of me. Got me a new dress. New shoes. We went to a suite at a flash hotel on Park Lane. What wasn't to like?'

Jake felt a clawing dread in the pit of his stomach, like a stone being thrown into a well. He'd desperately wanted his detective instincts to be right, but by being right, he now realised that pain would dull any victory he could claim.

Claire's eyes welled up as she continued. 'I was excited. I had a nice time. Nothing happened…' She exhaled. 'Not that time anyway. Everyone was really friendly. All I knew was they were people who were very important, and we had to make them happy so that they would buy British. It was Uncle Frank's job to look after them – he managed the MOD contracts. He paid for everything for them, even down to chartering a Boeing 747 cargo plane just to fly their shopping home to Riyadh.'

'Your uncle got you to work as an escort?' Jake asked incredulously.

'It was never meant to be like that. I went to a few more parties. The Saudi princes were so polite and charming at first. I enjoyed the attention. They started buying me pearls, Chanel handbags – giving me money. We'd have so much fun together, all of us in a big clique at the casino, or after a West End show. They'd tell us how they weren't allowed to drink or mix with girls back home, because it was against the law; how it was all a big adventure in London, and how it was only with us that they could let their hair down. I believed everything they told me – all of the girls did. We thought we were so special.

'Then one of the princes took a shine to me. Took me under his wing. Treated me like I was his girlfriend. He was so charming. So charismatic. I felt important. Before I knew where I was, we were having sex. I was fifteen. There were other girls there. Mostly younger, like me. They liked young girls. Sometimes a different prince wanted me. That's when I would get drunk. It was just easier that way. There was cocaine there. I knew that Uncle Frank was probably aware of the sex, but he was never actually around when it happened.'

'They paid you to have sex with them?' Just hearing the words come out of his own mouth made him feel hurt and disgusted all at the same time.

'Money was just left in envelopes for us. Thousands. Sometimes two, sometimes even five thousand at a time. I had nothing. My mother was an alcoholic. My dad couldn't have cared if I'd existed or not. The princes, they got me a gem-encrusted Bulgari watch. They called us their "London girlfriends". I started to realise that we probably weren't the only ones. It turned out it wasn't even the Saudis' money. They never liked to admit they were paying for sex. Uncle Frank would leave the money. He would buy the gifts. That was his job. It was all MOD money, from the arms sales.

'And the videos?' Jake asked.

'One day, Uncle Frank told me that he had to keep videos of us all. Collateral. Insurance. In case the princes reneged on their deals – in case the girls decided to speak up. We didn't know they were filming us at the time. We were all so naive. I could put up with all the goings-on, because I knew I was building a nest egg for the future. But then Frank—' Claire stopped, close to tears now.

'What?' asked Jake softly.

'He… he wanted personal attention. He started touching me. He said if I wanted to stay as the Saudis' favourite and his highest earner, I'd have to sleep with him too. It was like he'd become obsessed with me. I refused, but then he threatened me with foster care. Threatened to tell my father about the videos.'

Jake shook his head but said nothing.

'I gave in, gave him what he wanted. There was sex and drugs and illegality all around me. What could I say? It was like I didn't know right from wrong any longer. None of us did… I'd saved up tens of thousands of pounds, part of which paid for the deposit on this place. But that was it. That was the last straw. First the Saudi princes and now my uncle? It all stopped overnight. The whole thing. It was too much. It had sapped my sense of self. I was just an object for them to possess. And now my uncle wanted to possess me too. I moved out, used some of the money to pay for boarding school, then went to university, locked it all away…'

'I can't believe it…' said Jake.

'So you know all that stuff that went on back in 2005, during Operation Theseus? When I knew someone was watching me and I went into hiding?'

Jake nodded, not trusting himself enough to speak right now.

'Well it's obvious to me now. It was Frank stalking me. He must have been worried that I would talk to the SFO during the height of their investigation into the Saudi deals. I know that now – that's why I didn't need you to go any further…'

'You were a prostitute, Claire…' Jake shook his head in disbelief.

'Not exactly.'

'How else do you describe having sex with men for money then?'

'I didn't stand on street corners is what I meant.'

'No, you went to hotel rooms and did it with fat old Arabs instead!'

Claire took a couple of steps forward and thrust the glass at him, launching the contents directly into his face. He spluttered as the cold water caught him off guard, splashing down on to his shirt and shoes. 'I'm not fucking proud of myself for it you know!' she screamed.

'No, and neither am I – and what's more, I won't put up with you using me to do your dirty work. You've got me into this shit, and now you're throwing glasses of water in my face? You can fuck off!'

Jake's plans to listen and be understanding had all crumbled into dust at the anger coursing through his veins.

'Get out! Get the fuck out of my house and don't bother coming back!' shouted Claire, pointing toward the door.

'With pleasure!' he shouted as he marched down the hallway. He could hear her sobbing, but he didn't turn round. He opened the front door and stepped outside, slamming it behind him with a huge bang. It echoed down the deserted hallway like a gunshot.

He took the stairs; he didn't want to wait for the lift. Didn't want to stay one more minute in the building she'd moved into on the back of the proceeds from her sordid activities.

Jake was fuming. She'd got herself into this for money? There was no way he was going to be alone and stew over this – not tonight. As he made his way down the stairs, he pulled out his phone and called Sara.

'Hey, Jake!' She picked up the phone almost immediately. 'I wasn't expecting to hear from you.'

'Well today is your lucky day…'

'And it's my birthday!' she screamed down the phone. She'd evidently had a fair bit to drink already.

'It is. Where are you? I'll come and join you.'

'Can you make it to St Martin's Theatre? I've got spare tick-ets – Tracy hooked up with some bloke we met in a bar and Rebecca cried off with a migraine.

'I reckon so – I'll come straight there.'

How the hell was he going to be able to carry on with this job at work now, knowing what he did about Claire's past?

44

His flat was a wreck. Jake was lying in bed, browsing the news reports he'd printed from the internet, hunting for as much background as he could get his hands on about the dead spy. Adham Marmora had a murky past. Jake wasn't sure how events from so many years ago were going to help with a death that had happened just a few weeks previously, but he had to look all the same. The answers weren't going to come knocking on his front door.

His phone rang, startling him.

'Hey, it's me.' It was Sara. He'd not spoken to her since the night of her birthday.

She'd caught him off guard.

'Hi,' was all he could muster. He was never sure what the appropriate etiquette was in these sorts of situations.

'You've not called?'

'No. I thought it best that I let things cool down. It wasn't professional of me to have allowed that to happen between us.'

'I could say the same thing,' she mused.

'True.'

'We sacked Jenny yesterday.'

'Why?'

'We did an audit of all the things she had access to – it seemed wise after you found those documents on the industrial estate. She was up to something. We don't know what yet, but she was looking at all sorts of things that she shouldn't have been. Printing things off from investigations that she had no reason to look at – well mainly just the Al Yamamah investigation – and tons of documents are missing too…'

'Wow. What did she say when you spoke to her?'

'Not much. She didn't even seem that bothered. We're looking into how she managed to swing the job in the first place. Looks like there's been some sort of naughtiness going on with the recruitment manager. He reckons he was blackmailed into making sure she got the role. Looks like he'll be disciplined and sacked too.'

'Blackmailed?'

'I don't understand it all yet. We're looking into it. But I have Jenny's recruitment file at the office if you want copies of it?'

'Yes, that would be great. I'll collect it on Monday morning if that suits you?'

'Yeah. I'll be in the office then.' Sara paused. Jake heard a deep breath. 'I was wondering what you were up to tonight? Whether you fancied doing something?'

'Tonight?'

'Yeah…' She paused again. 'Look, I don't know anything about your life, or whether you're even single or not, but I had a good time the other night – with you.' She stumbled over her words nervously. 'I wanted to ask you… *are* you single?'

'I am single. But my life is a bit complicated, Sara. I've just come out of a very messy relationship that I'm still extricating myself from. And I've got an ex-wife, whom I adore, and two girls, who I think I really shouldn't have walked out on. I'm in a strange place relationship-wise at the moment; I'm best left alone. You're a lovely girl, and I'd only be a problem for you. You deserve better.'

'We could just have some sex? We had really good sex the other night. I'd be happy with just that – no relationship, just friends with benefits,' she blurted.

'I think it's best I just come and see you on Monday morning.'

'I've got tickets to the theatre tonight. And I'll wear suspenders…' She giggled.

What was he going to do tonight if he didn't go? Read about dead spies while eating a meat-feast pizza?

'Suspenders, you say?'

45

There had been nothing noteworthy among the desk drawer of items left behind by Jenny Reynolds, however her personnel file *had* piqued Jake's interest. It indicated that she didn't live with her mother, as they'd suspected, but had a flat of her own, on the Barnsbury Estate in Islington. Remembering her accent, Jake wondered if that was where she'd grown up.

The estate was just off the Caledonian Road, half a mile north of King's Cross station. Jake knew the place. Anyone who had worked in organised crime knew Islington well; it was riven with drugs and controlled by one of the biggest organised-crime families in the country.

The drive to Caledonian Road didn't take them long, despite the heavy traffic. Jake wondered if Jenny had walked to the office when she wasn't visiting her mum's place. It would take no longer than fifteen minutes.

Her flat was located on the first floor of an unattractive, flat-roofed, sixties block. Lenny parked outside the front. There were no off-road parking spaces, which explained why Jenny's flashy car had been located at her mother's house. Security was poor. There was no intercom system. They went straight up the stairs and found an old, wooden front door bearing the number given in her personnel file.

After banging it for what seemed like an eternity, they were eventually greeted by a bleary-eyed Jenny, wearing a pink, towelling dressing gown, her hair unwashed and unbrushed.

'I wondered how long it would be before you came to see me,' she said as she moved to aside and ushered them in toward the living room. 'Can I get you a cup of tea?'

'No, thanks,' said Jake, walking into the small lounge. He noted the luxurious, brown-leather corner sofa. An extravagant-looking reindeer hide was draped over it. This place wasn't what Jake had expected. The exterior was a dump, yet inside the place dripped with money.

'Do I need a lawyer?' she asked flatly as she sank into an armchair opposite the television.

'It depends if we arrest you or not, Jenny,' he replied, looking her straight in the eye.

'Are you going to arrest me?'

'That really depends on you,' he said.

'In what way?'

'Whether you want to do this the easy way or the hard way.'

'What's the easy way?'

'We ask you questions now and you answer them. Depending on what you say, we might be able to avoid you being arrested.'

'What do you want to know?'

'Tell me why you've been diverting case paperwork for the Al Yamamah investigation and sending files to places they shouldn't be,' he said, sitting down on the soft mottled fur of the reindeer throw.

'I was just doing what I was told to do.'

'Talk me through exactly what's gone on,' said Jake, pulling out a notebook from his pocket.

'Like what?'

'Maybe start with explaining how you found yourself working at the Serious Fraud Office?'

'I never wanted to work in an office. Why would someone sell themselves for forty hours a week, for £25,000 a year, to push some paperwork around? I can earn that in a month, and I don't have to sit in some boring office, staring out the window and fantasising about drinking champagne in some fancy hotel. I can actually live the glamorous life.'

'How?' asked Jake, though he feared he already knew the answer.

'People take me out, treat me nice, buy me nice things. It's not for everyone, but I think it beats sitting in some shitty little office. Other people, office girls, they sell themselves for a pittance and then they still have to put up with being groped and leched over by the boss. I get paid a lot of money and get respect in return for it. Sex is only one part of what they want. But if they want it, they have to pay for it,' said Jenny matter-of-factly.

There was a pause. Lenny glanced at Jake, trying to catch his eye. The absurdity of the situation was not lost on him. Here was a young woman in her twenties, sitting in a plush armchair, wearing her dressing gown, a pair of fluffy white slippers on her feet, twirling her hair as she talked to two strange men about how she had sex for money.

Jenny broke the silence. 'I'm not ashamed that I'm an escort – not at all. Why should I be?' she asked.

'You can call yourself whatever you want,' said Lenny quietly, 'but however you sugar-coat it, at the end of the day, it's just prostitution.'

'Men take women out and expect sex for free. If you're really lucky, you might get a Nando's in return. I'm just charging for something that I was doing for nothing anyway.'

'But how can you force yourself to sleep with someone who's really grim?' asked Lenny, curious now.

'I'm not stupid. I know how to disassociate my body from my mind. I may not fancy them, but they don't repulse me either – most of them are mainly middle of the road.'

Jake shook his head but said nothing. He didn't want to get into the rights and wrongs of prostitution. He sold himself to the Met every week. Sometimes he enjoyed the work and sometimes he felt violated by the way they treated him. Maybe she was right.

'So what do you think we're here about, Jenny?' he asked, trying to steer the conversation back to the investigation.

'It's the other stuff I've been doing. The stuff I'm embarrassed about.'

'You mean your double life at the Serious Fraud Office? I thought you said you didn't stoop to office work?'

'Look, I'm being honest with you here. I don't dress myself up as anything else... Well not unless they pay me more – then I'll dress up as anything they like. What I mean is, people understand who I am and the purpose of our relationship. They pay me to spend time with them. At least that's how it was – until this.'

'Go on,' replied Jake. Jenny sounded like she wanted to talk, and he was happy to listen.

'A while back, I told my mum I wanted to buy a proper big house and move out of town; out of this shithole,' she said, pointing to the street. 'But I needed to get a nest egg together. My mum introduced me to a man she knows. He worked for the government. She's supplied him with girls for years. He wanted someone to be available to assist some special clients of his. I wasn't sure at first, but the money was good and the Arabs, well they were all right. They paid really well and I had a steady stream of work. Easy.'

'What's this bloke's name?'

'Frank is all I know. I've got his number in my phone. So about eighteen months ago, he gave me a photo of some bloke. Asked me to go and meet this fella in a pub, befriend him. Said the bloke was a mate that was down on his luck and wanted to pay me to be his friend. But he didn't want me telling this bloke I was actually being paid – or that I was an escort. Unusual request.'

'So why did you do it?' asked Jake.

'He offered me a lot of money – £30K for several weeks' work. It was easy. The man was nice. I quite liked him. Ben, his name was.'

'Where did this happen – what pub?'

'Islington. He drank in The York on Islington High Street. It's a decent boozer. Right next door to my hairdresser's.'

'And you met this guy and befriended him easily?'

'Yeah. First couple of times it was just normal, you know – sex at his. I'd go home afterwards.'

'And then?'

'Then Frank started asking me questions about Ben: where he lived, what it was like inside his flat. That's when I realised he didn't really know this bloke at all. He started asking me to do things – like take pictures of stuff, borrow mobile phones or swap them round with ones that looked identical. Get copies of keys cut for his flat for them. I realised then that the escort work was just a means to an end. They were actually paying me to spy on this man.'

Jake noticed a subtle shift. Jenny had stopped saying 'he' and 'him' and started talking about 'they' and 'them'.

'The bloke you were asked to spy on, Ben – who was he?' Jake asked.

'He ran a campaign group. He was against the UK Government, reckoned they were all corrupt, that they shouldn't be selling weapons to certain countries.'

'What was the name of the campaign group?'

'It was called AGARMT – Against Arms Trafficking. Their offices were in a big old building on the corner of New Oxford Street and High Holborn. It's seen better days. Their armchairs were threadbare. They'd tried to cover up the cracks, but it was pretty grungy. Ben didn't have much money.'

'Why did you go to his office?'

'Frank told me to. I didn't feel comfortable, but Frank was very persuasive. But that's when it started getting really out of hand.'

'How?'

'Frank wanted to get his stooges inside Ben's campaign group. He asked me to help infiltrate it by recommending people to Ben. To say that they were my friends. But they weren't. They were people that Frank was planting to watch what was going on.'

'Can you remember any names?'

'One of them was called Javed Saleem. Dark skin, foreign accent. I can't remember the other one.'

'How do you know they were plants?' asked Jake.

'One day, Ben said that he'd found a listening device in his office. He showed me it; pulled it out of his pocket and practically threw it across the table to me in the pub. One side of the box was magnetic. Inside the box there was space for two batteries, and at one end was a tiny SIM card. I'd never seen anything like it. He said that the cleaner found it on the floor one morning under his desk, thinking she may have knocked it off when she'd been dusting. Did I know anything about it, he asked me.'

'And did you know anything about it?'

'I didn't, not at the time. Thing was, the office was always locked, so it was someone who had a key. It had to be one of the staff.'

'What happened?'

'Well I became a bit paranoid. I'd already introduced two people to Ben that had ended up working for him. I realised then that Frank was bugging Ben to find out what he was doing.'

Jake thought about Claire's paranoia and how she'd said she was constantly being watched. He thought about the way she'd been behaving. He hadn't cut her anywhere near as much slack as he should have done. This sort of thing could easily tip people over the edge.

'Ben told me,' continued Jenny, 'that he'd started to notice people following him. He hadn't ever paid any attention to that sort of stuff, but it sort of became obvious when he started to look. Then he had all his emails and Facebook hacked. His flat was broken into. They took his laptop, searched all his drawers and stole all his thumb drives and bank statements too. Yet they didn't break in in the traditional sense – no windows or locks broken. They had keys.'

'And you'd given Frank copies of Ben's keys?'

'Yes. And I'd gained the passwords to his online stuff.' Jenny shook her head. 'I was disgusted with myself for having this completely deceitful relationship with this man – that the things that were happening to him were a result of what I was being asked to do.'

Lenny shifted in his seat. 'Why did you—'

'Why did I do it?' Jenny interrupted him, giving him a hard stare. 'At the time, I'd had to give up all my other regular clients. Being with Ben was a full-time role. I'd been solely with him for weeks. I was trapped by the money. I didn't know what else to do.'

'Why was Frank so interested in him?' Jake tried to move her account on, make it more about Frank and less an interrogation about her personal behaviour.

'Back then I had no clue. I didn't really know Frank. He worked in some government department or other, but I didn't even know his last name.'

'OK. What happened then, after the bug was found?'

'Frank asked me to break up with Ben. Told me to have one of those "it's not you, it's me" conversations. I did. In the pub. That's the last I saw of him. Ben didn't know my real name, where I really lived. The phone I had was pay as you go, so I just changed my number. Frank kept on paying me for doing nothing, like a retainer. It was good money.'

'So you broke up with Ben and that was that?'

'No.'

'What?'

'They asked me to do the same thing again. Only this time I was to befriend the HR manager at the Serious Fraud Office. Take compromising videos of him – me shagging him with a big black dildo – that sort of thing. He was married. Frank then blackmailed him to get me the job as a clerk in the office, so I could get access to the SFO paperwork.'

Jake looked across at Lenny, who was shaking his head in disbelief. Was it really this easy to infiltrate organisations like the SFO – perhaps even the police?

'And it was when I started working there,' Jenny continued, 'that I realised the SFO were investigating all the problems with the Al Yamamah contract, and that's exactly what Ben had been doing at his campaign group. He was digging up things about the government's dodgy involvement in that contract and giving the info to the papers. It was actually Ben and his anti-arms organisation that had kick-started the SFO investigation in the first place. It was all connected. I wanted out of it. I wanted no part of it, but they wouldn't let me leave.'

'How did they stop you? Give you more money?'

'That Javed, the one that I'd introduced to Ben – he turned up at my door one night. I didn't even know they knew where I lived. He asked me if I wanted to go out on a date. I refused. But he said I should reconsider, that it wasn't always polite not to do things that people were asking of me. I realised he wasn't talking about the date, that he was talking about my refusal to do what Frank wanted. He said he could make people disappear and make deaths look like suicides. That he could get bodies minced into pet food.'

Jake would have struggled to believe the story he was hearing, it sounded so outrageous, yet he had heard Frank telling someone to put serious pressure on Jenny. He assumed it must have been this Javed Saleem she now spoke of.

'I told him to fuck off and I shut the door,' Jenny continued, 'but a few days later, I climbed into bed and found a pig's ear in it. An ear cut off a pig – can you believe it? Massive thing – it scared the life out of me! There was blood all under the duvet. Then I noticed things had been moved around in my bedroom and some underwear had been stolen.'

'What did you do?'

'I told my mum what had been going on. She said that Frank and Javed weren't the type you went to the police to complain about. That it would just make it worse. I did report a burglary. Mum said it was best there was a record of it with them, just in case things got out of hand, you know? But she told me to keep working at the SFO, to do what Frank said.'

'How comes you're telling me now – if Frank *isn't the type* you go to the police about?' asked Jake.

'Well the game's up now, isn't it? It's either him or me. I'm not covering up for him – that just makes me look guilty, like it was all me, and I ain't having all this on *my* shoulders. I might as well talk to you now, get it out in the open—'

'Jenny, we're going to need to put all this down on paper, in a signed statement,' Jake interrupted her. 'I'm happy to treat you as a witness in this case at present, but I need to do all this properly, on tape, as you've got yourself mixed up in something nasty here.'

'I've got a doctor's appointment in an hour. Can I do it in the morning?'

Jake knew that this was going to take several hours, possibly a whole day, by the time she'd come down to the station, documented everything on tape in an interview room and they'd debriefed her properly. She'd got herself mixed up in a serious crime – it wasn't a simple process of taking a quick written statement from her.

'OK,' replied Jake reluctantly. He couldn't have her backing out. Although she'd been helpful and open up until now, it was easy to lose the cooperation of a witness and have them withdraw their assistance. Better to give her some leeway. Making her miss the doctor's appointment might only cause her to turn on him. He'd give her some space for the rest of the day.

'I'll meet you at Islington police station at 9 a.m. tomorrow morning. OK?' he said.

46

Jake had heard nothing from Jenny and she was over an hour late. Her phone was going straight to voicemail. He wondered if she'd had second thoughts about helping them, or whether she'd just had a late night and overslept like yesterday. Maybe they could go and rouse her at her flat.

'What are you going to say to her if she's decided not to help?' asked Lenny as they stepped into the rear yard where their car was parked.

'I don't know. Cross that bridge when we come to it.'

The drive from the station took barely a couple of minutes. They were at Jenny's door in no time.

'Jenny?' Jake called out as he banged on the door. There was no bell or door knocker. Jake rattled the letterbox to make some noise and called out again. He paused. No answer. He rapped on the glass panel with his hands. No response.

Lenny peered through a kitchen window to the right of the door.

'Anything?' Jake asked him. Lenny shook his head.

Jake crouched down and looked through the letter box. He could make out the glow of a TV in one of the rooms toward the back of the flat.

'There's a TV on in there...'

'Is there?' Lenny looked at Jake as if he might not be telling him the truth.

'Yes, there is. Look for yourself if you want!'

'No, you're all right – if you say there is, there is.' Lenny winked at him.

'Look through the letter box yourself.'

'Jake, if you want to kick the door in using section 17 as the reason, I'm right with you. You don't have to pretend anything to me.'

Section 17 gave them permission to force entry to save lives or prevent injury. It was a rule that was frequently abused by certain police officers.

'No, Len – I don't *want* to kick the door in. There really *is* a TV on in there. Look for yourself.'

If a TV was on, it was almost a cast-iron guarantee that someone was in. But if nobody was answering the door, they might be injured or incapacitated and unable to answer, meaning Section 17 could rightfully come into play.

'For God's sake's, guv! Are you going to do the door or not?'

'Yes, I'm going to force entry,' said Jake, backing up.

Lenny moved backwards, giving him some space.

Jake ran at the door and made contact with the sole of his foot. The door stayed intact. He reversed and did it again. Still it didn't budge. Jake did it several times – until he was out of breath – but the door remained closed.

Lenny laughed. 'Call yourself a copper? You're rubbish!'

'It's solid. Shall we do the kitchen window instead?' replied Jake, having now caught his breath.

'Nah – don't fancy it. Have another go at the door, guv.'

'Blimey, Len. You're a bossy arse today. Don't you believe me when I say it won't budge? How about you have a go?' he said, crossing his arms.

'All right. No problem,' said Lenny, gearing up for a charge. He took a run at the door and kicked it as hard as he could. The frame splintered immediately and the door flew open.

'Ha! I've still got it!' he shouted.

'Yeah, yeah, but only after I'd done all the hard work for you, old man!' said Jake.

They walked into the small hallway. Other than the splintered wood littered here and there, the place looked clean and tidy. The kitchen to the right of the hall was spotless, the washing-up done, a fresh tea towel neatly folded on the work surface. To their left was a small bathroom. Doorways ahead led to a bedroom and a living room, where they'd sat and spoken to Jenny previously. Both were tidy.

There was no sign of Jenny.

The TV screen that Jake thought he could see through the letter box turned out to be a computer monitor, on in the bedroom. Jake went to have a closer look. The bed was made. A pair of black, plastic strappy shoes with a transparent high heel sat on one side of the computer desk.

A printed sheet of A4 paper lay across the keyboard.

By the time you read this I'll have done what I'm going to do. I can't take any more of it. My head's a mess. I can't face another year of this. I feel like there's no point carrying on.

Jenny

Jake squinted at the monitor. The words he'd just read were mirrored on the screen. The letter had been typed on the computer and printed out.

Jake pointed to the sheet of paper without saying anything.

'Oh bollocks,' Lenny said when he'd finished reading. 'She's topped herself somewhere.'

'Maybe...'

Just as Jake was about to deliver his thoughts to Lenny, he caught something out of the corner of his eye. Two uniformed police officers were standing at the front door. Both male. One of them looked no older than twenty, the other perhaps in his mid-fifties.

'Hello, sir. Are you a friend or relative of Miss Jenny Reynolds,' asked the younger of the two.

Jake walked up the hallway. 'No mate, Counter Terrorism Command,' he said, pulling his warrant card out. The younger officer appeared very confused. Jake looked him up and down. His uniform was brand new. Fresh out of the packet – a raw recruit.

'Why are you here?' asked Jake.

'Well, sir, we've been sent round to try and locate someone who knows Jenny Reynolds.'

'Fantastic. Where is she?'

'Thames have her, at Wapping,' said the older officer.

'Jeez,' said Lenny.

Jake's heart sank. Wapping was the home of the Marine Policing Unit, where corpses that had been pulled from the Thames went.

'What happened?' asked Jake through gritted teeth.

'Miss Reynolds was recovered floating in the water by Tower Bridge,' replied the older officer.

This wasn't a social call – they'd found her body and were looking for next of kin to identify it.

There was no time to process how he felt. He had to snap into action.

'OK. This place is a crime scene. I want a photographer here to document everything. There's a suicide note sitting on top of the keyboard in there.' Jake pointed into the bedroom. 'Looks like it's been written on the computer. I don't want you touching anything. I want the computer left on and the keyboard left just as it is. I want the place sealed up; steel shutters put on all the windows and doors, padlocked. I'll come and get the keys from Islington nick later on.'

'Yes, sir,' the older one said.

'Come on, Lenny. We've got to go and check it's actually her they've got at Wapping and not some bloody mix up,' said Jake, as he stalked past the two officers and out the front door.

47

Lenny pulled up outside a yellow-brick Victorian building – the home of the Marine Policing Unit. Just a stone's throw from London Bridge, it looked like a typical police station, though behind the facade there was little more than a few offices and some storage areas.

Many officers saw Thames Division as a plum post; something they aspired to do. It was a great place to work for those who loved the water and wanted a forty-seven-mile stretch of it to swan up and down in a police boat.

Jake thought differently.

The Thames was a magical and bewitching river. It charmed onlookers as they watched it sweep past the iconic landmarks of London. But the Thames had a secret. It was the biggest serial killer in London and killed at a rate of two a week – sometimes more. The officers of Thames Division saw more dead bodies in a year than the average murder detective in the provinces did in his or her career. Most of the bodies were treated as suicides. Yet Jake often wondered how many of those had been pushed in deliberately. In many cases there was no telling. The corpse of someone who had been pushed or thrown into the river looked very much like the corpse of someone who had committed suicide.

The Thames was tidal. Its waters rose and fell more than twenty feet, twice a day. If you went into the river fully clothed, the five-mile-an-hour currents, together with the eddies and undertows, made it very difficult to stay at the surface. Even the strongest of swimmers could get dragged under, not surfacing again for four or five days.

Thames Division would be called whenever someone saw a body in the water. They'd pull alongside it, latch it to the side of the boat using a net and then transport the corpse to Wapping.

Jake and Lenny were led through the building to the river's edge, down a jetty and on to a floating pontoon that was about thirty feet from the edge of the river. Standing alongside one of the moored boats was a man in a boiler suit, hosing something down over a large stainless-steel basin. As Jake drew closer, he saw what it was. Lying in the basin, her skin yellow and puffy – which suggested she'd been in the water a while – was the lifeless body of Jenny Reynolds.

'I've hosed her down as best I can for you!' the officer said, stopping what he was doing.

With around 39 million cubic metres of raw sewage finding its way into the Thames every year, the river was a filthy place. From what Jake could see of the debris left in the basin, Jenny had been found entwined in weeds, a selection of brightly coloured iced-lolly wrappers, a couple of green bags containing used nappies, some lengths of kitchen roll and a great deal of river sludge.

'Thanks,' said Jake.

He made a mental note of what she was wearing – a pair of jeans, a white blouse and a bomber jacket – but he found it difficult to look at her face, having seen her alive only twenty-four hours ago. A biting coldness gripped him, making him want to gasp as if he'd been in the Thames himself.

'How did you identify her?' Jake asked the boiler-suited officer.

'Had her driver's licence on her. We asked the local police station to go to the address on the licence. Guess that's where they found you? They said you wanted her home treated as a crime scene?'

'Yeah, just covering the bases, you know how it is.' Jake didn't want to give any information away right now. 'Anything else on her? Did you search all her pockets?'

'Mobile phone and a purse – over a hundred quid in that. All over there. Suicide note found at her home according to what the local boys said?'

'A note was found at her place, yes,' said Jake, crouching down to examine Jenny's clothing.

'Why are Counter Terror interested in this bird? She was a bit of a looker, weren't she? She doesn't look much like a terrorist to me though,' said the officer jovially.

'What does a terrorist look like? You met many?' Jake shot back at him.

'No, sir,' he replied sheepishly. 'Er, I'll wait up in the office. We can get our coroner to deal with this – unless you have other ideas?'

'Yes, wait in the office. I'll let you know,' snapped Jake.

The officer nodded and wandered off without saying anything else.

'He's only doing his job, guv,' said Lenny quietly, once they were alone.

Jake didn't reply. He knew the officer had probably dragged several dozen bodies out of the Thames this year already. The fact that Counter Terrorism Command were interested had probably made that bloke's day just a little less monotonous. Nevertheless, loose lips sank ships and nosey parkers with questions didn't make this process any easier for Jake.

He began checking Jenny's clothing for punctures, trying to work out if she'd been stabbed or shot. There were no points of entry that he could see. But it was difficult to tell when it was so wet.

You don't think it's suicide?' asked Lenny tentatively.

'I won't be surprised if the post-mortem finds that she died of drowning. But I will be surprised if she got in the river all by herself, Lenny.'

'Why's that?'

'Just a feeling. Give me a hand to turn her over so I can look at her back, please, mate.'

Lenny bent down, and between them they rolled Jenny face down in the large basin.

'How are we going to prove that?' said Lenny as he stood up.

'We might never be able to.' Jake grimaced. 'For all that she was involved with, it's still such a shame to see her like this.'

A moment of quiet descended on them as the waves lapped against the jetty.

As the wind whipped up, harsh screeching from a colony of yellow-beaked gulls, who'd taken an interest in Jenny, broke the calm.

Jake felt his chest constrict and a knot of desperation tighten in his gut. This was not a normal investigation. They were so very rarely in this situation as detectives. He'd seen many bodies, but that was exactly it – only after death. It was rare for police to see people in both life and death. Sitting in her pink fluffy bathrobe, so animated just a day ago – and then dragged out of the Thames, bloated and lifeless, the next.

Just like the baby in the fire. Another one he couldn't save.

'Lenny…' Jake's voice cracked. He cleared his throat.

'Guv?'

Recovering his composure, Jake began barking orders. 'Get that phone down the lab. See what they can recover from the memory. Get me her billings and cell-site data for the last forty-eight hours. I'll go and arrange for their coroner to deal with the post-mortem. I don't think it's going to tell us much, but we can't just sit around here all day and wait for the bloody seagulls to get involved.'

48

They'd driven back to Islington police station to collect the keys to the steel shutters that had been put on Jenny's flat. As they unlocked them, a communal light outside the front doorway switched itself on to fight the creeping dusk. It cast feeble shadows into the hallway and bedroom.

'What are we looking for here, guv?' asked Lenny.

'I'll show you.' Jake headed to the bedroom.

The uniformed officers had done as they'd been told. They'd left the computer turned on and hadn't touched anything. The light on the machine's CPU tower, sitting under the small desk, glowed an eerie yellow-green.

'Put them on,' said Jake, passing Lenny two sets of surgical gloves – doubling up as always, just to be on the safe side.

Lenny pulled on both pairs and looked awkwardly around the room, not entirely sure what he was supposed to be doing.

'How long do you think Jenny has been dead?' asked Jake.

'I don't know, some hours. Looked like she might have been in the river all night maybe?' replied Lenny, looking confused.

'Move that for me,' said Jake, pointing at the wireless mouse sitting on a dog-eared mat to the right of the monitor.

Lenny pushed the mouse gingerly with a pointed finger. As he did so, the computer screen sprang to life and the Word document containing the suicide note appeared on the screen. It looked exactly as it had when they'd been at the flat earlier that day. The monitor filled the room with a blue-tinged glare.

'So?' said Lenny, looking at Jake and shrugging.

Jake pulled out his phone and looked at the time. 'Patience,' he whispered.

'I don't get it.'

'You will. In a few minutes. Just wait,' replied Jake,.

Eventually the screen went dark again, as the computer went into sleep mode.

'There you are, right on schedule,' said Jake. 'When we arrived here this morning, that computer screen was on. That's why I forced entry to the premises, thinking that Jenny was in here. It goes off after ten minutes of inactivity – just like it has now.'

'So someone left this desk within minutes of us being here this morning – we just missed them?'

'Yes, and it wasn't Jenny, that's for certain.'

'You think someone else wrote that note on the computer and printed it off – *after* Jenny was dead – to make it look like suicide?'

'It's possible. They didn't find any keys on Jenny's body; they might have fallen out in the water, or someone might have taken them. That's why I wanted the steel shutters on the windows and doors.'

'Good work. Are we packing all this stuff up now?' Lenny asked.

'No – I've had problems when I've done that in the past. Unplugging it and turning it all off can mess with the timings of things. Call the guys from the Hi-Tech Unit to come and examine it here, in situ.'

Lenny nodded, pulled out his phone and made his way out to the external walkway at the front.

Jenny's flat was now in almost total darkness. Standing there, Jake wondered what else their suspect might have done inside the flat this morning, just before they'd arrived. He tried to imagine the person who'd been here; what he or she might have been up to.

Lenny wandered back in after finishing his call and turned the lights on, illuminating Jake.

'Why were you standing there in the dark, guv?'

Jake shrugged and changed the subject. Trying to use the twilight to think like a bad guy seemed like an idiotic response. 'What did the Yard say about the Hi-Tech Unit?' he asked instead.

'Two or three hours. They've got to call a guy out from home.'

'Where does he live – Outer Mongolia?'

'Don't shoot the messenger, Jake. He's probably at home with his wife and kids, enjoying his evening, eating a nice dinner or something. Some people do have lives outside of what goes on within the Met. I know you don't, but some of us do,' said Lenny, patting him on the shoulder.

'I did have a wife and family once, you know…'

'Yeah, and look what happened to that!'

'What's that supposed to mean?' Jake was starting to feel like Lenny was having a dig.

'Maybe if you'd spent more time at home, eating dinners with your family, and spent less time at work running around after the bad guys, you'd understand why a few hours isn't that outrageous.'

'Jenny needs me to catch these people.'

'Jenny's dead though – there's no bringing her back. Doesn't matter how hard you work; doesn't matter to Jenny how long it takes for the Hi-Tech man to get here.'

'Do you need some time off, Lenny? Is that what this is about?'

'No – well maybe… That's not what I meant. There's always a crusade with you, Jake. You're always on a mission.'

'Give it a rest, Lenny. I'm not in the mood. Dead people get the five-star service; it's the only time the Met gives *anyone* a five-star service. Ring them again, tell them I want them here faster.'

'Sometimes – just sometimes – people don't always share *your* priorities in life; they think spending time with the people they love is more important than chasing bad guys, terrorists, killers or people who've done bad things, Jake – that's all I'm saying.'

'Any time you fancy clocking off, feel free, Lenny.' Jake turned his attention to the bedroom they were standing in.

'And who's going to look after you? Drive you around? You fancy doing this by bus, on your own?' said Lenny sarcastically.

'This wouldn't be half as much fun without you, Lenny. You know that. You're like Watson to my Holmes, the one with all the sensible bits. And no – I don't fancy going it alone,' said Jake, studying the bed intently.

Lenny followed his gaze. 'Why are you so fascinated by the bed?'

The overhead light threw shadows on to the covers, revealing a slight indentation in the quilt. Jake had failed to spot it earlier in the gloom of the creeping dusk.

'Did you sit on it?' he asked Lenny.

'No, I haven't. I can't even see what you're looking at.'

'Come and stand here.' Jake moved to one side and pulled Lenny to the spot he'd been standing in. 'See it now?' Jake pointed at the hollowing in the bedcovers.

'Yeah, I see it. Nope, wasn't me.'

'OK. Don't go near it. If the bad guy has been sitting on the bed, we've got fibres from his trousers on there. Get hold of the two blokes in uniform that were here this morning. Find out if *they* sat on the bed. And get me a scene examiner to do some fibre lifting *please*, Watson – and don't tell me they're two hours away too…'

'Stop calling me Watson!' said Lenny, pulling out his phone and disappearing outside again.

49

Sitting in Helen's office on the fifteenth floor, the three of them sipped lattes Jake had bought up from the canteen. He hoped the caffeine would give him a lift. The night before, to drown out the thoughts of Jenny, he'd been to the off-licence to buy whisky. Drinking at home, alone, was something he hadn't done in a very long time.

'You two have a lot to bring me up to speed with,' said Helen, pulling the plastic lid off her takeaway cup.

'Yes, we have. The missing-documents case at the SFO has taken an odd turn,' replied Jake.

'I heard. The superintendent in charge of the Hi-Tech Unit phoned me, wanting to know why his staff were being called out so late on a summer's evening. He was keen to know the operation name and cost-centre code for the overtime, before he would authorise them attending. You need to keep me updated, Jake. I don't like being put on the spot like that.' Helen peered at him sternly through the steam of her coffee as she took a sip.

'It all moved rather quickly – my apologies that you didn't know.'

'Right. So where are we going with this, Jake?'

'The SFO paperwork thing *was* panning out nicely, and I mean *was*. We were speaking to a witness – a prostitute who was basically being paid to spy on people and blackmail them. I was looking to use her as a witness rather than a suspect. I'd

208

intended to debrief her properly, on tape, at the nick, and seek the advice of the CPS, because she was involved in some pretty serious criminality, I think. But she didn't turn up.

'So we went to her place, forced entry and found a suicide note sitting on her keyboard, printed out from her computer. A minute later two local uniform boys turn up at the door, looking for a relative of our chief witness, because she's just been pulled out of the Thames, dead.'

Helen's eyes remained fixed on Jake.

'We go down to Wapping and look at the body...' Jake could feel himself getting animated, 'and it looks like she's drowned. But here's the problem... Her home computer was on when we got to her flat. Lenny and I checked it. It times out in ten minutes and shuts the screen down into sleep mode.'

'So you're saying it wasn't the lady in the Thames who wrote the note?' asked Helen.

'Yes, that's why I needed the Hi-Tech guys, to look at her computer in situ. I wanted to see if we could get an idea of when that writing on the screen had been done, before we turned it all off and removed it.'

'And what did they say?'

'It was written on the computer twenty-three minutes before we arrived.'

'So the lady in the Thames couldn't have written it, and it's a murder. Have you involved Homicide Command?'

'It might be a murder – we don't know yet. We have no real evidence at the moment, other than this *anomaly*.'

'*Anomaly*? It sounds like a murder to me.'

'Homicide team won't touch it unless we have direct evidence that it was murder – it could be some suicide pact for all we know. And that's what the Homicide team will say, trust me on this. That's why I've kept it for the time being.'

'OK,' said Helen reluctantly.

'Whichever way you look at it, Jenny *didn't* write the note,' said Jake firmly. '*Someone* was poking around in there just before we arrived. Lenny and I must have missed them by minutes.'

'Who has keys to the place?' asked Helen, buoyed by Jake's conviction.

This was good. Jake had been worried that she wouldn't believe his theory and might insist on the Homicide team having it. The fact that she was asking probing questions was a favourable sign.

'That's part of the mystery. She had no keys when they pulled her from the Thames. She made no bones about being an escort, but she was struggling to reconcile herself with her new line of work.'

'And who was she being asked to spy on?' asked Helen.

'An anti-arms activist – Ben somebody. The people she worked for specialised in blackmail, but if that didn't work, coercion and threat of violence was next, and so on.'

'And you think this is all connected?'

'Well despite working for them, she wasn't immune to them using similar tactics on her. Yes, they'd pay her, but if she didn't do something, or refused to do it, they'd resort to other methods to persuade her. She recounted a story to me about coming home recently and finding a pig's ear in her bed—'

'A pig's ear?' exclaimed Helen.

'Yeah, under the covers – she didn't find it until she got into bed with it.'

'Why a pig's ear?'

'Ben runs an anti-arms campaign group. As well as spying on him, she was ordered to introduce moles into his group; help embed them from within. At least one of these moles turned out to be a spy for the arms industry and completely freaked her out. Told her that he was paid to *take care of things*. Boasted of making deaths look like suicide and said he'd previously disposed of bodies by getting them minced up and used as pet food.'

'And you think the pig's ear is a reference to an abattoir?'

'Possibly. She was *politely* told by him, fairly recently, that she needed to get a move on with something she was supposed to be doing, just before she found the pig's ear in her bed. She said some underwear was taken too. She reported it to the local police apparently.'

'The guy that threatened her had keys to her flat?'

'It seems possible, yes.'

'You need to find him and talk to him,' said Helen. 'Probably while he's in custody would be our safest bet, I'd say.'

'Yes, boss. My thoughts exactly. I was going to arrest him on suspicion of the burglary, without mentioning that Jenny is dead. Search his home, see what we find. See what he says…'

'You know who he is?'

'Yes. His details are on the crime report, when she reported the burglary. Shouldn't be a problem to track him down.'

'Sounds good. Just keep me up to date, Jake – I don't ask much of you other than that.'

'Of course.' Jake rose from his seat; Lenny followed his lead.

'Jake…' Helen called as they left her office.

'Yes.' He turned.

'Good work – well done,' she said, smiling at him.

'Thank you, ma'am.'

50

'Good morning, Jake. How are you?' asked Shirley.

'I'm OK.' Jake wasn't OK, but giving anything other than the de facto response seemed odd.

He pondered how often he answered questions of '*How are you?*' with an honest reply. Very rarely. People didn't really want to know, did they? Nobody ever expected an honest answer to that question.

'You asked to see me this morning, hence I think that things are *not* OK?' she said, breaking into his thoughts.

'I've been thinking about what you said to me, right at the beginning, when we first met – that it was good to share things, not bottle them up. I thought about it a lot. I thought that this morning I just needed someone to talk to, you know, away from the office…' Jake felt himself break out in a sweat, beads forming on his brow. 'Thanks for seeing me at such short notice.'

'It's fine. You look stressed, Jake. What's happened?'

'I had to deal with a dead body.'

'That can't have been very easy, but you've dealt with plenty of dead bodies before, yes?'

'Of course.' Jake nodded. 'I've dealt with hundreds of them.'

'Why was this one different then?'

Jake thought about the first time he'd dealt with a dead body. A man in his thirties had jumped thirteen floors to the pavement below. When Jake had arrived he'd still been breathing, though he was in a terrible mess. Jake had tried, but failed, to save him. The man had died right there in front of him. After they'd taken his body away, Jake had found his flat and looked around it. It had been clean and tidy. There'd been photos of the man with children – his children – now without a father. There'd been stacks of pennies, counted into neat piles of ten on the table by the open balcony door – £1.04. In pennies. There had been no note. No one else had been involved. The man had just jumped. To this day Jake didn't understand why. No one did. Only the man knew. Jake had assumed it was to do with money.

He suddenly remembered the utter feeling of despair he'd felt, standing there in the man's flat, looking at the neat piles of pennies. Jake would have given all the money he had for that man to still be alive. For those children to have had the past fifteen years with their father. He couldn't even remember his name. Had there really been that many bodies since?

Jake tried to sort through the pictures in his mind of the bodies he'd had to deal with at various crime scenes during his career. Drug overdoses, stabbings and road accidents; heart attacks, hangings and slit wrists. Bodies that had been punched to death or impaled on spikes. Bodies that had been burnt or poisoned. Bodies that had been blown up. And now *another* drowned one. He couldn't even remember how many drowned bodies he'd dealt with. One girl had even drowned in her own bath.

'Hundreds of them. There are hundreds of them. Hundreds and hundreds…' muttered Jake, staring at the window behind Shirley, 'and hundreds and hundreds and hundreds…'

'So what makes this one different, Jake?' Shirley asked him again.

'I knew her when she was alive. It was someone that I'd met previously…'

Shirley was giving him a puzzled look.

'They were only ever a body to me,' Jake continued. 'Of course it's sad whenever you have to deal with a dead person, but that's partly how you stay detached from it. Most of them, there was nothing I could have done to stop them from dying. You console yourself with the fact that they were gone before you could have got there.'

'I see…' Shirley still looked slightly puzzled. Jake didn't think she understood at all. Maybe he wasn't explaining it very well.

'Most of the bodies I've ever dealt with were dead when I first encountered them. Apart from Jenny yesterday – and there was once a baby in a house fire, and a man who jumped off a building. They were all alive. There were things, decisions I made, that meant that—'

'Jake. They're not your fault though, are they?'

Jake shook his head.

'You would have helped if you could have done?' Shirley nodded, trying to encourage him.

He felt hot tears welling up in his eyes. They rolled slowly and silently down his face. He was shaking.

'Take your time, Jake.' Shirley slid a box of tissues across the desk.

'I feel in some way responsible for the ones I couldn't save. I can't seem to shake off this sense of apprehension, almost like guilt. And the more I think about it, the guiltier I feel that… I couldn't save them.'

'Tell me about the baby.'

'I don't want to talk about the details – it was awful. She died in a fire. I couldn't get into the flat where she was, because I couldn't break down the door and the fire was too strong. She was alive when I got there – I could hear her crying in her cot. But she was dead when I left. The same with Jenny, the dead body yesterday. Alive one day, and I'm talking to her – and the next day I'm checking over her body to see how she died and investigating her death.'

'You must have saved some lives, Jake?'

He thought about it. 'I don't remember those – I can't think of any. On bad days I can only see the dead, and on really bad days all I think about are the ones that dig into me and gnaw away inside me, like that baby.'

214

'This recent death has brought back feelings that you've suppressed for a long time?'

'Yes, sort of. I think that fire at Glasgow Airport brought it all back. It's been getting steadily worse since then. Jenny's death has made me realise that I should have dealt with those feelings before now,'

Jake ignored the box of tissues. He wiped the tears from his cheeks with his sleeve, though they were quickly replaced with fresh ones. 'I just know that I can't carry the feelings of guilt about Jenny's death with me like I have that baby's. I just can't.'

'That's good – dealing with something at the time is far better than bottling it all up. Has the death yesterday made you want to drink again?' asked Shirley. 'We talked before about triggers for that behaviour.'

It was as if she could see straight into his soul and knew that he'd downed an entire bottle of whisky the previous night.

He nodded. 'I did have a drink last night,' he said quietly.

'And how do you feel about that this morning?'

'My head hurts, and I don't intend on repeating it tonight.'

Shirley smiled. 'Jake, I know this is hard, but I do think that you're starting to make some inroads into dealing with your emotions. The fact that you've chosen to come here today to talk about it, and admitted that you've had a drink after feeling down, are very positive steps.

'I need to get back to work.' Jake rose from his chair. 'Thanks for seeing me today.'

'I'm going to book you another appointment,' she said, smiling at him. 'You took a huge step today. You know that?'

He managed a nod, noting down the time of the next appointment before he strode out the door.

51

Standing on the pavement outside the office, Jake's thoughts were interrupted by a low irritating hum; the motor of the revolving Scotland Yard sign whirring as it slowly rotated. Claimed by some to be the capital's second-most-photographed location, after Buckingham Palace, Jake knew it wouldn't be long before the next coachload of tourists arrived to snap some photos next to the huge silver sign.

They'd spent the whole morning trying to establish where Javed Saleem, the man who'd threatened Jenny and planted the pig's ear in her bed, lived. Despite a thorough search, his pre-pay mobile number had led them nowhere. If they were going to get any further with this, they needed some help.

He looked at the latest text message he'd received from Claire. *'Don't shut me out. I'm all alone here in the cold with this stuff.'* He hadn't replied yet.

He was struggling to get past how she'd behaved when he'd confronted her about the Saudi princes – the anger he had seen in her, the look in her eyes. For a split second he'd wondered if she would strike him with the glass after she'd thrown its contents in his face. It was a side of her that he hadn't seen before. He hadn't known that she could react violently and it troubled him.

At the same time, he wondered how it had been for her, having carried those secrets with her all her adult life. Having been betrayed by an uncle she'd loved, by people she'd thought were her friends.

He dialled Claire's work number.

She wasn't allowed to take her mobile into her Thames House office. All devices had to be turned off and left in one of many small, lockable metal cages at the entrance of each office door. Corrupt employees had been known to collect data using their mobiles. Even worse, a handset could be compromised by a foreign security service, who could use it to look or listen in on them.

He skipped their usual pleasantries. Never engage – never explain. She was on a work phone line – they could talk about it in person later.

'You busy?' he asked.

'What's up?'

'Can I meet you for a cup of tea? We need to talk, and I need a favour.' Jake looked up at the sky, wondering if he also needed a coat. It looked grey and overcast.

'See you in twenty minutes. Yeah, usual place,' she said, and hung up.

Their usual place was a Pret A Manger outlet on the corner of Great Peter Street and Marsham Street. It was almost halfway between their two workplaces and directly opposite the new Home Office building; a modern, £311 million, multi-coloured glass palace that looked as though it housed a television studio, rather than some branch of government.

Thousands of civil servants worked in the Home Office, which meant the queue in the café was practically out the door as Jake arrived. It wasn't an exceptionally relaxing spot to choose at lunchtime, but the sheer volume of footfall afforded a degree of anonymity to two people discussing things they shouldn't be discussing.

On reaching the front of the queue, Jake picked up some snacks and drinks. He hovered incongruously for a while, until two customers sitting in a corner, away from the door, got fed up with his presence and finally vacated their table.

'Hi,' said Claire, sitting down opposite him, her shoulders hunched.

'Hey, you. Got you a fruit-yoghurt pot and a tea,' he said, pushing the granola-covered yoghurt and cardboard cup toward her, trying hard to sound upbeat.

'Wow. Is that your way of saying sorry to me?' She smirked, but he sensed she was still hurt.

'I'm sorry about the way I reacted. It's a tough thing to find out about your girlfriend.'

'I'm not your girlfriend though.'

'You were once, and when we broke up, we both agreed that we would see how things went and reassess. And right now that doesn't seem to be going too well.'

'I can tell you're still angry, Jake. I should have been honest with you, I get that, but maybe I wasn't ready to talk about it. Maybe I'm still not ready to talk about it. Maybe I still want it kept a secret. You know when things are tough it's easier not to talk about them.'

'That's not what my shrink says. She says it's best to get things into the open. But that said, I reacted badly. I was hurt – I felt you should've told me.'

'It's not always just about how things make *you* feel, Jake. One day you'll realise that.' She looked upset for a moment but quickly regained her composure. 'So I'm guessing that these delicious treats I see before me aren't an apology. It's going to cost something?'

'You got me started on this investigation by dragging me to the Forest of Dean to remove that bug, and now someone is dead.'

'What?' Claire was genuinely shocked.

'A girl...' Jake deliberately avoided using the word escort or prostitute through fear of Claire's reaction, 'who was being paid to spy on the SFO has somehow drowned in the Thames. I think she was helped into the river and it's been made to look like suicide.'

'Jesus!' she exclaimed. 'And this is connected to Uncle Frank how?'

'The girl we're talking about is the girl he was talking to on the phone on those recordings you made. It's Jenny – Jennifer.'

Claire shook her head. 'I knew he was a monster, but murder? I didn't think he was capable of that.'

'Not long before her death, Jenny was threatened by some bloke. I've got a name and phone number but nothing else. You remember we heard Frank telling someone to put pressure on Jenny?'

Claire nodded.

'Well I think this is the same guy, but we've nothing on our intel systems to help identify who he is.'

'Name?'

'Javed Saleem,' replied Jake.

Claire pulled the lid off her drink to see if Jake had put milk in it. 'Never heard of him,' she replied, looking up. 'Can you get me a spoon for my yoghurt please?'

Jake stood up and edged past her seat, where there was little space to move.

Anyone looking would think that they were two lovers, meeting for a quick five-minute break, a bit of eye gazing, some suggestive whispering. He straightened up and walked off to the counter.

On his return, he handed her a burgundy plastic spoon. 'I need to move fast on this, Claire, before it gets handed to someone else. The bosses could pass it to Homicide Command at any moment. You need to eat that at your desk,' he said, giving her a kiss as he slid a piece of paper into her hand with Javed Saleem's number on it before sitting back down.

'You need this information *now?*'

'Yes. Sorry to put you under pressure.'

Claire nodded. 'I've just remembered that I've left something for you back at the office. Can I see you back here in an hour?' she said loudly, playing the game for the benefit of any onlookers.

Jake nodded and remained seated.

One hour had stretched into two. Jake was on his third cup of tea and beginning to wonder if Claire was coming back.

Just as he was about to get up and head back to the Yard, Claire walked through the door and sat down opposite him.

'Got it,' she said in hushed tones, the place quieter now. He hadn't noticed it before, but her eyes were bloodshot, like she'd been crying or not sleeping properly.

'Interesting?'

'Very,' she replied, looking cagily around the café.

'Go on.' Jake leaned over the table, edging closer.

'This phone number,' Claire said furtively. 'We know it. We don't know who uses it, but the people who call this number use the names 'Javed' and 'Saleem' when speaking to the person on the other end—'

'You've got intercept recordings of it?'

'Sort of. There will always be a few people that we're monitoring all the time. Hooked-up phone-line monitoring – twenty-four-seven, I mean. One of them is a Libyan intelligence officer who's based here in the UK. Anyway, we intercepted some chat between him and your phone number. It was all coded. It was a few weeks back now. Couldn't work out what it was about, but it sounded dirty. We spoke to the lot at Vauxhall Cross, gave them what we had, asked them if it tied in with anything. They've gained some intelligence that suggests there was a plot to assassinate a Saudi prince. They intended to do it in the lobby of a hotel, I think.'

'What? Why haven't they given that info to us at Scotland Yard? This is a police matter.'

Claire waved off his protestations. 'The assassin was already in the country when we got that intelligence. Our surveillance on him didn't show up anything much. The surveillance team think that they were compromised and he knew he was being followed. The intercept can't be used in evidence. Nothing Vauxhall Cross had could be passed to the police. So the Home Secretary was briefed, the assassin was on a tourist visa, his visa was revoked and he was removed from the country. Local police and the Immigration Service assisted us with that. All very hush-hush.'

Jake nodded. 'So where does Saleem fit in with that?'

'Saleem appears to be part of the support network around the assassin. I would call them Saudi dissidents, people who oppose the Saudi royal family and want them deposed.'

'Politics?'

'Politics is a dirty game,' said Claire gravely.

Jake noticed her chin wobble as she spoke. This didn't seem like the strong, capable woman he knew. Maybe their argument had hit her harder than he'd realised. Maybe the stress of the whole situation was taking its toll.

A tall thin man in a business suit caught the back of her chair as he walked past, slopping some of his coffee on to his round metal tray and apologising profusely.

Claire jumped to her feet. 'Look, I need to get back,' she said skittishly, sliding a piece of paper across the table to Jake.

'Are you OK?'

'I'm tired. I've not been feeling well. They're watching me like a hawk in the office.'

'What's this?' he asked, unfolding the piece of paper and seeing a long series of numbers on it.

'That's the credit-card number that's being used to top up the credit on Javed Saleem's phone. You might get something from that. Be careful,' she said, unblinking. She kissed him quickly on the cheek before rushing out on to the street.

Jake wondered what had gotten into her.

52

The National Terrorist Financial Investigation Unit was a huge department that occupied one entire end of the seventeenth floor. The place felt as if it had been stuck in a time warp with ancient furniture that Jake hardly ever saw at the Met now. Desks had dark wooden legs with a heavy-duty inlay on the tabletop, and the atmosphere in the room was just like the furniture. Dull. Everyone was old – grey suits, white shirts, dark ties. The staff had been there as long the desks, but they were experts at what they did.

'Can I help you?' asked a woman with short hair and a deep voice, sitting a few desks down.

'I'm looking for DS Charlie Bedford?'

'Down the end on the right,' was the response, before she buried her attention back into a foot-high stack of old, Nat West bank statements.

'Thanks,' he replied then walked toward the back of the office.

A balding man in his late fifties with a slight paunch was sitting at a computer terminal, poring over an Excel spreadsheet.

'Charlie Bedford?' asked Jake.

'Yep, that's me,' said the man, swivelling round on his chair.

Jake extended his hand. 'Jake Flannagan.'

'Good to meet you at last, Jake. Heard a lot about you...'

'You have? All good I hope?'

'This is the Met. Rumours are never good, are they?'

'True enough, I suppose.'

'You're here about the production orders on Sharon and Jennifer Reynolds – the madam and her daughter, aren't you? Your DS – Lenny Sandringham – wanted to access some information on their financial records? I've got the orders here somewhere...' Charlie began hunting in earnest through the pile of folders next to the computer.

'Sort of, Charlie. I'm here about something connected.'

'Oh. What's that then?'

'Jennifer Reynolds is dead.'

Charlie raised his eyebrows. 'Is she?'

'Her body was found in the Thames. We're trying to establish how and why she ended up in the river. Whether someone helped her into it, that sort of thing...'

Charlie nodded. 'OK.'

'I'm trying to identify a suspect that threatened her previously and was probably involved in a burglary at her flat. I've managed to track down a phone number for this suspect, but it's a pay-as-you-go account. I've got the credit-card number that's being used to top up the phone, and I was wondering if you could make some enquiries with the bank about the card?'

'Make some calls?'

'Yes. I can't do the normal routes of production orders. The credit-card number isn't evidence, it's intelligence only – I can't put it to the court.'

'We can give it a go. So all you have is the number? Is it a UK credit card?'

'I think so.'

Charlie wrinkled up his nose in thought. 'They won't give me much without a production order,' he said ruefully.

'Will they say what recent transactions are on the card?'

'It's debatable... Look, I do have some good contacts who owe me. And if we don't ask, we don't get. You got the card number handy?'

Jake passed Charlie the piece of paper that Claire had given him.

'That's HSBC,' Charlie said instantly. From the first six numbers, he'd already recognised which bank the card had been issued by. Guys like Charlie, who did these things all the time, knew the codes off by heart. 'Give me a few hours. Let me see what I can get for you.'

53

They drove in silence. Rain hammered the top of the car and ran in soupy rivulets down the side windows, the rhythm of the windscreen wipers slightly mesmerising.

Lenny had been in a mood all morning, but this was the first time he'd been alone with Jake.

'You've still not told me how you got hold of that credit-card number in the first place, guv.'

Jake ignored him.

The credit-card company had revealed that there was very little expenditure on the account Claire had alerted him to. The card had mainly been used in filling stations to pay for fuel and to purchase vouchers with which to top up Javed Saleem's phone. The only thing of note that they'd let slip was that the Hilton on Park Lane had popped up on the records. On checking directly with the hotel, they'd discovered that Javed Saleem had been booked into a suite for two consecutive nights.

'I'm not happy about this,' said Lenny as he looked across from the driver's seat. They were on their way to the Hilton to hunt for Saleem, with an arrest team following behind them in a second car.

Again, Jake said nothing.

'This is a mistake. I'm telling you, Jake. I can feel it in my water. You're going to end up in trouble – again. Where did this job originate? How did we come to be sniffing around at the SFO about that paperwork in the first place?'

'I've told you. I saw a suspect on a roof. I followed him. Fell through the skylight and found the documents hidden in a cannabis farm,' he replied, hoping that would be enough for Lenny to drop it.

'So you were there by chance? We both know that is *utter bollocks*. I know you – I've worked with you for years, and I know how you work. And I know your bollocks when I hear it. Where did that credit-card number come from?'

'I just want to catch the bad guys, Lenny. That's my job, and I do it to the best of my abilities.'

Lenny shook his head.

'Someone is dead, Lenny. And—'

'You've not been straight with me,' Lenny interrupted him, sounding more than a little annoyed.

The rain was starting to clear and the sun was coming out. The weather was as changeable as Jake's mood. On the edge of Belgravia, a woman in skintight jeans, white stilettos and a white jumper walked out of a doorway, dragging a small black poodle by a lead on to the pavement. The poodle had a white jumper on to match its owner's outfit. Jake thought about pointing it out to Lenny, who was oblivious to the scene, but then decided to keep it to himself. Lenny was usually happy to run on Jake's gut instincts, but he really wasn't playing ball with him today.

Jake sighed. 'They pay us to detect, Lenny. That's why they call us detectives – we find things out that other people don't want us to find.'

'Where did you get that number from, Jake?'

There was a pause.

Jake took a deep breath. He didn't like keeping the truth from Lenny. They went way back.

'Claire,' he replied, finally deciding that honesty was the best policy.

'I knew it!' Lenny thumped the steering wheel. 'Why did she give you that? Is she involved in this?'

'Look…' Jake paused, unsure how to answer. Lenny rarely got this upset with him. 'The SFO thing originated from her

– it was never official,' said Jake, deciding to level with him. 'It's connected to her uncle somehow – Frank.'

'For fuck's sake!' Lenny hit the brakes on the car and brought it to a skidding halt. 'I fucking knew it. You do this all the time, Jake! You are going to lose your job!'

At a standstill in the middle of the road, cars behind them began to sound their horns.

'It's fine. I'm telling you the truth about the documents. They really *were* on a cannabis farm and I really *did* fall through a skylight. It's a genuine police operation that I've introduced as something that I came across, because I can't just say, "Oh it's connected to Claire." They'd take me off the job, or I might compromise her safety or position at work. I've told you because you asked and you're my friend—'

Lenny hit the steering wheel with the palm of his hand again. Jake had never seen him like this before. 'Why? Why do you do it?' he shouted as the traffic continued to queue up behind them in the road. 'You're like a one-man crusade! It's not on.'

'Not on?'

'No, it's not on. Why are you doing it? The bosses won't support you when the complaint comes in – you're turning into a liability to work with.'

'Liability?' Jake sighed and shook his head. 'A young woman is *dead*, Lenny.'

'And why is she dead?'

'Because someone wants to cover up why they were getting her to shift documents from the SFO and spy on anti-arms campaigners.'

'So you've had me chasing after this Javed Saleem at one end of the investigation when you've known all along that it was Frank?' Lenny said through gritted teeth.

'Yes,' Jake conceded.

'Jesus,' said Lenny, rolling his eyes.

'Lenny, you know as well as I do that when you're working with protected intelligence, you can't just jump from one place to another – there has to be a chain of evidence that shows how we've connected up the dots; otherwise everyone will know that someone has been talking – that there was an informant or a secret source of information. And when they know that, there'll be a witch-hunt. Witch-hunts never end well.'

Lenny thumped the steering wheel again.

'They killed Jenny to stop her talking!'

'And she's not even the main source of the bloody intelligence…'

'I don't think they knew that. I didn't want this to happen, but it has, and now we've got to deal with it.' Jake sighed. 'It's gone too far to back out now – now she's dead. I can't just drop it and walk away. And Claire might be at risk too. We've got to carry on. We've got to do the right thing.'

Lenny looked across at him. He remained silent, though some of the anger had drained from his face.

The vehicles behind them continued to honk, and Lenny finally realised he was blocking the road. 'The right thing?' he asked, putting the car into gear and moving off.

'You know what I mean by the right thing.'

Lenny shook his head. 'Do I, Jake?'

They slowed down to wait in traffic again. The wind had changed direction and the hint of sunshine was gone; rain had started to beat heavily on the windscreen again. Jake could sense Lenny needed some convincing.

'Look, one of the very first jobs I ever ran as a new detective was on a couple of drug dealers,' he began. 'Both of them were operating the same patch but working independently of one another – a bloke and a woman. We had covert cameras to record what was going on. I stayed in the control room and directed things from there. The woman was easy to catch – she was dealing in the street. We had loads of footage of her selling drugs. You know where she stored her stash?'

'No, guv – but I've a feeling you're going to tell me,' Lenny played along, clearly unsure where all this was going.

'To avoid being caught with the drugs on her when stopped and frisked, she stored them right up inside her vagina. She just pulled out an individual wrap ready for when the punters wanted it. So we grabbed her off the street one day – dragged her down the hospital. We had to hold her down whilst the doctor forcibly removed eighteen plastic wraps of heroin from her snatch.'

Lenny made a face.

'The bloke was more difficult,' continued Jake. 'People would come to his house. They'd go inside, do the deal and leave. We arrested several people with drugs who had left his house. We believed he was dealing, but we needed to catch him with them on his person.

'There was some intelligence that said he went in a cab somewhere, picked up the drugs from his supplier, brought them home and then cut them up. So we waited. Waited until we saw him getting out of a cab…

'The plan was to target him when he arrived home; when we thought he had the most drugs on him.

'I saw the cab arriving one morning on our cameras. I called on the arrest car to deploy and jump on him. They got caught behind another car as they were coming down the street. Delayed them by about thirty seconds.

'The guy didn't go into his own house. He knocked on the old dear who lived next door to him instead. Door opened just as the arrest car screamed to a halt, and they missed him. He ran into her house and dumped all the drugs on the floor. Denied they were his. Said they belonged to the 68-year-old woman who lived there.

'No one from the arrest car saw him drop the drugs on the floor. The senior detective in charge of the whole job, an old timer, said to me and the team: "Someone *must have* seen him drop those drugs – you *must have done*, because if you *didn't*, he's gonna walk away from this!" No one spoke up or agreed to say that they had seen him drop them. They all wanted to do it by the book.

'When we searched the old dear's house, we found that he was using it to store lots of stuff – all his drugs, all his money. He was a sneaky bastard. Even if we'd done his address, we'd have found nothing, because it was all next door. But we couldn't prove it was his. He walked away scot-free from that. The old woman got two years because she admitted she knew the drugs were in her house.

'Three weeks later, after we'd seized all his drugs and all his money, he broke into another old woman's house and robbed her of her life savings. That old woman tried to stop him, and he beat her up so badly that she nearly died. She was in hospital for weeks. Never really recovered. Went to live with her son for the rest of her days. She was too scared to ever live on her own again.

'I decided that day – no criminal would ever be allowed to go on and hurt someone else because I wouldn't *do the right thing*, Lenny. No one was ever going to walk away from things like that drug dealer did. He ruined two old ladies' lives. I ruined two old ladies' lives because I wouldn't do the right thing…'

Jake paused as he thought about seeing that old woman in hospital, in her eighties, beaten black and blue and to within an inch of her life.

'The bad guys *have* to lose, Lenny – otherwise people get hurt. And people die. The bad guys don't follow the rules. All I want to do is mess with them, Lenny – mess with the ones that ruin lives. I don't do this stuff for me. It's the right thing to do.'

Lenny didn't answer. He didn't need to. The traffic began to move again, and he just drove, eyes ahead. The agreement was unspoken.

54

Jake and Lenny made their way to the reception desk. The rest of the team stood by the lifts, waiting on the nod to go upstairs.

The exterior of the concrete-framed hotel reminded Jake of a nasty tower block on a sixties' council estate. The place had been the target of two IRA bomb attacks. The first back in 1975, killing two people, and the second, in 1992, destroying the toilets on the ground floor – thankfully with no fatalities. It made Jake wonder whether bad people were attracted to places with an unfortunate past.

The hotel's interior was far more impressive than the outside. An opulent rug, patterned with huge sunbeams, partially covered the lobby's expensive marble floor tiles. On top of it, a table held orchids in an oversized vase. Beyond the orchids, a semi-circular wooden desk nestled between two large pillars.

A petite, auburn-haired girl tapped away at the computer with exquisite precision. She looked up from the desk as Jake approached. A badge, pinned into a spot right next to her cleavage on an impeccably ironed, white blouse, stated 'Lucy, Head Receptionist'.

Jake pulled out his warrant card. 'Hello, Lucy, I'm a police officer. Can I speak to the duty manager please?'

'Ooh, hang on a moment.' She picked up the phone, punched in some numbers and then spoke very animatedly to someone.

'He's on his way.'

'Thank you, Lucy.'

'What's happened? Are you here about the man in room 1019?'

Lenny raised his eyebrows and Jake chuckled. 'No, although I'm sure that would be much more fun than what we're doing.'

Lucy's smile faded. 'Oh… well there was a big to-do here last night. Someone smashed up one of our rooms.'

'I don't think you'd get people like me here for that. I'm a detective.

'No.' She giggled. 'We'd get one of those policeman in uniform normally.'

Lucy's accent was northern – Mancunian, thought Jake.

He smiled. 'You worked here long, Lucy?'

'Five years now. Money's rubbish, but I get lots of perks *and* I get to meet lots of very nice people like yourself…' She smiled warmly at Jake, flirting now.

Her smile cooled abruptly as a gentleman in a smart blue suit and red tie walked across the foyer. 'That's the manager, walking toward you there.' Lucy nodded slightly in the man's direction.

'Thanks, Lucy.'

Jake turned to greet the man, who extended his hand for Jake to shake.

'Good afternoon. Graham Prendergast – General Manager. You're the gentleman from Scotland Yard? How can I help?'

'DI Jake Flannagan. I'm from the Counter Terrorism Command. We have a search warrant for room 614 – nothing to worry about as such. I was hoping you'd open the door for us rather than us having to force it open?'

'Yes, of course. We don't want the door damaged… Could I see your identification please?' asked the manager, extracting his master key card from an inside pocket.

'Yes, my detective sergeant here' – Jake pointed him toward Lenny – 'will show you everything you need to see, Mr Prendergast. We really appreciate your help in this matter,' he said, ushering them both toward the lifts.

Lenny looked at Jake oddly – a question.

'I'll wait down here Lenny,' said Jake, winking at him. 'You go and see what's going on up there.'

Lenny shook his head and headed for the lifts.

Jake returned to the main lobby desk and Lucy's considerable charms.

'Lucy, whilst they're busy up there, I wonder if you could help me with something?' he asked with his biggest and brightest smile.

55

'You not going upstairs with your friends?' Lucy asked with a coy smile.

'No, I thought I'd stay here with you. I wanted to ask you something...' Jake moved to stand squarely in front of her at the desk and leaned in closely.

'Ooooh, I hope it's not rude. My boyfriend wouldn't like that, Mr Police Officer,' she replied with a giggle.

Jake lowered his voice and put his lips to her ear. 'We wouldn't have to tell though, would we, Lucy?'

'No, that's very true!' she replied, her cheeks flushing a rosy pink.

Jake put his hand out to greet her properly, hoping physical contact would strengthen the emotional connection between them. 'My name's Jake – good to meet you,' he said, shaking her hand and holding it slightly longer than necessary.

'Good to meet you, Jake.'

'You too, Lucy.'

'So what is it that you were going to ask me, Jake?'

'There were a couple of things actually. The first was about the man staying in room 614. We're about to search the room and arrest him. I could do with knowing some of the information you hold on your computer. Forwarding address and anything else you can give me...'

'And there I was thinking you were going to ask me out or something!'

Jake laughed. 'You said you had a boyfriend!'

'I did say that. It doesn't stop you asking though, does it? All us girls like to know that we still have it,' she said, winking, before she started tapping at the keyboard. 'So let's see what we've got here for you then…'

Jake leaned over the desk, craning his neck round to see if he could get a glimpse of what was on her screen. He nudged into her, and she giggled again, blushed even deeper than before.

'Room 614…' Lucy said, staring at the monitor in an attempt to concentrate. 'Mr Javed Saleem. Gives his home address as some place in Ilford. There's no telephone number… room paid for with a credit card… Hang on, let me just have a look at that. I used to work in bookings, so I'm pretty handy on that system.'

'You do seem to know your stuff,' replied Jake, nodding in agreement as she touch-typed.

'Oh, all my favourite guests say that,' she said, laughing. 'Now let me see. The room was booked by phone in advance – five weeks ago. We've got a record of the number they called from. Dialling code starts 01594. Oh, he's a member of our gym club – there's a photo of him here. And he had Thai green curry on room service last night. That any help to you, Mr Police Officer?'

'All sounds very interesting, Lucy, especially the Thai green curry part. Can you print all that off for me please?' Jake peered at the photo on her screen.

'Of course,' said Lucy as she filled the paper tray with one hand whilst clicking print with the other.

'What's he done, this bloke?' she asked, handing the printed sheets to Jake.

'We're not sure yet. He—' Jake paused mid-sentence as a commotion erupted from the other side of the foyer.

'*STOP!*'

He turned around to see Lenny by the lifts running after a man wearing jeans and a bright yellow T-shirt. It took a moment for Jake to register what he was seeing. Lenny's nose was bleeding and he was chasing the man from the gym-membership photo. It was Javed Saleem.

'Shit!' Jake sighed. Losing a prisoner *after* an arrest was a big problem. It was a disciplinary matter. Not that it ever happened. There was always a cover-up story concocted that made it clear the suspect *hadn't* been arrested before he legged it.

Jake wasn't in the mood for a foot race, but he knew Lenny wasn't going to catch a younger, fitter man who thought he was running for his freedom. Where were the rest of the team?

Lenny and Saleem were out of the main door before Jake could even get into his stride. He knew he'd have to follow.

'Fuck it!'

Running out into the road, he was temporarily dazzled by the sunlight that had broken through the clouds. Squinting, he could see Saleem already some way up Old Park Lane at the back of the Intercontinental hotel.

Jake pushed off as hard as he could, building his speed with each step and concentrating only on his breathing, just like he used to in his running days. Focus. Block everything else out. The only sounds he could hear were the beating of his heart and the pound-pound-pound of his feet on the pavement.

He quickly gained on Lenny, who was slowing down and starting to give up on the chase.

'Call the office!' screamed Jake as he ran past him.

Old Park Lane led down a hill and joined directly on to Piccadilly, just a few hundred yards to the east of Hyde Park Corner.

Where was he running to? Where could he go?

Jake could see Saleem's yellow T-shirt about twenty yards in front now. The man hadn't looked back once. Jake turned to glance quickly over his shoulder. Lenny was on his mobile. There was no one else chasing. It was Jake versus Saleem.

Saleem reached the end of Old Park Lane and paused for the first time to look back at Jake pelting toward him in his suit and tie – and behind him, Lenny on the phone with his bloody nose.

Jake could see him wondering, thinking for a moment. Then it seemed to click. Jake saw his eyes. That recognition.

He'd put two and two together and realised that Jake was a police officer.

But in those few short moments, Jake had gained fifteen yards on him, and the panic was visible on Saleem's face. He turned and headed straight for the railings at the edge of the road.

Jake knew why the railings were there. He knew exactly what stretched out beneath them.

But it was too late.

Saleem jumped.

56

Congestion had always been a problem at this junction, which was why, in the sixties, the area had been remodelled and an underpass built to ease the flow of traffic.

An underpass into which Saleem had just jumped.

How high was it? Maybe a twenty-foot drop?

Jake heard the screeching of tyres, skidding, then a loud bang – a thud – the twisting of metal.

There were two lanes going in either direction beneath the railings at the end of Old Park Lane – a dual carriageway underneath Hyde Park Corner roundabout that had served as a racing track for the mods back in the sixties.

More squealing of tyres. Another loud bang. The breaking of glass; the shattering of plastic.

Jake kept running until he hit the barrier himself.

He looked over.

He could see a white van, its front end embedded into the concrete wall of the underpass.

The windscreen had a large break in it, a dent – from the inside out. The driver hadn't been wearing a seat belt. Jake could see steam rising from the crumpled front end. A red car was rammed into the back of it, its driver sitting motionless.

Saleem was alive and limping into the underpass, against the oncoming traffic, which was slowing down because of the accident.

Jake looked around him. It was too far to jump – way too high. Toward him came a courier on a battered Yamaha Thundercat. Jake stepped into the road and put his hands up to flag down the driver. The bike stopped.

Jake pulled out his warrant card. 'Police. Off. I need your bike now!'

Saleem was going to get himself killed or cause another accident in the underpass if he didn't act fast. Jake practically elbowed the begrudging courier off the vehicle before jumping on and kicking it into gear. 'Wait here,' he said. 'I'll bring her back – don't go anywhere.' And he revved the engine before pulling away.

He headed down the slip road and then did a U-turn into the underpass, against the flow of oncoming traffic and back toward where he had seen Saleem.

Twisting the throttle hard, he accelerated past the accident and up the middle of the two lanes of now-stationary traffic. Saleem was limping ahead of him, his yellow T-shirt like a beacon among a sea of vehicles.

Jake closed on him quickly. Saleem was clearly exhausted. As Jake moved up behind him, he extended his leg and, sole first, shunted Saleem square in the buttocks as he rode past him. Saleem went flying, banging his head on a car bonnet. Jake pulled alongside him and kicked him again, causing him to fall to the ground.

Jake stopped, placed the bike on its stand and went over to where Saleem lay on the ground, panting.

All the adrenalin pumping through Jake's body caused him to erupt. 'You're nicked! What the fuck is wrong with you? You fucking stupid idiot! Look at the carnage you've caused! You could have killed yourself and others – and if I find out that my DS's bloody nose was caused by you, I'll give you a proper hiding!'

Saleem just stared up at him, dazed, saying nothing.

Jake looked down at Saleem's leg. It was an odd shape, probably broken, and Jake started to regret his tirade. It was unsuitable conduct for an officer of the law, and verbally attacking someone who was obviously injured wouldn't look good to those people sitting in their cars – whatever they thought the chase was about.

As Jake grabbed his mobile to call for an ambulance, it rang. It was Claire.

He answered. 'Hi, I can't—'

'It was great to see you the other day,' she said, cutting him off. 'I was wondering if we might get dinner together?'

'I can't discuss this right now – I'm in the middle of something.'

'Tomorrow?' she asked.

'Claire…'

'Don't say it,' she interjected. 'I can tell by the tone of your voice what you're going to say. You're busy then too. And then it's going to lead into "maybe we should cool off a bit", isn't it?'

'Claire!'

'Fuck you, Jake.'

'Claire!' He was shouting at her now. 'I need to make a—'

'No, fuck you, Jake fucking Flannagan,' she said, getting more frenzied. 'None of that stuff I went through when I was a teenager was about you. But you *always* make it *all* about you. I expected you to understand. Not blame me for my mistakes as a fifteen-year-old. I'll sort this out myself. Thanks for fucking nothing,' she screamed.

The noise on the other end of the line sounded like she'd was slamming the handset down several times on something hard before it went dead.

57

The three of them took their seats in Helen's office – Jake and Lenny on the sofa and Helen opposite them, looking as elegant as always. She was wearing a dove-grey trouser suit, her black hair secured in a neat coil at the nape of her neck.

'Good afternoon to you both. Sorry I've not seen either of you for a while – I've been very busy on Seagram,' said Helen.

'How's that going? I've not heard the latest from anyone,' replied Jake.

'It's tough going. You'll have seen Sudeep Murthy died from his burns…'

'Did you ever get to talk to him?' asked Jake.

Helen sighed and shook her head. 'No. The whole thing is turning into a bit of a nightmare.'

'Oh, why?'

'Mark's relationship with the commander is causing me some problems. He's going over my head in order to get decisions directly from those higher up, which totally circumvents any instructions I've been giving him. It's incredibly frustrating. I suspect this might not be happening if I were a man.'

'For what it's worth, I think it has less to do with you being a woman and more to do with him being on a little power trip, trying to show everyone that he's top of the tree because of his friendship with the commander,' said Jake.

'Whatever it is, it's causing trouble for the investigation. We aren't going to get very far with anything right now. We have

241

just the one suspect left alive, and one or two others who might have had some prior knowledge but aren't talking.'

Jake shrugged and pulled a face. 'If that's what this commander wants, then that's what he wants, guv.'

'He's all about being in a place to absorb the next investigation when it happens – he's not interested in digging too far under the surface. "Get it done – move on to the next one."'

'But there will always be a next one unless we get to those at the top. It's no good just sweeping up the leaves. If you don't want leaves, you have to cut down the trees.'

'You're preaching to the converted,' replied Helen, before opening her folder. 'I need an update from you about the two jobs you currently still have on the go. Let's start with the dead spy. We've not spoken about that for a while.'

'Yes. The inquest date has been set. We've taken the job from the guys who were dealing with it at borough level.'

'Oh? Why?'

'There are a couple of things that bothered me about their initial investigation. Having said that, we've turned up very little since. Lenny has worked hard and done all the usual legwork. There's no CCTV, no witnesses, no forensic evidence and the body was released to the family before we were able to ask for any form of special post-mortem on it. Toxicology on the body shows traces of antidepressants, no alcohol or drugs…'

'So there's nothing?

'Nothing that we've found so far – though there is a possible motive for wanting him dead.'

Helen learned forward in her chair. 'Go on.'

'His memoirs. A few people have talked about them to Lenny. But no one has seen them, and no one knows what's in them. There are claims that he was going to write a book. I'm thinking maybe someone wanted something kept secret.'

'Or he did just jump after having a bad day?' asked Helen.

'We've been trying to establish what his state of mind was – glean what he was doing the day of his death, look at his call history. Suicide looks unlikely as there's no note. He was due to fly to the US – his bags were packed and waiting in the hall. And his wife says he also had an upcoming holiday booked with her and their five grandchildren.'

'I see what you mean,' she said.

'There *were* signs of stress though. On the day of his death, he'd refused to attend a board meeting at one of his companies due to a dispute with another director. In the weeks that led up to his death, his nearest and dearest had mentioned that he'd become increasingly paranoid about the idea of someone trying to harm him. There had also been a meeting on the morning of his death with someone at a hotel.'

'Have you been able to identify that person?'

'No – despite the extensive work we've done on his mobile phone.'

'So where does that leave you?'

'If I'm honest, we've got nothing. There's no evidence of anything at the moment. Almost like it was a spontaneous decision to kill himself. But that thinking then brings me back to where I was with the memoirs. Was someone putting him under pressure about a secret he was going to reveal, and threatening him, so he jumped?'

'Anything either of the intelligence services can tell us?' asked Helen, making notes.

'I'm meeting with someone at the SIS to see what they have – if they're willing to tell us.'

'Good. The SFO enquiry and the dead prostitute – what's happening with that? I hear you made an arrest?'

'Yes. We managed to identify the burglary suspect and tracked him to a hotel.'

'Yes. I heard about the chase into the underpass and Javed Saleem's broken leg.'

'How did you hear that?' asked Jake.

'Jake, you must know that people are keeping an eye on you, just waiting for you to mess up. They're looking for ammunition. Make sure you keep me updated.'

'Yes, ma'am. The suspect is in hospital. We're waiting to interview him, just as soon as he's discharged. We've conducted a home-address search. Some computer media has been taken. There's nothing really of note at his home. The post-mortem on the dead girl, Jenny, shows that she drowned – lungs full of water.'

'How did you identify this suspect, Jake? You've not explained that. Was he named on the crime report following her burglary?'

'Sort of. It's a long and boring story – you don't want to sit through it…' Jake glanced at Lenny, looking for some support, but he shifted his gaze to the floor and said nothing.

'Good. Just play by the rules, Jake, please.' She sighed. 'On another note – have you been submitting your expenses correctly on your Amex?'

Police officers in specialist operations were provided with credit cards to pay for incidental expenditure. The Met had used American Express for years. They looked like standard credit cards and had the officer's personal name on them but came with no limit. All the bills went to the bosses, who could never be bothered to check them. Everything was always signed off and paid in full without question.

'I was suspended and then stuck in the office, so my card hasn't been used in the last eighteen months – except on my visit to Glasgow recently. Why do you ask?'

'There's an audit underway. Up until now, no one has been looking at what expenditure has been going through. Apparently there are some outrageous transactions on there. I've not been given any names yet, but I'm told that there are four officers on the command that are going to get arrested for theft and fraud.'

'And you thought I might be one?' said Jake, laughing.

'No – I didn't think that. I'm just forewarning you that there's an audit going on – but it's not personal. Everyone's card is being looked at, including mine.'

'Thanks for letting me know.'

'It's going to cause a few problems. I just hope the four that are getting collared aren't anyone we've had anything to do with. Idiots…' Helen shook her head.

Lenny and Jake said their goodbyes and left the office.

On the way up the corridor, Lenny turned to Jake. 'I meant to give you a heads-up about this, guv – I heard it was going to happen.'

'Did you? How?'

'I've got a mate who works up at the MPA. Apparently there are some people who've bought all sorts of crazy stuff on their work credit cards...'

The Metropolitan Police Authority had been set up in 2000 with the aim of making the police democratically accountable. Their role was intended to be a strategic one, and while they didn't get involved in the day-to-day delivery of policing, they *did* get involved with the finance side of things.

'What did they buy?' asked Jake, curious.

'You'd never believe it if I told you,' replied Lenny, smirking.

'Go on – try me.'

'Well, amongst other things... sex toys and breast implants was what I heard!' Lenny guffawed.

'What!'

'Yeah. Crazy. Who'd be that stupid? It was the cash withdrawals that brought it all to light apparently.'

'Cash?'

'Thousands and thousands withdrawn over the counter – that's why they started looking at the card usage for everyone.'

'I didn't even know you could do that with those cards.'

'I didn't either, but...'

'Bonson,' said Jake firmly.

'Sorry?'

'That day in the car – when we went to the FEL about the car bombs. You remember? Gavin Bonson dropped his wallet on the back seat. It was stuffed full of cash and withdrawal slips.'

'Bonson never struck me as the thieving type. Smarmy, but not a thief,' said Lenny, shaking his head.

'Can you find out from your mate if he's one of the people being looked at?'

'I suppose so, but what does it matter?'

Jake wondered if he were putting two and two together and making five. Sometimes you could focus so much on a case, you'd miss obvious things going on around you in the workplace. Bonson's reaction that day had been strange. Was Mark involved? Was that why he was being so difficult toward Jake? Perhaps he was overthinking things.

'I just need to know.' Jake put his hand on Lenny's arm and squeezed slightly. 'Please?'

'Yeah, OK, I'll ask him. I'll ring him at home tonight. He'll be at work today. I can't ask him while he's there.'

58

The café in the east wing of the building served good coffee. Metal, folding bistro tables and chairs were set outside in the magnificent Georgian courtyard of Somerset House. The place was an oasis among the hustle and bustle of the north bank of the Thames, but sitting there, Jake was sweating for two crucial reasons.

Firstly, the courtyard was an elevated suntrap, the mix of limestone and granite magnifying the heat of the morning rays. Only the foolhardy spent any amount of time there on a hot August day without applying sun cream – as Jake was fast realising.

Secondly, he'd sent Lenny to get an update on the inquest into the spy's death and was anxiously awaiting news. He wanted to be sure that the coroner hadn't turned up anything important during routine enquiries with the family. He needed to clear this off his desk. It was no good having things left unfinished, especially if he was going to try to prove that Jenny had been murdered – which wasn't going to be easy.

A baritone voice with gliding vowels broke into his thoughts. 'You must be Mr Flannagan?'

Jake looked up from his latte to see a tall, slender man in chinos and a freshly pressed, red-and-yellow chequered shirt. He looked to be in his early fifties and had a mane of white hair that was parted to one side. He reminded Jake of a mature model in a catalogue aimed at the moneyed cruise market – tanned, well groomed and well travelled.

247

'Sebastian Williams?' asked Jake, standing to greet the MI6 contact he hoped might be able to help fill in the gaps on the dead spy.

'That's me.'

They shook hands. Jake noticed he had a slight limp as he manoeuvred himself into his seat.

'Thanks for agreeing to meet.'

'You're welcome. Strange venue for it,' he said.

'Neutral surroundings. Not my place of work, not yours. Neither of us have to worry about who's listening – and the coffee is good. Can I get you one?'

'Please. Skinny flat white for me. The gammy leg would thank me for losing a few extra pounds,' said Williams, patting his stomach.

'I noticed you had a bit of trouble with it when you sat down,' said Jake, nodding toward Williams's left side.

'Yeah, long story. All in the line of duty. It doesn't stop me doing too much – although outrunning the bad guys is pretty tough these days.' Williams gave him a wink followed by an intriguing smile.

Jake went off to get the fancy-sounding drink and found to his amusement that it was just a bog-standard coffee with milk.

'Where did you get my contact details from?' Williams asked him, as Jake returned to the sunshine of the courtyard and passed him his drink.

'Thames House suggested that you were the right man to speak to about our enquiries surrounding Adham Marmora – the spy found dead outside his flat.'

'Ah, I see. And why me?'

'It was suggested that you might have met him a few times and that you might have some intelligence you could share.'

'Was it?'

'It was.' Being subtle clearly wasn't working here, and Jake was in no mood for playing games. 'Look, I'm told you're an agent runner for the SIS. You recruit sources, try to get them to work for you and they provide you with information.'

It struck Jake how different the two intelligence services were. The British Security Service at Thames House, known as MI5, seemed to be made up mainly of fresh-faced graduates. But when Jake looked at MI6, over the river at Vauxhall Cross, he saw a different story. The people that Jake met there all tended to be older and more worldly-wise. All seasoned operators who'd dealt in foreign intelligence. Just like Williams, with his tanned skin, faded cover-boy looks and mysterious limp.

Williams sipped his coffee, deep in thought, before replying.

'If I answer positively here – if I agree that is or was my role, and that I knew Marmora – well then I would be in breach of my oath of confidentiality.' Williams smiled at him and sipped his coffee again. 'And I can't do that.'

'Look, I need your help. The man is dead – you can't breach his confidentiality. If he were sitting here with us, I'm sure he would implore you to help me,' said Jake, frustrated now.

'Perhaps he would…'

'I'm just trying to uncover how he came to find his way off the balcony. If he was thrown off, or if he jumped. And if he did jump, why he might have done so.'

'You were right about the coffee. I see why you chose this place,' said Williams, putting his cup down on the table. 'Let's just say I can't answer your question about my role and why I knew Marmora. I do, however, know a little bit about him. So if you have specific questions, I might be able to answer a couple.'

In a roundabout way, Williams seemed to be telling him that he had at least tried to recruit Marmora, though it seemed highly likely to Jake that Marmora had worked as an MI6 source.

'Maybe you could give me some background on him?' he asked.

'Well he'd certainly led an interesting life in his sixty or so years on this earth. In his youth, he dated the President of Egypt's daughter. The President suspected that Marmora's main interest in his daughter was due to her status, not his love for her, but eventually allowed Marmora to marry her anyway.'

'That sounds like it might have been a difficult relationship – with the President, I mean?'

'Yes. Marmora and his new wife moved to London, in the late sixties,' Williams continued, 'but there was conflict about them being here. Her father wasn't happy about it – or their lavish lifestyle. He ordered the couple back to Cairo. It was around this time that Marmora *allegedly* walked into the Israeli embassy, here in London, and began telling them that he wanted to be a spy, perhaps as some form of vengeance for the President curtailing whatever activity was funding his lavish lifestyle.'

'And what was funding their lifestyle?'

'The sale of weapons,' said Williams, frowning.

'Marmora sold weapons as well as spying?' exclaimed Jake. 'You didn't know this?'

Jake shook his head. 'No.'

'Marmora made billions in the arms industry. He sold weapons to terror groups such as the Palestine Liberation Organization and the likes of Gaddafi for many years. Even when he was ordered back to Egypt, he carried on selling weapons.'

'So he was an Egyptian citizen who was married to the Egyptian president's daughter and was spying for Israel?' asked Jake, confused.

'Yes,' replied Williams.

'But the PLO and Gaddafi were arch enemies of Israel, and he was selling them weapons – to attack Israel and Israeli targets?'

'He was. And at the same time as he was selling arms, he was gleaning as much information about the activities of the terror groups he was selling to as he could. Then he'd feed that information back to the Israelis. He made himself a lot of money because he was paid for both activities.'

'Did the Israelis know that he was doing that?'

'I don't know for certain, but I'd be surprised if they didn't.'

'So he might have been tasked to do that for them?'

'Yes, that's possible, though I think it started off as a free-lance job for him in the early days.'

'And he became a billionaire off the back of it?' Jake mused.

Williams smiled. 'Yes. There was money to be made from the Israelis by providing them with intelligence about their enemies. But the really big money was to be made by brokering the weapons deals to the very same enemies he was informing about.'

'Was his decision to work for the Israelis simply based on money?'

'I don't think it was *just* money, but it played a big part. Marmora's decision-making always hinged on what was in it for him.'

'Just like his marriage?'

'In a way, yes.' Williams sipped his coffee and paused for a moment before continuing. 'So the Israelis had someone at the absolute heart of the Egyptian government – and paid Marmora handsomely for it. He was the most unlikely spy – the President's own emissary. There was nothing that didn't pass over his desk. Spies didn't come better placed than Marmora.'

'Is that why they called him a double agent? Was he actually working against the Israelis, whilst feeding it all back to the Egyptians too?' asked Jake.

'There are those that want the world to believe that Marmora was a double agent or worse – it suits the picture they want to paint, but that's not what I believe.'

'No?'

'No. Marmora was a spy, but he wasn't a double agent. The whole exposure of Marmora as a spy, as a *double agent*, was carefully crafted, done by people who have a vested interest in portraying him in a certain light—'

'I'm confused.' Jake frowned. 'The newspapers were awash with him being a double agent?'

'Him being a double agent, even him being a spy, came from the same sources. Those people want Marmora to look like a double agent...'

'Why?'

'Have you ever heard mention of the Yom Kippur War? Some of the intelligence that Marmora gave about that impending event was ignored, shortly before Egypt went to war with Israel. Careers were ruined when it was found that he shouldn't have been ignored. By calling him a double agent, it leaves the door open for them to have been at least partially right to have treated what he was saying with caution.'

'But none of this would have had any influence on his death, would it? He was exposed as a spy some years back?'

'Well there's been a lot going on in Israel recently – court cases asking who named Marmora as a spy, when it was illegal to do so. There have been people trying to clear their names, people trying to erase what's written in the history books, to *reword* what's written, so that their own career failings aren't recognised. If it could all be blamed on Marmora and his spying, lots of people stood to clear their names.'

'But would they have benefitted from Marmora's death?'

'I don't know the answer to that. Marmora's deepest, darkest secrets were about to be revealed to the world – either in his own words in his memoirs, or by forces hostile to him. But dead men can't talk. And they certainly can't defend themselves. You can say anything you like about a dead man.'

'Sounds rather extreme, killing someone so that you can rewrite the history books.'

'You're assuming that someone killed him?' Williams frowned as he sipped his coffee.

'Rhetorical question – what do you think?'

'Perhaps he had been painted into a corner, so to speak…' He sounded hesitant.

'Why would someone do that?'

'Because they want a reaction,' continued Williams. 'A reaction from the Libyans, or a reaction from Marmora. They didn't care which, as long as they got a reaction that produced something they could use against a spy to expose the past. Gaddafi is one of the most unstable leaders in the world – deeply entrenched in terrorist activity and funding all sorts of disparate groups – but to him, the Egyptian president had always been a hero – so why kill his son-in-law? But Gaddafi was also prone to overreaction, and well known for assassinations.'

'So paint our spy into a corner – take away all his choices – the only way out is to ruin the freshly painted floor where the exit is, and that's going to look bad for him?'

Williams smiled and nodded. 'You've got the picture. Maybe Marmora had no choices left? He had to go public, to try to put the record straight. And perhaps writing it all into some memoirs, exposing the whole truth, was his only option.'

'But that might not have been what certain people wanted?' asked Jake, though the question was more to himself than to Williams.

He could see the predicament that Marmora might have found himself in, that morning on his balcony, with the feeling of nowhere to run and having no control over what the future held – a catch-22.

'I hear the dead spy's memoirs are missing?' Williams moved on, ignoring Jake's question.

'You've heard that too?'

Williams nodded. 'Yes.'

'No one has actually seen them,' replied Jake. 'We don't even know if they actually existed. But his family says that a draft manuscript disappeared from his bookshelf – a manuscript that threatened to expose secrets of the Middle East's intelligence agencies. That might have upset some people.'

'Possibly. We all trade on our reputations, Mr Flannagan. If our reputations are in tatters, we are worthless.'

Jake's thoughts drifted to Claire. It was almost like Williams could have been talking about her and not Marmora.

'What do you mean?'

'At one point in his career, Marmora was even in charge of supervising the collective development of the Arab defence industry. He was prolific in the weapons-sales business. Perhaps that's where you need to look for the answer to this, Mr Flannagan?'

'Do you think he was murdered?'

'That's your job – that's what you need to decide. I don't honestly know. What I do know is this – we all have secrets we say we'll never tell. And if you're on the verge of telling them, there will be those that will want you to stay silent.'

'Would people in the arms industry have wanted to kill him?' Jake thought of Jenny – how she had effectively become a spy, infiltrating different organisations on behalf of those connected to the arms industry – and how her death was now being made to look like suicide by someone.

'You may want to look into a group known as the Savoy Mafia. There may be some answers for you there. Listen, I've got to get back' he said, getting up from the table. 'I wish you luck in your quest, detective.'

Williams shook Jake's hand and smiled warmly at him.

'Good to meet you,' said Jake as they parted.

As he watched Williams limp his way across the cobbles and out of the sunlit square, Jake thought about how Marmora might have been working for MI6 too. London seemed an odd place to come to if he'd been working *just* for the Israelis. Who else had he been selling information about or to?

Jake called Lenny.

'Hey.'

'What did the coroner say?' he asked, eyeing Williams's empty cup on the table.

'He's ready to set the inquest date. They've got no more information. I told them that we hadn't either.'

'Are you still there? At the coroner's office?'

'Yes.'

'Could you ask them if they'd be happy to delay the inquest if I had something new?'

'*Have* you got something new? Where've you been all morning? I thought it was odd you didn't come with me.'

'Just ask him,' said Jake.

There was chatter in the background as Lenny spoke with the coroner's team. Jake couldn't make out exactly what was being said.

'I think he's happy to, if you've got some new leads to work on. What have you got?' said Lenny, coming back on the line.

'I think it's possible that Marmora's death is in some way connected to Jenny's.'

'What? How?' Lenny sounded incredulous. 'Where has this come from?'

'I will explain all. Ask him to push back the inquest. And then can you come and pick me up from the Strand please, mate?' asked Jake. 'I think there's more to all this than meets the eye.'

59

Charing Cross was one of the busiest police stations in London and had more prisoner cells than any other in Europe. On any given lunchtime there, it seemed to Jake like the entire station was clamouring to be fed at once, the canteen always packed out and noisy.

Back in 1834, the building had housed Charing Cross Hospital and despite the clamour in the canteen, it still had the same feel of a Victorian infirmary, with wide open corridors designed to make it easy to manoeuvre beds and wheelchairs around, and large windows to let in the light.

Lenny and Jake had arrested Saleem upon his discharge from hospital. The irony that they'd then transferred him here, to a former hospital building, wasn't lost on Jake.

'You going to give the brief any disclosure?' asked Lenny as he stuffed a fork load of sausage and hash brown into his mouth. He was referring to Saleem's solicitor, who was currently downstairs with her client in a private consultation.

'About the original burglary?' Where Jenny had been threatened, her underwear stolen. 'Yeah, why not? We want a productive interview if we can get one,' replied Jake.

'And the clothing we took from his house?' They'd seized all the clothing Saleem possessed to see if they could find a match for the dark-coloured fibres they'd lifted from Jenny's bed. Various computer storage devices and phones had also been seized from his home, together with a Range Rover.

'I just intend on asking if they are his clothes, but if the brief is any good, they'll stop him from answering. I certainly won't be disclosing why we've taken the clothing – or that Jenny is dead.'

'You're not even going to ask him about Jenny's death?'

'Not yet. We've got no evidence of anything except the burglary right now, have we? If we turn up something from his phones, computers or his clothes, then we'll ask him, but we've got zilch to put to him just yet.'

'The missing documents, the weapons sales... are we asking him about them?'

'Of course – that's all part of the burglary, isn't it? We're going to say that the burglary was done to put pressure on Jenny, to make her continue working for them.'

'Are you going to ask him about Frank?'

'Yes, it's a legitimate question. Jenny mentioned the name to us. It's evidence – we can ask him.'

'OK. Do you want me to do the interview with you?'

'No, I'll do it. I want you to go and get his Range Rover from the Technical Support Unit. They plumbed it for audio and video and put a tracking device on while he was in hospital getting his broken leg fixed up. I want you to give the vehicle back to him after we've finished the interview.'

Saleem's legal representative was a slim black woman with a slight Caribbean lilt to her voice who went by the name of Alva Lyle. Her business card identified her as a barrister based at the Temple in London. Jake could count on one hand the number of times a barrister had attended a local police station to be present for one of his police interviews. And in those incidences, every single suspect had been deeply involved in organised crime.

She wore a sharply tailored designer suit and carried a leather Mulberry bag in the same shade as her lipstick. The bag looked to Jake as if it had cost more than he earned in a month – and here she was, representing Saleem in an interview about a small residential burglary.

The expensive-looking woman had listened to the reasons Jake had given for Saleem's arrest then spent another two hours in private consultation with her client.

As Jake waited patiently for her to reappear, curiosity got the better of him. Why was she taking so long? He could bear it no longer and grabbed the opportunity to Google her name.

His hopes of a productive interview were all but dashed when he realised which chambers Alva Lyle came from. She'd been involved in putting a lid on the SFO investigation into the British–Saudi arms deal.

Things weren't looking fruitful.

It was gone 5 p.m. before Alva finally emerged from the meeting and said she was ready to proceed with the police interview. She beckoned Jake in with one finger, and he watched her suspiciously as they took their seats. She made little eye contact as she concentrated on making notes with an elegant Montblanc pen, Saleem sitting alongside her, a defiant look on his face.

As Jake finished the police caution, she spoke without prompting, 'I have advised my client to answer "no comment" to all of your questions. I see from the custody record that you have taken a large amount of clothing from his house *and* a car. You have not disclosed to me why you have done that – I cannot properly legally advise him, at this stage, without understanding what that is about,' she said, her voice calm.

'I have advised you that he is here to answer questions about a burglary. I've outlined the case against him to you. I believe that I've given you sufficient information to advise him in return. I will continue to ask questions,' replied Jake.

'Like I said…' She looked up from her notes and into Jake's eyes for what seemed like the very first time, 'I've advised him to answer no comment. You understand that, don't you, Mr Saleem?' She looked across at Saleem, who then nodded and smiled at Jake, tilting his head mockingly to one side.

'Your chambers represent some of our country's most successful arms companies, don't they, Ms Lyle?' asked Jake, trying to mess up their carefully pre-planned interview responses.

'Mr Saleem is the one being interviewed here, Inspector, not me. Your questions should be directed at him.' She forced a smile.

'I know. But this interview is about a burglary, a burglary that might have been perpetrated on behalf of one of your other clients, Ms Lyle. That's the allegation we have here. My research indicates that your chambers have represented British Aerospace in their recent discussions with the Serious Fraud Office, which means that you might have a conflict of interest in this case, does it not?'

She put down her pen. Jake could see annoyance flicker over her face. He'd succeeded.

'Inspector, it is for me to decide if there is a conflict of interest – not you. I do not know of one. I will continue to represent Mr Saleem.'

'You know best,' said Jake sarcastically.

'Well, *ain't* that the truth?' she replied, mocking Jake's south London accent.

Jake laughed at her. Saleem was looking at them both, bemused.

'Are you going to get on with the interview, Inspector? My client has been in custody a considerable time already...'

'We've waited several hours for you to turn up, Ms Lyle, then another two as you undertook a private consultation with your client. And now you're complaining that your client has been in custody too long? Give me a break!' Jake fired back at her.

The stench of arms-industry money was everywhere he looked, and Alva Lyle was beginning to push his buttons. Her, Saleem, Jenny – was there anything that the weapons companies couldn't buy?

Reluctantly he began the machinations of the interview, knowing it was going to be a waste of all of their time.

60

Jake was running late – he'd overslept. Awake until the early hours, he'd been trying to work out where he was going to get the evidence to prove Saleem guilty of Jenny's murder. Jake was loath to ignore his hunches, and his intuition was telling him the whole thing was linked to Marmora's death in some way, yet he had very little to go on.

He slammed the door to the flat and made his way down the stairs, fishing in his jacket pocket for the keys to his Saab.

The car was parked by the sari-shop window. As Jake reached for the driver's door handle, there was a tap on his shoulder and he jumped a mile. When he turned round, he found a diminutive figure in a pale-blue tunic and leggings standing behind him – the sari-shop-owner's daughter. A pair of Hoxton-cool, white-framed sunglasses held back a thick mane of freshly washed hair from her face.

'Don't do that to me!' said Jake as he came back down to earth.

'Hi, Jake. Sorry. I didn't mean to scare you. I need you to come and look at something,' she said, tugging him away from the car and toward the main entrance of the sari shop.

'I've not seen you for ages,' he replied as he followed her into the store, past rolls of shimmering orange and pink fabric, piled high against the wall, past the glass counter and out into the rear storeroom.

'I've been away in India with my parents at a big family wedding,' she replied. 'We just got back. We've had friends looking after the place for us...

'Stand there a second,' she ordered as she switched on the lights.

He did as he was told, wondering what on earth to expect.

'Our friends, they thought those were ours,' she said, pointing to a pile of pillows arranged in the corner – to the family of black kittens playing around it.

Jake couldn't work out how many of them there were, they moved so quickly, falling over themselves as they chased each other around the room. And watching over them from on top of the stack of pillows, looking pleased as punch, was Ted, her fur a glossy onyx; groomed and well looked after.

'They've brought her a bed and put a cat flap in the back door for her... They found her in the airing cupboard. She had her babies in the dark, all over the new season's fabric collection. She's got good taste, your cat, I'll give her that.'

Jake stared at the litter of... six, he finally managed to count, and began to laugh. 'I've been worried sick about her – not seen her for weeks. I thought she was dead! I've had posters up all over the place trying to find her. Thank God she's safe!'

'That's what cats do before they give birth. They slink off and find a safe, warm place away from prying eyes,' said the girl.

Jake went over and tried to pick Ted up, but it was impossible with the kittens all vying for their mother's attention. She looked at Jake and made a little squeak before she began purring loudly and licking their heads in turn. Jake looked at them and shook his head, lost for words.

So just like the terrorists, he thought, Ted had done a runner and disappeared off the radar for a while. But whereas this clever cat had set out with a plan, the failed bombers had high-tailed it back to Scotland with no real clue of what to do next. Had the Glasgow Airport attack been a half-arsed, last-ditch decision to go out in a blaze of martyred glory?

Jake gave up trying to cuddle Ted and went back to admiring from a distance. 'What a handful! We'll have to figure out what to do with them, but thank you.' He pecked the girl on the cheek.'

'I'll find that cat more often, I think,' the girl said, grinning.

Jake looked at his watch. 'Shit – I'm going to be late for court!'

61

The traffic had been awful. He just hoped the legal proceedings at the court were running as far behind schedule as he was. It was the day of Stephanie's careless-driving hearing, and he called her from the car to promise he'd be there as soon as he could.

After parking his car, he sprinted hard down the busy main road toward the imposing, Edwardian building where the case was to be held. He wanted Stephanie to understand that she didn't have to plead guilty; that he was there for her if she needed him to be. They were starting to become good friends again. It had been a long time since he had felt that trust from her, and it was important to him that he kept it that way.

Once they'd identified who Jake was, the security guards weren't interested in searching him. Jake had always thought Greenwich Magistrates' Court was unusual like that. In every other court he'd been in, they would search everyone, including police officers, before they were allowed entry. Here they were very trusting of the police. That or they were aware of Jake's feisty reputation and were leaving well alone.

Stephanie was standing outside Court One, leaning against a column of grey stone. No solicitor – she didn't need one if she wasn't planning to fight the charge.

'Thanks for coming, Jake – I really appreciate it,' she said, looking nervous.

'No problem. Are you feeling OK?' Jake asked, pecking her on the cheek.

'I'm fine,' she said resignedly. 'It's just a quick "I'm guilty" and then it's done. Hopefully it's just a big fine and not a driving ban.'

'None of this is right. Honestly, they're taking the piss, Stephanie. It's never careless driving – it's rubbish. Just an unfortunate chain of events. The police officer is out of order for—'

'Shhh… That's him coming in the door there.' She pointed to a uniformed police officer. 'PC Husher.'

Jake looked over at the officer with whom Stephanie had had so much trouble; the one who'd abandoned her at the side of the road, after criticising her driving and telling her the accident was all of her own making.

The name Husher rang a bell somewhere in Jake's brain.

And then it hit him.

PC Husher lived with the brother of Gavin Bonson. The smarmy little shit that had managed to get Jake his driving ban.

This wasn't about Stephanie at all.

This was about Jake and making his life as difficult as it could be. This was about what they thought *he* must have done after seeing all that cash in Gavin Bonson's wallet. Lenny had told him Bonson was one of the officers about to be prosecuted for fraud, so either they were seeking revenge on Bonson's behalf… or they were two of the others being investigated by the Metropolitan Police Authority.

A small rotund woman came out of Court One's door. 'Stephanie Flannagan,' she called.

'She'll be one minute,' said Jake to the woman, grabbing Stephanie by the arm and pulling her away from the door.

'Listen to me,' said Jake quickly. 'PC Husher's flatmate works up at Counter Terror. I think both he and the Bonson brothers are about to be arrested and lose their jobs for a work credit-card scam. They think that I grassed on them and started all their grief off, but the truth is it's nothing to do with me. They've tried to get me into trouble at work – and I think he was following you, which is why he was there so fast when you had that accident.'

Stephanie's mouth was hanging open. She looked too shocked to reply.

'They're all a bunch of corrupt bastards,' said Jake, 'and you've been dragged into this through no fault of your own.'

Stephanie was shaking her head. 'This is because I've kept my married name? They think we're still together?'

'You've got to plead "not guilty" – this isn't right,' he insisted.

'Jake, I can't—'

'Yes, you can. Trust me. Listen carefully to what I'm about to say, and you'll be all right...'

PC Husher was standing in the dock of Court One. With its stunning double-height ceiling, the huge room was typical of an Edwardian courtroom. Dark wood panels on the walls matched the magistrate's raised bench and witness box. Dark green leather adorned the seats. The only modern fittings in the room were speakers on the walls and some inconspicuous microphones on the desks. Defendants from one hundred years ago would have had exactly the same view as the defendants of today.

A female magistrate who looked to be in her mid-fifties positioned a pair of rimless spectacles on the end of her nose and peered at PC Husher from her elevated position as he began to explain the series of events.

'The car had mounted the pavement very clearly at some speed and struck the lamp post. There was extensive damage to the vehicle, likely several thousand pounds' worth.'

'No other cars were involved?' asked a female solicitor from the Crown Prosecution Service. She was wearing a dark trouser suit and standing just in front of the magistrate.

'No, just the defendant's car, a silver Volkswagen Golf,' PC Husher replied. 'There was no evidence that another car was involved, your worship.'

Though it was customary for questions to be asked of witnesses in court by the solicitor representing either the prosecution or the defence, the witness had to direct their answers to the magistrate. It was he or she who would make the decisions in the case.

'Any skid marks? Any indication that the defendant applied the brakes near to this *car* that pulled out in front of her?' The CPS solicitor had a way of accentuating things she wanted to draw the magistrate's attention to. Court rooms were often a big game, to see who could outwit whom, and the real justice often became secondary to the game of *I win, you lose*. Jake's heart sank.

'No, there was no evidence that she attempted to brake – none at all,' replied PC Husher.

'We know there was a car that pulled out in front of her though, because the defendant's ex-husband, who is a police officer, obtained the CCTV from a nearby garage. That is not in dispute here, is it, PC Husher?' asked the magistrate.

'No, your worship. I didn't doubt that there was a near miss on the roundabout – that was never disputed. Rather it was the defendant's speed which was the contributing factor here, thus her carelessness, which caused the accident.'

'I'm sure the defence will ask you, so I will get it out of the way,' the magistrate interjected. 'Why didn't you seize the CCTV from the garage? Surely that should have been part of your initial investigation? That's not the ex-husband's job, police officer or not, is it?'

'It was an oversight on my part, your worship. I didn't think that the cameras would cover the roundabout, and in any case it doesn't alter the fact that the defendant actually had the accident – it's mitigation rather than evidence…'

'Hardly, Officer. It assists the defence case that she swerved to avoid a car, and without the court being able to have seen that video, we would have been asking, "Was there a car in the first place or is she making it all up?" Though I'm sure that's not what your intention was when you failed to seize the CCTV,' replied the magistrate, shaking her head.

Husher's face turned bright red – embarrassed at being outed for covering his tracks.

Jake's stomach was doing somersaults as he listened.

'It was hardly mitigation,' the magistrate continued. 'It goes to the very heart of the defence case. It's rather fortunate that the ex-husband went and looked for the CCTV, isn't it? That he did your job for you?'

Husher didn't answer.

There was an awkward silence in the court. PC Husher obviously didn't want Jake to have the satisfaction of seeing him agree with the magistrate. Risky behaviour. The sort of thing that those in court hated. This was their jungle, and you were a guest. Never piss off the king, or in this case, queen of the jungle, thought Jake.

'Did you speak with the defendant?' the CPS solicitor asked, breaking the silence.

'Yes. Yes, I did…' Husher turned from the magistrate and then began answering directly to the solicitor, another subtle sign that he was flustered. The magistrate would be looking down on this escapade and wondering what sort of amateur clown she was dealing with here.

Husher continued, 'I asked if she were the driver of the car at the time of the accident. She said she was. I then cautioned her using the standard police caution.'

'And what was her reply?'

'She said…' Husher read verbatim from a small book in his hand, "I'm really sorry – a car pulled out in front of me. I swerved and hit the lamp post."'

'I have no further questions, your worship.' The solicitor sat down.

The magistrate turned to Stephanie, who sat in the dock opposite. 'As you're representing yourself, Mrs Flannagan, do you want to ask any questions of the officer before we ask if you intend to give evidence?'

Stephanie shook her head and smiled.

PC Husher stepped down from the witness box and left the room. Another mistake, thought Jake. Good officers would sit in the room and listen to the defendant's evidence, in case they could assist the prosecution solicitor further.

'OK. Good. Are you intending on giving evidence in your defence?' the magistrate asked.

'Yes, I am.'

'Please go to the witness box.' With her spectacles now in her hand, the magistrate motioned to the area on her left-hand side.

Stephanie made her way to the box and gave her oath.

'Mrs Flannagan, normally we would have a defence solicitor asking you questions, but you've elected to represent yourself. So if you say what you want to say, I will then ask questions to clear up any ambiguities. Is that clear?'

Stephanie nodded.

'Please begin,' said the magistrate.

'Well I just want to say that I've been a driver for fifteen years, I passed my test first time. I've never had any penalty points on my licence – ever. I've never even been stopped by the police before. I'm a really careful driver. Other than this incident, I've never had an accident before—'

'Mrs Flannagan.' The magistrate held up her hand and motioned for her to stop talking. 'This isn't how we normally do things. We need to understand what happened on the day of this accident – how you came to hit the lamp post. That's what we are concerned with initially.'

'Yes, I was getting to that, sorry. I was on my way to meet a friend for lunch. We were meeting in Blackheath. I'd not seen her for ages. I left with plenty of time. I wasn't in any rush. I've driven that route hundreds of times. I was driving across the roundabout, but I wasn't going fast – I don't drive fast.' Stephanie was waffling. She did this when she was nervous. Jake willed her to stay calm.

The magistrate interjected again. 'OK, Mrs Flannagan. We understand all that. Now tell us exactly what happened on the roundabout please.'

Stephanie paused, took a deep breath and composed herself. Jake dug his fingers into his palms. He hoped she would stick to the plan.

Stephanie began again, more slowly this time. 'Yes, your worship. Sorry. So halfway across the roundabout, the sun shone in my eyes…'

'Yes?' asked the magistrate, motioning for her to continue.

'And, well… I sneezed.'

'You sneezed?'

'Yes. I automatically closed my eyes, as you do when you sneeze. When I opened them, there was a car in front of me, on the roundabout. I had right of way, but it had pulled out in front of me. I don't know why. There was no time to brake. I had just enough time to swerve out of his way because I really didn't want to hit him. By the time I had done that, I was on the pavement and had hit the lamp post. That's it.'

'So you sneezed?' the magistrate asked.

'Yes.'

'The officer makes no mention of this in his evidence. Did you tell him that? This is very significant.'

'I was trying to tell him, but he wasn't listening. If I'm honest, it felt like he'd made his mind up, well before I'd even spoken to him, that for some reason I was going to have a day in court.'

'Is that all you wish to say, Mrs Flannagan?'

'I think so…'

'Does the prosecution have any questions?'

'No, your worship,' said the solicitor, displeased, not even bothering to rise.

Stephanie made her way back to her seat.

The magistrate asked for PC Husher to be found and recalled to the witness box.

Jake was smiling inwardly. The failure to gain CCTV images had already made PC Husher look utterly incompetent. It had been a deliberate attempt on his part to ensure that Stephanie couldn't defend herself, but it had backfired spectacularly on him when the magistrate had realised it was Jake who had collected the CCTV. And Husher was now about to be ambushed with something else he hadn't prepared for.

Standing in the witness box again, Husher looked at the magistrate. It was fairly unusual to be called back into the box after having exited the courtroom. When it happened, it meant someone had called your evidence, or even your competence, into question.

'PC Husher…' The magistrate pronounced his name in a staccato way that made her irritation with him abundantly clear. After a slow start, Stephanie had turned into a convincing witness and had clearly won her support. The magistrate continued, 'The defendant has said that she sneezed on the roundabout after the sun shone in her eyes. Do you recall her telling you that?'

'No, your worship, she didn't tell me that. I would have recorded it in my notes if so, and I've no record of that,' he replied, throwing Jake a hard stare. He knew the game was up.

This charade – a product of spiteful personal and totally misplaced vengeance – should never have gotten to the courthouse, thought Jake. And he was silently praying it would be over soon.

'You are aware,' said the magistrate, 'as I'm sure the prosecution are, that when one sneezes, we automatically close our eyes? It's called an automatism, and it's a defence to careless driving.'

'Yes, your worship, I'm well aware of the defence in law, but—'

'You failed to even collect the CCTV from the garage, Officer. This is *the most basic* of investigations. The defendant would not have been able to defend herself had her ex-husband not had the foresight to do it on your behalf. And now there is a dispute as to what you were told at the scene. The defendant said that she attempted to tell you, directly, about a defence to the very crime that you accuse her of but that you would not listen.'

'But, your worship—'

'You are excused from the witness box, Officer. I shall retire to chambers to consider the verdict in this matter,' the magistrate said, gathering herself to leave.

'All rise,' called the clerk. Everyone in the court stood up as the magistrate left the bench and exited through the large wood-panelled door behind her.

'She didn't tell me that – it's a lie!' Husher protested to the CPS solicitor who was shaking her head and shrugging at him.

Stephanie smiled at Jake.

'This is outrageous!' Husher stepped down from the box and began walking toward the exit, red faced and angry.

'I'll be seeing you, Husher,' said Jake under his breath as he walked past.

'Fuck you,' Husher said, as he left the court without turning round.

'Thank you, Jake!' Stephanie hugged him outside the court-room, thoroughly delighted.

'I'm really sorry you ended up here in the first place. It's obvious to anyone that it was a simple accident. I couldn't fath-om why anyone was taking it to court – until I saw who it was and remembered who he's mates with. Anyway, glad it's over. Sorry we had to bend the rules a bit to sort this out.'

'What will happen to him, after what the magistrate said?'

'Nothing. All the Job will know is that he lost the case. You got a not-guilty verdict. They won't find out that the magis-trate questioned his ability or anything like that. Though, to be honest, what the hell a bloke like that is still doing in the police...'

'Can I get you dinner tonight? We'll go out – my treat for the help you've given me?'

'Sure, that'd be great,' he said as Stephanie landed an unex-pected kiss on his lips.

Ring me later,' she said over her shoulder as she walked away from him. He was unsure what that kiss meant. Was she just happy – friendly?

But it felt just a fraction too long for that.

62

After Jake had exchanged the usual pleasantries in the Financial Investigation Unit, Charlie began wading through some folders on his desk, updating him on the details of Jenny's financial records.

'Well large amounts of money were being paid into Jenny's bank account – thousands at a time. She was getting regular payment for her work as a filing clerk by the SFO, and then there were these sporadic but fairly large payments from a bank account at HSBC,' said Charlie, pointing at some bank statements.

'Do you know whose bank account that is? Where those HSBC payments are coming from?'

'We're on it, just waiting for the information back from the bank, but I've already noticed something odd.'

'Go on,' said Jake, peering at the paperwork that Charlie was looking at.

'It looks like her second wage was being paid by Paxol Ltd. That's the same company whose credit card was used to pay for Javed Saleem's phone top ups.'

'Well that's looking good – looks like we're making some headway. Can you let me know when you have some details from the bank please?'

'Sure, I'll do some digging around the Paxol company registration and their accounts too.'

Jake's phone started to ring. Lenny's name flashed up on the small screen.

'Hi, Len,' said Jake.

'The computer guys…' Lenny sounded panicked. 'They found details of flight bookings on Saleem's devices. He's got a seat reserved – he's travelling to Riyadh with British Airways.'

'When?' asked Jake.

'Now! He's about to leave the country. I've just dialled into the tracker that we put on his Range Rover. He's at the airport. Do you want to let him run or try to stop him?'

'We've got to stop him! Meet me in the car park!' Jake got up from the desk and, without explanation, made a dash for the stairs.

By the time Jake had reached the bottom of the steel staircase, Lenny was already sitting in the car, waiting for him. Jake climbed hastily into the passenger seat.

'What are his flight details, do you know?' asked Jake as Lenny accelerated up the ramp, past the security guard and switched on the sirens and blue lights.

'BA263,' shouted Lenny, as he wove his way through traffic toward Victoria.

'What time is it due to leave?'

'At 1003 hours. Terminal 3.'

Jake checked his watch. 'That's in twelve minutes, Lenny!'

'I know. I know!'

'We'll never make it in time.'

'I've called Special Branch, Ports.' A car pulled into their path unexpectedly and caused Lenny to hit the brakes hard. Jake dropped his mobile phone into the footwell.

'Are you deaf? Can't you see?' Lenny yelled at the driver of the small red car as he passed it on the wrong side of the road.

Jake retrieved his phone from the footwell just as it started to ring. 'DI Flannagan,' he answered, pushing his index finger into his left ear as he strained to hear what was being said on the other end.

'Sir, it's DS Bray – Ports officer at London Heathrow. I've been asked to give you a call.'

'Yes. BA263 – going to Riyadh from Terminal 3. Has it boarded yet?'

'I'll have to log on, sir. What time is it scheduled to leave?'

'At 1003 hours I think…'

'That's less than ten minutes, sir…'

'You poxy fool! Look at what you're doing, you stupid bloody idiot!' Lenny screamed at someone else on the road in front of him.

'Was that directed at me, sir?' asked Bray.

'No, that's my driver. We're on our way to you—' Jake put his hand across the phone as Lenny began going the wrong way down a one-way street, 'Fuck me, Lenny. Be careful!' he exclaimed, as cars heading straight for them were mounting the pavement to avoid a head-on collision.

'Right, I've logged on, give me a second here…' said Bray. There was a pause. Jake could hear the tapping of the keyboard in the background. 'That flight has boarded. It's on the runway, sir. What's the problem with it?'

'Move. Don't just bloody sit there. Move!' Lenny screamed out of the window at a car blocking their way.

'There's a suspect on it. We need him off the flight. The passenger's name is Javed Saleem,' replied Jake.

'I'm not sure we can do that. Is there any risk to the plane or the passengers? What's the offence?'

'He's on bail for burglary. He's obviously leaving the country deliberately…'

'I'm afraid that won't be enough to stop the plane, sir.'

'But we also suspect him of being involved in a murder that's linked to organised criminal activity,' added Jake quickly.

'I'll see what I can do.' The line went dead.

Lenny was now on the dual carriageway section of the A4, heading across the Hammersmith flyover. With luck Heathrow could be reached in ten minutes.

'What did they say?' asked Lenny as the road ahead of them cleared slightly. He killed the sirens for the first time since they'd left the yard.

'The plane's already on the runway. He's checking to see if they can pull him off the flight.'

The minutes were ticking down. Jake wondered about the levels of authority that Bray would have to go through, internally within the police, before he could even speak to the control tower directly – the conversation Bray would be having with those in direct contact with the plane, as it taxied slowly down the runway. What the pilots themselves would say to the control tower as they sat there on the end of the tarmac. He wondered if Saleem's heart was beating as fast as his own right now, anxious for that plane to get in the air – gripping his armrest, willing the pilot to start accelerating.

'Have you ever done this before – got a plane stopped?' asked Lenny, breaking Jake's train of thought.

'No, Len. This is a first for me. Not tried it before. Just like that sixty-miles-per-hour drive in the wrong direction up a one-way street back there. That was a first for me too, mate!'

'We're alive, we didn't crash, and I'm only a few miles off Heathrow now, so don't give me grief! At least I'm not banned!' Lenny laughed. 'What about getting him arrested at the other end, in Riyadh – can we do that if he gets airborne?'

'If they grant him permission to enter the country, then we'd have to extradite him – but I don't think the Saudis even have an official extradition treaty with the UK right now. So you can guess how long that might bloody take. Put your foot down. The road's clear ahead of you. Go!'

Lenny accelerated. They raced toward the access tunnel underneath the runway and headed toward Terminal 3. Jake suddenly realised he had absolutely no idea what he was going to do when he arrived.

Lenny screeched to a halt outside departures. Jake jumped out and began heading toward the terminal entrance. He looked at his watch. It said 1012 hours. His heart sank.

63

Terminal 3 looked very different from how Jake remembered it, though he hadn't flown from there for some time. It was all long-haul flights nowadays. The drab sixties frontage was gone, replaced by an entrance framed by a modern-looking canopy and lush plants, which Jake narrowly avoided colliding with as he sprinted in through the sliding glass doors.

He glanced at his watch again. Had they managed to hold the flight?

Jake was hunting around for an information desk as Lenny came running into the building behind him. His phone rang as he scanned the area for the best person to speak with. Where the hell were the Ports officers located?

'Sir, it's DS Bray,' said the voice on the other end of the phone.

'I'm here in Terminal 3 departures. Where do I need to go?'

'I'm afraid I wasn't able to get them to stop, sir. The flight took off a couple of minutes ago, sorry.'

'OK.' Jake pulled the phone from his ear, hit the end-call button and screwed up his face in anger.

'Bollocks!' shouted Lenny, realising that their chase had been in vain. 'We must be able to get him at the other end! There must be a way?' he asked.

'I don't think there is. We'd need paperwork from the CPS and all sorts I'd imagine. We won't get that in a few hours – it would take weeks or months. How long is the flight to Riyadh?'

'It's certainly not a few months,' said Lenny, before he headed toward a British Airways information desk in a filthy mood.

Jake looked around the airport, remembering the footage he'd seen from the Glasgow Airport attack and thinking how lucky they'd been that nobody apart from the assailants had been seriously hurt in the blaze.

Inside Terminal 3, people were rushing around with their cases. Jake saw excited faces in casual clothes, plainly about to jet off to warmer climes. Others more smartly dressed were checking into VIP lounges. Jake imagined Saleem on his plane. Had Lenny said whether he was travelling business class? Going somewhere for work – not running away? No, but… the flight information was already in his computer when they took it from his house – this had to be a pre-planned trip.

'Six and a half hours until he gets there,' announced Lenny, breaking into Jake's vision of Saleem lounging in his seat.

'The guys that found this flight booking on his computer – did they give any indication of why he was going to Riyadh?'

Lenny looked a little confused. 'They didn't say anything other than he was booked on a flight.'

'It was obviously booked before we arrested him, Lenny. Those tickets and that information were already in the computer. I want to understand why – if Jenny's death was pre-planned, is this trip in some way linked to her death?'

'OK, I can ask…'

'Get back to the Yard. See what else they've got. I'm inclined to think that he'll probably come back, as long as we don't spook him too much. I'm going to find out what I can about his flight via the Special Branch guys here. I'll get the train back.'

64

Jake needed some time to think. His chat with the guys in Ports had told him very little.

Saleem was a frequent flyer to Saudi Arabia and Iraq – which seemed at odds with what Claire had said about him being 'a Saudi dissident'.

How was he allowed in and out of the country so freely?

Jake settled in a café in the terminal building. Dark walnut wood contrasted with the sea of steel, glass and grey-tiled floor of Terminal 3.

From his table, Jake watched people scurrying around like hot-footed mice in the desert, all running in different directions.

Steam rose off his cup of English breakfast tea and spiralled up his nose. Alongside it were some scones and cream. It wasn't much, but a pit stop made his brain slow down. He was angry – angry that Saleem had evaded him. Even if it wasn't personal – it felt like it was. But he needed to focus on the investigation, focus on where it was going. Saleem wasn't all of it. He was just a single component. It was no good becoming fixated on one part. He needed to see the whole picture.

Jake slid a knife through one of the scones. The two sides fell apart on the plate, their bready interior exposed, sweet sultanas bursting out here and there. He could never work out which was supposed to go on first, the jam or the cream.

He decided to prepare both scones differently to see if he could taste the difference. A woman on the next table watched him intently. She could see what he was doing, and a smile spread across her face.

'I'm just a mere boy at heart,' he said, smiling back at her. 'I never learned which one should go on first, so I'm experimenting,' he said, as he spread jam then cream on one, then alternated for the other.

The scones looked very different. One was almost entirely red and one almost white. He picked up the first, the one with jam on top, and took a bite. Then he tried the other one.

'Makes no difference,' said Jake to the woman, and she laughed as he wiped the excess off his lips with a serviette.

So despite looking very different, they both tasted exactly the same...

'Things can look totally different, but in reality, they're the same...' Jake mumbled to himself.

Saleem wasn't a Saudi dissident. Someone just wanted it to look that way. He certainly wouldn't be able to fly in and out of Saudi Arabia like he was doing. Someone was manipulating the truth. Someone with the power to decide what you saw – the jam on top or the cream on top.

After finishing his cup of tea, Jake made his way through the terminal building and picked up the Heathrow Express. It was little more than an expensive commuter train into Paddington, but it was quicker than the Tube, slightly cleaner, and it meant that Jake could get a signal on his phone throughout the journey – even in the tunnels.

On the way back into London, Lenny called.

'How's it going, Len?'

'OK. I'm back with the computer guys going through Saleem's computer. I've found out something a bit odd. I'm not sure what to make of it.'

'OK, what's that?

'Saleem was asked to go to Riyadh by British Aerospace – something about collecting some documents. It's in an email from them...'

'Good work. Not sure how that helps yet, but at least we know why he's gone there, and I suppose that now links Saleem to the arms guys, if only at a very minor level.'

'Er, yeah, but that's not the only odd thing that I found – not as such…'

'No? What was it then?' asked Jake as the train began pulling into Paddington.

'The postal address on the email from British Aerospace. It was from one of the senior managers. He has one of those automatic signature things that pastes the information on the bottom of it.'

'They're based in Hampshire, aren't they?'

'Well, that's what I thought, too – but it turns out that their senior leadership team are based in London.'

'Oh, OK…'

'Yeah, but that's the thing – it's *where* in London they're based.'

'Get on with it, Lenny – you're killing me here. Where?'

'Six Carlton Gardens,' he replied.

Jake paused while he thought about it for a moment. 'Carlton Gardens? I'm not sure where that is.'

'Carlton Gardens is a continuation of Carlton House Terrace. British Aerospace's registered office and senior management are in the same road that our spy, Adham Marmora, died. Their offices are just 150 metres away.'

'What?'

'Probably just a coincidence. But an odd one, when you consider that Marmora is an arms dealer, and that we've been pointed in that direction to look for clues about his death. Funny how all this is linking together.'

'That *is* odd. Anything else?'

'No – not yet. I'll keep looking.'

'Good. I'm off to see Sara at the SFO. I think we've missed something.'

Lenny groaned. 'OK. Just don't get yourself into trouble, guv.'

65

Sara had suggested they meet near her office, in a venue she'd described as a pub. When he got there, however, Jake was pleased to find that it was more like a busy restaurant. The pressure to imbibe alcohol didn't weigh so heavily on his shoulders.

She was sitting at a round wooden table in a large, open-plan seating area. Mismatched chairs gave off a shabby-chic air, and high up on the back wall, sitting above steaming hot plates and smoking griddles, a series of chalkboards carried an extensive British menu with a Continental twist.

'This is the place that coined the word gastropub. Did you know?' asked Sara as he sat down.

'Really? No, I didn't know that.'

Jake looked around at the vintage furniture and bare floorboards.

'Yeah, in the nineties they turned it from a dowdy pub with sticky carpets into something a bit special. I like it here. Good menu, good atmosphere – owned by a couple of chefs. I'm told that they even chip the crockery deliberately to give it that rustic, lived-in feel,' she explained.

Jake nodded as he watched the kitchen staff. Flames flew up from the griddle, causing the chef to step back, as he flambéed what looked like two large steaks in a pan. Even in restaurants, Jake realised that he struggled to look at large flames without being reminded of burnt corpses.

'So what can I do for you, Detective Inspector Jake Flannagan? I'm guessing this isn't a social visit,' said Sara, wrenching him away from the scene in the kitchen.

Jake frowned at her. 'What makes you say that?'

'Well, you virtually told me it was a one-night thing when we last spoke. Or should that be two-night thing now?'

'It's work-related, Sara,' he said, trying to sound firm.

'It's like you're expecting me to cling to you, in floods of tears and beg you to never leave me.' Sara tutted and shook her head at him.

'Well…'

'Relax. It's fine. I had a good time – you had a good time. We can still be friends. Women can occasionally initiate sex, you know, without necessarily wanting it again. Or having a nervous breakdown.'

'I thought you were after a relationship?' asked Jake tentatively.

Sara laughed. 'Yes. Just not with you!'

'OK. Now I'm totally offended,' Jake pulled a face.

'We're working together and we ended up having sex. I fancied you, but we're work colleagues. How unprofessional does that make us? You're a nice bloke, but I'm not prepared to lose my job over you,' she replied matter-of-factly.

Jake nodded.

'Let's park it and leave it at that. Do you want to eat while we talk? The steak is pretty good in here.' She nodded in the direction of the bar.

'I've not got time, Sara. I'm up against the clock. I need some information,' he replied, getting down to business.

'OK.' Sara looked confused.

'Jenny's dead,' he said flatly.

'What? How?'

'Drowned in the Thames.

'Oh God, that's dreadful. She was so young.'

'From the outside, it looks like a suicide, but I don't think it was. What's the latest on your internal investigation at work?'

'I've not heard anything in the office. The HR manager, the one we suspended when we found out how Jenny had got her job – well he resigned. So there's been no need for a disciplinary process.'

'You're not doing anything about it?'

Sara shrugged but said nothing.

'There are criminal offences there. We could look at your HR bloke, prosecute him...' Jake filled the silence. Was she really going to let this go – just like that? The infiltration of their organisation, the theft of sensitive documents?

'I don't think the management wants all of this to go public, Jake,' she said, cutting him off. 'It's all rather embarrassing.'

'You may have no choice – if I can get my suspect before the courts, then I *will* need to speak to your HR bloke, and it will all be public.'

'Suspect?'

'Yes. I've identified someone that may be involved in Jenny's death. And not just hers – there's been another death that looks suspicious and may also be linked. That's one of the reasons I wanted to talk to you today.'

'Oh?'

'Have you heard of a man named Adham Marmora?'

Sara nodded. 'Yes...'

Jake was shocked. How the hell had he missed this? How had Marmora been linked to this all along, without him knowing? He felt like a complete fool.

'I *have* heard of him, yes,' she continued. 'He's a middleman, a fixer.'

'Can you explain?'

'He acts like a bridge between people who legitimately buy and sell weapons, and those who can't. Certain countries can't sell arms to other countries due to embargoes or sanctions. He passes the weapons around, bypasses any regulations and puts his markup on the deal. Why did you want to know about him?'

'He's dead too.'

'What can I get you two?' interrupted one of the waiters, wearing denim dungarees and bright red Dr Martens boots. He was sporting a long but perfectly kept beard, as red as his boots.

'Can we just get two coffees?' Jake didn't wait to ask Sara what she wanted.

'Sure, what type?'

'Mocha for me,' chimed Sara.

'Ordinary white for me, please.'

The man in the red boots walked off toward the bar.

'Bloody hell,' replied Sara. 'Small world. Marmora was on the board of the British Egyptian Society. Quite a few of their big-name members lobbied hard for the SFO enquiry to be dropped... This suspect of yours, how is he linked to Jenny and Marmora's deaths?'

'He threatened Jenny shortly before she died, probably broke into her house. We were very lucky to have identified him in the first place. He has a number of linkages to British Aerospace, not least because he was spying on the anti-arms campaign group on their behalf. It seems he also has links to your lost paperwork too.'

'What's his name?'

'Javed Saleem – heard of him?'

'No.'

'What about the Savoy Mafia, that ring any bells?' asked Jake.

'I've heard of *them*, yes.'

'Who are they?'

'Oh God, where do I start? The Savoy Mafia are a group of businessmen. They include arms dealers, money men, MOD officials, secret-service personnel and politicians. They're so called because they hold their meetings at the grill in the Savoy Hotel on The Strand.'

'What's the Mafia part about?'

'They have a common goal – a desire to abuse UK foreign aid and a little-known government loophole to make lots of money. Millions and millions of pounds at a time. And there are lots of rumours about people who get on the wrong side of them – people who disappear; die in odd circumstances. How true that is I have no idea – but there are rumours.'

'What's the loophole?' Jake asked.

'The loophole is the Export Credit Guarantee Scheme – it's basically an insurance policy, underwritten by the British government. A British company sells its goods or services abroad, normally to another state. Ultimately, if the foreign country can't afford the goods for any reason – then the British taxpayer has to find that money. And the biggest beneficiary of the Export Guarantee Scheme is the weapons industry. '

'Was that part of your Al Yamamah investigation?'

'Not as such. It's clear there's corruption occurring on a massive scale, but we were told to stay away from it. Not our remit.'

'Why – if it's serious fraud?'

'We were just looking to whom the bribes had been paid, not *how* they were paid.'

'What do you mean?'

'Well some of the bribes paid to the Saudis in Al Yamamah were funded initially through the Export Credit Guarantee Scheme and the Foreign Aid budget.'

'So you're telling me that the taxpayer paid the bribes to the Saudis?'

'Of course.' Sara looked at him oddly, as if this was common knowledge. 'But it's not unique to Al Yamamah. It's used a lot. In just about every arms deal or potential arms deal, there are bungs paid as a sweetener. In this case, the money was all paid through a number of Swiss bank accounts. We could see the money going from UK Government accounts to Swiss bank accounts. We were in the process of serving orders on the Swiss to disclose who controlled the accounts and to trace where the onward payments went to, but—'

'Tony Blair stopped your investigation?'

Sara nodded, a look of resignation on her face. The man with red boots returned with their coffees. Jake smiled when he saw that his 'vintage' cup was chipped.

'You don't think all the money was going to the Saudis, do you?'

'I know for certain that it wasn't just the Saudis receiving bribes. There were all sorts of senior people and officials involved.

Lots of people right here in the UK were getting very rich from it. It'll all come out eventually – in twenty years or so.'

'How?'

'Most of the early details about who profited and why are locked away in a National Audit Office report. It has secret stamped all over it, and no one can get access to it. I'm sure in there the abuse of power, the nepotism and the outright corruption at the heart of this deal are laid bare. It'll tell the real story of why Margaret Thatcher resigned. Forget Europe and all the Poll Tax nonsense – it was the arms deals that were the really damaging stuff. And it was the family business that orchestrated her rise to power and positioned her as the acceptable face of arms. People forget that,' said Sara coolly.

'Look, my suspect is on a plane to Saudi Arabia. I need something – something to stop him being given entry to the country at the other end, something you've not done, something that might turn me up some evidence… Where have you not looked?

'We've not done much around DESO – the Defence Export Services Organisation.'

'No?'

'No. Do you know what DESO is?'

'Yes, I know what they do – they're a trade delegation loosely attached to the MOD. They do the same sort of thing that the British tourist board does to attract foreign tourists – but rather than promoting UK holidays, they're promoting our weapons. They basically encourage foreign regimes to buy British arms.'

'Yes – and more. They smooth all the ripples and handle all the "special payments". Brown has said he's going to close the whole department. I'm hoping he'll remain true to his word, but he might just change its name and move it somewhere else because there's so much pressure from the arms industry to keep it going. It's headed up by various executives of defence companies who are officially seconded from their employer and continue to receive their salary. At least one third of DESO's five hundred staff work on the Al Yamamah contracts with Saudi

Arabia. There are some really desperate people wanting certain secrets to be kept quiet and things to continue as they are.'

'Jeez, so you're saying our government puts commercial business people with their sights firmly focussed on selling their own company's arms and weapons inside a government export department?'

'Yeah, I know. It's bizarre. It's like a weird form of nationalised arms industry, with its own rules. It's almost as if it's an actual part of government. Unlike any other sector. Hang on. There was a name that kept coming up from inside DESO...' Sara looked to the ceiling for a moment, as if the name she was searching for might be written on it. 'He was suspected of being part of the Savoy Mafia too...' Her voice tailed off.

Jake sipped his coffee, trying to curb his impatience. His knee wriggled up and down absentmindedly. He needed this.

'I think the first name began with an "F"?' she said suddenly. 'Was it Fred? Fraser? We never actually spoke to him in the end, but he is on the list. He might be a good bet to have a chat with? Actually, I'm not sure of the first name. Surname was Ricks-something – Rickson, or maybe Richards?'

Jake felt the pit of his stomach lurch.

Frank Richards. Claire's uncle. It had to be.

Sara continued, blissfully unaware of Jake's predicament, 'I might look him up myself, thinking about it,' she said. 'It might help the Yanks now that they've taken over with their own follow-on investigation. We can have a look at him together if you want?'

'Best keeping it separate, Sara. You crack on,' said Jake, downing the rest of his coffee as he stood up. Making his excuses, he thanked her and left.

He needed to get to Frank Richards – alone. Quickly.

If Frank was linked to Jenny's death, it was very possible he was also linked to Marmora's. And now Frank was involved in this Savoy Mafia ring too? If it all came into full view without the right management, Claire could lose her vetting – lose her job.

Or worse, if she'd got too close to all this – she could lose her life.

66

Jake had told Lenny to forget trying to reach Saleem; this thing was way more involved than either of them had realised. Saleem might even be connected to Marmora's death, but they needed hard evidence. That was all going to take time.

Jake picked up his battered Saab and drove straight to the Forest of Dean. It was a gorgeous evening. After storms, deluges and flooding, the weather patterns had turned fine and dry, yet it was three months too late to be heralded as the official appearance of summer.

As on his previous visit with Claire, Jake left his vehicle in the car park and hired the last bike of the day, promising he wouldn't be long. Thankfully, the spotty youth who'd served him last time was nowhere to be seen.

Taking the same route he'd done that day with Claire, he made sure to hide his bike safely in the bushes before climbing over the high wall at the rear of Frank Richards' house and making his way up and through the orchard. Despite the summer floods, the boughs of the trees still drooped heavily, laden with a kaleidoscope of apple, pear and plum varieties.

Jake's feet met the edge of the lawn. As he walked across the lush, manicured carpet from the direction of the forest, a voice called out to him. He looked up to see Frank Richards seated at an ornate wrought-iron table on the rear terrace, his head bowed, buried in a book.

'I've owned this house for twenty years. Always loved sitting in this spot, looking toward the forest in the evening. Living in the countryside, it's a real pleasure. You see all sorts of animals walking across the garden from this vantage point,' he said, not even bothering to look up at Jake.

'It's me that's the animal?' he responded, as he drew closer to Frank. It infuriated Jake that this man – a man who had sold and abused his own niece; a man who could kill – would refer to him as an animal.

'Animals are straightforward. They eat, they sleep, they move with the change of season. They don't harbour grudges or desire revenge,' said Frank creepily as he finally looked up from the book he was reading.

'I would have used the front door, but I didn't fancy the fun and games of talking via the intercom,' replied Jake, stepping on to the patio.

'So you just scuttled over the wall, like a rodent,' sneered Frank, looking Jake up and down before scanning the end of the garden. 'So no search warrant, no gun, no handcuffs, no backup? What is this, a social call?'

'You know who I am?'

'I know who you are. I just didn't realise you plods could do that. Aren't you always at work? The law's the law, isn't it – you either have the evidence or you don't? Isn't that how it normally works?'

'I'm just here for a chat at the moment. Man to man,' replied Jake as he pulled out a chair from the table and sat down opposite Frank. 'How do you know who I am?'

'I ran over you with my car. I had no idea who you were back then. But after you'd arrested Saleem, I made it my business to find out who was poking their nose in. It didn't take me long to get hold of a photo of you, and when I did, I realised that you'd already been here. Probably with that filthy little slut of a niece of mine.'

Jake wondered how much Frank really knew about him. If he had sourced a photo, did he know Jake had kids? How dangerous was this, not just for him, but for his family too?

'What is it that you want today, Jake Flannagan?' he asked imperiously.

'The game's over. I know how it all fits together. I don't have every single last piece, not yet, but I know where to look for it. And I wanted to talk to you first…' Jake paused, 'to give you a chance to do the right thing.'

'Really, like what?'

'Claire.'

'What is there to say about her?'

'We wouldn't be here if it wasn't for the way you treated her, what you did to her. This probably would've all been forgotten about.'

'I don't feel any regret. I've never done anything wrong. She did what she did of her own free will.'

'She'd lost her mum, been virtually deserted by her father and was in your care. You should have been looking after her, not taking her to dodgy parties.'

'I took her along to those parties as a favour at first. I never expected her to become involved like she did!'

'You took her along because she was a pretty young girl, and the Saudis liked her around. You were already plying them with prostitutes. You must have known there was potential for her to become involved! Why didn't you take your own daughter?'

'Claire was down, needed cheering up. I got her a new dress, new shoes. Took her out. That was it. Honestly. The next thing I knew, one of them had taken a shine to her. It was difficult to pull the reins in. I didn't expect her to become the life and soul of the bloody party!'

'She was fifteen. You were her legal guardian, supposedly looking after her! She was in a vulnerable position. And you took her to parties with booze and drugs, where prostitutes were on hand to service the needs of your clients…'

'It was my job to look after the Saudis. That's what I was paid to do by the government – authorised at the highest level. I was there to ensure they continued with the deal. "*Show them a good time, whatever they need,*" were the instructions. Our country had been on its knees thanks to the miners' strike and the coal not getting through. Thatcher knew we were fucked unless we had more oil to burn. Keeping the Saudis happy was our number-one priority – she *had* to swap weapons for oil to avoid running out of fuel again.'

'So you're laying it squarely at the feet of the coalminers? You're saying that's why we had to do everything possible to keep the Saudis happy – to guarantee fuel supplies?'

'Yes.'

'And if the Saudis *needed* your niece, you just had to let them have her too?'

'It wasn't like that – it really wasn't. She just came along. I didn't expect her to start fucking them!'

'But she did. And you didn't stop it. You carried on letting it happen, even paying for it—'

'I didn't give her money – they did.'

'Don't treat me like a fool. That money came out of the slush fund from the MOD. It came from the kickbacks on the weapons deals. Just like it did for all the other prostitutes. You provided the Saudis with the money that they gave to her. And you knew why they were giving it to her, because you'd seen it on the videos.'

Frank looked surprised at Jake's level of knowledge.

'You can't pull the wool over my eyes, Frank. Claire's told me everything.'

'Go on then.'

'I know about the secret videos you had made. The ones she was in. The ones designed to blackmail the Saudis should it all go wrong. The insurance policy.'

'I suppose she told you that I raped her?' said Frank, shaking his head. 'Well, I didn't,' he added, before Jake had an opportunity to answer.

'No?'

'No, I didn't rape her. She wanted it.'

'She was your niece; vulnerable; missing her mother; a mess – whether she understood what she wanted or not at that time.'

'She was almost sixteen!' he retorted.

'She was your niece, Frank! And by today's standards it was rape!' Jake shot back.

'What do you want from me?'

'I want the videos. Claire wants them, so they can never see the light of day. So that she can put this behind her – for good. That will be the end of anything related to Claire, at least as far as the charges are concerned.'

'Charges? What happens then, to me – with the rest of what you've been investigating?'

'Well you can come clean – about everything. Tell me the lot. Go Queen's – tell me about the bribes, about the Savoy Mafia – about silencing the SFO investigation – about Jenny and Marmora. Let's get it *all* out in the open...'

'I wasn't involved in the bombing.'

'What bombing?'

'You're in Counter Terrorism Command, aren't you?' said Frank with disdain.

He could only be talking about Operation Seagram. Jake's mind raced for the answer.

Marmora had fallen to his death, thirty-six hours before the car bomb had been planted outside Tiger Tiger. Marmora's flat and the rose garden where he fell were just metres from the site of the car bomb in Cockspur Street and the blue Mercedes that had been towed away to the underground car pound. Frank could only be talking about that.

Jake said nothing, waiting for him to continue before he decided how to play this.

'That wasn't me. Nothing to do with me. That was the Saudis,' said Frank, filling the silence. 'They were just trying to stop the SFO enquiry reopening. They'd threatened to cut off security intelligence if it was. This was to be a sign, show just how much intelligence they could provide and how important it was that we all play nicely together. They were so desperate for that investigation to be stopped before the SFO uncovered all the pieces...' Frank tailed off and began staring at something behind Jake.

Jake turned and looked to see what Frank was staring at. Walking toward them, very slowly from the corner of the house, was Claire.

She was holding a gun. She gripped it in two hands, at shoulder height, ready to fire. Her eyes were red and wild. Frank raised his hands in the air.

Jake stood up slowly and stepped away from the table. The gun remained pointed in Frank's direction. Frank was now standing too.

'You raped me,' she said through gritted teeth. 'How dare you say I consented!' Her hands trembled as she edged closer. Jake could see that she'd been crying.

'It was a long time ago. We are both very different people now,' said Frank, trying to placate her.

'It was like it was yesterday for me. Every day I live with it,' she snarled.

'Claire, put down the gun,' said Jake.

The weapon looked old. A revolver of some sort with a long barrel.

'No, I will not put down the gun. You stay right where you are,' she said sternly, gesturing to Jake with her head. 'He's got two minutes to tell me everything. Why he was bugging my house; why he was stealing those documents; where the videos are – and who else is involved. Then I decide if I let him live.'

Frank looked at Jake – there was real fear in his eyes – but Jake remained where he was. He figured that getting between Frank and the gun was a bad move at this point, and besides, he wanted answers to those questions too.

'Now!' Claire shook the gun at Frank.

'We didn't know who was talking, who was helping the SFO,' he began slowly. 'Lots of people knew small parts, bits and pieces. We didn't think that their investigation would ever get off the ground. Most of that deal was kept secret, locked away all these years. We tried to control the information flow.'

'The bug in my flat, in 2005 – that was you?'

'Yes. You knew what my role was back in the eighties. You knew more than most about the things we were doing, the deals we were making – and you were in a position to give that to your employer. So when the SFO investigation kicked off, I didn't know if it was you who was doing the talking—'

'You came into my home?' she shouted, stepped closer to him, shaking with rage.

'Not me, no, not me,' said Frank, obviously realising that would have made it worse. 'It was a man we hired. He did all that. I didn't go anywhere near your home.'

'Who?' asked Claire. A single tear rolled down her left cheek.

'A man named Saleem – he did all that. I'm not the lead in all of this. It's bigger than me. I'm just a bit part, the little man.'

'You didn't sound like the little man when you were ordering that Jenny girl to lose the documents from the SFO investigation.' Claire shuffled closer and closer to him as she spoke, the gun outstretched in front of her. 'And you forget, I know you – I know how you operate. I've watched you, seen you around other people. You're always in charge. I've seen the way you bully people, manipulate them to do what you want them to. I had sex with you because you threatened to tell my father about the videos, about what was going on with the Saudi princes. And you said that if I didn't, I would end up in a foster home.' Claire was now standing within a few feet of Frank, the gun pointed right in his face, talking through gritted teeth. 'So don't you fucking dare pull that this-is-bigger-than-me shit.'

'So if I don't say what you want me to say, you're going to kill me? It's better that I just tell you what you want to hear?'

'Sit down in the chair,' ordered Claire gruffly.

Frank obeyed. Jake stayed well away from where the gun was pointed. Claire looked crazed enough to pull the trigger at this point.

'Who is Saleem?' she asked, moving behind Frank and poking the barrel of the gun into the back of his skull.

'He's a Saudi secret-service agent.'

'Who does he work for?'

Frank's head jolted forward as Claire jabbed him in the back of the head with the gun.

'He works for the Saudis, but he's under my control in the UK.'

'And who're you working for in all this?'

'I worked for DESO. The Defence Export Services Organisation – part of the MOD. My job was to makes sure the Saudis bought British arms.'

'Who knows about the videos? The MOD? This Saleem? The arms companies?'

'No one knows – just me. They were insurance, for me, just in case I needed them.'

'Why did you need insurance?'

'It was all illegal. The bribes we were paying on the Al Yamamah contract, what Downing Street were telling me to do, supplying the Saudis with whatever they wanted, to serve their every whim. It was wrong. All of it. I knew. The Saudi princes knew. Downing Street knew. I wasn't going to be the one without a chair when the music stopped. I needed insurance, bargaining chips, get-out-of-jail-free cards. That's all they were intended for.'

'Where are the videos?' demanded Claire.

'They're locked in a safe place – only I can get to them. We can go and get them together.'

'No, you tell me where the fuck they are – or I kill you right here, right now,' she growled at him, jabbing him in the back of the head again.

Frank looked terrified.

Jake wasn't sure if Claire was bluffing or not, given how disturbed she looked.

'Claire, why don't you put the gun down?' he asked as he moved slowly forward, trying not to startle her.

'You stay where you are!' she said fiercely, actually shifting the gun to point at Jake for a moment as she spoke. Jake froze on the spot.

Claire returned her focus to Frank. 'The bombings in London – you mentioned them earlier. How are they linked to this?'

'Tony Blair successfully shut down the SFO investigation on national-security grounds. The Saudis told him what would happen if he didn't. They threatened him with another 7/7. They control all this, all the terror groups. It's their money that keeps it all going, so they can orchestrate when and where things happen. So he shut it down. But then the anti-arms campaign group – they wouldn't leave it alone. They were challenging the decision in the courts. Parliament wouldn't leave it alone either – debate after debate. We tried our best to silence anyone that would talk. Nicely. We didn't want deaths or bombings – none of us here did. We tried to steal the case files. Then that spy, Marmora, was going to release his memoirs about the arms deals, and the anti-arms campaigners started talking to MPs—'

'So you killed people?'

'Not us, not me. The Saudis. This is them. I'm just a small part of this – trying to keep the lid on it. They are desperate to avoid being named, and even more desperate not to lose their money. That's all they care about. They were even prepared to assassinate members of their own family, because they thought they were leaking information. They're crazy. Life means nothing to them. They gave us warnings that they were going to go through with something. We didn't know what. They warned us they were going to send a message to the government, send a message to the SFO, that the investigation into the bribes had to stop. Marmora was found dead, then there were the two car bombs in London, then the attack on Glasgow Airport.'

'You knew they were going to do that?' Jake suddenly found himself shouting at Frank, angry and frustrated.

'We didn't know what, when or how – then it was too late when it all started.' Frank didn't take his eyes off Claire as he replied.

'How would those things have stopped the investigation? That doesn't make sense,' said Jake.

'Because the Saudis wanted it to look like they had intelligence in advance of the attacks. They wanted to make us believe that, had they been talking to us, they could have supplied that intel, and we could have stopped the bombings. But the intelligence is all false – it's made up. They're organising these things, doing the bombings, and then supplying intelligence on their own agents and saying, "*Look what we had! Look how we could have helped, had you not been messing about with that stupid SFO investigation.*" And to prove their point, a few days after the Glasgow Airport attack, Ayman al-Zawahiri, the deputy head of al-Qaeda specifically singled out the Al Yamamah defence contract as corrupt. They are not our friends. They are monsters. They manipulate the intelligence all the time – to make themselves look good.'

Jake interrupted. 'We've got to take him in, Claire – this is massive. This involves the government at its highest levels. It can't carry on.' Jake began moving toward Frank again.

'Not until he tells me where those videos are.' Claire tightened her grip on the gun.

'What are you going to do – shoot him *and* shoot me?' he shouted at her.

'If I have to. This ends today. Now. I'm not living with this any longer. Tell me where the videos are or I blow your fucking head off.'

67

What was the best way out of this God-awful mess?

As Jake began to formulate a plan of action, out of the blue, Frank stood up, wheeled around and shoved Claire hard into the glass panes of the French doors. Jake ran toward her instinctively.

He wasn't sure what happened first. Did he hear the bang or feel the warm blood on his face?

There'd been a flash from the muzzle of the gun… the shot so loud it made his head judder. He stopped where he was, just inches from where the gun had gone off, his head vibrating, ears ringing. He stood there, rooted to the spot, for what seemed like an eternity – trying to fathom what had just happened.

The blood ran down his face, over his lips, its salty taste in his mouth, his hands, stretched out in front of him, ready to grab hold of the swirling mass of arms that was the struggle between Claire and Frank. His hands and arms were covered in deep red splatters and chunks of pink and white flesh.

He knew this was actually all happening in a matter of split seconds, but the duration seemed longer. His brain was receiving massive amounts of data to process, altering his perception of time, trying to allow him to react quickly to a dangerous situation.

He realised that it wasn't his own blood.

Frank was falling to the ground in front of him.

298

Falling to the floor, his body limp. His face barely recognisable.

Frank had been shot. Just under the chin, the bullet exiting near his nose. There was only a large hole where his eyes and nose had once been. He hadn't hit the floor yet. He was half-way down.

Gobbets of skin, tissue and muscle continued to rain down, a raw bloodied mess settling on Jake's outstretched arms.

Claire stood there against the cracked French doors.

The bang was still ringing in Jake's ears. It was disorientating, the buzz jarring his bones as it vibrated across his skull from left to right.

Frank Richards was dead.

The smell. The ammunition. It was old. Cordite. An odour like fireworks. Modern ammunition didn't smell like that when fired. The propellant used was different.

Claire was in shock, her face spattered with blood. The gun firmly in her hands, finger still clasped around the trigger.

He watched as she began to weep openly, but he could only hear that buzzing in his head.

Time gradually returned to its normal speed as the ringing in his ears subsided. Jake looked at the gun she was holding. A revolver. It was something from World War II or before.

Black. A little dirty. He could see a wooden handle through her fingers.

Her grandfather. She'd mentioned the gun before. He remembered now. She'd talked about it being an antique, but he'd never seen it until now. He'd assumed it was decommissioned. That it could no longer be used – that there was no ammunition with it. It had to be the same gun.

Vintage. But lethal.

'What the fuck?' were the first words out of his mouth.

'Sorry. I'm so sorry,' she choked out, shaking her head.

Jake didn't dare to approach her. Had she totally lost it? Had the paranoia of being bugged become too much? He didn't know.

'Why?' he shouted at her, the adrenalin still coursing through his veins now threatening to erupt.

'He abused me. Repeatedly. And let me suffer at the hands of men who paid to have sex with me. He's made me feel worthless ever since I was fifteen. And then, just when I thought I was beginning to heal, beginning to put it behind me, it all starts up again and I'm constantly looking over my shoulder thinking it's going to come back and destroy my life for a second time.' Her voice cracked and she began to sob again.

'You killed him. You killed him in front of me. What the fuck are we going to say?'

'The gun... It's his...' She was crying as she spoke. 'From his loft. My grandfather's.'

'What?'

Claire's tears stopped. Her eyes changed, pupils dilating. She didn't need to say what she was thinking. Those words were enough. The look was enough. It all answered his question. The question about what they were going to do.

She wanted to set the scene up and walk away.

'Help me. Please. I need you,' she said, calmly holding out the gun in front of her. 'It was an accident – I didn't mean to shoot him.'

She was asking him to make a murder look like suicide. The very sorts of crimes he was now investigating.

Jake stared at her pleading eyes.

He needed to make a decision. They had little time to spare and there were few choices.

His brain kicked into gear. He analysed the possibilities.

Arrest her – that's what would be expected of him. That's what he should do. Murder. She could say that it was an accident. Maybe she'd get a manslaughter verdict. There was mitigation – it was not a defence. She'd planned this. She'd threatened him with the gun. Yes there had been a struggle, but maybe she'd not intended to kill Frank. She'd go to prison for five to ten years for manslaughter. But that was looking at it positively, with the judge taking pity on her for having to relive in the witness box every single time that she'd been coerced, groomed, sexually assaulted or raped by her uncle and others;

hoping that the minimum tariff would be lower, because of the mitigating circumstances of those traumatic teenage years.

What would that mean for his career? His life? What was he doing here? This wasn't official. He'd climbed over the back wall to avoid any CCTV on the gate. He couldn't claim to have just been having a friendly chat with a man now connected to two strange deaths, a man that had been on the periphery of a terror attack in London three months ago.

Jake felt enough like a madman: referred to Occupational Health – Lenny and Helen asking him if he was all right. He'd virtually admitted he was an alcoholic to Shirley. They'd use Shirley's notes against him. There'd be evidence of him being unhinged. Gross professional misconduct. He'd lose his job – easily. He wouldn't get away with another investigation into Claire – him being here, with her, while she shot someone. And that was if they didn't try to pursue him as an accessory. The content of the bugs Claire had placed were on her computer at home. They'd surely connect that to what he was doing at the SFO. They'd arrest him too. Search his home.

Cover it up, Jake. Make it look like suicide. Walk away… the voice in his head said.

Jake stayed still, thinking; running through the chain of events that would follow either decision he made.

Burn your clothes. Wash off the blood. Claire gets to live her life. Frank was a monster.

He could live with that, couldn't he? A monster that was dead. Not of his doing.

He looked again at the gun. Then at Claire.

'Please,' she whispered to him.

It was decision time.

68

'My aunt will be home soon,' pleaded Claire, her back against the cracked pane in the French doors, the flagstones of the terrace now awash with blood from Frank's head.

He looked at her, saying nothing.

'Please, Jake…'

'You just killed him, Claire. What am I supposed to do? I'm a police officer. I'm supposed to put people before the courts for things like this. Regardless of what's gone on in the past, who you are, how bad a man he was. None of that stuff should matter. The law is the law. This isn't bending the rules. This wouldn't be cheating just a little bit, so that the good guys win, telling a few lies. That's a dead body there – the body of a man who was alive just a few moments ago.'

'And what was I supposed to do?' she shouted back at him, enraged, her sudden change in tone catching him by surprise. 'I didn't ask for my mother to be an alcoholic. I didn't ask my father to abandon me to an uncle that would end up abusing and raping me,' Claire carried on shouting. 'I didn't ask him to have videos of me – to be left living in fear of when all this was going to come out. I'd put it behind me and built a life, away from all that shit. My life was mine. I owned it. I was proud of me, proud of what I'd overcome. It was all behind me – buried. And then suddenly it's all out in the open again, and it was going to cost me everything! Don't talk to me about laws! Where's the justice for me, for what I've been through?

Where's the justice in me losing everything for something that happened twenty years ago? Something that wasn't my fault?'

'Claire…'

'Don't fucking *Claire* me. You bend and break the law all the time – so don't you fucking dare give me that *the-law-is-the-law* bollocks. Have you any idea what it's like to have something like this hanging over you? To know you're being followed, bugged; your every move watched?'

Jake shook his head. 'Claire, if I go along with what you want, that's exactly what my life will become. I will always be looking over my shoulder, wondering when this is going to come back and bite me, waiting for the rug to be pulled from under my feet.'

'Welcome to my reality! All you've got to do is walk away and forget about this. Just tell me what to do. I'll set up the scene here. You were never here – you've done nothing wrong.' Claire sounded calmer now. 'He shot himself. That's his father's gun. My aunt will say that, I'm sure. She knows how much stress he's been under from the threat of the SFO investigation being reopened. You can still do all of the things you were going to do – you just won't have to bother prosecuting that piece of shit. And I get my life back without having to worry if he's going to use those videos somewhere.'

'Do you know how the police will investigate this, Claire? Do you know about bullet trajectories? About muzzle burns on the skin when a gun is fired close to it? About gunshot residue on the hands, face and clothes after you've pulled the trigger? If you did, you'd know that all of those things, if checked, will paint a very different story to the one you want to tell. The crack in the window behind you – how did that happen on its own? Your feet are surrounded by blood. It's on the soles of your shoes, so when you walk away, you're going to leave bloody footprints… Already this doesn't look like a suicide, Claire.'

'Then you've got to help me do this. I can't set it up alone!' Claire struggled to look at the watch on her right wrist. 'We've got time before my aunt gets home. She's at line dancing. It finishes in an hour, and add on to that a twenty-three-minute drive back here. And, by the way, she hates him – he's a bully and frequently knocked her about. So he won't be missed.'

'We'll go to prison for this – both of us – and I didn't do anything…'

'Eighty-two minutes and counting – that's how long we've got,' she said, without taking her eyes off her watch.

69

Four thousand bulbs illuminated the bridge, intensified by reflections from the surface of the Thames. This was usually one of Jake's favourite spots at night – looking eastwards along the river in the direction of the derelict Battersea power station. The bridge was known to many as the Trembling Lady, because it would shake as people travelled across it. Traffic flow was restricted, and when winter came, the metal plates that made up its surface froze and became slippery as hell.

Claire was dead.

She'd turned the gun on herself when he'd said it was too late to help her; that he wasn't prepared to help cover up her crime. She'd done it without warning, no final attempt to convince him. 'OK,' she'd said simply, before placing the barrel of the gun in her mouth.

He wondered if he would ever forget the look in her eyes, just before she pulled the trigger.

As he stared over the side of the bridge and down into the murky depths of the Thames, he felt hollow – utterly defeated. The tide was ebbing. The water was slipping out toward the Thames Estuary and into the North Sea. An image of Claire's face stared up at him from the still, dark water beneath.

He'd walked away from the house in the forest leaving both Claire and Frank lying there in their own blood. The man she'd hated so much in life, the man she detested, was now her partner in death. They were together again. The exact opposite of what she had wanted.

He hadn't a clue how to deal with what had happened. Looking into the water wasn't helping. The tide was ebbing faster now, and he wondered how cold it was, how long it would take to drown – whether he had enough time. How painful it would be.

Claire's face disappeared from the surface of the river.

70

'Come in, Jake.' Helen motioned to him from the other side of her desk.

The sun was shining in through the window, the room warm. Helen got up to lower the blinds slightly and alleviate the glare before sitting back down behind her desk.

'Morning, Helen,' he said as he sat down opposite her.

'How are you?'

'Could be better,' he replied, knowing he must look awful – tired and drawn.

'I'm really sorry to hear the news about Claire. Is there anything that you need – time off perhaps? I can grant you some compassionate leave?'

'No, it's fine. I just want to get on with things, forget about it.'

'I've spoken with the Gloucestershire police. They say, from initial investigation, that Claire shot her uncle and then shot herself – they aren't looking for anyone else. Had you spoken to her recently?'

'No. Last time we spoke was a few weeks back. We weren't on great terms toward the end.'

'OK, I understand,' she continued. 'Mrs Richards said that her husband was under a lot of stress apparently. The weapon was a family heirloom from the attic. She said that her husband had admitted to having had some sort of odd relationship with Claire in the past and she believed that was the driver in Claire killing him. Were you aware of this?'

'She'd told me a little, not much. She wanted to keep it confidential.'

'The uncle – he was part of the SFO investigation. Have we had any contact with him? I'll have to inform the IPCC if we have.'

Jake phrased his words carefully. 'No, we've had no contact with him from a police perspective.'

'I'm sorry to press you on this now. I appreciate it's probably difficult.

'It's fine.'

'There seems to be a lot of death surrounding that SFO investigation, a lot of suicides among those connected to it...'

'Except that Jenny didn't commit suicide, and I have grave doubts about Marmora. I believe he's connected in some way too.'

'Can we prove differently? Can we prove they were killed?'

'We're some way off. I don't think we're going to get anywhere with Marmora – there's simply no evidence, just some suggestions he was involved, but with Jenny, it's looking a little better. A pair of trousers that we found in the wardrobe at Javed Saleem's house are a positive match to fibres we found on Jenny's bed – and vice versa, there are fibres from the duvet on the trousers.'

'So that proves he was in her flat at some stage, but it doesn't prove that he killed her, does it?'

Jake sighed. 'Not yet, no.'

'When is Saleem due to return to the country?'

'We don't have a return date – not yet.'

'I think this is a good point for us to pass this on, Jake. Put a port warning on Saleem so that when he comes back in, we know he's here. Pass the paperwork you have on to whichever murder teams deal with where those bodies were found, and let them deal with it. I don't want you involved in it now that Claire has become mixed up in it all. We don't want any conflicts with you – not again. So that's the end of it. Leave it all alone, and let the SFO get on with whatever they need to as well.'

'But—'

Helen waved him off as he spoke, cutting off his protestations before he started.

'It's for the best. Honestly. I want you to just leave it now. I was pleased to see you get stuck in and pleased to see you back to your old self, turning up leads, but it's nothing to do with us. It's the SFO's job to sort out who was stealing their papers – they have their own directions, which are nothing to do with the Met. And if Jenny or Marmora was murdered, then Homicide Command is the place for those investigations. I don't want you working on them – it'll only make it more difficult and messy for everyone after what's happened with Claire.'

Jake shook his head but said nothing.

'I believe the US Department of Justice has taken over the investigation into the arms-deal bribery where British Aerospace are concerned. They *will* get their just desserts. Besides, it's not all bad news. I'm giving you a team back. The next job that comes in is yours, if you're up to it?'

Jake was genuinely surprised. He nodded in agreement.

'The commander is more than happy with your progress. Well done.'

'Thank you. Which team is it?'

'Team One, Mark's old team. He's being moved. I don't know where yet. I take it you've heard about the arrests at work today?'

'No.' Jake shook his head.

'I thought everyone knew. Two people from the command have been arrested. Fraud and theft. They've spent thousands on their job credit cards. Personal stuff. You must have heard about it? Holidays, plastic surgery… intimate personal items, which shall remain nameless. The commander is fuming.'

'Which teams are they from?' asked Jake.

'Both are within Team One.'

'Team One falls under you?' he said tentatively.

'Sadly, yes. But I don't scrutinise their credit-card statements – that's the DI's job. They're signed off by Mark Castle.'

'So which team members?' he asked bluntly, though he was certain he knew the answer.

'Gavin Bonson and Pat Husher. I don't think he was even looking at their spending. They've really duped him. Both their brothers are also involved, so I'm told. Husher's brother is a traffic officer.'

The traffic officer that had caused all that trouble for Stephanie. Jake hadn't forgotten.

'Will Mark be disciplined for lack of supervision?'

'The commander doesn't want it formal, just wants him spoken with, moved on. They're mates, so unless Mark was actually involved himself, he's never going to discipline him, is he?'

Jake shook his head. 'They dropped me in it over the use of a car...'

'You dropped yourself in it, Jake.'

He nodded.

'Now that Bonson's gone, and Mark is being moved, that team needs kicking into shape. There's a vacancy for a DS on there too, so you can have Lenny with you, if you'd like.'

'Thank you.'

'That's all I wanted. Stay away from what's gone on in Gloucestershire please.'

'Of course.'

'If Mark is outside, would you show him in for me,' she asked as he got up to leave.

Jake found a strained Mark Castle standing in the hallway outside.

They exchanged looks. Mark stared back, stony faced. Jake remembered the driving ban he still had to work off and the way Mark had been so dismissive of his detective work. He felt his pulse quicken; his hackles rise.

For a split second he thought about all the things he wanted to shout in the man's face.

The door to Helen's office was still ajar.

A phrase from his grandmother echoed in his ears.

If you've nothing nice to say, it's best to say nothing at all.

He passed Mark silently and walked off down the hall.

'Jake,' Mark called after him.

Jake turned and looked at Mark. They were about ten feet apart.

'I'm sorry,' said Mark.

'For what?'

'About the car. I should have spoken to you about it directly, not gone to the boss. Bonson was winding me up, playing me. I realise now it was because you'd seen his wallet and credit-card slips. He wanted to try and take you out of the game. I thought you were just causing trouble.'

'You think his arrest and the investigation is because of me?'

'Is it not?' Mark looked confused.

'No. It's not. They were both playing you good and proper. The MPA started that investigation of their own volition. It's nothing to do with me at all.'

'But Gavin said—'

'Can you not see it? They were trying to set me up, because they thought I was the source of the credit-card investigation into them.'

Mark nodded, his mouth slightly agape. The man's detective skills were far worse than Jake had realised.

'Mark, they were keeping you busy with pointless, silly little things, like me driving cars with blue lights. They were winding you up in the background with all these niggles about me, so that you were too busy to scrutinise their credit-card statements. And if I lost all my credibility, I was less useful as a witness in that case. It was a win-win for them.'

Mark sighed but said nothing.

'No hard feelings, Mark. We all make mistakes sometimes. Bonson and the rest of them deserve everything that gets thrown at them for stealing that money.'

'Well… I am sorry,' he repeated quietly.

'Put it behind us. We've both learned something from it, that's the main thing,' said Jake as he turned to walk away.

'Come in, Mark. Sit down, and close the door please,' he heard Helen say in stern tones just before it did. She was using that strident formal voice that no officer wanted to hear. Jake didn't envy him.

On the stairs, he called Lenny.

'Hi, mate, you OK?' he answered.

'Yeah, not too bad. Boss has given me a team back, and there's a DS vacancy on it, as luck would have it, so we're back on proper jobs together…' Jake paused, expecting some response from Lenny.

There was silence.

I'm not sure I'm up for that, to be honest, guv,' he said finally.

'No?' Jake was surprised. They'd worked together for years.

'I'm not getting any younger, Jake. I've got to think about my pension. You sail so close to the wind, the chances of us getting in trouble… I don't think my heart can take it. And, well, there's a vacancy on the CCTV-viewing team for a DS, so I think I'm going to apply for that.'

'Bollocks to that, you are! Meet me in the canteen, Lenny. We need to have a chat.'

Lenny sighed. 'Yes, Jake,' he said – and hung up the phone.

DISCUSSION POINTS FOR BOOK CLUBS

'The truth costs nothing, but a lie can cost you everything.'

In *The Detriment*, everyone has secrets they're trying to keep buried for as long as possible. From the Government, to the spy, to Claire and her uncle Frank – even right down to Ted the cat.

Should Jake have helped Claire? How far would *you* go to keep the truth hidden? We all have skeletons in our closet. Sometimes, morally, things don't seem cut and dried. Can actions be illegal and right, but legal and wrong – or is the law always black and white?

Would her reality have become his? A life filled with secrets and running away from the truth. Would he have looked complicit in events if they'd been found out? How trustworthy was Claire? Did the skeletons that Jake was already carrying from his last case impact on his decision-making this time around? Was it a choice about potentially forfeiting his life as a father, or did he owe it to Claire to help her? Could they really live happily ever after or would they always be looking over their shoulders after what had taken place?

Did Jake make the right decision or not?

APPENDIX: THE FACTS

Al Yamamah

The Al Yamamah arms deal is the biggest sale of anything in history – ever. It is an arms contract between the UK and Saudi Arabia.

Al Yamamah is an ancient, nostalgic name for a historical region of Saudi Arabia. The headquarters of the Saudi Government in Riyadh is known as the Palace of Yamamah. Al Yamamah is also said to mean 'The Dove' in Arabic.

(All times given as British Summer Time, BST)

HISTORY

10 June 1983 Prime Minister Margaret Thatcher is re-elected in a landslide victory. The Tory government begins a programme of privatisation and deregulation, trade-union reform and tax cuts.

Early 1984 The British government begins intensive efforts to sell military equipment to the Saudis, including Tornado and Hawk aircraft in return for payment in Saudi oil.

The British coalminers' unrest begins, leading to strikes.

2 January 1985 The Al Yamamah arms deal is under negotiation. With enthusiastic backing of British arms companies, Margaret Thatcher tells King Fahd of Saudi Arabia she is delighted relations between the UK and his country are warm and friendly. She also agrees to Saudi demands for secrecy. 'You may be confident of our complete discretion,' she tells King Fahd.[1]

3 March 1985 The British coalminers' strike formally ends. At its height, more than 50 per cent of Britain's electricity is being supplied by oil-fired power plants rather than coal. The cost of buying extra fuel oil to crush the miners' fifty-three-week strike tops £3.3 billion (which would be around £10 billion in 2017). Oil needs are so large that they move the global oil price. Without the oil, experts now believe that the miners would have won their confrontation with the National Coal Board and the British government.

1 April 1985 A secret meeting is organised for Margaret Thatcher, to be held in Riyadh, Saudi Arabia. Richard Evans of British Aerospace (BAe) calls his old friend and fellow rugby enthusiast Denis Thatcher, the Prime Minister's husband, and arranges for a secret, last-minute refuelling stop on a flight back from Japan.

Margaret Thatcher's private secretary and foreign-policy advisor Charles Powell writes:

> We should not add anyone to the prime minister's party for the visit to Riyadh. To include someone from MoD sales would only serve to draw attention to the Tornado aspect (given that there will be 25 journalists aboard the aircraft).[2]

14 April 1985 Margaret Thatcher makes the crucial stop off to see King Fahd. They enjoy a private lunch in the Saudi capital, Riyadh. An official record of the meeting makes no mention of Tornados or an arms deal. However, in a letter to the king the following day, the Prime Minister mysteriously writes:

> I was glad that we were able to discuss a further matter privately over lunch. I look forward to receiving your majesty's personal envoy soon, in order that we may conclude this matter successfully.[3]

26 September 1985 The UK and Saudi defence ministers sign a memorandum of understanding at Lancaster House in

London for aircraft, weapons, radar and training. Margaret Thatcher meets with the Saudis and agrees 'offset' arrangements and 'payment methods'.

February 1986 Part one of the Al Yamamah contract is signed.

18 March 1986 The Export Credits Guarantee Department sets out its support for the Al Yamamah deal. It will underwrite the contract to the tune of £1.9 billion, which means that the British taxpayer is now liable for that amount should the Saudis not be able to pay for the arms in oil or cash.

29 August 1986 A letter about the Al Yamamah deal from the Export Credits Guarantee Department to HM Treasury states:

> We have consulted our Solicitor and in his view this letters [sic] does not contain legally enforceable obligations on the part of the Saudis to continue to make oil available to meet all the costs of the Project … in the event of the oil lift arrangements falling through … the earlier contractual documents are also imprecise[,] the legal framework is imperfect and it is very doubtful if the Saudi commitment would be enforceable in the courts.[4]

1987 A £1 million Mayfair house in Eaton Terrace is purchased on behalf of Mark Thatcher, the Prime Minister's son, by an offshore company connected to a billionaire Al Yamamah middleman.

January 1987 An opaque company is formed in Panama City to buy Flat 12 in Rosebery Court, an apartment block in Mayfair. A Swiss director of the company confirms that he set it up on behalf of an Al Yamamah middleman, solely to buy the flat. The property later passes into the ownership of Richard Evans as the chairman of British Aerospace (BAe), a British arms manufacturer and key beneficiary of the Al Yamamah arms deal.

A senior source at the Serious Fraud Office will go on to tell *The Times* newspaper in February 2013 that they suspected the flats may have been bought for Richard Evans as a 'kickback' from the slush funds used by BAe to woo the Saudi royal family into buying British arms.

1988 Margaret Thatcher agrees to give £234 million of UK Aid to Malaysia to help them build the Pergau Dam near the Malaysia–Thailand border. A few months later, Malaysia agrees to buy $1.95 billion worth of arms from British Aerospace. The Export Credits Guarantee Department backs the project with three guarantees, issued between 1991 and 1992, for a total of £600 million. The contracts for the dam are awarded jointly to Balfour Beatty – a company with close links to the then governing British Conservative Party – and Cementation International, a company that employs Margaret Thatcher's son Mark as an advisor.

Tim Bell, Margaret Thatcher's public-relations advisor, is an advisor to the Malaysian Prime Minister Mahathir bin Mohamad.

Charles Powell, Margaret Thatcher's foreign-affairs advisor, is a director of the construction firm Trafalgar House; its subsidiary Cementation International is one of the contractors on the dam project and other aid programs in Malaysia.

Mark Thatcher denies claims by some Malaysian parliamentarians that he had connections with the arms deals through British Aerospace.

3 July 1988 A British delegation flies to Bermuda. Part two of the Al Yamamah contract is signed by the defence ministers of the UK and Saudi Arabia.

1989 The Export Credits Guarantee Department begins to provide insurances and indemnities to British Aerospace in respect of the Al Yamamah programme.

April 1989 Following rampant speculation in the press about huge bribes being paid to all involved in the Al Yamamah negotiations, the National Audit Office launches an investigation. There are many who claim that nepotism is hard at work in the centre of government, with Mark Thatcher 'cashing in' on his mother's name, yet Denis Thatcher's close friendship with Richard Evans of British Aerospace is not mentioned.

1990 Richard Evans is appointed Chief Executive of British Aerospace.

February 1990 An Overseas Development Agency review concludes that the Pergau Dam in Malaysia was a 'very bad buy' and the Department for Trade and Industry proposes a review of the Malaysian power sector. Both the Malaysian government and the UK government are determined to proceed, regardless.

22 November 1990 Margaret Thatcher unexpectedly resigns.

December 1990 Denis Thatcher is made Sir Denis, 1st Baronet of Scotney. The title will pass to his son, Mark Thatcher, on his death. It is the last hereditary honour to be bestowed outside of the Royal Family before a complete halt is placed on this type of honour. It is highly unlikely they will ever be granted again.

29 January 1992 The National Audit Office investigation entitled 'Saudi Arabian Air Force Project (Al Yamamah)' finds that the British government has paid no bribes. However, the investigation only focuses on the Government and fails to look at the Ministry of Defence, British Aerospace (BAe) or the Defence Export Services Organisation (DESO).

12 March 1992 The House of Commons Public Accounts Committee (PAC) agrees not to publish the findings from the National Audit Office investigation into Al Yamamah, which have taken three years to produce. PAC chair Robert Sheldon will state later: 'We were not able to follow public money outside the department once it is paid to the contractors, so we do not know what was done with it.' Sheldon makes it quite clear that the reason the report was not published was the 'highly sensitive situation regarding jobs in the defence industry', and that 'the Saudis may have become upset'.[5]

2 May 1997 Tony Blair's New Labour sweeps to power and he becomes Prime Minister. He ousts the Tories on election pledges to clean up British politics and remove sleaze from government. Shortly after Labour's victory, Tony Blair appoints Jonathan Powell in the official role of Downing Street Chief of Staff – a new position with the power to issue orders to civil servants, unprecedented for a political appointee. Jonathan Powell is the brother of Charles Powell, who was previously foreign-affairs advisor to Margaret Thatcher.

12 May 1997 The British government's foreign secretary, Robin Cook, delivers a mission statement which says: 'Our foreign policy must have an ethical dimension and must support the demands of other peoples for the democratic rights on which we insist for ourselves.' According to government insiders, this statement was disparaged by some. Jonathan Powell was reported to have stomped through Downing Street chanting: 'An ethical foreign policy is bollocks, an ethical foreign policy is bollocks.'

1997 A second National Audit Office report is commissioned into Al Yamamah. This second, secret report is never disclosed to Parliament and its existence is only discovered in 2006 following the Serious Fraud Office investigation.

30 November 1999 BAE Systems is formed by the £7.7 billion merger of British Aerospace (BAe) and Marconi Electronic Systems (MES).

8 June 2001 Peter Goldsmith, a long-time ally of Tony Blair, is appointed Attorney General.

February 2002 UK Parliament toughens up the law on bribery and corruption, outlawing payments to foreign government officials.

1 December 2002 A Sunday newspaper alleges that convicted conman Peter Foster boasted to business contacts that the Prime Minister's wife, Cherie Blair, asked him to negotiate the purchase of two luxury flats in Bristol. It is alleged that Thales, a government defence contractor, then pays the Blairs £60,000 a year to rent the two flats, which were said to be for the Blairs' son, Euan, for student accommodation, but were left unused by him. A similar flat in the same block is going for a rental price of just £2,600 per month.

Thales is a defence firm involved in government contracts worth more than £5 billion. The company has a 50 per cent stake in the build of two aircraft carriers for the Royal Navy in a joint project together with BAE Systems.

Since the Thales staff in Bristol who are allegedly renting the Blairs' property are working on a government-funded contract, which is funded by the Ministry of Defence – Tony and Cherie Blair are effectively receiving taxpayers' money in rental payments from their tenants.

Late 2002 Lady Thatcher speaks at a dinner in Hampshire. One of the guests asks her what her greatest achievements are and she replies, 'Tony Blair and New Labour.'

Autumn 2003 A Serious Fraud Office investigation into the British Aerospace payments made to Saudi princes is triggered.

20 October 2003 Robin Cook, a British Labour MP, publishes a book about the Blair government, which includes extracts from his diaries. In one part he explains how he had attempted to introduce an ethical foreign policy in government, but failed due to 'repeatedly running into a brick wall called BAE Systems'.

During his time spent as Leader of the House of Commons between 2001 and 2003, he also famously recorded in his diaries: 'The Chairman of BAE Systems appeared to have the key to the garden door of No 10. Certainly I never knew No 10 to come up with any decision that would be incommoding to BAE.'

June 2004 Richard Evans steps down as chairman of BAE Systems, moving to a part-time 'customer relationship' role in which he will earn almost £1.5 million to advise the company on its relationships with Saudi Arabia.

September 2004 Future Tiger Tiger bomber and Glasgow airport bomber Kafeel Ahmed arrives in Cambridge to begin his PhD studies at the Anglia Ruskin University.

5 May 2005 The Labour Party wins its third consecutive general-election victory under Tony Blair.

July 2005 Senior Saudis meet with Tony Blair to discuss the Serious Fraud Office enquiry into the Al Yamamah arms deal. The Saudis come away with the impression that the enquiry will be stopped.

August 2005 Mike Turner, then CEO of BAE Systems, says that BAE, and its predecessor British Aerospace (BAe), have earned £43 billion in twenty years from the Al Yamamah contracts, and that it *could* earn £40 billion more if part three of the contract is allowed to go ahead.

8 October 2005 The British press reports that Tony Blair is employing Charles Powell as his special envoy to Brunei whilst he is also on the payroll of BAE Systems. BAE is currently in a dispute with Brunei over the purchase of three warships. Charles Powell is Margaret Thatcher's former foreign advisor and the brother of Tony Blair's Downing Street Chief of Staff, Jonathan Powell. Their brother, Chris Powell, an advertising executive, had previously been responsible for organising the advertising of the New Labour brand.

14 October 2005 The Serious Fraud Office issues a statutory notice to BAE Systems requiring it to disclose details of payments to agents and consultants in respect of the Al Yamamah contracts. BAE lobbies Attorney General Goldsmith directly to get the investigation dropped. This eventually leads to the unusual situation of the Attorney General seeking views of 'interested government ministers' on the relevancy of continuing the investigation.

November 2005 BAE Systems sends a confidential letter to Attorney General Lord Goldsmith stating that the Serious Fraud Office investigation is straining UK–Saudi relations and placing the arms programme at risk.

12 December 2005 The governments of the UK and Saudi Arabia sign a memorandum of understanding for a new phase of the Al Yamamah arms deal, which involves the sale of Typhoon aircraft to replace RSAF Tornados and other aircraft.

January 2006 The Serious Fraud Office investigation continues when views of ministers are known.

16 March 2006 BAE Systems is ordered to reveal the identity of its agents and middlemen that it uses to make murky multi-million-pound commission payments to those abroad, through secret Swiss bank accounts. The payments are alleged by anti-arms campaigners to be channels for bribery.

July 2006 Saudi officials learn that the Serious Fraud Office investigation may now be about to obtain details of Swiss bank accounts and they threaten to pull out of the latest part of the Al Yamamah contract involving the sale of Typhoons, during a meeting with Jonathan Powell, Tony Blair's chief of staff.

25 July 2006 Ministry of Defence police and the Serious Fraud Office ask to see the National Audit Office report into Saudi arms deals, which has been kept secret since 1992, but the National Audit Office refuses to hand over documents to police relating to the Al Yamamah contract.

Summer 2006 Future Tiger Tiger and Glasgow Airport bomber Bilal Abdullah visits family in Iraq. It is during this visit that many say his views harden. He meets a mystery 'emir' who tells him it is time to 'open a jihad front' in Britain.

Kafeel Ahmed resigns abruptly from his technology firm in India. Since December 2005, he has worked as a senior aeronautical engineer for Infotech Enterprises, an Indian outsourcing company that designs aircraft parts for clients including Boeing and Airbus. He leaves his job in August 2006.

It is understood that he has detailed plans on his computer hard drive that cover the purchase of five acres of land in or around Bangalore on which he wants to build a housing complex that would be governed under Sharia law.

It has never been established how he would finance the project or who would provide the funding for it.

18 August 2006 Part three of the Al Yamamah contract is signed between the British government, BAE and Saudi Arabia. It includes seventy-two Eurofighter Typhoon multirole fighters at a cost of £4.43 billion. The full weapons system is estimated at a total cost of £10 billion.

Early September 2006 The Serious Fraud Office pursues evidence that millions of pounds of BAE Systems cash found in Swiss accounts is potentially linked to the Saudi royal family and corrupt individuals involved in the Al Yamamah deal. The Serious Fraud Office makes formal requests to the Swiss authorities to provide the bank records, but the Swiss have already officially informed one of the account holders, who is a billionaire middleman involved in the Al Yamamah deal.

A source close to the investigation is reported as saying that the Saudis have now 'hit the roof' as a result, and regard the disclosure of banking information from Switzerland and the Ministry of Defence as a totally unacceptable breach, claiming the Al Yamamah deal is protected by sovereign national immunity.

A twelve-page letter drawn up by a Saudi law firm is delivered by a Saudi diplomat to Jonathan Powell, Blair's chief of staff, demanding a detailed explanation as to why the SFO investigation is still continuing. The letter claims that the British government has broken an undertaking to keep details of the Al Yamamah deal confidential. The senior Saudi diplomat informs the British government that Saudi Arabia is prepared to suspend diplomatic relations and to stop sharing intelligence on al-Qaeda if the SFO investigation is not halted.

7 September 2006 Tony Blair unexpectedly announces that he will step down as prime minister within the next twelve months.

September 2006 Kafeel Ahmed visits Bilal Abdullah, who is working at Inverclyde Hospital in Scotland.

End of September 2006 A confidential Defence Export Services Organisation (DESO) report, released under the Freedom of Information Act, reveals that Iraq and Libya are now 'priority' markets for their British-arms sales push, as are Colombia and Kazakhstan – both criticised for human-rights violations.

27 October 2006 Al Yamamah bribery suspicions intensify after the British government accidentally releases documents to the National Archive that detail the cost of each aircraft. These reveal that the price of each Tornado was inflated by 32 per cent, from £16.3 million to £21.5 million. It is common in arms deals for the prices of weapons to be raised so that commissions can be skimmed off the top. The total figures indicate an inflation of £600 million in additional payments, the same amount believed to be paid in secret commissions to Saudi royals and intermediaries in London.

19 November 2006 It is reported that the Serious Fraud Office is about to, or has already, obtained the details of Swiss bank accounts that may implicate certain members of the Saudi royal family in secret Al Yamamah arms-deal commissions of more than £100 million.

21 November 2006 The British ambassador to Saudi Arabia, Sherard Cowper-Coles, meets Saudi rulers, who tell him 'all intelligence cooperation is under threat' if the Serious Fraud Office investigation continues. Cowper-Coles subsequently meets with the Attorney General three times between this date and early December to lobby him to drop the investigation.

28 November 2006 BAE Systems announces its Eurofighter deal with the Saudis has stalled. BAE chief executive, Mike Turner says: 'We don't want to interfere with the judicial process [of the SFO investigation] ... but we do want to see a resolution. It is damaging for our business.'

1 December 2006 Saudi Arabia gives Britain ten days to halt the Serious Fraud Office investigation or lose the Al Yamamah contract. They say they will make it easier for terrorists to attack London by cutting vital intelligence links that might forewarn of an attack – unless corruption investigations into the Al Yamamah arms deal are halted.

8 December 2006 Blair writes a 'secret and personal' letter to Attorney General Goldsmith demanding he stop the investigation into Al Yamamah. He says he is concerned about the 'critical difficulty' in negotiations over a new Typhoon fighter sales contract, as well as a 'real and immediate risk of a collapse in UK/Saudi security, intelligence and diplomatic cooperation'.

Politicians normally have no right to interfere in a criminal case.

11 December 2006 In a meeting, Attorney General Goldsmith and Prime Minister Tony Blair discuss shutting down the Serious Fraud Office investigation.

11 December, 2006 Prince Turki al-Faisal, Saudi Arabia's ambassador to the United States, flies out of Washington after informing the US Secretary of State that he will be leaving his post unexpectedly after only fifteen months in the job. Prince Turki is one of the persons of interest in the Al Yamamah Serious Fraud Office investigation.

13 December 2006 A decision is made to halt the Serious Fraud Organisation investigation but is not yet made public.

14 December 2006 Tony Blair becomes the first prime minister in history to be interviewed by the police. He is questioned over the cash-for-honours corruption scandal. On the same day, the Government releases the findings of the enquiry into the death of Diana, Princess of Wales, which dominates the news.

An official announcement is made stating that the Serious Fraud Office investigation is to be dropped on the grounds of national security:

> The Prime Minister and the Foreign and Defence Secretaries … have expressed the clear view that continuation of the investigation would cause serious damage to UK/Saudi security, intelligence and diplomatic cooperation.[6]

15 December 2006 There is disgust in the British media at the fact that Tony Blair is said to be behind the move to persuade Attorney General Lord Goldsmith to halt the Serious Fraud Office investigation.

Tony Blair argues that pressing ahead with the Serious Fraud Office enquiry would be 'devastating for our relationship with an important country with whom we cooperate closely on terrorism, on security, on the Middle East peace process'. He goes on to say that it would threaten 'British lives on British streets'.

The head of the Secret Intelligence Service (MI6) rejects the assertion that the Saudis would sever links should the SFO investigation continue. He personally refuses to sign a dossier stating that MI6 endorses this assertion.

Clare Short, MP, Mr Blair's former cabinet colleague, says: 'This government is even more soiled than we thought it was. It means that BAE is above the law.' She adds, 'The message it sends to corrupt businessmen is carry on – the Government will support you.'

6 January 2007 The Saudi Defence Minister says the country is looking forward to receiving seventy-two Eurofighter jets from BAE Systems 'very soon'.

7 February 2007 A debate in the House of Commons questions the ethics and conduct of the British government in relation to the Al Yamamah contract. MP Vince Cable pressures the Government to come clean about its conduct.

During the debate, Cable states that there is information that suggests the vast proportion of Mark Thatcher's personal fortune came directly from the Al Yamamah contract.

On the subject of the government shutting down the Serious Fraud Office investigation, Cable states in the debate:

> One of two conclusions must emerge. The Prime Minister has done what he did in the case of Iraq, which was to exaggerate and distort the advice received from the security services; alternatively and much more alarmingly, he was right, and the Saudi authorities, who are supposed to be our allies, *are threatening us with terrorism*.[7]

8 February 2007 In a shock announcement, Sir Sherard Cowper-Coles, UK ambassador to Saudi Arabia, will move to become ambassador to Afghanistan. The announcement comes as a surprise to everyone, as Sir Sherard would normally have been posted for at least another year in Saudi Arabia. Cowper-Coles had persistently lobbied Robert Wardle of the Serious Fraud Office to drop the investigation into Al Yamamah, telling him at one point that 'British lives on British streets were at risk' and that the Saudis were, in effect, willing to see UK citizens murdered by terrorists if they did not get their way.

Sherard Cowper-Coles is a member of the British Egyptian Society.

One of the British Egyptian Society's directors is Egyptian billionaire Ashraf Marwan, son-in-law of the former Egyptian president, informant to the Israeli secret services and infamous arms dealer.

23 February 2007 Anti-arms campaigners make their first formal application to the Government for a judicial review into their decision to suddenly drop the Serious Fraud Office's investigation into BAE Systems' dealings with Saudi Arabia.

26 February 2007 Internet messages between the terror plotters Kafeel Ahmed and Bilal Abdullah indicate that 'experiments' will get underway. This is the first recorded message to indicate that work on their bomb plot has begun. The conversation concludes that they will agree a timetable in a week or so.

1 March 2007 Vince Cable applies further pressure on the British government by requesting information on any Serious Fraud Office liaisons with the US Department of Justice in relation to Al Yamamah contracts.

8 March 2007 In Scotland, Bilal Abdullah sets about finding a bomb factory. At 3.48 a.m. he emails Kafeel Ahmed to ask him: 'Flat or house?'

'Flat with garage, if possible,' Ahmed replies, later responding, 'Inshallah [God willing] hee hee.'

12–14 March 2007 The Organisation for Economic Co-operation and Development (OECD) criticises the UK's implementation of the Anti-Bribery Convention and decides to 'conduct a further examination of the UK's efforts to fight bribery'. It reaffirms its serious concerns about the UK's discontinuance of the BAE–Al Yamamah fraud investigation and outlines continued shortcomings in the UK's anti-bribery legislation.

April 2007 Anti-arms campaigners The Corner House and Campaign Against Arms Trade (CAAT) apply for a second judicial review into the sudden and unexpected decision to close the Serious Fraud Office investigation.

17 April 2007 Bilal Abdullah views a rental property in the village of Houston.

18 April 2007 BAE Systems admits to paying private investigators to infiltrate anti-arms campaign groups. Suggestions later arise in the press that certain offices may also have been bugged, including those of Portcullis House, belonging to Members of Parliament.

28 April 2007 Although he does not require a place to live, as he is staying in hospital accommodation, Bilal Abdullah signs the lease on the Houston house, near Glasgow.

2 May 2007 The US Department of Justice announces that it is in talks to establish whether it can launch a formal enquiry to pursue allegations of bribery against BAE Systems. Mike O'Brien, the Solicitor General, acknowledges that the UK's Serious Fraud Office (SFO) has met with the US Department of Justice to discuss allegations of corrupt practices by defence company BAE.

5 May 2007 Kafeel Ahmed joins Bilal Abdullah at the house he has rented near Glasgow. Soon after Abdullah and Ahmed move in, they place a black bin liner over the inside of the garage window, so that neighbours and passers-by cannot look in.

10 May 2007 Tony Blair officially announces that he is to stand down as prime minister on 27 June 2007.

28 May 2007 Red Diamond, an opaque BAE Systems company registered in the British Virgin Islands, is liquidated. Over the years it has been used to channel payments to arms middlemen and agents all over the world via accounts in London, Switzerland and New York. Secret payments were eventually traced to agents in South America, Tanzania, Romania, South Africa, Qatar, Chile and the Czech Republic.

Red Diamond was also used to make payments to UK citizens who were working as consultants and lobbyists for BAE. These citizens included David Hart, who also advised Margaret Thatcher heavily in relation to the coalminers' strike.

BAE never disclosed the existence of Red Diamond in its published company accounts and has never explained why.

29 May 2007 Kafeel Ahmed drives to Keighley, West Yorkshire, and buys tools and a large quantity of nails and screws from B&Q. In Beeston, Leeds, he buys the first patio gas canister and a propane regulator.

Between 2 June and 16 June 2007 Bilal Abdullah and Kafeel Ahmed buy five cars located in various different parts of the country by answering private car adverts in *Auto Trader* magazine.

5 June 2007 The bombers pay £650 in cash to a Liverpool man for a Mercedes, before driving the car to Liverpool's John Lennon Airport and abandoning it in a car park after discovering that the man they bought it from is an off-duty police officer.

11 June 2007 The BBC broadcasts an episode of its flagship *Panorama* show on BBC One entitled 'Princes, Planes and Payoffs'. It examines the allegations of massive corruption surrounding the largest arms deal in history and claims that when the Serious Fraud Office got close to uncovering the truth, the Government forced it to drop its investigation.

On the same day, Lord Woolf, the former Lord Chief Justice of England and Wales, is appointed by BAE Systems to head its own internal review of business practices – criticised as a cynical PR move by many in the media.

22 June 2007 Lord Goldsmith announces his resignation as Attorney General late in the evening.

25 June 2007 BAE Systems acknowledges that the US Department of Justice has decided to investigate the company's compliance with US anti-corruption laws, particularly the 1977 Foreign Corrupt Practices Act, in its Al Yamamah deals.

27 June 2007 Gordon Brown, former chancellor, becomes the UK prime minister after Tony Blair resigns following ten years as PM. Brown is expected to reshuffle the cabinet and address new priorities for the country.

27 June 2007 Ashraf Marwan, son-in-law of the former Egyptian president, informant to the Israeli secret services and billionaire arms dealer, is found dead, having somehow fallen five floors from his apartment balcony. It is believed that the Egyptian businessman died shortly after 1.30 p.m. in the private rose garden at number 24 Carlton House Terrace. His home is located approximately a 200-metre walk north-east of the registered offices of BAE Systems, and a 200-metre walk south-east of the Cockspur Street location in which a car bomb will be planted within the next thirty-six hours.

28 June 2007 Bilal Abdullah and Kafeel Ahmed prepare their two vehicle-borne improvised explosive devices in the two Mercedes sitting in the garage of 6 Neuk Crescent, Houston, Renfrewshire, Scotland. They call and test the mobile phones used in the home-made detonators in the early hours of the morning. In the afternoon, both cars begin the journey to London.

29 June 2007

12.39 a.m. The cars are caught on traffic cameras at Marble Arch. They drive along Weymouth Street, Portland Place, Regent Street, Piccadilly Circus, Coventry Street, Panton Street, Haymarket, Pall Mall and Piccadilly Circus for a second time.

1.18 a.m. Ahmed parks the blue Mercedes, registration L708 VBB, in a bus stop in Cockspur Street, just a 200-metre walk away from Ashraf Marwan's home and a 400-metre walk from BAE Systems' registered offices.

1.24 a.m. Abdullah parks the other car, a light, metallic-green Mercedes, registration G824 VFK, in Haymarket outside the main entrance to the Tiger Tiger nightclub. He spends several minutes inside the car pouring petrol in the footwells and across the seats and arming the electrical circuit. He is caught on the nightclub's CCTV running across Haymarket, but both men use umbrellas to conceal their faces from cameras – umbrellas that were purchased during the drive south.

1.40 a.m. Nightclub staff and paramedics who are dealing with an unconnected matter outside the venue raise the alarm after noticing suspicious fumes. The cars and their devices are eventually recovered intact for forensic examination, and both are found to contain petrol cans, gas canisters and a quantity of nails, with a mobile-phone-based trigger.

30 June 2007

1.34 a.m. Kafeel Ahmed uploads his will and suicide note into the drafts folder of his Google Mail account.

5.29 a.m. Bilal Abdullah sends an email to his boss at the Royal Alexandra Hospital, purporting to be from his sister, in which he claims to have been severely injured while on holiday and unlikely to walk again. This email was sent while the pair were inside the Houston bomb factory.

Just after 8 a.m. The two men, having packed their Jeep with fuel and shrapnel, drive north from Houston, Renfrewshire, to Loch Lomond where they remain until 2 p.m. During this time, Ahmed sends a text message to his brother explaining how to access various Google Mail documents.

3.04 p.m. CCTV cameras at Glasgow Airport capture the dark-green Jeep Cherokee arriving.

3.13 p.m. The Jeep smashes into the entrance doors of the international terminal, impaling the front of the vehicle on a metal security bollard outside the entrance. Kafeel Ahmed throws petrol bombs from the passenger seats before dousing himself in petrol and setting himself alight. CCTV from inside the terminal shows hundreds of holidaymakers and passengers running for safety, many abandoning luggage to escape.

The two men are tackled by members of the public and police officers. They are eventually detained and arrested.

Kafeel Ahmed is severely burnt in the ensuing fire and five members of the public are injured.

Both occupants of the Jeep are apprehended at the scene, and all those injured are taken to the Royal Alexandra Hospital in nearby Paisley.

Police identify the two men as Bilal Abdullah, a British-born, Muslim doctor of Iraqi descent, who works at the Royal Alexandra Hospital in Paisley, and Kafeel Ahmed, an engineer and the driver of the Jeep, who is treated for burns at the same hospital.

Kafeel Ahmed suffers burns to 90 per cent of his body and is not expected to survive.

3 July 2007 A British vicar in Baghdad claims that an al-Qaeda leader warned him that 'the people who cure you would kill you' months before the terrorist bomb plots in Glasgow and London. Canon Andrew White, who runs the Iraqi capital's only Anglican parish, claims that he met an unnamed al-Qaeda leader on the sidelines of a religious reconciliation meeting in Amman, Jordan.

4 July 2007 Kafeel Ahmed is revived twice in hospital. Newspapers report that Britain's NHS is paying over £5,000 a day to keep him alive, while security sources said this amount reaches £30,000 if security costs are included.

5 July 2007 Al Jazeera shows a new video from al-Qaeda which features Ayman al-Zawahiri in his eighth message this year. He is outspoken against what he terms as the corrupt and repressive governments of Saudi Arabia and Egypt. In an unusual turn of events, he singles out the Al Yamamah defence contract between Britain and the Saudi kingdom, in which large bribes were reportedly paid to Saudi princes. Although the video is believed to have been filmed some time ago, its broadcast comes just days after the attacks on London and Glasgow.

6 July 2007 Bilal Abdullah is charged with conspiracy to cause explosions in London and at Glasgow Airport.

26 July 2007 Prime Minister Gordon Brown announces that the Defence Export Services Organisation (DESO) will be transferred from the Ministry of Defence to the UK Trade and Investment department from April 2008. It will now be called the UKTI Defence and Security Group. Uniquely, however, the Al Yamamah contracts shall remain within the remit of the MOD.

17 September 2007 The British government agrees to supply seventy-two Eurofighter Typhoon combat jets to Saudi Arabia, in a deal that will include training, spares, ground support equipment, plus technical support and manpower.

9 April 2008 A ruling from the High Court announces that the Serious Fraud Office director, Robert Wardle, failed to stand up to threats from the Saudis when he closed the investigation into the Al Yamamah deal. It says the SFO and the British government made an 'abject surrender' to 'blatant threats'.

10 April 2008 In a surprise decision, the High Court announces that the Saudi regime successfully 'perverted the course of justice in the United Kingdom' by getting the Serious Fraud Office investigation dropped.

12 May 2008 The US Department of Justice, investigating bribery allegations in the Al Yamamah arms deal, detains Mike Turner, chief executive of BAE Systems, and Sir Nigel Rudd, a non-executive director, issuing them with subpoenas as they land at Houston Airport.

30 July 2008 The House of Lords rules that the Serious Fraud Office acted lawfully when it halted its investigation into the Al Yamamah bribery allegations. The Law Lords ruling says, 'The SFO director (Robert Wardle) was convinced that Saudi Arabia wasn't bluffing.' The judgement outlines the incredible pressure placed upon the SFO director's shoulders to drop his investigation. Those who pressured him hard to stop the investigation included the Saudi Arabians, BAE Systems, the Ministry of Defence, the Attorney General Lord Goldsmith, and the former prime minister, Tony Blair.

16 December 2008 Bilal Abdullah is convicted of conspiracy to cause murder and explosions. He is sentenced to life imprisonment with a minimum of thirty-two years.

12 July 2010 A coroner's inquest begins into the death of former spy and billionaire arms dealer Ashraf Marwan.

18 February 2011 Sir Sherard Cowper-Coles, the former Saudi ambassador and senior British diplomat who played a central role in pressuring the Serious Fraud Office to drop its investigation into British Aerospace over the Al Yamamah arms deal, is hired by the defence group BAE Systems to become International Development Director, focussing on the Middle East and Southeast Asia. The move causes uproar among anti-corruption campaigners. It raises further questions over the close relationship between the British government and BAE, and the circumstances in which the Serious Fraud Office investigation was controversially dropped.

12 September 2013 The Serious Fraud Office is forced to admit that thousands of confidential documents it has lost over the years were discovered on a cannabis farm in London Docklands. The SFO admits in total it had lost at least 32,000 documents, eighty-one audio tapes and other electronic media from fifty-nine sources. The data includes the identity of a major prosecution witness in a £43 billion fraud case against defence giant BAE Systems. It emerges that the files were put in a self-storage warehouse in London's Docklands, which was used to house stolen goods and as an illegal cannabis farm.

21 July 2016 The National Archives release hundreds of government records under the thirty-year rule, but two relating to the late Margaret Thatcher's son are staying closed and will not be released until 2053, when Sir Mark Thatcher will be ninety-nine. The decision to keep the files closed is taken by former Culture Secretary John Whittingdale, who served as Mrs Thatcher's political secretary.

Ten years on At the time of writing, the British government is currently defending a High Court challenge by anti-arms campaigners who say that it is breaking its own arms-export licence criteria by continuing to sell arms to Saudi Arabia. Documents revealed in court show that the head of the Government's own Export Control Organisation has recommended that arms sales to Saudi Arabia be stopped but that this advice has never been adopted by ministers.

The reasons for the death of Ashraf Marwan – the Egyptian billionaire, former spy and arms dealer, who was found in his rose garden having somehow fallen from his balcony just metres away from, and hours before, the 2007 London car bomb attacks – are still disputed.

At the inquest, the coroner could not decide how or why Marwan came to have found his way off the balcony and the reasons remain unexplained. His family claim that vital evidence, such as the shoes that Marwan wore at the time of his death, are missing. They vow to continue their search for the truth. Shortly after his death, details about Marwan's spying activities and arms dealing with Colonel Gaddafi emerged.

His memoirs have never been found.

Between 2003 and 2007 there were at least two plots to assassinate members of the Saudi royal family while they were in London. All were thwarted by police. No one was ever prosecuted. At least one of the plots was funded by Colonel Gaddafi, whose agents planned murder on London's streets as he was courted by the British government and his family enjoyed close relationships with the then prime minister, Tony Blair. The events remain shrouded in secrecy and the motives for the assassination plots have never been fully established.

Thanks to Al Yamamah, Britain sold more arms to Saudi Arabia between 1973 and 1997 than did the United States.

The 1992 National Audit Office report into Al Yamamah has never been published and British Aerospace's role never clarified. It is the only National Audit Office report never to have seen the light of day.

An unnamed analyst is widely quoted by anti-arms groups as once saying: 'There is a feeling in the City that BAE is run by a mafia, and that they are a law unto themselves.'

At the time of writing, part four of the Al Yamamah contract is currently under negotiation between the Saudis and the British government. This is despite everything that has gone before, and despite new evidence that British-made weaponry is killing civilians in Yemen.

Few people know that public money has been used to support the export of weapons. In the eleven years prior to 2002, the British Export Credits Guarantee Department

(ECGD) lost €976 million on arms deals according to government figures obtained by the European Network Against Arms Trade.

Money that came from the taxpayer's purse.

The UK is believed to have paid Saudi royal-family members, middlemen and others around £6 billion in commissions in the Al Yamamah deal. It remains the biggest corruption scandal in history. No direct convictions for involvement in Al Yamamah were ever made.

Britain remains the second largest arms exporter in the world today.

---

1. Declassified document in National Archives. Letter from Margaret Thatcher to King Fahd, dated 2 January 1985, from offices of 10 Downing Street.

2. Declassified document in National Archives. Letter from Margaret Thatcher's private secretary and foreign policy advisor, Charles Powell, to the Foreign Office dated 1 April 1985, marked 'Secret'.

3. Declassified document in National Archives. Letter from Margaret Thatcher to King Fahd, dated 15 April 1985, from the office of 10 Downing Street.

4. Declassified document in National Archives. Letter headed 'Confidential' from ECGD to HM Treasury dated 29 August 1986 entitled 'Saudi Arabia: Defence Deal (Tornados) (now called the Yamamah Project).'

For reference, this letter can also be viewed at: https://www.caat.org.uk/resources/countries/saudi-arabia/al-yamamah/pj5-40-ay-revised-aug.pdf

5. Taken from: Select Committee on International Development. Memorandum submitted by the Campaign Against Arms Trade, Appendix 3 (September 2000).

For reference, it can be found here: https://www.publications. parliament.uk/pa/cm200001/cmselect/cmintdev/39/39ap04.htm

6. Extract taken from Official Report, House of Lords, 14 December 2006; Vol. 687, c. 1712.

7. Extract taken from: House of Commons Hansard Debates for 07 Feb 2007. Al Yamamah Arms Agreement from 1.41 pm, Column 867.

For reference, can be found here: https://www.publications. parliament.uk/pa/cm200607/cmhansrd/cm070207/debtext/ 70207-0007.htm

The Police Dependants' Trust

David Videcette is proud to support the work of the Police Dependants' Trust through his books, including the development of the National Welfare Contingency Fund. The fund has been designed to assist with the mental-health needs of police officers following a major terrorist or other national incident.

Visit www.pdtrust.org for more details.

If you've enjoyed this book, please review it on Amazon. Just a few words will help fellow readers make more informed buying choices.

Have you tried *The Theseus Paradox* – the first book in the Detective Inspector Jake Flannagan series?

Coming soon!
Jake Flannagan will return in a third adventure based on true events.

For the chance to win a signed copy of the next Jake Flannagan thriller, drop in your email address at:
http://www.davidvidecette.com/title-reveal

Lightning Source UK Ltd.
Milton Keynes UK
UKHW04f0626300818
328037UK00001B/81/P